"And if we can make Jantar just taste that misery, would you not be avenged? Tell me, rani. Would you not be pleased to have Farin's head at your feet?"

Her heart thundered. Her desire, on his lips, made her sick, thrilled. Around her, Elena could feel the hot rage of the inferno, the cold stares of the ghosts. *Vengeance.* For her people, her father, Ferma, Yassen, *herself.* The desire rippled through her with a slow heat, her every breath scraping the inside of her throat like a finely toothed comb. Elena watched the inferno with a new mixture of horror and wonder. *Vengeance* lay at her fingertips.

At theirs.

"How," she began, and stopped when she met his eyes. Because in them, she saw her same fury reflected—*tenfold.* Only his was colder, crueler, a wrath that seemed at once unfathomable and endless. If he harbored that much fury, what kind of god was he? A savior, like the stories said? Or a monster, like she had once believed? Elena paused, uncertain. Yet below her alarm, she sensed an awareness tugging her belly with an incessant urgency, and as she considered it, she felt his Agni twinge in recognition. *Like knows like. Fire knows its brethren.* The realization hummed through her bones, filling her ears with a buzz that built until all she could hear was the steady murmur of the inferno as it knelt before a cursed god.

A god who offered her his hand.

Slowly, Elena raised hers.

"Will you help me, then?" she said.

Samson smiled. A crude, vicious smile.

A butcher's smile, she thought.

He took her hand. "We start with Ravence."

Praise for

THE PHOENIX KING

"Fiery, inventive, and full of yearning and vengeance. A wonderful read."
—Tasha Suri, World Fantasy Award–winning
author of *The Jasmine Throne*

"A captivating adventure from a gifted new voice."
—Peter V. Brett, *New York Times* bestselling
author of the Demon Cycle

"The kind of book you sit down with to read one chapter and end up spending the whole day on. Come for the science fantasy worldbuilding and stay for the characters you just can't get out of your head."
—Vaishnavi Patel, *New York Times* bestselling
author of *Kaikeyi*

"A heady and seamless blend of sci-fi and fantasy infused with Indian inspiration. An engrossing read that will have you quickly turning through the chapters."
—R.R. Virdi, *USA Today* bestselling
author of *The First Binding*

"Elegant and intelligent storytelling that starts out as conniving and treacherous intrigue and transforms into an exhilarating adventure without losing that touch of mystery. Perfect for fans of S. A. Chakraborty."
—*Library Journal*

"A riveting page-turner."
—*Booklist*

By Aparna Verma

The Ravence Trilogy

The Phoenix King

The Burning Queen

THE BURNING QUEEN

THE RAVENCE TRILOGY: BOOK TWO

APARNA VERMA

orbit

orbitbooks.net

Copyright © 2025 by Aparna Verma

Cover design by Alexia E. Pereira
Cover images by Shutterstock
Cover copyright © 2025 by Hachette Book Group, Inc.
Map by Tim Paul
Interior illustrations by Ngoc Nguyen
Author photograph by Aparna Verma

Orbit
Hachette Book Group
1290 Avenue of the Americas
New York, NY 10104
orbitbooks.net

First Edition: November 2025
Simultaneously published in Great Britain by Orbit

Orbit is an imprint of Hachette Book Group.
The Orbit name and logo are registered trademarks of Little, Brown Book Group Limited.

The publisher is not responsible for websites (or their content) that are not owned by the publisher.

The Hachette Speakers Bureau provides a wide range of authors for speaking events. To find out more, go to hachettespeakersbureau.com or email HachetteSpeakers@hbgusa.com.

Orbit books may be purchased in bulk for business, educational, or promotional use. For information, please contact your local bookseller or the Hachette Book Group Special Markets Department at special.markets@hbgusa.com.

Library of Congress Cataloging-in-Publication Data
Names: Verma, Aparna author
Title: The burning queen / Aparna Verma.
Description: First edition. | New York, NY : Orbit, 2025. | Series: The Ravence trilogy ; book 2
Identifiers: LCCN 2025016280 | ISBN 9780316523028 trade paperback | ISBN 9780316523158 ebook
Subjects: LCGFT: Fiction | Fantasy fiction | Novels
Classification: LCC PS3622.E7456 B87 2025 | DDC 813/.6—dc23/eng/20250613
LC record available at https://lccn.loc.gov/2025016280

ISBNs: 9780316523028 (trade paperback), 9780316523158 (ebook)

Printed in the United States of America

LSC-C

Printing 1, 2025

To the sons and daughters who fight and claw and endure, this one is for you.

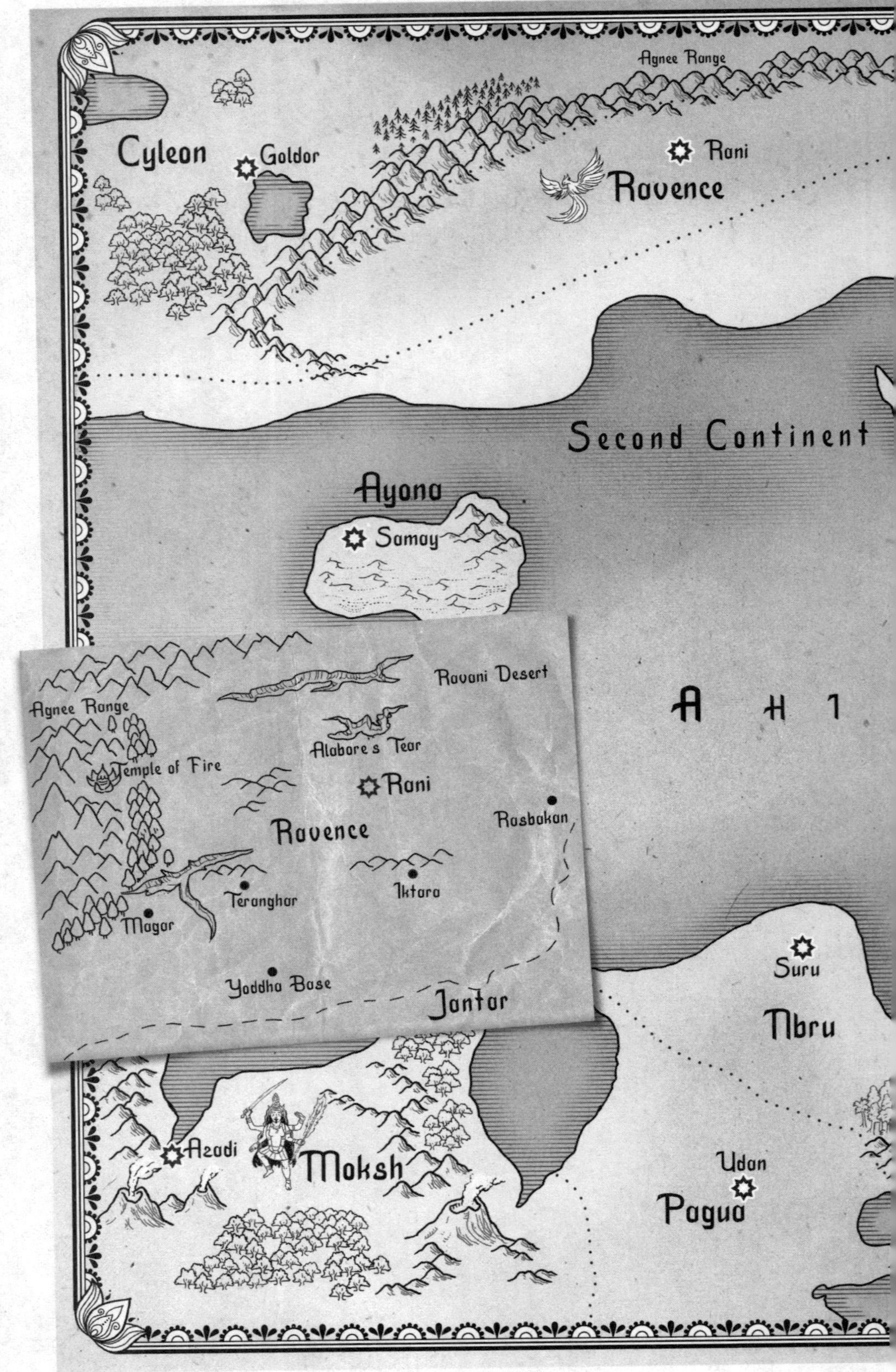

Agnee Range
Cyleon
Goldor
Rani
Ravence
Second Continent
Ayona
Samay
A H 1
Ravani Desert
Agnee Range
Alabore's Tear
Temple of Fire
Rani
Rasbakan
Ravence
Teranghar
Iktara
Magar
Yoddha Base
Jantar
Suru
Nbru
Azadi
Moksh
Udan
Pagua

Karven
Sard
Veran
Amirin Mtns.
Eravan
Jantar
Rhea
Sona Range
Tsuana
Janoon
Rysanti
S E A
Ajgar
Seshar
First Continent
The Claw
Mandur
Narasir
Map by Tim Paul

THE PHOENIX KING RECAP

*T*o be forgiven, one must be burned. That's what the Ravani say. They believe fire will cleanse one of all sins and bear them anew. But they have said nothing of the inferno's wrath.

Leo Malhari Ravence believed he could defy the Eternal Fire and defeat its Prophet. Through burning, subterfuge, and murder, he attempted to catch her—until he learned that the Prophet was not a woman, but a man. By then, it was too late. He had killed the priests of the order and made an enemy of the gods. Perhaps it was divine retribution, then, that led to the Arohassin attack. On the day of his daughter's coronation, the great king knelt within the Eternal Fire, and the Arohassin bombed his city and temple. But theirs was not the blow to kill him. For you see, the Eternal Fire had tasted his sins and claimed its due. The Phoenix demanded Her sacrifice. Thus, Leo Malhari Ravence, Guardian of Fire, Son of Alabore, the Divine Grace of Desert and Sky, and the Twentieth Phoenix King, died by his own making.

Within the chaos and clamor of the attack, an assassin of the Arohassin found himself embroiled in a battle of another kind—one of the heart. Yassen Knight had sworn allegiance to the Arohassin. After his botched assassination of King Bormani of Veran, he was given a chance to win back his freedom by sabotaging the new queen's coronation. He infiltrated the palace. Obtained the position of bodyguard to the heir. Laid the trap. But there was one thing our assassin did not anticipate: the heir herself. Elena Aadya Ravence became his undoing. So on the eve of her destruction, Yassen Knight made a fatal decision. He saved the new queen. He led her to safety within the Sona mountains of Jantar. He hid her within his father's cabin and told himself he had done so selfishly—to redeem himself. But the heart is a strange tormentor. Somewhere in between her anger and his regret, their sorrow and loneliness, he came to understand her. He learned every inch and curve of her face, every tremble of her lip. The wants of her desire, the edges of her pain. He would know her face even in the darkness of death. Perhaps that is how love begins—as forgiveness.

As surrender.

He told her of his broken past, and she told him of her grief. He admitted how his ache for belonging had never eased, and she showed him a home worth saving. The heart is a strange tormentor, yes, but it is also a great revealer of truths hidden from oneself. When the Arohassin and Jantari attacked the mountainside, when the mines burned and the fires pinned them down, Yassen Knight discovered one final, lasting truth: He did not need a home. He had Elena, and she was worth saving. So our brave knight, our lonely bleeding boy, told Elena to run. He would find her, he said.

You'd better, she replied.

She did not turn back when the bullet sliced through his chest. She did not stop running. Elena Aadya Ravence escaped into the dark bowels of the mountains and howled in agony. She had learned how to wield fire through the scrolls. She had even learned how to withstand the Eternal Fire and walk the Agneepath of her forefathers. But she had never learned how to handle this sudden, weighty grief. In the span of a month, she had lost her Spear, her father, her lover, and her kingdom. What was left other than to despair? But the heart is a strange tormentor. It refused to wither. She refused to let their deaths be in vain. So Elena Aadya Ravence, the queen of Ravence and last of her name, crawled through the shadowed tunnels of the mountain and found refuge among the Black Scales. Little did she know that they had been waiting for her.

That he had been waiting for her.

Samson Kytuu rose from the ashes of her dead kingdom. He shattered the eyes of the false god and proclaimed himself Prophet. He was no longer the puppet of a metal Jantari king, or the servant of a mad Ravani one. He was a god, and he will wage a war greater than Sayon has ever seen.

THE BURNING QUEEN

PROLOGUE

ELENA

The desert howled around them in rippling waves, spitting sand and rock against the curved window of the hoverpod. Even through the thick glass, Elena could smell the desert: its dry camphor, underlaid with something bitter and savage.

"Brace for landing," the pilot called.

Elena did not sit. She placed her hands against the sill and leaned forward so that her nose pressed against the glass, leaving a smudge of ash. She needed to see it with her own eyes, to affirm that the rumors were real. That these, the dark amorphous forms of billowing sand, were wraiths of a god made alive.

A god so cursed that the desert raged before it.

When the mountains of the Agnee Range snapped up through the storm, Elena went rigid. There, nestled between the dark teeth of the cliffs, was the Eternal Fire. It licked the open sky as if sensing her approach. She began to shake. Not long ago, she had come to these same mountains with the blazing, glorious hope of a kingdom behind her.

Only ghosts followed her now.

The pod docked, and Elena stumbled after the Black Scale soldiers as they ascended the temple stairs. The winds were not so fierce this high, but she could taste salt in the air, intermingled with the acidity of smoke. With it, memories came flitting back: the hot breath of the inferno, the piercing note in her father's screams, the temple crumbling like a crushed flower underneath a cruel hand.

Elena faltered on the steps. Above, in the ruins of the temple where she had been crowned queen, the ghosts awaited. Her father, Ferma, the guards, all those who had died in her name. All the ones she could not save. She felt their unearthly stares prick her flesh with the cold, tender care of a carver's blade cutting through a skinned bird.

Ahead, one of the soldiers turned. She had dark, liquid eyes and a tattoo of a skull hand wrapped around her throat. She smiled, and the ghosts wailed.

"Come, he's waiting," she called.

With a stuttering heart, Elena let go of the crumbling railing. The wailing of the ghosts manifested into a keen, needling down her ears and setting her teeth on edge. Elena slipped her hand into her pocket and grasped Yassen's holopod. She traced its familiar scratches, and her chest loosened a degree. He had led her this far. Been so brave, so fierce. She borrowed courage from it and from him, wherever he was.

Elena trudged toward the Eternal Fire, blinking furiously as its heat buffeted against her face. Fallen columns and crushed diyas littered the ground. Scorch marks marred the white marble foundation, but her gaze, like an arrow flying true, settled on *him*.

The man basking within the inferno, as if it was the most natural thing in the world.

Her heart ratcheted up a notch, and all her earlier anticipation came crashing back. The flames sensed it. They trembled at her approach, rising, singing in soft hisses. As they grew louder, Elena felt the air tighten until it grew sharp, physical, like a match poised to strike.

The man turned.

The match struck, and Elena felt a deep, burning sensation ripple through the air and her body, cauterizing her nerves.

Eyes too blue, she thought. *Eyes cursed in the desert.*

They drank in the sight of her: the tousled hair of a month of no sleep; the cuts on her arms; the darkened skin of her hands. A slow smile spread across his face.

"I knew we'd find you," Samson said.

His voice seemed to come from the flames themselves, a thick, crackling song. The flames swooned. Her mind teetered between disbelief and fear. He could not be alive. He *should not* be alive. But then Samson stepped forward and took her hands, and the shock of his touch, warm and tender like the flames she summoned, jolted her back.

"You're alive," she said.

He smiled again, so bright and blinding that for a moment, Elena felt her fear dissipate, flooded out by relief.

"*You're alive*," she gasped. She crushed him in an embrace, and Samson laughed, the flames rumbling with him. He smelled of smoke and ginger, like spices roasted and set alight. His arms were heavy and strong as he pressed her into his chest and rested his chin on top of her head.

"I am, my rani," he said.

That was when she noticed the flames.

Not the ones of the Eternal Fire, but the *others*. They crawled up the staircase, encroaching on all sides. Blue like an unblemished sky. Blue like the roiling sea. Blue like his cursed eyes.

Elena pulled away. A question, the one that festered inside her like a parasite as the Black Scales had smuggled her out of Jantar, rose in her throat. She did not want to say it and make her fears real. But Samson only looked at her, expectant. And she saw then that his smile had never reached his eyes.

"How?" she said, her voice a low rasp. "How did you survive?"

Samson spread his hands, and blue flames rolled down his shoulders, spiraling around his arms. "I am the Prophet, darling."

There is a new god, the soldiers had told her. *A god that the desert bends to. A foreign god that your people never anticipated.*

"But—you—you're." Her tongue twisted in on itself. "H-how can that be possible? You're Sesharian. You don't believe in the Phoenix. And you—your fire…"

"Fire knows its brethren," he said, watching her. "We are the same, you and I."

She took another step back, watching the blue flames with a mixture of wariness and fascination. She could not deny that she felt a *pull*. Deep inside her, something ancient and raw. A burning that seared her veins with a heady potency and a creeping alarm, like when two predators in the wild see each other from a distance and awareness of their own danger flows between them. "I can wield fire, but I am not the Prophet. What makes you one, then?"

Samson considered her, his head tilting in an achingly familiar gesture that reminded her of hot afternoons spent on her balcony discussing their vision for Ravence. But there was something sharp in the slant of his mouth.

"Let me show you."

He turned to the Eternal Fire, and in that moment, Elena felt a mysterious sensation begin to build within her. A foreboding, a curiosity. It heightened as he raised his hand and the Eternal Fire, the one she could not control, the one she had spent months trying to even hold, *bent*. All its heads, all the angry, biting flames, *bent*.

Elena stared, stunned. Her mind raced, going through the stories of the Prophet, the Phoenix, her father's hunt, and all the while, that terrible sensation grew stronger.

"Where is the Phoenix?" Her voice was barely a whisper above the hiss of the flames. "The stories say that you were supposed to rise with Her."

When he spoke, the flames spoke with him. "There is no Phoenix. There never was. Only a lie, conjured by con men. The true master and architect of the Eternal Fire is the Great Serpent, and you and I, Elena, are of Her like. *We* are the gods now. *We* will take back Ravence and Seshar and watch the world bend."

Ravence.

The very name sent an ache through her. Her home lay ruined and burned, occupied by enemies. And before her was the very god the stories claimed would free it.

Stories that, according to him, were no longer true.

Samson must have sensed her hesitation, because he stepped closer, holding out his hand. In the light of the inferno, she could see the ash streaks on his cheeks, the spark of madness or genius in his eyes.

"I know what it means to burn," he said softly. "I know its misery. Its hunger."

Elena flinched. He drew closer, his voice low, dangerous.

"And if we can make Jantar just taste that misery, would you not be avenged? Tell me, rani. Would you not be pleased to have Farin's head at your feet?"

Her heart thundered. Her desire, on his lips, made her sick, thrilled. Around her, Elena could feel the hot rage of the inferno, the cold stares of the ghosts. *Vengeance.* For her people, her father, Ferma, Yassen, *herself.* The desire rippled through her with a slow heat, her every breath scraping the inside of her throat like a finely toothed comb. Elena watched the inferno with a new mixture of horror and wonder. *Vengeance* lay at her fingertips.

At theirs.

"How," she began, and stopped when she met his eyes. Because in them, she saw her same fury reflected—*tenfold.* Only his was colder, crueler, a wrath that seemed at once unfathomable and endless. If he harbored that much fury, what kind of god was he? A savior, like the stories said? Or a monster, like she had once believed? Elena paused, uncertain. Yet below her alarm, she sensed an awareness tugging her belly with an incessant urgency, and as she considered it, she felt his Agni twinge in recognition. *Like knows like. Fire knows its brethren.* The realization hummed through her bones, filling her ears with a buzz that built until all she could hear was the steady murmur of the inferno as it knelt before a cursed god.

A god who offered her his hand.

Slowly, Elena raised hers.

"Will you help me, then?" she said.

Samson smiled. A crude, vicious smile.

A butcher's smile, she thought.

He took her hand. "We start with Ravence."

THE HERO

CHAPTER 1

ELENA

I have woken to a strange world where heroes have turned beasts,
and beasts turned men. Where the heartless grow merciful, and the
merciful—heartless.
        —from the diaries of Priestess Nomu of the Fire Order

It was impossible to distinguish the smell of rancid metal from that of
burning flesh. Elena pressed herself against the canyon wall, trying to
breathe through her mouth, but the stench crawled down her nose and sat
in her throat. She could taste their fear. Her people, already dying.

Carefully, Elena scaled the canyon, the fine webbing of her gloves and
kneecaps sucking onto the rough faces of the rocks. The cliffs of southern
Ravence towered above her, red and severe, their stiff, craggy faces unlike
the soft, ever-changing curves of the dunes. Their silence swallowed her.
She felt like a beetle. Small. Inadequate.

She paused on a ledge and flexed her tired arms, wincing. They had
been climbing for hours. Behind her, the others vaulted softly onto the
ledge. Visha did not stop to rest. The strategist was already flicking open

her pod with a gloved hand, studying the maps. The holos cast a pale blue light on her face, leeching the color from her cheeks and making the sharp angles of her nose and chin as stark as the cliffs.

"I say we have about a few more minutes' climb before we reach the base of the tower," she said. She elongated her *s*'s, savoring them like morsels of meat caught in her teeth. Behind her, the twins, Akino and Akiri, were unbuckling their pouches, sliding out various weapons: stun grenades, hand-sized explosives, pulse guns, and of course, their daggers. They were Black Scale issued, with a winged serpent on the hilt.

Elena had warned them not to carry too much weight. The climb was long and narrow, but while she leaned against the wall, trying not to pant, the Black Scales moved with calculated ease, each move measured, bouts of energy managed. Visha was barely sweating.

"We've lost connection to the comms," Akiri said, checking her pod.

"So…it's only us…from here," Elena said.

Akino glanced at her and must have noticed the sweat on her brow, for he turned away, frowning.

"Lucky bastards," he said. "They're down there while we have to deal with this smell."

"Skies above, it's horrid," Akiri said. Her eyes avoided Elena's. "And we've been moving *so slow*. And taking too many breaks. If I have to smell this another minute—"

"Quit prattling," Visha snapped. The twins immediately quieted. "Phoenix set the pace. We've made good time, even if we are on the later side."

Elena's cheeks burned, but she ignored the slight. "I say…we rest another minute. Then head up. The tower is just ahead of us…" She sucked in air and blew out slowly. "So that means the rocks above will be crawling with Jantari. I can take lead and—"

"Let me," Visha interjected.

Elena paused. Though Visha met her eyes, there was a force in her voice that left Elena unsettled, like someone had run a wet rag down her sweaty arms.

"I did recon. I know the area. I can scout the cliffs ahead and make it back without losing too much time," Visha continued. "I'll move… quicker."

Elena wrestled the urge to panic. *They aren't disobeying me*, she thought. This was her mission. Her orders. Her team. After two months of studying Black Scale military tactics, suffering their grueling training, and planning the operation down to every single minute, every second, she had *earned* her right to lead. Never mind the fact that every Black Scale, including the three before her, had once vowed to serve her and her kingdom. They were her men, in name. But in spirit? Elena felt that same odd uncertainty, the unease that skittered like the fast-fading vestiges of a dream. Crouched before her, dressed in their black battlesuits with their silver horned shoulders, the Black Scales looked like sleek, vicious gargoyles. Demons of a god.

They will *follow me*, she thought furiously.

"We'll move together," she said, hoping her voice didn't betray her misgivings. Visha's face remained carefully neutral, while Akiri scowled, and Akino glanced at his sister.

Mine, she thought desperately.

Something flickered at the edge of her vision. Elena whirled, but the soldiers flew into movement. Their speed astonished her, even now. Visha with her throwing knife, poised and ready; the twins with their guns, one red, the other blue, both stamped with the seal of their leader. The black serpent.

The shadows flittered again. Elena was reaching for her gun when the shadows paled, then diminished as a bright, searing light flooded the top of the canyon.

"Get down!" Visha hissed.

Elena shrank back. The searchlight skimmed over them, every indention, every nook in the wall, suddenly bright and visible, before the light passed and the shadows rushed back with uncanny swiftness.

She waited a beat, then straightened slowly. Visha checked her pod.

"The tower is on," she said.

"But I thought—" Akino began.

"We're late," Akiri said flatly. Though Elena was facing away from her, she could feel her glower. "And those fucking junk brains are right on time."

They were supposed to have reached the tower base before the searchlight activated. Elena had made it a point in her briefing. Planned it, in the minute-by-minute breakdown. And now *it's on me. I moved too slow, took too many breaks.* She watched the rocks above, heart bleating. *Fuck, fuck, fuck.*

"We can still make it," Visha said.

Akino collected his weapons, but Elena noticed an added urgency in his movements. Visha pocketed her pod. Akiri was no longer scowling, but there was a dark, almost murderous look in her eyes. Elena could almost imagine her thoughts: *If I die because of this Ravani bitch—*

"We *will* make it," Elena said. She met their gazes, biting back her nerves as they stared, eyes like flint. She fished hurriedly in her pockets for her pod, not Yassen's, but the other. It was smooth and unmarred, face clean of scratches. *A novice's pod*, she thought suddenly as she drew it. *Not a captain's.*

"Here, look at this," she said, highlighting a route in red. It indicated a path that diverged from their planned route, hugging the rocks and then climbing up the steep cliffs of the western side of the tower. There was a sheer drop of several hundred feet on this side, which Elena noted. "But it will work," she said hastily. "We can't go the eastern route like we had planned. The Jantari guards will be out. But they won't expect someone creeping up the cliffs because—"

"It's a suicide mission," Akiri said.

Visha shot her a look. "Not if we move carefully. And quickly."

Akiri opened her mouth to retort, then seemed to think better of it. Akino belted on his gun, flexed his hands. His scar, hanging down from the edge of his eyebrow like a thin crescent moon, scrunched as he smiled.

"I'll beat you to it, di," he said to Akiri.

She sniffed. "Like hell you will. I was born two minutes before you."

The searchlight swung back, and they hid in the crevice again. By the time it receded, Elena felt heat building in her arms, something gritty on her tongue. It took her a moment to realize it was ash.

Her Agni was stirring.

Which could only mean that he was growing impatient.

"We should move forward," Visha said.

"On my signal," Elena cut in.

Visha met her gaze, eyes narrowing. "Right. Captain."

Elena crept up the wall. She could feel Visha's cold, disparaging gaze on her neck, could feel all their eyes boring holes into her shoulders like perfectly round pulse wounds. She had a sudden, irrational fear that if she looked down, she would find their guns pointing at her. *She got caught in the pulse fire,* she could almost imagine Visha saying. *Poor, poor queen.* Elena gripped her gun. She did not look down.

She climbed up onto the next ledge and sidled along the wall until she found the path cutting into the cliff. Once they reached it, she began to move quicker, rounded the corner, the others on her flank.

The corridor sloped upward, then veered left, but the swollen curve of a boulder blocked the view ahead. *A blind spot.* Elena crept forward. She strained to listen past the blood pounding in her ears for any sound, any indication of something waiting ahead. Nothing. Even the wind held its secrets.

Cautiously, Elena continued. The boulder loomed above her, its red face dark in the moonless night. Twenty paces, ten, five . . .

As Elena reached the turn, she spotted movement in the shadows in the corridor ahead. She held up her hand, signaling, but then the shadow morphed, and a man stepped toward the far wall, his back to her. He had a jagged silver weapon strapped to his shoulder. *Zeemir.* Elena backpedaled. The soldier had not seen her. He was too busy fiddling with his pants, the jangle of his belt bouncing through the air. She stepped back and crashed right into Visha.

The strategist hissed, and it was this sound, so quick and innocuous, that made the soldier whirl around. His eyes widened.

"The devils—" he began, reaching for his gun. But Visha was already moving, a blur of armor and knives and bright teeth, her dagger slicing cleanly into his neck as his pulse shot ripped through the fragile quiet. It cleaved through the boulder, rock and dust exploding in the air. Elena dove to the ground. An alarm wailed, and the searchlight swung around, its white, searing light washing out the rocks, Visha, the twins.

The memory came rushing back, pinning her to the ground.

The hoverpod's searchlight. The burning mountain. Yassen, grasping her hand.

Elena, run.

She clawed onto her knees. Shapes swam in and out of her vision. Her men, where were her men? Elena clutched her gun, calling. Suddenly, someone grabbed her elbow.

"Come on!" Visha shouted.

She pulled her up and they sprinted through the western passage as the searchlight whirled, trying to find them. Elena heard soldiers shouting over each other. Some went down the southern path, away from them, while others turned to the canyons in the east. A few came rushing toward the western cliffs. Toward them.

"Down here," Visha said. She rushed to the edge of the path and hopped down on the ledge jutting underneath it. Elena followed, just in time as the soldiers rounded the corner and ran past. They were heading in the direction of their fallen comrade.

"The twins—" Elena began.

"Don't worry about them," Visha said. "Now climb."

Above them, Elena saw the western watchtower pierce the night sky like a cold, sharp talon. Unlike the canyons, the watchtower was fashioned of obsidian rock. Its red veins shone with a dim, violent light.

Miles below, beyond the lip of the cliff, the city slumbered in fitful sleep. Magar, the Walled Oasis. A large wall ringed the city like a wedding band of sandstone. Elena spotted lights glowing along its ramparts. Only the city center was a dark, silent mass.

The Jantari had enacted a curfew. According to Visha's intel, citizens were corralled in the city center and had to be given special permission, or escort, to approach the wall.

As she stared down at the silent city, Elena felt bitterness growing within her. Tonight was Laal Joon. Today, her people were supposed to celebrate the founding of Ravence. They were supposed to light diyas. Bathe the city in showers of crimson powder so that every building, every man and woman, looked to be on fire.

But no diyas lit the street. No songs rumbled through the canyons.

There was only a chilling winter wind, and the far, cold stars to bear witness.

They crawled upward and finally climbed onto the flat ground of the tower. A sentry spotted them, but before he could shout, Visha's gloved hand flashed, quick as a snake. The sentry cried out as her blade buried into his shoulder. He fumbled for his gun, but Visha had already crossed the distance and slipped off her gloves.

With an almost tender gesture, she touched her bare hands to his face.

He screamed as his skin began to bubble.

The poison in her hands corroded his cheeks, darkening his chin, his lips, until he was choking on his own spit. He sagged in her arms. Visha removed her hands, and he slammed to the ground, like a tree toppled.

Elena looked away from his glassy, white-rimmed gaze.

There was a reason the Black Scales called the strategist the vicious vishkanya.

Visha already had her gloves back on as she sidestepped the dead man.

"Here," she said, but Elena backed away as she tried to hand her the explosives. "It's all right. My body's poison won't harm you."

Still, Elena made sure not to touch the uncovered skin of Visha's wrist. Her hands shook as she took the explosives. If Visha noticed, she made no comment. Elena pasted her three explosives around the western base as Jantari soldiers raced out of the eastern front. She ran back around, trigger in hand, to where Visha was placing her explosives.

"Check the city wall," Visha said, handing her a heat scope.

Elena peered down the cliff, picking up heat signatures. She spotted three soldiers patrolling the ramparts of the wall directly below them. Two more were on the far corner, immobile.

"There are five. Three sentries, two for relief on the southeastern side," she said, sweeping her gaze. "Several more huddled within the wall, possibly their barracks. In the west—" she began, turning, and stopped abruptly. Something had caught her eye. Elena swept back south, picking out the human-shaped signatures. What had . . . ?

Suddenly, she saw it. A small heat signature, too small to be human. It flickered like a flame. A candle.

A diya, she realized.

There were diyas scattered alongside the Jantari barracks. Diyas that Ravani had left out to light the way for Jodhaa and Alabore and their kin as they made their way through the desert. Diyas to celebrate the marking of Laal Joon. Elena picked them out, slow horror constricting her throat.

"I thought you said all the civilians are kept in the city center," she said. "What?"

"There are civilians just inside the wall," she said. "They're the ones who put up the diyas. Look."

Visha surveyed the wall below, her lips pressed into a thin, hard line.

When she handed the scope back, there was no flicker of guilt on her face. No remorse. "We're still sticking to the plan."

"You knew." Elena stepped back. "You knew there were civilians close to the western wall. Phoenix Above, Visha! You told me we'd hit *only* Jantari guards—"

Visha calmly placed the last explosive. "Give me the remote."

"No."

"Great skies above, if you don't—"

Elena took another step back, sparks crackling up her wrists. "Try me."

Visha puffed out her cheeks and then exhaled slowly. When she spoke, her voice was flat and toneless. "If you don't give me the remote, they'll still die. But then so will the thousands of Ravani trapped in the city."

For a moment, Elena hesitated, but it was all Visha needed. She launched forward, and as her gloved hand neared Elena, some irrational part, some part still fearful of her poison, made Elena flinch. Visha snatched the remote, and before Elena could stop her, she pressed the button.

The world erupted.

Elena was thrown off her feet as earth and sky bled into pools of red. She flung out her arm, clawing the air desperately, and found stone. Gasping, she hugged the boulder just as she saw the tower *snap*. Like a finger broken from a hand, a branch severed from its tree. It crashed down the cliffs and cleaved the wall below, shattering stone, lights—people.

Somewhere, Visha let out a whoop. The wall had been breached. The signal had gone out, and on the northeastern wall, *he* would saunter in. But Elena felt no sense of victory. All she could hear, all she could see, were the alarms screeching into the night and the diyas, smashed beneath sandstone. Ravani, civilians, crushed to death by her hand. Snuffed out, like a candle choked.

CHAPTER 2

ELENA

The Phoenix's love is strange. At once, it nourishes. Protects. And yet the kiss of fire is so gruesome that I wish to no longer bear Her worship.
—from the diaries of Priestess Nomu of the Fire Order

Smoke filled the breach. Elena felt it vine through her chest, squeezing her lungs as she climbed over fallen fragments of the wall. A small force of fifty Black Scale soldiers, those who had been lying in wait at the bottom of the cliffs, had already ripped through and taken the Jantari unawares. The larger, second force would break through the northeastern wall. Already, she could hear pulse fire in the distance. She should be running toward it, should be in position when Samson and his forces descended into the center.

But Elena did not hurry.

She surveyed the debris, the splotches of blood, the crumpled bodies. A mangled sensation built in her chest.

People.

Her people.

She swayed, trying to catch her balance, and a hand, broken and bloody, crunched under her boot.

She wanted to scream.

She fell, instead.

Her hands and feet began to move of their own accord. Distantly, Elena realized she had started to dig through the rubble. Stones bit into her skin. Scraped her palms. Her gloves were in ruins. She hissed as she felt the sting of the cuts, leaving bloody handprints in her wake.

"What are you doing?"

She whirled to find Visha standing in the breach, a hand on her hip.

It was the sight of Visha's unbloodied hands, gloved and spotless while hers were red and ruined, that made Elena bristle until all she could see, all she could think about, were those fucking perfect hands.

She rose, snarling.

Visha started, reaching for the urumi on her belt. It was too late.

The flame lanced through the air like an arrow, ripping the sword from her grasp.

"What the hells are you doing!" she barked.

"You lied," Elena said, stalking forward. "You told us after your recon that only soldiers manned the walls, but there were Ravani there. *Goddamn civilians*, Visha."

"Listen, I—" Visha said, taking another step back. Her heel struck the edge of a broken sandstone, and she tottered before regaining her balance. "We need to get to the others."

"We need to dig out the survivors," Elena said.

Visha laughed, short and harsh. "That's not our orders."

"Those might be yours. Not mine."

"We'll send rescue parties after we take the city."

"If we wait, we'll find only corpses."

"Well," Visha said, fixing her with a cold smile, "we better take this city quickly."

"Did he know?" Elena said as Visha turned. The strategist froze. "Did you tell him?"

Before Visha could respond, a drone filled the air. At once, Elena felt her fury fizzle, die. She whipped around to see three Jantari warbirds rise from within the center of the city and race toward the broken wall.

"Shit," Visha said.

"I thought—" Elena said, mouth suddenly dry.

"Shit, shit, shit." Visha grabbed her arm, pulling her. *"Run, Ravani."*

They barreled down the ruins as the jets roared. There was an earsplitting boom, like thunder cracking right above her head. Elena could not even hear her own scream. She slammed onto her back. The air rushed out of her, and for a moment, she couldn't see. Couldn't breathe. The world went black, then white. Elena blinked away bright, hot lights. The ground, the wall, everything was spinning.

A new section of the wall had been blown off. A gaping black hole, yawning into the dark canyons beyond. The warbirds circled overhead, no doubt searching for the mysterious army ensconced in the canyons.

We're already inside, you fools, she thought vehemently.

Something grabbed her hand. She blinked. Visha swam into her vision, ash streaking her face. She was pointing up, up, up.

But Elena felt them before she saw them.

The red sandstone beneath her rumbled as a steady thrumming reverberated through the air. The blackwings streaked past her from their journey within the Agnee Range, silver serpents rippling on their black hides as if alive. They shot past the warbirds, who scattered. One blackwing peeled away to the south while the other swung around, chasing after the warbirds within the canyons. It opened fire, long-range pulses lighting up the sky like red lightning bolts. Two Jantari jets managed to get away— but one was not quick enough.

A pulse ripped through its wing, shredding metal and severing it in two. The warbird crashed into the deeper canyons. A ball of gas and flames belched into the air like the dying gasp of some twisted beast.

Visha whooped. "Blast them, boys!"

Elena could not look away, even as the explosion split the air and blinded her. It was brutish and elegant and terrifying all the same. All that fire. She leaned forward as if to feel the brush of that distant inferno. She could feel its heat sear through her as if she herself had summoned it. It filled her with a deep, carnal pleasure, and a desire to *burn*. To do so much worse.

Soon, you will want to take everything, Samson had told her. *You will want everything to sing its song.*

But then her gaze slammed back to the fallen wall, and Elena tasted something acidic and vile on her tongue. Hot shame flushed over her. She swallowed the prickly torridity pushing up her throat and forced herself to breathe, to bury that treacherous desire.

"Come on. We need to get you to the center," Visha said.

Elena rose unsteadily to her feet, looking back to the wall. She wanted to stay. To sift through the rubble with her bloodied hands and rescue the survivors. *If there are any left*, she thought. How many were gasping for air right now, buried under rock? She almost took a step toward the wall when she felt a ripple, low in her stomach. A whine keened in her ears. And it began again. The *thud thud* in her veins as her Agni gnashed and roiled in frustration.

It was beginning.

He was calling.

"Elena, we have to go." Visha held out her pulse gun. "Come."

When she still did not move, Visha stepped forward and pressed the gun into her hand with a gentleness that startled her.

"How many more will die if we stay here, searching for what few survivors are left?" Visha said softly.

Elena turned to her, eyes red. Her throat ached. "Don't."

But Visha was already moving. She preferred to stay in motion, always. "There are more Ravani trapped in the city center, waiting for their queen. But you can stay here, mourning the dead. Don't bother with the living."

The words felt like a slap.

Burn, the Agni within her begged. It was as if the flames pulsed in want. *Burn*.

Slowly, painstakingly, Elena turned away. Everything within her screamed. Every step felt like a betrayal, and that feeling felt too familiar, too cruel. She pushed back the guilt. Swallowed it as she ran, listening to the rising chant of the flames as they called for her.

They hid behind a makeshift barricade as pulse fire shredded the air. In the tight lane, three Black Scales crouched behind a hovercar. Jantari soldiers, hidden behind a dilapidated storefront, fired from the other end, and Elena ducked as a pulse clipped off a store sign.

"Cover me!" Visha shouted.

Elena fired as Visha dove into the fray, joining the soldiers by the car. None of her shots hit their mark. Elena swore, warming up her barrel again when she saw Visha stand. The strategist ran forward as the Jantari fired. Elena and other Black Scales gave her cover, but a pulse, friendly or not, grazed Visha's thigh and she tripped, falling, but not before hurling a black ball toward the Jantari.

The grenade exploded. In the din of shouts and screams, Elena shot up and hauled Visha behind a cart full of shattered diyas.

"Can you walk?" she asked.

Visha nodded grimly, but Elena could see the blood blooming across her thigh. The other Black Scales had already run up, firing into the smoke.

They joined them to find five Jantari soldiers sprawled dead within the rubble. A comms crackled, and one Black Scale yanked the bloody device out of the fallen's ear with a sudden, vicious movement.

"There's another squad up ahead," he said as he listened. "Twelve of them in the northwest bazaar. They're calling for reinforcements."

"Soon all those bastards will be here," Visha said. "We have to move."

Their advantage was speed. That, and surprise. The Jantari had not known they would attack in the middle of the night. Twice. The black-wings picked off any escape hoverpods and warbirds as the infantry pushed in with a two-pronged attack, like a knife followed by a sledgehammer. A quick cut, then the killing blow.

"We just have to hold them off a little bit longer," Visha said. "When the second wave comes in, they'll crumble."

"Then what are we waiting for?" The soldier fitted the Jantari comms into his ear and grinned. It was his grin that reminded Elena of his name. Kavson. A tall brute with small ears and close-set eyes. Eyes that he fixed on her. "Let's take back the queen's city."

And save its people, Elena wanted to add, but they were already turning away.

They ran through a twisting alley that opened onto a wider road. Torn storefronts and sagging walls bowed to Elena. She spotted a body crushed beneath a wall, the legs splayed out, as if the soldier had been caught mid-leap. More bodies, some fallen Black Scales, mostly Jantari soldiers, were tangled within the rubble. She spotted a hand, half-closed. A shock of black hair, with the face squashed under stone. A boot, with no sign of its owner, sat alone in the middle of the road. As Elena picked her way past it, she saw that the foot was still within the shoe.

Visha turned as Elena vomited. Her face screwed up in contempt.

"Try to keep your shit together," she said.

"Visha, Visha," Kavson chided. He shot Elena a wolf's smile. "Don't make fun of our queen's delicate sensibilities. Not all of us are as lucky to have them."

"I'd rather shoot my eyes out," Visha said.

"What a waste," he said. "How will you find me in the dark, then?"

Elena wiped spit from her chin. She wanted to retort that she did not feel lucky, but then a high-pitched hum cut through the smoke. *Cruiser.* Before Elena could react, the armored vehicle burst over the rubble, guns firing.

"Everybody down!" Visha screamed.

Elena lunged to the side, ducking behind a crumbled wall. She saw a spray of blood out of the corner of her left eye, then heard a shriek. Visha dropped her grenade, fingers bloodied. Elena began to make her way toward her, but then the cruiser plunged forward, forcing her back.

She was trapped.

Elena shot up, trying to gun down the driver, but her pulses glanced off the shields. The cruiser hurtled closer. Fifty paces, forty. It switched on its headlights, blinding her. Thirty. Elena fired desperately. Twenty, ten—

The grenade shattered her eardrums. She screamed but did not hear it. Elena smacked into the ground, gasping. She tried to get up, but her limbs were heavy, slow. Blood leaked out of a gash on her forehead. She managed to climb onto her knees and peer at the world through a screen of crimson. She spotted Kavson ahead, yelling, or maybe he was laughing as he pushed a crumpled body out of the cruiser.

Visha and two other Black Scales were running up the side of the street toward Kavson. Elena wobbled to her feet. She called out to them, her voice far-off and foreign.

And then the air split.

At first, Elena saw only a blinding white light. *Grenade.* But the light was too bright, too sharp, and Elena felt it sear the air. It hit her with a physical force she did not expect. She slammed against the rubble, and this time, something pierced the armor of her battlesuit, straight into the soft flesh of her arm. She moaned. The light slowly faded, and when Elena gingerly opened her eyes, her heart dropped.

A hull blocked the end of the street.

It was a behemoth, tall as two men and wider than three. Thick metal coils hooked three Jantari soldiers within its belly. Where the men ended and the machine started, Elena could not tell. They were more metal than flesh, more weapon than man. The hull rolled through the street, crushing stone, limbs, soldiers. She watched it flick Kavson off his feet as if he were nothing but a fly. Visha fired, but it was useless. The hull came. Brutal. Relentless. Elena raised her hands to form the Lotus, the first form of her Agni, but her sparks fizzled in her palms, as bleary as her mind.

Suddenly, a sound pierced through the fog of her mind.

It was a hiss. Low and dangerous.

Her fingers smarted. Elena felt heat building in her arms, her legs, her throat as the fire that licked the buildings curved toward the sky. Every part of her, every cell, vibrated with the rhythmic hissing.

The inferno bent as if it too knew.

The Prophet was here.

CHAPTER 3

SAMSON

Son of sea, son of sea! See the horrors they have done unto me!
—from the hymns of the Great Serpent

*Y*our *eyes are too blue,* his mother had told him. *That is a curse.*

But I was born a god.

Samson relished the heat building through his arms, his chest, as he gunned the cruiser. He zipped past smoking rubble, racing toward the signal blinking on his screen as Chandi took up his flank. Behind them, the northern wall had already fallen. After the western tower had crumbled, the Jantari had been too distracted to notice his creeping assassins, and his Black Scales had made quick work after. The northern gates had *opened* for them. In his rearview mirror, Samson could see his Black Scales marching in, and he almost laughed at the sight.

He swung around a corner, and a shot rang out. Samson swerved. He saw the sniper—but Chandi spotted him first.

She fired her bloodsplitter, the icy-blue bolt slamming into the sniper with an electric keen and splitting his head in two. With something akin to amusement, Samson watched the Jantari fall. He wanted to see if the soldier had been a former mine overseer. Or, better yet, an island hunter. But the blinking light on his screen tore him back, and he pushed onward.

He could feel her Agni. Raw and powerful, flaring. He was getting closer, and he did not need Visha's signal to know it. Heat skittered through his body in anticipation.

A blue flame slithered down his wrist.

Wait, he told it.

"This way!" Chandi shouted and veered to the left. He followed as the wail of warbirds and sirens clanged through the air.

Wait.

They flew past a broken storefront. Past Jantari soldiers crumpled in the rubble. He could hear pulse guns in the distance, along with a strange, high whistle. The blue fire twisted tighter.

Wait.

They barged onto a side street, Chandi slamming through a soldier and sending him flying. His zeemir clattered to the ground. She was already off and grabbing the weapon as Samson leapt and broke into a sprint, the sounds of pulse fire rising, his Agni swelling with such desire, such *want*, that it took all his control to curb it as he burst around the corner.

She was the first thing he saw.

Black braids and bleeding lips. Eyes bright and burning as she raised her gun. She was several yards ahead, but she turned. Her gaze caught his for a moment, and Samson saw Elena's eyes widen, her mouth twist in... wariness? Relief? He did not have the time to understand because then he saw the hull in the distance marching toward her.

The blue flame hissed again.

This time, he answered it.

With one smooth movement, he unfurled the urumi around his waist. The long, snakelike blades whipped through the dirt with a sharp ring. Silver serpents spiraled up the twin tongues. It was the weapon of his people. The weapon the Jantari would come to fear. Samson flicked his wrist, and the urumi ionized with electricity as he closed his eyes and sought his inner Agni. He willed it to grow. To swell. To *devour*.

The blue flame on his wrist flared, rushing down the urumi.

Samson let it go.

The inferno sprang forth with a roar. Snapping. Biting. Tearing. He flicked his blades, and the flames bounded past Elena, barreling into the hull.

Glass popped. The hull, and the soldiers within it, screamed, batting at the flames. The huge machine stumbled, and he saw Elena raise her gun. *Wait! Just see!* he wanted to yell, but then he saw she wasn't aiming at the floundering hull, but at a Jantari soldier who had suddenly appeared from behind a fallen wall, lobbing a dark shape into the air.

With a snarl, Samson raised his blades, and a flame shot up. It caught the grenade and devoured the force of its explosion. Melded the heat into its own. Samson felt it surge through his body with an electricity that heightened his nerves, a giddiness that made the inferno cackle with glee.

He flew forward. Snapping his urumi, he directed the flames through the melee. The blue fire rushed past his Black Scales, instead latching on to any man who held a zeemir. Howls erupted as metal melted onto flesh. Samson whipped his urumi faster, the Agni beating within him, heat traveling through his limbs as the inferno grew larger, bolder. He saw Jantari soldiers running. Retreating.

"Cowards!" he crowed.

Sweat bathed his face. A buzz zipped through his bones, setting his teeth on edge, but Samson paid it no mind as his urumi crackled and his Black Scales pushed past the Jantari blockade.

A laugh started in his stomach. It rumbled through his chest, up his throat, and pierced the air. High and crazed.

Battle madness, his father would call it.

Victory is what he called it.

Samson slashed down, and the blue flames rammed into the hull. It fell with a clatter. Oil and something acidic filled the air as Samson slowly walked toward it. The fire hissed. It bowed to him like a devotee to its master.

Come, it chanted.

Elena was already kneeling, peering into the hatch.

"They're dead," she said.

Samson slowly crouched beside her. He could not make sense of the tangle of metal and flesh and coils. But he saw the metal eye of one soldier blink. Once. Twice. And then it stopped, fizzing.

He remembered the Jantari king with his robotic eye, the cold touch of his metallic fingers. *You are like a son to me,* Farin had said. He remembered the smell of oiled flesh. *And one day, you will look like this too.*

Samson spat. It hit the unblinking eye and dripped down into the mangled flesh and coils.

Elena turned to him in surprise as he stepped back to avoid the growing pool of blood. No sense in ruining his boots.

"Let's go," he said.

Blue flames brushed his feet, whispering. Elena inhaled sharply. She scrutinized the melted hull, but he knew she was looking past it, listening to what the fire had to tell.

"What do you hear?" he asked, hopeful.

"Men weeping." She stood, and the fire parted with a hiss. "They're all crying in the city center."

"You're getting better." He reached out, and a blue flame looped up his arm. It unfurled slowly as if testing the air. He brought it closer. "The fire tells me that the Black Scales have pushed the Jantari inward. They've barricaded themselves in the city center."

"You heard all this from the fire?" she asked, incredulous.

"Yes." He smiled as the flame slithered down his arm and waist. "You just need to listen."

"We penned them in. But we also trapped the remaining civilians."

"Elena—"

"They're hostages, Sam," she said. There was an edge of bitterness in her voice that made him bristle. "You made them hostages."

"The Jantari wouldn't dare to hurt them."

"How do you know?" She finally met his gaze.

Once, when they had danced under rose petals and soft lights, she had looked at him with something like hope. Tenderness, even. He had asked her how far she was willing to go to protect her kingdom, and her voice had cracked with complete conviction. *Far enough.* He had heard himself in that answer. Believed that perhaps they shared a similar sense of duty, of burden.

But the look she gave him now was unflinching, accusatory, an uncomfortable heat between his shoulder blades.

"I won't give them the option," he said firmly. He curled up his urumi, belted it back around his waist. "Neither will you."

He searched her face. She had not used her Agni yet, he could tell, and that worried him. "You won't hold back, will you?"

A muscle feathered up her jaw. She glanced between him and the roving fire, her face at once stricken and hard, a mask he could not tear off.

"No more civilian deaths," she said finally. Her eyes met his. "No more senseless killing."

She did not have to say *like this*, but he could feel those unsaid words. Smell the rancid sweat and fear of the dead around them. The fire hissed. It wanted to feed, couldn't she see? This was its nature. *Their* nature. But that was an argument he had lost before, and he did not have the energy to lose it again. No. Victory was lying a few miles away. His first real victory against Farin. He could almost taste the fire's hunger as it clenched his own stomach.

So he tried on a smile. "For you? Surely."

The horizon had begun to grey by the time they reached the inner city. The Jantari had set up a barricade of cars and tanks, cutting off access. But he did not need it. Samson stood with his hands in his pockets, waiting. Above, a floating streetlamp flickered intermittently. Chandi shifted beside him. The Jantari had allowed him to bring only one soldier for the parley, but his men were sprawled out and hidden in the buildings behind them. Just as the Jantari surely were spread out on the other side.

He felt a tug in his navel. *Elena.* She was getting into position. Serpent willing, Magar would be theirs by dawn.

"They're taking their damn time," Chandi grumbled.

"They'll come," he said. "Just wait."

Chandi paused, and it was this sudden hesitancy from her that made him turn. "What?"

Her eyes searched him, as if looking for something amiss. "How are you feeling? Otherwise?"

"Me? Swell." He grinned, nodding to the Jantari soldiers who were now stepping through the barricade, bearing a white flag. "And look. Here comes the catch."

"I don't mean that, Blue Star." There was a warning in her voice. "How is your…Agni?"

As if on cue, pain cracked up his shoulder. Samson wrestled back a gasp, gritting his teeth so hard he felt ash grind between his molars. It had started after he had summoned the flames. Like always. The pain was as loyal to him as his inferno, and the dichotomy of both almost made him laugh. Even now, it slithered down his shoulder, inched up his neck. He blinked quickly as the Jantari approached.

"It's fine," he said.

The Jantari general was a stout man with a face meaner than a blade's edge. From his thin cheekbones to his angled chin, he reminded Samson of Jantari steel. Pale, wicked, crude. Though he had not been subjected to metal transformation like other soldiers, the man reeked of metal. Samson could smell the oil, the tangy bite beneath. He could never forget the smell.

The general's lip curled as Samson offered his hand. He made no move to take it. "Sesharian."

"Jantari." Samson smiled, folding his hand behind him. Four Jantari soldiers formed a half ring around them, their zeemirs gleaming. "A pleasure."

"There's been a change of plans. Dismiss your commander and let us talk between each other."

Chandi started, but Samson stayed her, his eyes never leaving the general. "That would make it five to one. That's hardly fair."

"Let me revise: Dismiss your commander, or else I'll start shooting hostages."

Samson scowled. He was suddenly grateful that Elena was not within hearing; otherwise the general would not be standing now, and negotiations would have gone to shit. "You'd lose your leverage, then."

"I have thousands. Tick tock."

Samson rolled back his shoulders, sighing. "Go on, Chandi."

"Blue Star—"

"Go."

With a huff, Chandi relented. The general nodded, his eyes cool and triumphant, and Samson bit back a smile. Let him have a small victory, if only to give him a false sense of security. They hardly knew what was in store.

"Search him."

Two soldiers stepped forward. They frisked him, their hands harsh and coarse. When one touched the urumi looped around his waist, Samson winked.

"Careful, you might cut yourself," he said.

The soldier warily unlooped the blade and held it out in front of him as if it were a live bomb.

The general frowned. "You were supposed to come unarmed."

"I am, *now*. I give my weapon, my pride and joy, to you."

"Pride and joy of a Sesharian beggar," the general spat. He took the blade as the soldiers stepped back.

"He's clear, sir."

"See, Edmund," Samson said, reading the tag on the general's chest. "I'm true to my word."

With a flick of his wrist, the general snapped the blade open. It cut Samson across the cheek. A soldier drove the butt of his zeemir into Samson's side and he gasped, doubling over in pain. There came a shout from behind, from Chandi, but Samson held out his hand.

He wheezed and peered up at the general with a bloody grin. "Well, at least we're on a first-name basis."

Edmund said nothing as the soldiers propped Samson up. Gingerly, Samson touched his cheek. Pain shot up his cheekbone, into his eye. Samson winced.

"You betrayed our king," Edmund said, his mouth screwed up in distaste. "He was going to make you a Ravani king, and you slapped the hand that raised you."

"If I remember correctly, *your* king betrayed *me*. Partnering with the Arohassin to murder the royal family? Killing my soldiers on the wall? He never told me about that." Samson nodded toward the north, toward Rani. "I hear now that your lot is in a stalemate with the Arohassin in the capital. Funny, how in the end, they betrayed you too."

"Our reinforcements will be here soon," Edmund said, his voice flat. "We've taken down your blackwings. Your men are outnumbered. Save us all the time, and surrender."

"Quite the threat." Samson grimaced. He wiped off the blood from his fingers and met the general's gaze. "But it's utterly unconvincing."

"Not from where I'm standing."

Samson cocked his head. "Are you sure?"

Edmund narrowed his eyes as he gripped the urumi's hilt. "Make a decision."

"I already have," Samson answered. He stepped back and nodded up toward the sky. "Tell me, when exactly did you send for the reinforcements?"

At this, the general frowned. "What?"

Samson searched the empty sky. "A little bird tells me no reinforcements are coming."

"You're bluffing," Edmund said, but before he could say anything else, a rumble echoed through the canyons. They all looked up as a blackwing streaked in from the south. It wheeled around twice, and Samson smiled at the code.

"You see, the bird tells me that no messages have gone out in the past three hours. In fact, they've all been intercepted, rerouted back to you."

"Major—" Edmund turned to the man on his left, but he was cut short as loud snaps thundered through the city. One by one, the lights went out. The orb above them fizzled and died. The street plunged into darkness, and the soldiers let out little yelps.

"Hold," Edmund cried, but then he stilled. So did his soldiers. They heard it then.

The soft hiss.

It came from everywhere. From the city center to the Black Scale front line. The fire had been creeping around them for some time, low and quiet, embers waiting to rise. Slowly, the hiss grew louder until it seemed to vibrate from the air itself. Tiny flickering flames edged Samson's vision.

Elena had held to her promise. She had coaxed the fire, guided it as far as he had asked.

And what had she asked of him?

No more civilian deaths.

"I suggest you surrender, now, before you force my hand," he said.

"Are you mad?" Edmund snapped. "You'll burn us all down."

"Not us, just you," Samson replied.

And before Edmund could respond, Samson leapt forward, quick as a snake, and grabbed the urumi from his hand. With a flick of his wrist, the weapon ionized. The Jantari shouted, some reaching for their zeemirs, others for their guns. He whipped around, slicing two of the soldiers across their chests. Blood sprayed, hot. Fetid. Edmund backpedaled as the others scrambled for their triggers, but Samson was all momentum, a typhoon. He slashed down, cutting one soldier diagonally from neck to waist. He toppled in half. Samson whirled, blade singing—

"Kill the hostages!" Edmund howled as he ran for the barricade. "Kill the Rav—"

Red and blue flames burst forth, blocking his path, surrounding them. Edmund wheeled around just as Samson knocked the zeemir from the remaining soldier's hands.

"Tell. Me. Edmund," Samson said, each word punctuated as he rammed the hilt of his urumi against the soldier's head. The man wobbled, sank to his knees. Slowly, Samson gripped his chin from behind. "Do you know the smell of burning flesh?"

He whipped his urumi with a sharp crack, and the blue flames leapt. They swept past Edmund and jumped onto the soldier, biting and tearing, cutting his bloodcurdling screams short. Still, Samson held up the sagging body as the scent of burning flesh became unbearable and the soldier became a blackened, broken husk of a thing.

Edmund gagged, vomited. "Devil," he cried. "Butcher."

Finally, Samson let go. The corpse toppled as he bent down and slowly wiped his hands on the white flag. Then, carefully, he folded it. Held out the peace offering, its surface marred with blood, and smiled at Edmund.

"I think it's time for you to surrender."

CHAPTER 4

ELENA

We are a stubborn lot. Even when armies come to desecrate our temples and rebuke our god, we refuse. Perhaps that is our greatest rebellion, and our terrible tragedy—this refusal to stop believing.
—from the diaries of Priestess Nomu of the Fire Order

How many captured?" Elena asked.

"About eight hundred Jantari," Samson said. Blood flecked his jaw, dry and rust colored, but he made no move to wipe it off. She wondered if she too had blood on her that she had not noticed.

They had set up a rudimentary command center in the city square, in the hall that had once been filled with dignitaries and bureaucrats. The Jantari had taken it over, and Elena saw the remnants of their control: communication panels and pods, various headgears and military equipment, even a zeemir, recently polished. In the next room, the Jantari had kept their weapons arsenal and battlesuits. Chandi and Visha were in there, taking stock. Elena could hear their quiet murmur, the scuffle of their feet. The hall was a reprieve from the chaos of the city, but Elena found the quiet discerning, unnatural.

She nodded toward the control panel that had once been Edmund's.

"Are you sure no codes or messages were sent out? To Rani? To Farin?"

"None," Samson said. "We took out their communications tower in the south. They were in the black."

"And the Ravani army? How many soldiers were imprisoned?"

"Two hundred, or at least that's how many we found. They're in bad shape. But they're alive. And grateful."

A blue flame, half-formed, flickered like a ghost around his wrist. Ever since he had proclaimed himself the Prophet, Samson was more open with his powers. Fire, it seemed, was always around him. Even when she couldn't see it, she could feel it. Like awakening a limb that had fallen asleep, tiny pinpricks of awareness traveled through her bones. She could feel her inner spark, her Agni, ripple beneath her skin, yearning to be released. But she held it back. Something about so flagrantly flaring her powers filled her with distaste.

Samson's eyes slid to her. "What is it? You're fidgeting."

"You're wielding," she retorted, pointing to his wrist.

"A habit."

"One you kept conveniently hidden in Rani," she said before she could stop herself.

He sighed. "Again, Elena?"

She bristled at his tone, but more so, she felt the same sensation of slow strangulation. They had discussed this before. Samson was *the* Prophet. She had seen it, felt the awful depth of his powers. As a Ravani who had been raised on the stories of the Prophet, she knew she should *believe* in him and his fight for freedom. He had promised her vengeance. But in the months after she had taken his hand, her disbelief and unease had grown. He did not claim fealty to the Phoenix. He had allowed the order to be killed, watched her father fall into madness during his hunt—

"Elena." He took her hands, his voice gentle. "I told you, I had to hide. Your father would not have believed me, even if I summoned flames before him. He was already lost. His fate already written in the flames. Even I could not have stopped it."

"His fate," she said darkly, working against the lump in her throat. "I could have convinced him. Brokered a partnership—"

"The Eternal Fire had already claimed him. I could do nothing," he said.

"You could have warned him," she said.

"And it would have changed nothing," he responded.

They stared at each other—she, confused and hurt; he, wary and watchful. It was the same argument. The same patterns. They went around and around and arrived at the invariable conclusion. Silence.

Finally, Elena looked away. She felt her anger leaching out, replaced by a bone-weary grief that seemed to have never loosened its grip since Rani. All at once, she was acutely aware of the grime on her clothes, the blood in her hair, a filth that sank deeper than skin. She wanted to sleep. To scream. To scrub her skin until her hands felt raw and she saw the white gleam of bone. Maybe then this grief would leave her. Maybe then she could walk without this burden bearing down until it ripped through her stomach and left her bleeding.

Hollowed.

"We counted the survivors in the city," Samson said, breaking the silence. He hesitated, then placed his hand on her shoulder. It was warm, heavy. "Mostly Ravani, with some Sesharian refugees who settled south. They'll be in the square soon. You should address them."

"And the Jantari soldiers?" she asked.

"They'll be dealt with."

"We crushed civilians when we breached the wall. I sent out a crew to search for survivors, but they found none." She met his gaze. "Our intel said all civilians were kept in the inner city, under tight watch. But Visha reported her recons to you. Did you know they were there?"

A pause.

"You saved thousands of Ravani, Elena. Tens of thousands, in exchange for seventy."

"That wasn't an answer to my question."

"No," he said, and the flame on his wrist flickered, then stilled. "But you and Visha were right to continue the mission. We have Magar now. The city is free of the Jantari, thanks to you."

Thanks to you. A twinge of guilt reverberated through her ribs, hammering against her heart. "I regret it," she said.

Her voice, though soft, seemed to echo in the hall.

Samson stilled. Even Visha and Chandi in the room over must have noticed, because she could no longer hear their murmurs. Samson stepped closer, his eyes raking over her, through her, and she had the odd sensation of being stripped down, examined, and found lacking.

"Regret," he said slowly, pulling out the word as if tasting it for the first time.

"Yes," she said, uneasy. She was pinned between him and the table. With no escape, Elena faced him. She faced the Prophet and the darkness beginning to bleed into his eyes. "You are their Prophet, *our* Prophet. Surely you must feel regret for killing your followers."

Samson cocked his head and regarded her with a cold, almost reptilian focus. "I have had many regrets in my life, Elena Aadya Ravence, but this is not one of them. Tell me. Did you feel regret when you destroyed those Jantari mines and set off landslides, crushing the tiny village?"

She stared at him, speechless.

He drew closer, and she saw now how his blue eyes were not dark, but hot like burning coals. "You told me you wanted vengeance against the Jantari. This is part of it. These *sacrifices*," he said, and she flinched, as if struck. "There is no room for regret, or those who feel it. So, tell me, rani. Do you still want vengeance, or will I have to leave you behind?"

Elena swallowed. There was a fervor in his eyes, vicious and bright, like fire glinting off a sword. But when he hooked his fingers beneath her chin, drawing her in with a touch so gentle that the absence of pain felt like a prick, she realized the look in his eyes was more than just fervor. It was zeal. The unshakable belief of the righteous, who *knew*, without a tremor of doubt, that their actions were justified.

Because he was a god, and gods did not answer to the laws of men.

"Should I leave you behind?" he said, his breath brushing her lips.

Disgust, guilt, anger rippled through her as she wrestled for an answer. The long cool hall stretched onward, and outside the great doors, she began to hear the chatter of a crowd gathering. Survivors. Her people, freed because of him. Because of them.

"No," she spat.

His nail lightly scraped the underside of her chin. "Good. Because regret immobilizes you. Makes you weak. You are a god, Elena, whether you believe it or not. And gods do not fret about regrets, not when we have a war to win." He let her go. "I would hate parting ways with you, my rani."

He began to leave, but she hooked her nails into his arm and forced him to stop.

"I want to give the ones lost at the wall proper funerals," she said, her voice hard, firm. "It's the least we can do, *as gods*. Right?"

He looked down at her hand. For a moment, she thought he would refuse, but then Samson dipped his head. "As you wish."

"The queen!"

"Make way!"

"She's alive, she's alive! Phoenix Above, look!"

Elena blinked against the sudden brightness of the day, overwhelmed by the onslaught of voices from the crowd waiting on the hall steps. They swarmed her, shouting, calling. One older woman came forward and draped a mala, a garland threaded with fresh jasmine and marigold, around Elena's neck.

Already, celebrations were ringing through the city. People walked openly in the streets, drinking, singing, dancing, with no fear of curfew, no zeemir glinting overhead. Elena wanted to feel their exuberance. She wished for joy to sweep her up like a heady drug so that she forgot the deaths along the wall, the blood beneath her fingernails. She wanted to relish their victory. *Her* victory.

But Elena could only stand there, silent. With each passing second, her smile faded. She ducked her head and pushed past the crowd, muttering excuses, and with every hand that reached out to touch her, she flinched. She stumbled down the steps, heading—*where?* She did not know these streets, not like Rani, not like the dunes surrounding the capital. The city walls towered overhead, red and stark in the bright midday sun. *The breach*, she thought, but as soon as she thought of it, the strength left her legs. She staggered, sick. The idea of digging up the dead and creating more funeral pyres churned her stomach. She could not face the dead or yield her regret. Somehow, that juxtaposition of pain felt *right*.

Good, she thought savagely. *Let me suffer.*

At least it was something she deserved, unlike this joy.

She turned the corner and spotted the white marble steps of a temple.

It was small but ornate, with a tiny courtyard fenced in by sandstone pillars that led to an intricate doorway decorated with carved lotuses and reclining deities. On the spire, the Phoenix soared above. Her mighty wings spanned around the dome, Her eyes inlaid with a collection of jewels that made Her seem both prescient and formidable, divine and relentless.

Elena stopped.

Samson had told her that the Phoenix was a false god. A myth, and a lie. *The true master and architect of the Eternal Fire is the Great Serpent.* He had torn down the ruins of the high temple in the mountains and already begun erecting a new spire, one with the Great Serpent coiling around it. This one would go too. What was the use of pitying a fraudulent god?

But Elena ascended the steps, removed her shoes, and ducked into the inner chamber.

Clay diyas flickered in tiny alcoves set into the walls. A fine rug, threadbare now after suns of use, kissed her naked soles. Elena found herself pulled not to the Phoenix soaring above, but to the fire that burned within Her altar. She could recognize its song anywhere. The Eternal Fire's small child rumbled in welcome. Every temple fire in Ravence was created from a flame taken from the Eternal Fire, but unlike its mother, this small fire filled the inner sanctum with a gentle warmth.

Elena knelt slowly.

"I..." she began. Her voice rang through the chamber. All at once, she felt foolish, conspicuous, even though she was alone. A prayer book sat propped up on a stand. Elena stared at it—the delicate white pages, the scrawling black text—and her well of bitterness grew more acidic. She wanted to rip out the pages. Burn all the lies they told.

"Of all the betrayals, yours was the worst." She clasped her hands around her knees until she could see the gleam of fire against the white of her knuckles. "You don't exist. Your stories, your prayers, your songs, all blasphemy. I know. *I know.* I saw how the Eternal Fire knelt to Samson. He is the Prophet called by a god, and you are a false god made by a man. You made my kingdom a lie. You made my family a mockery." She raised her eyes, looking into the flickering ruby eyes of the Phoenix. "But why can't I stop believing in you?"

She had tried to come to terms with it. Tried to shift her faith to the true god, Samson's god, *the Prophet's god.* But even now, kneeling before the Phoenix and Her small fire, Elena could hear the songs sung in Her name. The lilting prayers, the melodious chants, the music of her childhood, her people, her family. Her parents had sat before the altars like this. They had dedicated their lives to a god—and for what? To learn that She had never existed? That their lives had been a waste?

"I refuse." She looked away from the statue to the ceiling, pitching her voice to the heavens above. "You hear me? Samson may be the Prophet, but my family was not *wrong*. I refuse to believe it. Because my mother believed. She wrote of the Phoenix, your grief, and your rage. And that cannot be a lie. She and my father did not throw away their lives for a lie," she said, and her voice broke. She stopped, wiped furiously at the corners of her eyes. The fire crackled, and Elena stood, glaring up at the Phoenix. "I will find proof of either your existence or your deception. And you or whatever god will have to confront me then."

The fire banked, wavering against her sudden movement, and for a moment, Elena thought she saw something in the flames. Eyes, golden and full of hurt. But when she peered closer, they vanished.

I am going mad, she thought.

Shadows flickered on her right, and Elena whipped around sharply. A woman cried out, stumbling. Her thali clattered to the floor.

"Sorry, sorry, I didn't mean to startle you," the woman said as Elena knelt to pick up her tray.

She gathered the offerings—sugared almonds, faded and worn apples, ladoos made of foxnuts—and placed them back onto the thali. "It's all right," she murmured, handing the thali back to the woman.

The woman made no move to take it. "Mother's Gold," she gasped. "It's you! The queen, in my little temple." She laughed, taking the thali. "Did you like the mala I gave you?"

It was only then that Elena recognized the woman as the one before city hall. She had changed into a priestess's garb, with a red sash around her wide waist and an orange dupatta draped over her head.

"Yes, yes." She shifted uneasily, moving away from the woman. "Thank you. I have to go—"

"Please, take some prasad before you go." The priestess quickly bent to the altar and swiped a slightly melted ladoo from a platter. She looked at it, blanched. "Sorry, maybe another— Oh! Come, I'll make a fresh batch. Just for you."

"I really must—"

"You really must try them." The priestess grinned. "Even the order at the high temple asks for my offerings specifically. 'Fetch us Kruppa's,' they say, and send a bored novice my way. Come, come!"

Fighting back her annoyance, Elena plastered on a smile. "I would love to, Kruppa, right? But I really must go to…" Her voice trailed off. She almost said she had to go to the breach, and the slip must have made her face contort, because Kruppa's eyes softened, and she squeezed her arm.

Elena looked away, flushing.

"I was there," the priestess said softly. "The day of your coronation, I was there at the temple, delivering my offerings. They wouldn't let me inside the sanctum, tight security and all, but I heard after how the king…" She paused, shaking her head. "It was a dark and horrible day. I cannot imagine the grief you must feel, but you have now given us hope. We can make those fucking bastards pay for what they did."

Elena laughed, a choking sound. "Kruppa, we're in a temple."

Kruppa covered her mouth, but a sly grin creeped between her fingers. "Sorry, sorry," she said, not looking the least bit apologetic.

Elena looked to her and the Phoenix, and something settled in her heart. Not her confusion or regret—those stayed tangled, ensnaring her. But within their cage, resolve hardened. Like a thorn, it cut her skin, ruthless and stubborn, intent on being recognized.

Elena swallowed hard, staring at the fire as if it could dry off her tears.

"Kruppa," she said finally, "can you help me to oversee funeral rites for the ones we've lost?"

Kruppa smiled, gentle. "I will see them across the threshold to our creator, Your Majesty."

Elena did not respond. She only glared at the Phoenix and the heavens in challenge.

See? she thought. *See how we refuse?*

CHAPTER 5

SAMSON

We will rise, like seeds buried. We will rise, and even the metal blades of the Jantari will bend to our fury.
  —from *The Lament of Seshar: A People's History*

The inferno purred to him as Samson watched the smoke-clogged horizon warm to an acidic orange. Even the sun couldn't break through the smoke of his flames. He didn't know whether to take that as a sign of triumph or an omen.

They're watching, the inferno murmured.

He turned his attention to the cage. It was a rudimentary perimeter made up of barbed wire and steel rods and Black Scale sentries. Set outside the city with the ruined wall towering behind it, the cage had the quality of a chained and ruined beast. The Jantari soldiers within watched as he drew closer. Some were sitting, others pacing, a few sharing a Rysanti-made cigarette that smelled like wet sulfur, but they grew still at his approach. Their eyes, pale and shrewd, pierced him. It brought an ugly memory, one of sand and dirt and screams ringing through salt air when similar eyes had watched from the beach, but Samson pushed the memory away as he joined the Black Scales.

Chandi glanced over as he neared. Still dressed in her black battle fatigues with her skull-hand tattoo wrapped around her throat, she looked like a shard of the black obsidian that lined the beaches of their island. *Like a fang of the Great Serpent*, he had joked with her once. Poised and always ready to strike. But Chandi had looked at him then just as she looked at him now, her eyes unpeeling him as if she knew whatever uncomfortable truth he was hiding beneath.

"You shouldn't be here," she said.

"And a warm hello to you too, Commander."

"You pushed yourself enough today. Go rest. If your Agni——"

"I'm all right, Chandi," he said firmly, though his body ached, and a tremor was already beginning to build up his arm. "I'll go after this, I promise. I just wanted to see them."

"To gloat," she corrected.

He grinned. "Maybe we should send a holo to Farin. *Greetings from Ravence. Signed, your beloved Sesharian pets.*"

Chandi said nothing, but a patrolling Black Scale chuckled. Samson, biting back a smile, surveyed their prisoners.

"How are they?" he asked.

"Snapping like snakes in a pit."

Chandi and his commanders had split up the Jantari throughout the city to minimize chances of riots. This prison only held a hundred soldiers, but still, Samson had asked for quick-fingered Black Scales to keep watch. Even a hundred Jantari soldiers could spell trouble.

Eight hundred Jantari soldiers left, in my care, he thought, and it sent a vicious thrill through him. Great Serpent Above, it felt *good*. Delicious. All these Jantari soldiers, defeated and imprisoned by Sesharians. Chandi may not prefer to gloat, but he savored the sight of their muddied uniforms and broken zeemirs. He had played a pet and puppet to Farin for so long that he had almost forgotten the sweetness of victory, selfish and hard-won. All these suns, he and his Black Scales had answered to Farin. Fought his petty battles, serviced his whims. Samson's victories had never truly been his—they had been for Jantar. For their king.

But this one, this one was his.

And Elena's, he thought after a beat. But unlike him, she did not revel in it, and it was this that made his smile falter.

"Elena regrets breaching the wall," he said.

"I told you," Chandi said. "She does not have the stomach for war. Or its costs. Let's go to the Sona Range and be done with her."

Samson said nothing, not because he did not agree, but because he did not wish to admit it. Chandi was right, in her own way. Elena had never fought battles, never led an army, never played an obedient puppet to a king. She was born into power, when he had had to claw for it, kill for it. And now that she had finally bloodied her hands, she whimpered. Regretted.

It filled him with fierce awe and envy, a pernicious tangle that ensnared him tight. She was of Agni. How could someone like her, someone *of* power and made *from* power, regret? But it was her capacity to even *feel* remorse that made him ache—simply because he had forfeited it many suns ago.

Remorse had made him feel more human, less monstrous. And he grieved for that lost part of himself.

"She is of Agni, Chandi," he said bitterly. "I owe it to myself to understand her powers. Maybe she'll surprise us."

Chandi scoffed but made no rebuke. He was her general, and like any loyal soldier, she knew when to hold her complaints.

Samson locked eyes with a tall Jantari standing by the fence line. The soldier was broad shouldered, with a thick neck and shaved head. Deliberately, he dropped his cigarette and, with his gaze never leaving Samson's, crushed it slowly with the heel of his boot. Stamped, again and again.

"That one's ready to charge. Like a mohanti," Chandi said. "Probably just as small-brained."

Samson did not flinch under the soldier's gaze, but he was not stupid. The Jantari would revolt. It was in their blood to squash opposition, like it was in his blood to cut down their metal hands. They were an inexorable pair. The tyrant and the rebel. Changing faces, spaces, but dancing the same song all the same.

They're always watching, the inferno purred.

Reflexively, Samson touched his lower chakra beneath his belly button, where the core spark of his Agni lived. Its hiss traveled up his abdomen, his chest, licking the insides of his throat. He could taste its hunger.

A few Black Scales who were warming themselves around a small fire suddenly jumped back as the flames swelled. Even at this distance, Samson could hear the inferno call to him.

But he clenched his hand, and the flames coiled back, hissing in displeasure. A shooting pain, sharp and electric like hitting his elbow against a corner, traveled through his arm and across his chest. Samson gritted his teeth. If it weren't for the Jantari before him, he would have gasped.

"Blue Star?" Chandi asked, a tinge of worry in her voice.

"I'm all right, I'm all right." Samson ran a hand through his hair to nonchalantly shake off the pain in his arm. His mouth felt strangely dry and swollen. The scar across his chest began to itch, but he fought the urge to pick it. *Not yet.*

"What happened to Edmund?" he asked, hoping Chandi would move on.

But she studied him, her eyes flicking from his arm to his face. "It's getting worse, isn't it?"

No, he thought desperately. *Not yet.*

"Is that him?" Samson said, pointing to a man hunched over in the far corner. The Jantari general was talking fiercely to a group of angry, exhausted men. They seemed to soak in his every word. Ripples began to move through the prisoners, more turning toward their surviving leader.

"Shit," Chandi said.

"Move Edmund," Samson said. "Get him out before we have a riot."

He glanced back at the glaring soldier. He had become deathly still, his shoulders taut like a pulled bow. *Skies above, he does look like an ox.* Uneasily, Samson looked away.

"Execute any pilots and their remaining commanding officers. That should shut them up for a bit."

Chandi nodded and motioned to one of the sentries. "How many tonight?"

"All of them."

Keeping the officers alive would only lead to a counterattack. Edmund may have his brawn, but without the brains of his operation, he couldn't even lead a petty skirmish.

Samson turned to go when he felt a hiss travel down his spine to his navel, the inferno flaring in warning just as the tall brute flung himself against the fenced wall with a death keen. The rudimentary fence quivered. For a moment, everyone stilled. The rods teetered, the barbed wire rattling like scorpions in a pit. And then a singular rod fell—right at Samson's feet.

He stared down at it and then back up at the soldier. The man grinned and grabbed the barbed wire.

The air erupted.

At once, Jantari soldiers rushed the fence. Chandi bellowed for the Black Scales to shoot. Edmund jumped to his feet, screaming. Shots crashed through the grounds, quick and percussive. A few Jantari went down. But the stampede built, soldier after soldier, pressing against the fence as it jerked in sharp, erratic movements like a branch in a winter wind.

Samson moved to unravel his urumi. One slash, and he could cut the tall soldier's hands clean off—but something in the man's eyes made him freeze.

"Butcher," the soldier called him. He reached through the barbed wire, blood spilling down his hands as he grabbed the metal rods. "Farin treated you like a son. Raised you from the dirt. Trained you to fight like us. But even with all of that, you could never hide your true filth, could you, *boy*."

The fence bent, groaning.

"Climb so high," the soldier said as the fence bucked wildly, "in filth you lie."

With a horrid crack, the fence snapped.

Chandi roared as pulse fire cleaved through the stampede. There was no order to it. Shoot at will. Soldiers collapsed. The tall man dashed toward Samson before he could react. The Jantari grabbed his wrist, pulling him close as he raised his other fist. Reflexively, Samson drove up his arm to block the soldier's punch and gasped as the man's fist collided with his forearm. White-hot pain jittered up his arm, his side. More soldiers rushed through the opening, streaking past.

Kata, kata, kata, kata.

The rapid, percussive sounds of magazine pulses ripped through the air. The fleeing soldiers toppled, one by one.

Samson wheeled, trying to push the big man off him, but the Jantari used his weight to lock him in. His next punch landed right below Samson's sternum.

He cried out. Black spots danced in his eyes, and his knees buckled. Around him, Samson was faintly aware of the rushing and falling bodies, of the small fire hissing as the soldier wrapped his thick fingers around his throat.

Use us, the flames said.

But he remembered the last time he had wielded his Agni in a weakened state: the pain ripping up his arm, an electric sensation scorching through his body as the cold bit into his flesh.

It won't be like last time, the inferno purred. *You are stronger.*

Samson backpedaled, slamming his arms onto the soldier's forearm. Distance, he needed distance. But the man moved so quick, and his next blow connected with Samson's chin.

The world spun. Samson tasted iron in his mouth, then dirt, and then he realized he was lying on the ground.

Climb so high, in filth you lie.

The soldier raised his boot, and Samson rolled over. He scrambled to his feet, clawing his waist for his urumi just as the soldier lunged for Samson's weapon.

No one touched his urumi.

He roared, slamming his elbow into the soldier and kneeing him in the liver. The Jantari gasped, coughing. Samson ripped out his urumi, and the sound of it unsheathing, like a chord being struck in a wide blue lake, filled him with such fierce relief, such calm, that all the fear melted away until he felt one thing only, one truth that encapsulated everything he knew, everything he was, that he laughed to think he had ever thought otherwise.

I am a god.

The blue flames screeched. They flared down his urumi like a torch, striking so suddenly that the Jantari soldier didn't even know that his arm was burning until he raised his fist and saw it aflame.

He screamed.

Samson cut down, down, twins blades tearing through the soldier's thick neck, through skin, tendon, down to the bone and then clean to the other side. His head sailed through the air.

Samson whipped around, momentum now.

The flames leapt and crashed over each other, momentum now.

The inferno laughed, shattering, biting, momentum now.

When Samson stopped his dance, when his twin blades finally floated down to the earth like wings come to rest, the fence was gone. The fleeing soldiers were too. Only black mounds, chipped bone.

The survivors were corralled at the back of the pen, hedged in by Black Scales with pulse guns.

Chandi ran to him. "Edmund, have you seen him?"

A sudden cry made them both turn as a Black Scale held up a ruined uniform. Even from here, Samson could see the glint of stars on the shoulders.

Chandi hissed. "We were supposed to use him as a bargaining chip."

The realization, like a touch of cold steel against his skin, made Samson still amid his battle lust. He blinked at Chandi.

"The general was our prized hostage. We need some hostages for—"

"We have seven hundred others." Samson swayed on his feet even as he belted his urumi. His bones buzzed. The pain, ever present, came back with relish.

Sulfur in his nose. Electricity in his blood. He needed to leave, now.

"Samson, are you—"

"We were supposed to execute their officers." Samson turned, his boots trudging through the remains. "I just started it for you."

She caught him before he fell, and he sagged into her shoulder. "You fool."

He could barely hear her.

Pain crashed through him, fast and fierce. Chandi shouted, and then he found himself in a cruiser, then on a cot. Clarity returned, and he recognized his quarters, an old family home set behind the city center. Shakily, he unbuttoned his shirt. His scar began to sting, and when he looked down, he saw that it had darkened too.

He had pushed hard today, perhaps too much. Heat prickled down his spine, and Samson felt sweat break on his forehead. He opened his palm. He tried to summon sparks, but his hand remained empty. Hollow.

He had spun his Agni so completely, so vehemently, that it had devoured *him*. He couldn't differentiate the inferno's hunger from his own. It frightened him, in a way that made his insides shrivel as if unearthing a dirty secret. Even now, he could taste its hunger, like a morsel of food stuck stubbornly between his teeth. It hooked into his spine and began to tug.

But then a wave of tiredness washed over Samson, sucking him down into a dark, black sea.

It was always this way. Sound seeped out. The hammering in his chest slowed until he could hear nothing at all. Familiar panic rushed through him, and Samson tried to fight, tried to claw his way back to the surface. A distant part of his mind worried that Elena would call upon him and see him like this, weak and vulnerable, but then another wave crashed over him, and Samson was sinking. The soundless black sea drowned everything out. All he could hear was the quiet. So loud, it felt like a roar. And then a voice, so, so far away.

"It's all right, Blue Star." A gentle hand touched his forehead. "Rest now. It's only me."

And he slipped beneath the sea, unmoored.

CHAPTER 6

SAMSON

*"What is the most dangerous opponent of fire?" the son of sea asked.
"Nothingness itself," the Great Serpent hummed. "Be wary of absence.
Even Agni cannot burn on its own."*
    —from *The Legends and Myths of Sayon*

He dreamed of men pressed against a cage, clawing at him with large metallic hands. He stared up at them and realized with a start that *he* was in the cage. Above, the men laughed. With ease, they broke through the bars and grabbed his hair, his face, sinking their hungry teeth into his flesh and chewing nonchalantly, as if he was simply a thing they had already claimed and thus found no particular hurry to enjoy. He roared for his Agni, but his waist was bare, his urumi gone. No flames leapt to his aid. Metal teeth grated through his stomach, and he yelped as a dark mouth ripped out his Agni, the spark already fading. *Come back*, he cried. *Come back!* And then he was sinking. A deep, terrible void surrounded him, pinning him down as if it was a physical weight. Like waves, it pushed him down farther and farther to a bottom he could not see, could not feel, but the knowledge of its absence filled him with a wild, animallike fear. He screamed. The sea vibrated with laughter, and suddenly he was on the wet floor. Someone kneeled on top of him. Pale hands gripped his throat, metal nails breaking through skin. He tried to hit the attacker, and they jerked away to reveal eyes as golden as the sun. Horrible and familiar. He reached—

The void reached back, claiming him.

Samson gasped awake. His throat burned. Ash on his tongue, iron clacking between his teeth. He tried to sit up when he noticed the hot coals on his body. Three were lined down his naked chest and abdomen, placed above his chakra points. Their heat spread through his bones, and gradually, Samson relaxed. There was no chill in his blood, no empty feeling in his gut. He opened his palm and blue embers sparked between his fingers. His Agni, whole and alive.

Chandi stirred beside him.

"Warmer now?"

He lay back against the pillow and took a long, shuddering breath. Relief, edged with fear, rippled through him. He touched his lower abdomen, where metal teeth had ripped out and stolen his Agni.

"Yes," he said.

Chandi drew her chair closer. Tired shadows ringed her eyes, but her gaze was bright and alert.

"You—"

"I know," he said quickly. Then, in a softer voice, "I know."

Chandi said nothing, but her eyes were still fixed on him like the sharp, dark shards of ore they found underneath the Sona mountains.

After wrapping her hand in a scarf, she took off the coals and placed them back in a metal pot. The room was so warm he could feel his skin tingle, as if every fiber of his being was drinking in the heat. Already, he could feel his strength returning.

Samson sat up. Chandi did not retie the scarf around her neck, and he could see sweat beading on her forehead. The room was too hot for her.

"You should rest—" he began.

"It took longer to revive you this time," she said. Her mouth was pressed into a thin line, her face pinched with an inwardness that he knew, after many years of fighting together, meant she had been chewing on a topic for some time.

"How long?"

"Five hours."

A year before, it had been one. A cold panic broke over him, gooseflesh prickling across his chest. He reached for his shirt with a forced calm.

"It's just that I pushed too hard. That's it. No reason for concern."

Chandi simply stared at his chest, at the scar that scraped down his left pec to his lower abdomen. It had turned a vicious crimson like fresh blood.

Chillingly soft, she said, "At the rate you're going, how long will it take until your Agni withers away?"

"It can be replenished," he said, but he did not meet her eyes. "I just need fire prana. And we have the Eternal Fire now. If I sit in the flames and soak in its prana, I'll be as good as new."

"You're expending your Agni far more than you are recovering it, like pouring water into a leaky bucket." She sat forward so that he was forced to meet her gaze. "A sun's worth. That's what you estimated was left of your Agni before it..."

She did not say it. She did not have to.

Samson felt the panic resurface, this time with a chill that crept down the back of his neck. He touched below his navel, the point of his Agni and the most powerful chakra. Every person had seven main chakras, seven centers in which they could channel the power of the heavens and achieve something *more*. There had been a time when gods walked the earth. A time when dragons and great creatures raced through the skies, and his people built their kingdoms in the clouds.

"But men began to desire the physical pleasures of the earth," his mother had said. They sat before their altar of the Great Serpent, incense wreathing around them, and he had wondered then if the smoke was the very breath of the Serpent, blessing them. "They fell to the illusions of mortal life, and their chakra points closed. They forgot about the Great Serpent and Her lesser gods. So She faded. And men began to walk among men, not gods."

The shells of her headdress tinkled softly as she turned to him. Gently, she had touched his navel.

"But you, my cursed Ruru, are blessed by Her. And your chakra here is still open. If you focus, you can summon Agni through it. But you must keep it balanced. Whole."

He had placed his little hand over hers, and replied solemnly, "Yes, Mama."

He had spent suns under her guidance of opening his navel chakra until he felt an almost metaphysical spark in his body. Agni was not a physical object. It was a power *made* physical, a manifestation of the gods. He had learned to nurture and strengthen his navel chakra until his Agni flared with a sure, heady assurance that vibrated through his blood. Reminding him of his deathly, beautiful purpose.

He was a god.

But every day that his Agni grew, so did the promise of ruin.

That was his curse, and his gift.

When he summoned his Agni, the pain was the first warning. It would begin with his sword arm. A chill would creep through his fingers, then up his elbow, across his shoulders. If he was not careful, it would spread. Down his chest, toward his navel chakra. Cold, and the nothingness it brought, would slowly surround his Agni and choke it out, like a flame gradually deprived of air. In time, he would fade.

To where? Men had the ability to be reborn, to live infinite lives. But he was a god. He did not know where the graveyard of his kind was kept.

"You have to seriously consider the Sona operation," Chandi said, bringing him back. "The Eternal Fire may sustain you now, but what if you summon too much, or you're too far away? What then, Samson? How will we be able to save you then?"

He turned to her, surprised by the anger in her voice.

"You can't put it off," she said. "It endangers not only you, but everyone. We should take Elena and—"

"I told you before, Elena is of Agni." He stood, buttoning his shirt. "And hers is deep and powerful. Maybe I can learn how she sustains it. Maybe she has the answer."

"But—"

"Enough, Chandi, please." Though a part of him knew Chandi spoke with reason, it annoyed him to hear Elena attacked, and he did not fully understand why. "We haven't exhausted all our options yet. If there is no other way, then we will go to Sona, and I'll tap into Elena's Agni."

"Then learn from her soon. And quickly." Chandi nodded to the scar on his chest. "It's fading."

He looked down. Indeed, the scar had washed out to a ruddy red.

"See?" He rapped his chest. "Good as new."

Chandi rolled her eyes. "Inconsiderate prick. You didn't even thank me."

"Thank you, Chandi the Great, Chandi the Marvelous, Chandi the Killer Who Can Gut Out Jantaris in the Dark—" He finished buttoning up his shirt and shrugged on his jacket. "Is that adequate, or should I go on?"

She leaned back in her chair, crossing her arms. "Continue."

"Chandi the Savior, Chandi the Brave, Chandi the Hero We Don't Deserve but Who Saves Us Without Complaint." He paused, catching her eyes. "Chandi the Flirt Who Has Women Running in Circles Simply Because She Can't Settle Down—"

"Okay, okay." Chandi stood, her cheeks coloring. "You ruined it."

She pushed past him, muttering obscenities as he grinned. They left his chambers, bickering, and went out into the bright sun of Magar and the warm roar of the festivities. Songs floated up the street. Somewhere, around the corner, he heard drunken laughter. A soldier offered him whiskey. Samson took a swig, then another, making Chandi scowl, but even as she reached for a drink, even as laughter rolled through them both at her sudden grimace, Samson could not shake off the ghostlike hand of remembered pain. It lingered, like the gritty salt of the sea after a swim. A reminder of his nature, and the curse that came with it.

CHAPTER 7

ELENA

The ancient gods of Sayon oddly have more similarities than dispar-
ities. Take, for instance, the Great Serpent and the Phoenix. Both
goddesses of fire, both ruthless to the core. Is it possible, then, that they
stemmed from the same protomyth?
>   —from *A Critique of the Ancient Gods*
>   (note: debunked by historians)

Elena listened to the crackle of the Eternal Fire and felt as if each pop, each spark, was a hot finger stabbing her stomach. The inferno burned freely, flames swollen and fat. It lazily tumbled past the pit, feeding on the ruins of the temple, but Samson had created a perimeter, and now, rather than being restrained by the altar created by her ancestors, the Eternal Fire was stayed by a god.

Samson stood beside her, slightly swaying. His eyes were closed, his head bent, as if he was listening to a sweet song rather than a savage hiss. Gone were the lines on his forehead, the bags beneath his eyes. Blue flames spiraled down his arms, so close she could hear their soft murmurs, so close that if she were not of Agni herself, the skin on her elbows would peel.

Elena shifted, not because of Samson, but because of the jittery energy building within her. Since the coronation, the Eternal Fire had regarded her differently. It called to her. She could feel it vibrate through the stones, up her legs, to the top of her head. She felt the *vastness* of its strength— deep, ancient, powerful. In a small, secret part of herself, half-crazed, half-formed, she desired its potency. Like a predator put before a fresh kill, she wanted to *feast*. To wield the flames and tear through the Jantari, eating, biting.

Come, the inferno chanted.

"Do you hear that?" he asked. His voice was buoyant. "They're pleased with our presence."

Elena nearly closed her eyes, overwhelmed. But then she caught sight of the ruins around them. She remembered her father's terrible scream as he tumbled into the inferno. Once, this place had held the promise of power for her. Now it was a memorial of all that she had lost.

"I don't," she lied.

"The Great Serpent blesses us, Elena. She *wants* us to win this war, and She will help us." He finally opened his eyes. "And She knows of you. Your Phoenix may be a lie, but the Great Serpent has not forgotten you."

"Touching," she replied.

Samson smiled. "You don't believe it."

Elena hesitated. Ash still lined her fingernails from the funeral pyres. All night, she, Kruppa, and a few soldiers had dug out the bodies, Ravani and Jantari alike. They had burned the Ravani, buried the Jantari, as according to their different customs, and sung prayers for the dead.

But those prayers were meant for the Phoenix, and the Prophet would have found them blasphemous. She studied Samson, measuring her words.

"I don't believe the Phoenix was a lie," she said carefully. "At least, not fully. Not yet. Gods, even fake ones, are hard to kill."

"Did you sing songs of the Phoenix when you lit the funeral pyres, then?" He was examining her hands, and Elena tucked them behind her.

"We did," she said. "The Phoenix is our faith, Samson. Even as Prophet, you can't change that. Maybe in time, people will come to understand and love your Great Serpent too. Maybe they'll find the Phoenix to be a lie.

But they need proof of the lie." She paused, looking to the Eternal Fire. "I need proof too."

"Like what?" He gestured to the mountains, the Eternal Fire, the ruins. "It's all around you."

"You can't drag every faithful Ravani here and demonstrate your powers."

"Why not?" He toyed with the fire on his wrist. "It would be convincing."

"You need proof for the Ravani. We're a fervent and religious lot, and simply calling our god a lie won't be enough.

"My mother studied the Phoenix. And she was a preeminent scholar, far more than any priest. She wrote me a letter saying that Alabore created his kingdom with a different power. A darker power. But she also said the Phoenix would still rise. She believed that the Phoenix would return. Do you see, Samson?" She stepped closer. "Even after uncovering Alabore's truth, my mother still *believed*. That's what you're dealing with. What *we're* dealing with. An unshakable faith."

She did not mention her hope. The hope that if her mother had still believed in the god, then maybe the Phoenix was true. Maybe her kingdom wasn't a lie after all. Elena felt it flutter against her chest, small and fragile, an ember barely given the ability to breathe. But it was there. *Hope is an ember you must keep alive in the dark*, her mother had said. Behind her back, Elena fastened her hands together as if to hold on to it.

Samson sighed. Slowly, the fire around his wrist withered away. "She jumped into the fire, didn't she?"

Elena nodded, fighting against the sudden tightness in her throat. "She did."

"Unshakable, indeed." He ran a hand through his hair, considering. "If you can gather proof that the Phoenix was a lie, then will you reveal what you've found?"

"Of course."

"To everyone. Even your own people?"

"If my kingdom was built on a lie, I want to know *why*. I want to know how." She met his eyes. "They deserve to know it too."

He did not flinch from her gaze but held it. She wished she could decipher his expression, the deepening of his eyes, the slight tightness in his jaw, but his face was a mask. Samson Kytuu was a man of many masks. Suitor, soldier—savior. She had made a mistake by disregarding that earlier, but now, as he stood before her, Elena felt the urge to peel back that mask. To find what truly lay beneath.

Finally, Samson nodded.

"Fine. Saayna is around somewhere. Why not start with her." He began to turn to the blaze but stopped. "Did your mother mention anything else in the letter?"

"She said there are three types of fire. That I'm one of them."

"She knew you were of Agni, then." Samson shook his head, a wry smile on his face. "Why do I get the feeling your mother must have run circles around Leo?"

Elena did not reply. Something nagged at her. *The Phoenix shall awaken, and She will seek Her Prophet and other brethren,* her mother had written. What had she meant by *brethren*?

But before Elena could speak, a flame of the Eternal Fire suddenly shot up.

It arced through the air, vivid and viciously bright, a weeping scar against the perfect blue skin of the sky, and then whipped around, barreling toward them.

Samson reached for his urumi, but Elena was already moving, curving her arms and framing her hands into lotuses. She caught the stray flame in her arms, but the impact nearly knocked her over. She gasped, stumbling back as the flame fought her control, its sparks spitting against her hands as if spittle from a beast. Elena felt its ferocious heat, its burning desire to *kill*, and for a moment, she was bewildered by the savage strength of that desire. With a grunt, she threw the flame back. It hurtled straight through the Eternal Fire, parting the flames like a knife, and collided against a broken pillar.

The pillar snapped. A large chunk fell into the Eternal Fire, and the flames swelled forward.

"Get back!" Samson cried.

But she only widened her stance. She was not going to allow it to burn this mountain. Not again. Elena faced the approaching flames, her heart thundering, her Agni a battle cry in her ears, when Samson whipped his urumi with a roar. The inferno stumbled, as if hesitating. He slashed down, and with an almost imperceptible groan, the flames rolled back.

Elena stared. "How did you—"

Samson swayed. She caught him by the elbow, and he sagged against her.

"I'm fine, just fine." This close, she could smell the sweet musk of his sweat, the ash on his skin. For a moment, he leaned into her, his forehead pressed into her shoulder, his hand curved around the nape of her neck. He was heavy, warm. His fingers delicate against her skin. Her heart clattered—in bafflement, unease, and a deeper, darker feeling she could not name.

"Samson," she said.

He straightened suddenly, pulling away. "I'm fine."

His face had paled, and she noticed how his hand trembled around the hilt of his urumi.

"I'm fine, Elena," he said, more forcefully this time.

She nodded, for his sake. "Shall we go find Saayna?"

"You go. I'll make sure the Eternal Fire is…" He hesitated, as if tasting the word. *"Cowed."*

She descended the stairs, and then looked back. Samson stood before the Eternal Fire, his shoulders stiff like a board. Though she could not see his face, she could feel his anger even from here.

Elena found Saayna and Kruppa together, talking quietly in the grove behind the ruins.

Most of the trees were blackened stalks, but the gulmohar tree remained upright, its bright red leaves a shock against the gutted landscape.

"Your Majesty." Kruppa bowed quickly as she approached. Saayna turned.

They had not seen each other since Elena and the Black Scales had left for Magar. Somehow, the high priestess seemed to have grown gaunter. Her skin stretched tightly across her cheekbones, her lips thin and nearly colorless. She no longer wore the orange sash of the order, which had been dissolved by the Prophet. Nor did she wear a tilak or any marks of the Phoenix. But Elena saw how she still grasped the same wooden prayer beads. Almost imperceptibly, Saayna hid the beads into her sleeve, touching her crimson shawl.

"You recognize this, yes?" she said.

It was a deflection. Saayna smiled kindly, but Elena could see the quick panic in her eyes.

How long will we dance around this? she wondered.

"Is that the one you wore during my crowning ceremony?" Elena asked.

"The very one. It was a gift from your mother, long ago."

They stood there, suddenly silent. The wind soughed through the gulmohar tree, rattling the dry leaves with a dolorous cry. Elena opened her mouth to say something just as Saayna began to speak, but they both fell back into silence. Kruppa glanced between them, smiling uneasily.

"Are you——" Saayna said.

"Does your burn still hurt?" Elena said at the same time.

Saayna blinked. Her shawl partly covered the mark, but Elena could see the dark coiling shape of a serpent on her cheek.

"It does not," Saayna said in a heavy voice, as if it took her much effort to admit it. "The Prophet is merciful in his blessings."

Merciful, Elena thought wryly as she looked upon the destruction around them. But she clamped down on the deceitful feeling beginning to stir in her chest. *He freed Magar. He will help me free Ravence.* She remembered his promise as they had stood in the inferno, months ago. *He promised me vengeance.*

"I spoke to the Prophet," she said slowly. "He wants me, *us,* to investigate the origins of the Phoenix. We don't have access to the royal library, but are there any scrolls left, Saayna, in the temple tunnels? Perhaps something of Priestess Nomu's? Anything that can prove that——" And here she stumbled. Saayna looked away, her lips pinched, as if she could sense what was coming. Elena took a deep breath. "Anything that can prove that the Phoenix is a false god."

The silence that followed was damning. Only the gulmohar spoke, singing its mournful song. Ash stirred at Elena's feet, but she ignored it, trying to catch Saayna's eyes. The priestess remained quiet.

It was Kruppa who broke the silence.

"Is it true, then?" she said, her voice small. "Is the Phoenix a lie? Is our Prophet born by another god?"

"Yes," Saayna said finally. She turned to them rigidly, her mouth set, her shoulders steeled, but Elena noted how her eyes were softened by sorrow. "Our loyalty belongs to the Prophet and the Great Serpent. To continue to worship the Phoenix is...heresy."

"Right," Elena said, but the word tasted foul.

"But if the Phoenix never existed—" At this, Kruppa made the sign of the Phoenix, tapping her forehead, chest, and then mouth, and froze as they stared. "Sorry, habit. But. If She never existed, then who did Alabore seek blessings from to create Ravence? Is he a lie too? A myth?"

I have read of a deeper, darker power. This power fed visions to Alabore, led him to the desert, and tormented him into subsequent madness, her mother had written. Not for the first time, Elena wished she had shown the letter to her father. She wished she had taken his counsel, heeded his warnings.

There were many things she wished she had done, and the regret laced her throat tight like a cruel noose.

Regret immobilizes you. Makes you weak.

Samson's voice rang through her as the gulmohar moaned, and the Eternal Fire filled the air with its ceaseless hiss. Elena stared at the priestesses, her response strangled by her own bitterness. She felt the inescapable sensation of being trapped, caught between performing as queen and her own wavering belief. Her allegiance was to Ravence, and Ravence to its Prophet. But she had once sworn to lead this kingdom in the name of the Phoenix too. She had knelt with her mother before their tiny altar. Grasped her father's hand as they sat in the inferno. The Phoenix was more than a goddess. She was a reminder of her family, her ancestors, and the burden they carried.

Elena slowly curved her hands and summoned a flame. It rippled to life with a soft hiss as Kruppa gasped.

"You're a prophet too?" she cried.

"If I am, of what god, then? The Phoenix?" Elena laughed ruefully. "I feel no special connection to Her, no sudden revelation. I do not know what I am, truthfully. But I am of Agni. My mother wrote that there are three types of fire. Perhaps Samson and I are two of the three. Who, then, is the third?"

She looked to Saayna, who stared at the flame in her hands. Gently, she said, "Saayna, you have studied the Phoenix for so long. What if She is real? Samson calls forth his power from the Great Serpent. Can the second god be the Phoenix?"

"But if the Prophet claims She is not real..." Kruppa shuddered. "Are there more gods?"

They both turned to Saayna then. The high priestess touched the mark on her cheek as she gazed past them, to the tips of the flames licking the sky. When she finally spoke, her voice was firm, hardened by pain.

"There is no true god other than the Great Serpent and Her Prophet," she said.

"Saayna," Elena began.

"I know where my allegiance lies. I have my proof," she said, lowering her hand from her cheek. "I will give you the remaining scrolls, but I will take no part in this blasphemy. Learn what you must and learn quickly."

Kruppa's face was an open wound. "How can you just turn away? *You* are our highest sister. You have spent suns studying the Phoenix. You know She is not a false god."

"The Prophet has shown me otherwise."

"But if we find proof that the Phoenix is real," Elena interjected. "Think, Saayna. Perhaps there are more gods and power at play."

"Have you thought of the consequences?" Saayna said, her voice like a whip. "Do you know what *he* will do?"

Elena heard the panic edging in her voice then. *She is afraid of Samson,* she thought. But she followed Saayna's gaze and saw that she was staring at the Eternal Fire, and a new understanding crept through her.

She is afraid of the inferno itself. Saayna had felt the fire's teeth tear through her flesh. She knew the pain of burning. *Like Yassen.*

Elena remembered his fear. He had hidden it, pushed through it, and it had led to his ruin. By following her, Yassen Knight had died. And the high priestess feared the same.

"Do not ask more of me, please." Saayna's voice trembled. "Please."

"I know my family has given you grief," Elena said softly. "My father was wrong to imprison you. But you believe in Samson solely because he healed you." She fluttered her fingers, and the flame grew, a steadfast beacon. "Here is your other proof, Saayna. I too am a god. I may not be *the* Prophet, but I will free my kingdom. And I will call on whatever higher power to do so."

Saayna looked down at the flame, and then at her. "Then I pray for the day when we will finally be free of you gods."

CHAPTER 8

ELENA

The Council of the Second Continent was last called during the invasion of Seshar. Leaders attempted to persuade King Harrow of Jantar to turn back his boats. They failed, miserably. Since then, the council has not convened. Some political scholars wager the kingdoms are fearful of Jantar's retaliation, while others believe the rulers are too ashamed of their historical precedent.

> —from chapter 43 of *The Great History of Sayon*

The hoverpod skimmed over the vast and shadowed canyons as Elena thumbed through the scrolls. There were only twenty-one left after the fires, and when Elena lifted one up, she could still smell ash.

"Any luck?" Samson asked.

"I haven't started reading yet," she said.

"What do you think, Priestess?" Samson turned to Kruppa, slipping on a devilish smile. "Do you believe I'm your Prophet?"

Kruppa returned his smile, though Elena noted how she twisted the end of her dupatta. "Yes, um, Your Holiness."

"Holiness?" He laughed. "I prefer Blue Star."

"Blue Star?"

"It is the Great Serpent's symbol." He pointed to the darkening sky, at the stars slowly waking. "It lies just above the horizon, pointing true north."

Kruppa hissed. Samson raised a brow, looking to Elena. She carefully slipped the scrolls back into their bag.

"The north is sacred to the Phoenix," she said, glancing at Kruppa, who had stilled, aware of her blunder. "Even the palace has no northern tower, just the east, south, and west."

"Ah, I noticed that. Well. Once we reclaim Rani, my rani, we'll have to build a northern tower," he said, holding her gaze as if to measure her.

She swallowed her retort. "Of course . . . Prophet."

He motioned for her, and Elena stood, squeezing Kruppa's shoulder, before following him into the inner office of the hoverpod.

Chandi and Visha snapped to attention as they entered. A bank of holos floated above the center table: reports, battle schematics, various maps. Elena pointed to the one closest to her.

"What's this?" she said.

"An offer," Samson answered.

He pulled out a chair, and warily, she sat down. He sat next to her, his hand resting on her armrest. As the others leaned forward, Elena had the strange sensation of being cornered in a pen, like a wild horse ready to be broken.

"An offer of what kind?"

"I think it's time we contact Cyleon," Samson said.

"I thought we were going to push forward and recover Teranghar and the Yoddha Base," Elena said. The other southern city was smaller than Magar, and several miles of canyons stretched between them. But if they were to regain Teranghar and Yoddha, they could free southern Ravence before they marched onward to Rani.

She explained as much, and Samson listened patiently, his eyes seeming to drink her in. When she finished, he leaned back in his chair, but his hand remained on her armrest.

"Pushing the Jantari out of the south will help us gain a stronghold, but it will only prolong the war," Samson said. "We need to hit Jantar where it hurts."

"How does that include the Cyleoni?"

"What if King Syla were to help? He has resources, troops. Cyleon is Ravence's ally, after all."

"But—"

"We need to partner with Syla if we want to win this war," Chandi cut in.

Elena turned to the commander as Samson scowled. Chandi ignored him, meeting her gaze. The blue light of the holos curved down Chandi's neck, limning the skull hand around her throat. It was an odd tattoo. Garish, morbid, and utterly fitting. Distantly, Elena wondered of its significance.

"Cyleon has old mines in its eastern mountains that ran dry because Jantar sucked it all from their side of the range," Chandi said. "Syla could do nothing. He lost his most valuable resource without the Jantari ever raising a weapon. He couldn't call a war then. But he can now, with us. He is angry and bitter and needs the right excuse to move against Jantar. We can become that excuse."

Elena shook her head. "Syla may be bitter, but he's no instigator. He'd rather sit back and let someone else do the killing for him. He is a puppeteer—and we will not become his assassins. No. If we recruit Syla, we must be smart." She drew a breath, steeling herself. "Syla has always loved playing the part of hero. So, we make him that. I think it's time we call for the Council of the Second Continent. Syla and I can go in together. We paint him the shining savior, me the deposed queen. The other kingdoms may not care for Ravence, but once they hear that Farin tried to kill a living ruler, they'll be afraid. They'll think he'll come for them next. They *will* move against him."

"*Council?*" Visha sneered. "Your precious council is a gathering of vain, chicken-livered rulers who did nothing when Seshar was attacked. They're cowards."

"The council—"

"The council hasn't met in nearly sixty suns because they know they're guilty," Visha snarled. "They can't show their faces. They won't come."

"They will," Elena shot back. "Those vultures came to my coronation to size me up. Now they think I'm dead. If I suddenly appear at the council, they'll know I've survived. They'll know Farin tried to have me killed."

"But we barely have enough leverage right now," Visha argued. "What do we have? A couple hundred men? One city? Farin still has a fucking army camped out in the capital. You think he'll just stand up and leave because the other kingdoms tell him to? *If* they even come."

"Let's start with Syla first," Samson said before Elena could retort.

She swallowed her bitterness as Visha returned her glare. Visha had not come to dig out the bodies along the wall, or even to attend the funerals after. And Elena could never forget her look of cold defiance as Visha said their orders were not to recover the dead, but to take the city. The strategist steepled her gloved fingers together and rested her chin on top in a mocking gesture. Elena scowled.

"We could send a hoverpod, with a gift."

"Like what?"

The answer was already on her tongue, and it surprised Elena how quickly and easily it came.

"A Jantari prisoner."

Chandi blinked, Samson smiled, and even Visha looked appalled.

"Now, that's the ruthless queen I know," he said.

She did not smile. "If there's one thing Syla loves the most, it's pawns to wield against Farin. Give him someone of note. The general, Edmund."

At this, Samson's face fell. He exchanged a glance with Chandi.

"What?" When they said nothing, she sat forward. "What happened to him?"

Visha laughed. It was a low, scraping sound, like sand whipping her skin. It grated her ears.

"He's dead," Samson said.

"What?"

"There was an accident," Samson said. "An uprising of sorts. We had to shut it down."

"So you executed him? You should have consulted me—"

"There was no time, Elena. I burned him." His lips curled back, as if the admission itself tasted poisonous. "There is no body to mourn. But it stopped the Jantari rebellion."

How easily he had burned through the men, how quickly she had crushed people along the wall. She remembered then how Saayna had looked at her with horror in her eyes.

I pray for the day when we will finally be free of you gods.

We did this, she thought. Just as Samson was complicit in the deaths of those along the wall, she was guilty of Edmund's death.

Shame, hot and sticky, scratched her throat as he refused to meet her eyes. Shame, not just for herself, but of *them*. For what they were. It tickled her throat, but no matter how much she coughed or hacked, Elena knew she could never get rid of that phantomlike sensation.

"You—" she began, struggling to temper her voice. "We need to go about this strategically, Samson. Logically. Edmund was *leverage*. If Farin finds out, he'll use it against us."

"I know," Samson said. His mouth twisted up into a slant, and he still did not meet her gaze. "It won't happen again."

Visha continued to laugh.

"Will you shut up?" Elena and Samson snarled at once.

Visha stopped, but her smile was slow, catlike. She rose. Her hands skimmed along the edge of the table, and she paused in between their two chairs and leaned forward, draping her arms around their shoulders.

"You know what I think?" she said. "Send them a couple of bodies, their throats slit by urumis. Syla will get the message. And if he doesn't, why, then we can send our precious queen, wrapped up in a pretty bow."

Elena stiffened. She had half a mind to cut *Visha's* throat, but she forced herself to not rise to her quip. The strategist laughed, dipping her head.

"Blue Star. Queen."

She left, the doors sliding quietly shut behind her.

Chandi rose. "I'll deal with her."

When they were alone, Elena turned to Samson. He leaned away, pulling his hand from her chair.

"She's valuable, so don't tear her head from her body," he warned.

"Valuable," Elena growled. "Right."

"Visha's had a…curious upbringing, but it's made her a weapon. One of Jantar's finest. My finest, now." He finally met her gaze. "And she's right. We don't have enough leverage to make the other kingdoms come to the council. Syla and you aren't enough. We need more. We need to target Jantar's northern mines."

"We barely have enough resources as it is, Sam."

"But with Syla's men, we will. Think. The mines aren't just Jantar's lifeblood, but the other kingdoms' too. How many of them use Jantari steel? How many of them have been forced to swallow Farin's exorbitant prices simply because he controls the flow of ore? Ore that *my people* mine for him." Samson paused, and she saw his anger, quick and spiderlike, skitter across his face. "If we take out the mines, Farin will listen. *All* the kingdoms will listen."

Elena hesitated, and at this, Samson's face softened. He reached into his pocket and withdrew an earring. It took her a moment to recognize that dark green jade, and when she did, her breath caught in her throat, the memory, the pain, suddenly all too fresh, all too real.

"Is that—" she began.

"Your father's. I found it in the ruins today." Gently, Samson unfolded her hand and placed it in her palm. Her fingers trembled, and Samson wrapped his hand around hers to still them. "Think what he would do."

She knew what Leo would do. He would call on the Phoenix, on his people's belief. Their faith entangled with their anger, building, burning. They would march with the songs of the Phoenix on their lips. But their god was a lie now. Crushed by the faith of another. How, then, could she call upon them? Whom would they follow, other than their Prophet?

Elena clutched her dead father's earring. "The Phoenix—"

She was interrupted as the doors slid open and Kruppa sprinted in, out of breath.

"Your Majesty, Your Holi—Blue Star." She stumbled over her words, gasping.

Elena rose. In their exchange, she had not realized they had already docked. She could see shapes moving beyond the hoverpod, could hear multiple voices rising outside. Loud and furious.

"There's a fight in the medic tents. The refugees—"

But Elena was already running, Samson shouting for men to clear the way.

Elena hurried to the medic quarters where, already, a small crowd was forming. As she drew closer, she could hear angry complaints, soft cries. A man turned, gasped.

"She's here," he hissed.

More people began to turn, make way. Elena slowed her pace. She did not want to seem flustered or disgruntled. Calmly, with eyes fixed ahead, she entered the tents.

Several beds were laid out in rows, each occupied by a patient. To the right, Elena could see the crumbling facade of the overrun city hospital. On her left, a group of people surrounded the bed of a teenager who cowered into his father's shoulder. A woman holding a bleeding child shouted hysterically as a harried-looking doctor stood between her and the cot.

"Give her the bed!" she cried. "Not *him*."

The doctor held out his hands in an almost pleading gesture. "Please, I need to treat—"

"They're Sesharians," the mother spat. "You need to help your own!"

The father frowned, his expression an exasperated combination of indignity and hurt, but before he could speak, Elena stepped forward.

"What is this?" she said.

They turned. The nurse beside the boy made a quick sign of the Phoenix, and the motion twisted Elena's stomach.

"Your Majesty!" the mother gasped. She stumbled forward, cradling her daughter, a child of no more than five suns. The girl's skin was flushed, her eyes hot and feverish. "Please, tell them to treat my daughter. She is burned and hurt. That Sesharian boy has nothing but a broken finger—"

"A Jantari soldier smashed his arm!" the father roared.

The mother whipped around with a sudden, vicious jerk. "Then your son shouldn't have gotten in the way! You Sesharians are always where you're not wanted. Your son is a man. My daughter is a child. A *Ravani*," she said, looking pointedly to the doctor. "And you need to treat her first. Please, Your Majesty. Please, I beg. Help my daughter."

Around them, Elena could see other patients and their families begin to turn, to listen. Almost all were Ravani.

"Ma—" Elena began.

She stilled as she felt Samson and the others approach. Out of the corner of her eye, she saw Black Scale soldiers file into the tent, and the mother noticed too, because she shrank back, her eyes darting from Elena to them.

"Is there a problem?" Samson said.

Emboldened, the father stepped forward. "This woman is refusing to let them treat my son."

"There's just been a misunderstanding," the doctor said, looking to the soldiers. "Please, tell your men to stand down. We already have enough injured patients."

"My daughter is dying and here you are treating a broken arm," the mother said.

"I will treat your daughter, ma, but you cannot kick out a patient from their bed—"

"Do you hear that?" the mother called, turning to the entrance of the tent, where more people were beginning to gather. She raised her daughter for them to see. "They refuse to help *us* first. We Ravani are not being treated justly here."

The crowd began to push forward. One man shoved a Black Scale, who tottered back, then fell. Another soldier shouted, telling the onlookers to stand back, and beside her, Samson bristled. Elena felt the air sharpen, smolder, just before the summoning of Agni.

"Stop, stop!" Elena cried. She blocked Samson's path. "Stand down. Now."

He looked at her, the anger so clear and alive in his eyes that it felt like a blow. She placed her hand on his chest, her touch light, pointed. "Stand down and let me deal with this."

He hesitated, but Elena used that moment to turn to the mother. "Come. I will treat your daughter."

The mother cradled her child closer. "But you—"

"Bring me a salve. And whatever clean sheets you have," she told the nurse and doctor. "She has a fever, so find something to bring it down. You, treat the boy's arm."

"Your Majesty—" the mother protested.

"He is a child too, ma," Elena said. Her voice softened. "Should we treat your daughter only at the expense of another sick child? Do you want his fate on her head?"

The mother looked at the Sesharian teenager, her face a war of confusion and grief, of bitter injustice. But Elena could see her hurt too, her aches, her misguided love that pushed her to threaten another child simply to save her own. Her daughter gave a soft whimper.

"Please," Elena said, offering her arms.

Slowly, carefully, the mother lifted her child, and Elena took the girl and cradled her to her chest. She was so light, so small. Elena could feel the fever on her skin, see the molted burns on her legs. The nurse dumped out dirty sheets from a box and turned it upside down, creating a make-shift table.

Elena turned to the crowd, raising her voice. "This girl needs medical attention and rest, but she can't sleep if you are all here. Please. I will see to her—you have my word as your queen. Go and let us do our jobs."

Chandi stood at the entrance of the tent now, and she turned to the crowd. "You heard your queen."

But no one moved. Around them, Elena could see more people gathering. She glanced at the Sesharians and saw how the father protectively stood by his son's side, his hands fisted, as if ready to fight.

She did not want another bloodbath on her hands.

Elena lowered the girl onto the box, calling for the nurse. Better to start treating the child now to mollify the mother. The nurse knelt beside her, unscrewing an ointment bottle, when suddenly Elena felt a tightening in her stomach, a rush of heat up her spine, and she turned to Samson, crying out, but it was too late.

With a crack, blue flames rushed down his arms. The mother gasped. The nurse shrieked and people outside shouted in alarm.

"Samson, wait—"

His flames engulfed the girl.

The mother screamed. She threw herself down, reaching for her daughter, when the fire suddenly died, disappearing as quickly as it had appeared. The child sat up.

Gone was the feverish glint in her eyes. Gone was the sickly pallor of her skin. Gone were the burns on her legs, replaced now by a coiling serpent.

"Phoenix Above," the mother said, touching her daughter's face, her hands, her legs, as if she wasn't real. "H-how?"

Samson looked at her, and then at the silent crowd and patients and doctors, his voice rippling with the crackle of fire.

"Because I am of Agni." His eyes caught Elena's, and she saw then his pride, his anger. "I am your Prophet returned."

Gasps rippled around them. Soft murmurs, confused cries, whispered prayers. But they raged like thunder in Elena's ears as she saw the mother kneel.

"O Prophet," she cried. "Forgive me!"

One by one, her people began to kneel. Sesharian, Ravani, the doctors, the soldiers—they all knelt to Samson. Elena remembered the fear in Saayna's eyes, along with her awe.

I know where my allegiance lies. I have my proof.

How easily they believed. How easily, in a land of burning, her people wished to be saved. The Ravani knew the pain of fire. Of course they would seek a leader who healed.

But Elena did not bend.

She remained standing, watching as Samson smiled, the slow, satisfied smile of a man who recognized power and found himself deserving of it. And as she watched her people bow to such a man, she felt the strange, unnerving feeling of being *undermined*. That she, Elena Aadya Ravence, had been rendered—in some sly, nearly imperceptible way—useless.

CHAPTER 9

SAMSON

I have read of a deeper, darker power . . . This power fed visions to Alabore, led him to the desert, and tormented him into subsequent madness . . . The Eternal Fire does not rage because it is angry; it rages because it grieves.

—from the letters of Aahnah Madhani Ravence

They trailed after him then, the believers. He recognized most from the medic tents, but there were new faces too. More bystanders began to stop and mutter as he left the medic tents and made his way toward the ruined wall.

"The Prophet."

"Is it him?"

"Did you see how he healed her burns?"

One man stepped back and spat. It landed right before Samson's feet.

"His eyes are blue and cursed," the man said. "He is no Prophet."

Beside him, Chandi stiffened. But then the mother strode forward, her child in tow. She stood before the man, her eyes raking him from head to toe, and laughed. Loud and strong, her body shaking. She laughed in the man's face and presented her arm, where Samson had blessed her with his sign.

"But your eyes are not cursed, are they, brother? See, then. See the proof."

The man sniffed, but his eyes skittered past her and met Samson's. "Well?"

Samson looked at him and then Elena. She stood apart, her lips pressed together, her jaw tight. He could sense her Agni roiling in agitation. She did not know how to hide it from him or how to read his. *So many things you don't know,* he thought. So many things he wished he could tell her.

But she refused to meet his gaze. Without a word, Elena turned, and while the crowd watched him, eyes wide and expectant for evidence of another miracle, he watched as she disappeared from his view. A strange ache traveled through him then—not the pain from summoning Agni, but a deeper, insidious sting as if someone had gently slid a dagger through his ribs without his noticing. He did not understand it, this new hurt. Nor why his throat closed as if he had tasted something sour and sharp.

"Prophet," the mother called.

He turned back to them. So many faces, Sesharian and Ravani, believers and nonbelievers, some leaning forward as if, by simply being closer, they could touch his godliness, while others stood back, wary yet watchful. Those were the ones on the precipice. The ones who just needed a simple push.

Samson counted the Sesharians in the crowd. Only seventeen, among fifty or so. And yet they watched him with a kind of hope that made him want to crawl away, unseen, and also rise above. To show them that finally, *finally,* they had a chance to be free. That they, the ones who had lost their home, who suffered the torment of various nations, could be victors.

He stepped forward. "I do not dance to your whims," he said to the man. "You have your proof. Buuut"—he smiled, drawing out the word—"who am I to turn away a man of god?"

He unsheathed his urumi from his waist. The sudden slither of steel hissed through the air, and several people stumbled back. The man blanched. With a flick of his wrist, Samson ionized the blades, and blue flames furled down, crackling with electricity.

"From now on, no man shall be denied healing. Ravani and Sesharian will be treated equally, and if you disagree…" He looked at the mother, who dipped her head, muttering apologies. "I can take away your pain, but I can also return it tenfold."

He turned on his heel, sparks flaring in his wake. He left them gawking as he hopped on a cruiser and started the engine with a roar. Though he did not know where Elena had gone, he could sense her Agni. It was bright and agitated, like a diya full of too much oil. He needed to find her—

Chandi slid into the seat beside him.

"What—" he began.

"Go to the wall," she said. "There's something I need to show you."

Before he could respond, she reached around him and gunned the engine.

They rode through the gates of the northern wall and stopped in a wide basin the color of rust. Black Scales snapped to attention.

"Blue Star," one said.

Though he was tall, he had a curved stoop to his shoulders as if he had been forced to walk through low spaces. A crescent scar hung from his eyebrow. A former miner, one Samson had dug out from the rubble and named his master of arms.

"Akino." Samson looked up the western face of the basin, where soldiers had set a perimeter. "What have you found here?"

"A…messenger," Akino said.

"From whom?"

Akino exchanged a glance with Chandi. "Will you climb?"

They scaled the basin, and when Samson pulled himself up over the lip, he heard a strange hum. Around the boulder, he saw that his men had formed a circle around an object. *No, not an object.* He walked closer, and Akino shouted a warning. There, seated in the center of the perimeter, was a man.

A man made completely of black sand.

Two sensors made of steel floated around the man as he—it?—sat serenely with pulse guns pointed its way.

"What is that?" he asked.

"We're not sure," Akino said. "But it's not safe to draw closer. If we do, it starts to melt."

"*Melt?*" Samson looked between him and the strange figure. "Show me."

Akino carefully crept forward. The man, the figure, the thing—Samson was still not sure what to make of it—made no move. Akino took another step. At once, the sensors gave a loud, singular hum.

Samson stilled. He heard his men shift, the soft creak of gloves curling around triggers. Akino glanced back, as if to reassure them. He then took another step. The sudden susurration of sand filled the air as the man began to melt. Sand spilled down. A cheek caved in, revealing a cold, metallic glint that sent a jab down Samson's throat.

He could recognize Jantari steel anywhere.

"Get back!" he barked. "Now!"

Akino retreated as the man continued to shift. A shoulder rippled down and swelled, the sand pooling around the knob of an elbow as if water around a bend. And then its right side gave a sigh. Samson gasped as he saw a blinking light, and then he was shouting, his men were stumbling back, and Chandi had her hand already on his arm, tugging him. But he could not burn, didn't she know? He wrenched himself away, only to realize, a moment too late, that Chandi wasn't pulling him back, but forward.

He cried for her to stop. She stood her ground, facing the man of sand as it began to stand. A blue blinking dot appeared out of its side, where its liver should have been had it been a real man. The sensors hummed twice. A warning.

"Chandi," he called.

"What is it that the Arohassin would tell you?" she said.

He blinked, momentarily too stunned to reach for her. "Chandi, that's a *bomb*. Move back."

"What was their training mantra?"

"They, they—" He remembered his mentor's voice, ringing through his ears as he lay on his stomach, wounded and punished. "'Be persistent, be obedient, be wicked.'"

As he uttered the last word, his throat closing and then spitting the last syllable, the humming stopped. The sensors swiveled away, and the man dissipated in a rush of sand that gushed forward and brushed his feet. Reflexively, Samson took a step back.

There, floating where the man had been, was a metal lotus. It reminded him of the ones used to power gamefields. A blue light blinked in its center, and then flared.

"Ruru."

And then he was drowning.

Salt water stung his throat as he swam with all his might. Blood darkened the water. He could not tell if it was his or his mother's. His sister's. But he could still hear their voices calling out to him. Warning him.

Run, Ruru, run!

The Jantari had rushed back to their boats, but he had ripped holes in their hulls with his urumi. A few tenacious fools jumped into the sea to chase him. *Plop. Plop.* Each successive dive rattled through his chest like the shock waves of a bomb, tightening his lungs as he spat out bloody water. *Plop, plop, plop.* The waves smashed him back. A stone pierced the wet, soft skin of his shoulder, and he opened his mouth to scream—and drowned.

Fishermen had found him, half-dead, holding on to driftwood.

A miracle, they called him. *Blessed by the Great Serpent.*

They had recognized him, of course. Son of the priestess, the last of his great family. They had ferried him away before the Jantari found his whereabouts, put him on a ship headed to Rysanti, only to whisper in his ear, with a deep urgency, to go to Ravence.

We refugees are welcome there.

But his arrival hadn't felt like a welcome. They had looked down on him, called him a rat. Told him he was unwanted. And it wasn't until he had found a boy with the eyes of a Jantari and the sweet tongue of a Ravani, a boy who had the same sharp angles and hunger in his eyes as he did, that he revealed his true name.

"Ruru."

The thing spoke again. A low, strangled sound escaped Samson's lips. He staggered, and through the haze of panic and pain and confusion, he was aware that the petals of the metal lotus had peeled back, revealing a small holopod.

"We come with an offer, old friend," the pod intoned. "There are no conditions other than you consider it carefully. We await your response."

The voice, clipped, staticky, ensnared him tight. It was faintly feminine.

Chandi moved to grab the holopod when the lotus blinked once more, and another voice spoke, one horribly familiar.

"Sam, old boy," Akaros said.

He flinched, as if struck. It had been many suns since he had heard that voice. A lifetime since he had been a broken boy bleeding out on the training floor, Akaros towering over him. *You should have listened, Ruru.* He moved to touch his back, his scars, before he realized what he was doing. Samson forced his hands down. He tried to steady his breath, but his heart tripped over itself.

"We know what you've been searching for. And we can help. Far more than your little queen." There was a pause, a slight rustle, as if Akaros was shifting, and Samson could almost imagine him, his old tormentor, his once protector, holding the pod to his lips. "Yassen's maps were true. Amrithi exists, but not where you thought." He could hear Akaros smiling, that brute. "Remember, Ruru, you must be wicked."

The light blinked off, and Chandi snatched the pod. The sensors and the lotus tumbled into the sand with a soft, muffled thud.

Samson stared. There was a wetness in his lungs, a pressure that swelled against the walls of his rib cage. If he spoke, he feared it would spill out. Bloody water so dark it could drown out the moons.

"Blue Star," Chandi said.

"General," Akino called from behind the boulder.

"They know." His voice was a low rasp. He looked up from the fallen sensors, the spilled sand. He could almost taste blood, metallic and sharp, on his tongue. "They know about Agni and the amrithi."

Chandi opened the pod, read the holos. Her mouth twisted. "They want an alliance."

"A what?" Akino said.

"They..." Her voice trailed off as she looked up at Samson.

He met her gaze, and his questions were mirrored in her own. If the Arohassin knew of the ore's existence, did they then know how to unlock it?

"Leave us, Akino," she said.

When they were alone, Chandi handed him the pod. "As soon as I saw this...thing, I suspected it was the Arohassin. The last time I saw black sand this far south, they left a rune for the old king. Purely to fuck with him." She indicated a holo. "Our intel was right. The Arohassin and the Jantari are in a stalemate, and it seems like the Arohassin want to break it, with us. They want to meet us, here in Magar."

"When?"

"In ten days." She studied him. "Are you okay?"

He made no move to open the pod. In fact, he had no desire to hold it, not when Akaros had held it too. Something brutish and dangerous stirred within him. Thick and black, seeping into his veins with a steady malice like Visha's poisons. The same familiar fury gripped his throat. If he was going to be in the same room as Akaros, he would kill him.

He had sworn it.

"Blue Star?"

"He's toying with us. With me." Samson clenched his hands, his skin stretched tautly over his knuckles. "This is another one of his mind games."

"A game we can play." She waved at the pool of sand. "Why do you think they sent us this thing? They want to show us what they have. Weapons. Tech. *An edge.* Don't you see? We can use them."

"We don't need the Arohassin," he snarled.

Sparks flared down his hand, unbidden, but Chandi did not shy away. She held her ground, eyes steady, mouth fixed, and for a moment, his anger wavered in the face of her defiance.

"You're not alone this time, Blue Star," she said softly. "He can't hurt you."

His throat closed. He still remembered the sting of Akaros's whip. The tremor in Yassen's desperate cries. It had been long ago, when he was a boy, helpless, weak. But he was a god now. Powerful, radiant. And yet, and yet…

"Forget the Arohassin," he said in Ambari, the old Sesharian tongue. "My Agni is enough. Or have you forgotten the Makara mines?"

The other half—*when I saved you, when I saved you all*—was left unspoken. Not as a threat. But a reminder. A reminder of all they had bled and sacrificed for, together.

"I have never forgotten Makara," she said coolly, though something flickered in her eyes, something he could not quite place. "I know my debts."

"Then trust me," he said. "We do not need the Arohassin. I've led you this far, yes? Look at what we've achieved, what we've soon to gain." He nodded toward the rising moons, to the Eternal Fire that blazed in the north. "We have my Agni. We have Elena's. We don't need Akaros or his mind games to win freedom now."

Chandi nodded slowly, though he could still see doubt in her eyes. But when she spoke again, her voice had lost its chilly tone, replaced now by a potency that reminded Samson of the riptide that had delivered him to the fishermen, to safety.

"So what's next, General?"

He slipped the pod into his pocket. "Cyleon."

"But I thought Elena did not want to attack the mines."

"She will." He turned toward Magar. "I'll make her see."

He found Elena simply by feeling for the pull of her Agni. It was warm and steady, a constant blaze that made him envious of its sureness.

She crouched among the ruins of the watchtower, and when he settled down beside her, she shifted to make room. Together, they watched the canyons change color. From red to rust to a deep purple, they bled forth until the twin moons rose and shadows marked their faces. For a long time, they sat in silence.

Finally, as songbirds trilled, Elena spoke.

"The mother was wrong," she said. "She shouldn't have demanded the Sesharian boy be thrown out. And the onlookers..." She shook her head, her face crumpling, and for a moment, he felt sympathy for her. Because he knew what it felt like to have your own people act against your morals. To feel your own faith break. When his father had bent to the Jantari, he had felt revulsion, but deeper yet, loss. As if something integral had been broken.

"If you hadn't acted, we would have had a mob on our hands." She glanced down at the city. The lights looked small and distant, little candle flames that could easily be capped, or enraged. "Do you think they'll tear down the temple themselves, or will you do it?"

He shifted away from the prick of her accusation. *You are as stubborn as Leo*, he thought. Both clung to their faith, even though they were not fervent believers. He supposed that was the nature of desperate men—to grasp the tattered remains of their belief as it burned down around them.

By tomorrow, word would have spread of his miracle. And they would come, the believers and the skeptics. They would come calling and leave bearing his sign. It was the natural progression of things.

The Ravani, the Sesharians, the Jantari—the world—would bow to his Agni. *Their* Agni.

But when he turned to her, he saw that she was folding into herself, shoring up, bracing for the worst, and at this, he felt true pity. Pity for her stubbornness, her inability to accept a new truth, however bitter.

The city temple was inconsequential. He had the Eternal Fire. He was in no hurry to push his god—the Ravani would do that for him. One day, they would raze temples themselves. And he hoped, with a tired sort of pity as one would feel for a moth who flings itself, relentlessly, against the burning glass of a lantern, that she would have stopped believing by then.

Chandi would call him a fool. Visha would laugh and then try to tear down the temple herself. But for the first time in his life, Samson retreated.

"Would you want me to?" he asked gently.

Elena blinked. She stared at him with wary hope.

"If you don't, then you have my word. I won't touch that city temple."

She searched his face, but he held still under her scrutiny, and after a while, she nodded. "Thank you."

"In exchange, I need your help."

"With what?"

For a moment, he considered telling her the truth. *With my own Agni. With the ore.*

His control of Agni had always been iron tight, precise to the point of obsession, but he had felt something tremble when the Eternal Fire had fought him. Its subtle defiance, like a cat nipping at your hand before you pet it. He had pushed back the flames with more force than he had needed before, and the effects of that effort still reverberated through him now. Samson clenched his fist as he felt a spasm of pain flicker through his shoulder and chest.

How could she understand the costs of his power when hers remained constant? He could sense the steady thrum of her Agni, the vicious energy humming through her veins. It was cruel. How it taunted him as his own Agni faded.

"For Syla," he said instead. "Draft a message. Something cryptic but familiar enough that he knows it's you. Ask him to meet us north of the temple, deep into the Agnee Range."

She pulled out a holopod. It was scuffed and battered, with scratches along the surface, but Samson recognized it at once, and his heart gave a strange shudder.

"That..." he began. He remembered Yassen's fingers brushing his own, the moonlight limning the bridge of his nose and the crown of his head as they sat in the small courtyard.

"It's his," Elena said softly. She rubbed her thumb along the face, and for a moment, Samson felt a hot, irrational rush of jealousy and the urge to snatch away the pod. It was ridiculous and stupid, and yet, his throat closed in.

He thought of how his friend had knelt beside him in that glittering throne room and sung the oath. How it had put him on the side of a burning mountain, dead.

It was not Elena's fault, he knew. Of course he *knew* that. But Samson wondered what would have happened if Yassen had not followed her, or if *he* had never offered the amnesty deal that had sealed his friend's fate. *What if?* He clung to that *if*. Trembled to think of *if*.

What a simple, cruel word. In its two letters, his world skittered off-balance, threatening to tip and crash, all the regret and guilt bubbling up like boiling water if he thought too deeply, too long, about *what if I had never called Yassen? What if he could have lived if not for me? What if*—

"Here."

Elena placed the pod in his hand. Samson jolted, blinking rapidly, shocked by the wet, crushing sensation in his eyes and nose. Her hand was gentle on his forearm.

"It's just full of old bank accounts and the maps you gave him," she said, and something in her voice told him that she sensed his pain, that it lingered in her too.

He took a small, shaky breath. "He was better than the two of us."

"He was—is—if he's still." She stopped. Drew up her knees and circled her arms around them as if to hug herself. "It's my fault. I should have listened to him and left the mines alone."

"I blame *me*." He laughed, short, acrid. "I should have never bargained his life away to Leo."

"It's not your fault—"

"I loved and lost him too, Elena," he said, and his voice broke at the end. He looked away, clenching his jaw to stop the trembling.

They sat there in silence, weighed down by their own sudden, private griefs. Samson traced the curve of the pod. He wished, more than anything, for it to ping with a message from Yassen, hurtling toward them in the dark. He wished he had had the courage to tell him earlier just how much he had loved him. How he had never forgotten him after all these suns.

"You're lucky," he whispered. "At least he knew that you loved him. At least he loved you back. I could never tell him myself."

"He did love you, Sam."

He smiled bitterly. *Just not in the way I wanted.*

His men had found no traces of the assassin in Jantar. Most of the mountainside had been burned or shredded by landslides. Yassen Knight was dead—of their making.

"I suppose gods do feel remorse, then," Elena said.

He choked out a laugh. "Yes, we do."

She gently took the pod from him and slipped it into her pocket.

Stay, he thought suddenly, wildly. He did not want to be alone in these canyons tonight, alone in his grief, watching a black horizon crowded by sharp shadows and distant moons. Elena began to rise, but then he reached for her.

She turned, her mouth shaping into a retort, and paused.

"Let's just sit here for a while. Before we go back." His touch was light on the inner skin of her wrist. "The world can wait for us a while, Elena Aadya Ravence."

She considered him for a long time. Her lips pursed, and for a moment, he thought she would leave him alone to face his monsters, but then a slow smile curved her lips. "Tired already, Prophet?"

"Exhausted." He leaned back. "Take pity on me."

She laughed. The sound rang through the canyons, soft and quick, like a beautiful bird darting through the sky—out of his reach.

"I have no pity for you, Samson Kytuu."

"None at all?" His hand was still on her wrist, and he felt her pulse jump. He smiled. "Why not?"

She considered. In the low moonlight, her eyes were large, luminous. "You don't pity gods who can destroy you."

He leaned closer, his breath brushing her cheek. "You are as much a god as me, Elena. You can destroy me too."

He heard her breath catch, and it sent a thrill through him. She was so close that he could feel the heat of her skin, smell the gentle aroma of her hair, like jasmine intermingled with sandalwood. Her Agni pulsed. Deep red soil and white sandstone, he need only to reach—

Elena stepped away, and his hand fell back to his side. Her chest rose and fell rapidly, and he tried not to stare, failed miserably. She mumbled something about the temple and hurried off, dark curls tumbling over her shoulders. He did not call her back. But the image of her Agni stayed with him, so vital, so furiously bright, and he realized, with gentle dismay, that Chandi was right.

Perhaps he would need to tap into Elena's Agni sooner than he thought.

CHAPTER 10

ELENA

The others have grown afraid of me. Perhaps it is out of reverence, but frankly, these fools do not have the spine to venerate me. They refuse to meet my eyes. Even the shadows do not dare creep closer.
—from the diaries of Priestess Nomu of the Fire Order

Elena tried to focus on the scrolls, but her thoughts, treacherous and twisting, returned to Samson. The hot brush of his breath against her cheek. His fingers on her pulse.

You are as much a god as me, Elena. You can destroy me too.

Despite the warmth of the temple fire, Elena shivered. She had no desire to go against a god, let alone destroy one. What would her people think, if she crushed their Prophet? She had seen their awe, their hope. It brought forth an ugly feeling, twisted, emulous, and though Elena tried to swallow it down, she could not push away the image of her people following a foreign Prophet.

Where would that leave her?

Without a throne, without a people, without a kingdom.

Alone, again.

Out of habit, she clasped Yassen's holopod. *What would you do?* She rubbed her thumb across the pod's scratched surface as if it could answer. Of course, it would not. It was not the first time she had wished Yassen was here, but now, Elena wished for it so strongly that her want became an ache that squeezed her chest until her breath became a thin rasp.

He would have found a way. Yassen Knight always found a way. With his gentle smile and quick hands, he'd manage to balance the scale between queen and Prophet, between her people and his. Yassen Knight could do anything.

But he could not come back from the dead.

Elena shuddered. She remembered the torn, forlorn look on Samson's face.

I loved and lost him too.

She did not know what to make of his grief. He, with his blazing swords and cursed eyes and vicious fire, *inflicted* misery. But for a moment, she had seen something broken and exposed, something awfully familiar. She had seen her pain reflected in him. It was unbecoming, like putting a bow on a tiger.

The diyas guttered, the temple fire whispering.

She half turned to listen when Kruppa sighed. The priestess set down her scroll, wincing as she cracked her back.

"Holy Bird, these old bones," she muttered.

"Careful. Say it near our Blue Star and he might behead you." Elena meant to keep her voice light, sarcastic, but it came out tired and worn, a pathetic accusation rather than a tease.

Kruppa rubbed her chin, her eyes slinking to the Phoenix statue. "He really means to tear down my temple, then?"

"No—maybe. I—" Elena shook her head. "I think we have more pressing matters to deal with than razing an old temple."

"Old?" Kruppa snorted. "These walls shine better than any of the holy homes in Rani. Name one temple more spotless."

Elena scraped her finger along the floor and withdrew ash. "I think you missed a spot."

"*That* is from the holy fire." Kruppa skimmed her hand along the edge of a diya, raking up the black ash, and then reached for Elena.

She dipped her head, and Kruppa drew a tilak on her forehead.

"There," Kruppa said. "Now who would want to behead a pretty face like that?"

Elena smiled at the priestess's attempt at humor, but a cold, clammy sensation prickled her skin. She imagined it: her kneeling in the ruins of the temple, Samson's urumi glinting over the soft skin of her neck as her people raised their hands for his offerings. She pushed the image away. No. Samson would not kill her. She was of Agni—*he needed her.* But the fire swelled, and the flames whispered, and she thought she heard its voice, soft and spiderlike, skittering across her skin like a warning.

To what end? it said.

Elena turned and picked up another scroll. She forced down the disquiet clotting her throat. The scroll was old and laden with a thick layer of ash. Blowing off the dust, Elena found it to be a journal entry from Priestess Nomu, dated before Alabore. Ash flaked off as she peeled back the edge, and Elena thought of the hundreds of thousands of scrolls and books burned during the invasion, the amount of her people's history—erased. She felt a great unwieldly loss, one whose shape she could not see or trace, but which spread through her with grey, phantomlike limbs. She should have read more. Asked more, listened to her mother *more.* There was so much more she could have done, so much she wished she had asked. Her mother had tried to transfer the scrolls to digital records, but that effort had ended after her death, when her father had sealed the royal library to everyone but themselves.

Grief led one to strange pursuits, but in her family, it induced them to do awful, ruinous things.

"'The inferno quakes with a different temper today,'" she read aloud. "'The high priestess says it's a sign that the Sixth Prophet will be chosen soon and take the flames. What a shame. I do not want it to leave. I've grown quite fond of the inferno's spirit, even if it mostly tries to spit sparks in my face.'"

Kruppa chortled. "She makes the Eternal Fire seem like an abusive lover."

"I suppose it is," Elena said, thinking of Samson standing before the inferno, the wrath scraping across his face as he forced the flames to bend.

She returned her attention back to the scroll when something struck her. "Wait. I thought the Sixth Prophet created the Eternal Fire. Why does it seem like it existed before her?"

"Because it did." Kruppa flipped through the prayer book, the pages rustling like the soft susurrus of sand against skin, and settled on a passage. "'And thus the First Prophet spoke: "This fire will burn in my stead to protect the land." Within the heart of the temple, the people saw a spark flare to a great inferno that burned the eyes of the sinners and healed the weak and the blind.' See? The Eternal Fire has been here since the dawn of time. Since the Phoenix and First Prophet."

Elena frowned, picking up another scroll. This one was a historical account labeled by a scrawling hand, *The Last Prophet*, dated after Alabore, author unknown.

"It says here about the Sixth, 'She spoke with the multitude of her former incarnations. "This fire will protect the land. Do not let it die." And so the Eternal Fire came to live in the heart of the temple.'"

"Let me see that." Kruppa took the scroll and read it fully, top to bottom, thrice. The lines around her mouth deepened. "This must be a mistake. Some priest must have gotten too high or loopy living underground in the great temple. The Eternal Fire has *always* existed, even before the Sixth. Priestess Nomu mentions it."

"She never names it, just calls it the inferno," Elena said.

Kruppa made an offended clucking sound. "It's one and the same. Eternal Fire, inferno, great blaze. I've once seen it written as the Flaring Fury. You know, we priests are quite inventive in our naming."

"How creative." Elena returned to Nomu's writing. For all her mother's adoration of the priestess, Nomu's diaries were chaotic. Dramatic even. She detailed inconsequential ceremonies, then followed up on trysts with rival priests so raunchy it would make a prostitute blush, but when Elena turned to the third entry, a scroll not as ruined by ash or dust, she paused.

"Listen to this: 'The first priests of the order have written that a sadness resides deep within these walls. I have come to feel it. Lately, I have dreamed of burning, of golden eyes speaking with a multitudinous voice that is both deafening and soft, that thunders through my skull and slithers through me in whispers. Always, there is a shadow within the flames. I think the inferno senses my unhappiness, because it has stopped spitting at me. Today, it tried to reach for me in what I thought was a comforting gesture, but it was a warning. The shadows were stirring. One snapped at my ankle, and I was overcome with such a vicious chill I thought my bones would freeze and break. But then the inferno gave a great roar that had all the others come running in. The shadows fled. Sister Madhu told me later how I had fainted, and when I was asleep, the fire raged for so long it took hours for the high priestess to calm it. But I have felt its sadness. It grieves for me, and I do not know why.'"

The entry ended there, but Elena flipped it over, her heart beating erratically in her ears. There, as she had suspected, was a signature.

A. M.

The Eternal Fire does not rage because it is angry; it rages because it grieves.

Her mother had read this scroll. She too had written not of the Eternal Fire's fury, but of its grief. And Elena still did not know why. She read the entry again. Held it up to the diyas, to the temple fire, but no secret passage appeared, no errant scrawl. The scroll remained markedly the same.

Kruppa carefully closed the prayer book.

"You know, sometimes, during my prayers, I can sense the inferno's sorrow too. Sometimes, it just curls into itself. The day you freed Magar, it became so small that I thought it would vanish." She stared into the temple fire as it crackled softly.

"If I were the Phoenix, locked in a mountain, forced to appear only after humanity had degraded itself to something monstrous, I would grieve too. I would mourn for all the things that have been lost, all the things I could not stop." She kissed the cover of the book and returned it reverently to its stand. "But then, that is Her duty. To give us hope when we have forgotten what it feels like. To remind us that we are soft and human too."

That is too simple, Elena thought. She looked into the glittering eyes of the Phoenix, at Her beak opened in an eternal frozen scream. What must it feel like, to watch for centuries as the people you loved and nurtured turned on themselves? She thought of her father welcoming Sesharian refugees and not giving them the means or resources to survive in a new home; the mother screaming as the terrified boy clutched his father; Samson smiling as her people bowed to yet another leader, another conqueror. It was the same cruel cycle. The ruinous march that led to new faces, new characters, but the same wicked fate.

She did not feel grief.

She felt rage, deep and dark and enduring. Centuries old, as dense as the desert, as unending, the kind stoked by unpunished sins and unrequited honesty. It echoed through her. Settled into her bones and began to make its home.

The Phoenix and Her Prophet were meant to inspire hope, to create justice, and with sinking, final clarity, Elena knew it was not her. She could never be her people's Prophet. How could she create hope when her Agni tasted this vicious?

The flames quivered. She turned to listen, but when she reached for them, they shied away, as if afraid.

I have read of a deeper, darker power. It imprisoned the Phoenix in a dark, stony hell.

Shadows danced around them, as if stirred by the wind. When they scraped her feet, Elena did not feel a chill like Priestess Nomu. She tasted salt and earth, something raw and untamed and at once grimly familiar.

And for the first time, Elena considered the shadows as they curled around her, kept back by only the faint, wavering hem of the inferno's light.

There are three types of fire, her mother had written. One had trapped the Phoenix.

Maybe that was why the Eternal Fire always raged when she came near. Maybe that was why it had tried to attack her.

What if my Agni imprisoned the Phoenix?

She could feel her Agni pulling beneath her fingers, itching to rush forward, to conquer, like all the ones who had come before her.

You are as much a god as me, Elena. You can destroy me too.

Samson's admission was also a warning. He could destroy her as well. Already her people were turning away. Already they called on another god. If Samson Kytuu truly saw her as an equal, then she needed to balance the scale.

She needed to make the Prophet bend.

CHAPTER 11

SAMSON

The urumi has become the symbol of Sesharian resistance. Thus, the Jantari have banned the weapon. To own one is punishable by imprisonment, to wield one punishable by death.
—from chapter 43 of *The Great History of Sayon*

Though verdant forests limn the horizon green, a new light rises in mountains where the gods convene. Two points past the scar, left by a man to consecrate the stars.'" He swept the holo to Visha. "Send it to the Cyleoni."

"What is this?" she asked.

"It's Elena's code."

"It sounds like gibberish."

"That's why it's a code."

"Or a bad rhyme written by a queen who fancies herself a poet—"

"And you're what, patron of the arts now? Go on, then. Give me a couplet."

Visha scowled, looking at Akino as he strode out of the weapons arsenal. "Ask our resident poet. I bet he can come up with a better rhyme."

"Don't drag me into this," Akino said. He set down Samson's urumi, the blades freshly shined and whetted, the silver almost blue in the early light. "Try not to let Jantari blood rust on the blades again. It was a bitch to clean."

"I'm afraid I can't promise that," Samson said as he ran a finger lightly, almost reverently, along the edge of his sword. It had been his mother's blade. An ancestral heirloom, passed down from her mother and the one before her, generations of priestesses who had prayed and sang for a son of the sea. For a god, cursed and radiant.

There had been a time when the old sky warriors wielded urumis with as many as five blades. One day, he would wield seven. One for each of the council kingdoms that had ignored Seshar's call for help, and one for Seshar herself.

For now, he wielded two blades to mirror the two antlers of the Great Serpent. Samson slowly belted the urumi around his waist, its weight familiar and natural. It felt like an extension of himself. For what was a god without his instruments?

"Just send the code," Chandi said.

Visha grumbled, but Samson noticed how her gaze lingered on Chandi, how her hand trembled, ever so slightly, inches away from Chandi's own. She began to encrypt the message, although not without another curse about untalented queens.

He searched Chandi, but his commander had not noticed. And at this, he felt a dull ache, sweet if only for its nostalgia. Once before, he had loved a boy who had never noticed. Once, he had hung on to every one of his gestures, every flick of his glance, to see if he *knew*. Because Samson couldn't bring himself to admit it. He had not the courage to say it first.

The memory of Yassen brought back a few nights ago, when he had felt the intoxicating pull of Elena's pulse and tasted the rich red earth of her fire, the vivacious flow of her prana. The *abundance* of her Agni. Even with his urumi, his Agni felt like a match flame compared with hers. It was *unfair*, that his Agni was the one fading when *he* was the stronger wielder; *he* knew more of their shared nature. Quickly, his grief flaked away under the strength of his disquieted envy. Samson stood, startling his officers.

"Give Elena an urumi," he said. "A singular silver blade, forged from the same fire as mine. You know the one."

Visha leaned back in her seat, curious, but both his commander and his master of arms frowned.

"You want to tap into her Agni now? Has yours—" Chandi said.

"I am fine," Samson said. "And I don't mean to tap hers yet. I want only to establish a connection."

"It would be dangerous to give her your twin, Blue Star," Akino said. "She can learn how to use it as a conduit, trace your Agni back to your own center. If she understood—"

"Tell me, when you and your sister added another blade to my urumi, why did you make a third?" Samson said.

Akino swallowed. "It was a safety measure, in case the second blade—"

"You were afraid I wouldn't be able to handle two tongues," he said softly. Akino flinched from his accusation, however gentle. Samson dropped his hand to his waist, touching the hilt of his urumi. "But I can handle more, Akino. When Elena uses the blade and channels her Agni through it, she'll open the connection to *her* own center. And then you will add the third blade to mine. And I will control both our Agni at once."

Akino's eyes widened in comprehension. He sprang to his feet and rushed to the arsenal.

Meanwhile, Visha reached into a black case and removed the remnants of the Arohassin's message: the floating sensors, the metal lotus, and the pod. She set them on the table and opened a holo. A transcript of the rebels' message rose before him, along with a new one.

"They're growing antsy," Visha said. "They want us to respond before—" But then her eyes floated above his shoulder.

"Your Majesty," she said coolly.

He whipped around to see Elena standing in the doorway.

"Who's growing antsy?" she asked.

"No one—" Visha said.

"The Cyleoni—" Chandi answered.

"We sent Syla your code," Samson cut in, throwing his officers a quick glance. "But we've received a report from our scouts in Rani that the Jantari are growing antsy. They seem to be planning a new counterattack. The sooner we meet with Syla, the better."

The lie, smooth and glib on his tongue, slipped out easily. Lies, he had found, were easier to tell than the truth. Truths were blunt and unwieldly, but lies required care and craft, and he knew how to feed them with the finesse of a butcher fattening a sow destined for dinner.

"Rani," she said, and the way her voice tripped, he knew she had bitten into the lie. "What kind of counterattack?"

"We don't know, but Syla might have intel," Samson said as Akino reentered holding a black suede bag. He started forward, but Samson gave a subtle shake of his head. *Not yet.* He would give Elena the urumi later, after he had earned her trust.

"Come," he told her. "There's something I need to discuss with you."

They entered the courtyard behind the hall. The Jantari officers had used it as a training ground, the stones still riddled with scars from zeemirs. The fountains lay grey, stagnant. Samson watched Elena survey the court-yard as he leaned against an old gulmohar tree.

"They're used to be sculptures here," Elena said, her voice carrying through the quiet. "Jodhaa and her sister, Sandhana, each holding a feather of the Phoenix. I wonder what they did to them." She turned slowly, and he saw the pain on her face then, perhaps not for the statues, but for the loss they represented—a destruction of her people, her culture, her history.

"When the Jantari invaded, they ripped out the golden medallion of the Serpent from the city temple. Now it sits in one of their museums. Maybe your statues will be there too," Samson said.

Elena smiled ruefully. "No, they will not. Farin will have them in his palace to remind himself who is truly the Phoenix King."

Her face darkened then, and Samson knew this was the time to broach his proposition. He carefully pushed off from the gulmohar, his voice slow, measured.

"I need your help, Elena," he said. "We need to understand each other's Agni. How it works, when it doesn't." *How to sustain it without consequence.* "Our Agni is our advantage over Farin. If we could hone it, strengthen it, the war won't even last a sun."

Across from them leaned a tall, cracked mirror. Her eyes connected with his within it. "You're the Prophet of our great god. Shouldn't you already know the nature of Agni?"

He ignored the edge in her voice and drew up beside her, her shoulder brushing his scar, and he felt a shiver—cold, fiery—crackling down his sternum. He watched her face within the mirror. A crack bisected it, he on one side, she on the other.

"You burned three Jantari mines down on your own, Elena. That's impressive," he said. She quirked an eyebrow but stayed silent, her eyes dark, watchful. "What if…we were to burn more? Enough to really make Farin notice?" He stepped closer, his face sliding over the crack in the mirror so that his reflection bent, one half alone, the other half hovering over her head. "For that to happen, we need to amplify our Agni."

He had known of her, known *her*, for a long time. When he had been a boy scavenging the streets of Rani, he had felt an odd sensation crawl up his neck. It tugged him, like a hook on one of his father's fishing rods, to Palace Hill. He had looked up at that austere, distant behemoth and thought something of him belonged there. Someone like him.

The feeling had grown when he met Leo for the first time in Rasbakan. Elena had accompanied her father, though she had been in another part of the compound when he had met the old king. The odd sensation, the one he had felt as a boy, rose within him then. As he spoke to Leo and offered his proposal of marriage, he felt a low burning in his naval chakra. It had been difficult to suppress his Agni and quench the sparks threatening to break from his fingertips. Heat thrummed through his spine not as a sensation but as a *physicality*, a buzzing that vibrated through his bones and teeth with such power he wondered why Leo and his Astra were not trembling like he was. He had felt then, with an awful clarity, that someone within the walls of this compound was the *same*. Just as wondrous, just as monstrous. It filled him with dizziness and elation—to be so close to someone of his nature, someone who knew the consequences of fire. Someone who knew his burden of burning.

It wasn't until he had seen her in the throne room, dressed in a resplendent lehenga, looking both beautiful and terrifying, that he knew it was her. He had wanted to rush over and take her hands, to feel the heat in her veins. *You and I are gods*, he had wanted to say.

Gods among men. The powerful among the weak. What was she doing, waiting, when the world could be theirs?

But she had proved to be a godling, not yet awakened. And he had watched her coming into her power with an impatient hunger, anticipating the right moment, the right people to be eliminated, before—

Elena strode forward, breaking him from his thoughts. She trailed her hand through the bowl of a fountain and flicked. Water spattered across him, though some drops caught her. A little bead of water trembled on her bottom lip.

"And how exactly can we amplify our Agni?" she said.

He was still staring at the bead of water on her lip. With great effort, Samson dragged his gaze away. "W-we start by understanding its true nature. I will show you everything I know of Agni, and in turn, you can show me what you know. We can start training tomorrow."

She considered this for a moment, and he noticed how her eyes seemed to turn inward, as if she was retreating into the chasms of her mind, finding solutions, back alleys, twists and turns. Some way to use him, manipulate him—just as he would her.

It delighted him, in a sick, perverse way. They were more alike than she knew, no matter what label she threw at him.

He began to speak again when she raised her hand. The air grew taut, and he tasted ash on his tongue. At first, there was a fizzle. Then a spark. Then a glare so bright he had to turn away. He didn't need to see it—he *felt* it. The sudden rush of heat emanating from his lower chakra, the electric buzz filling his throat, his ears.

When he turned back, there was a single red flame in Elena's hand. Brilliant and perfect, hissing with a power that reminded him of the sound of waves crashing against a cliff. He could feel its reverberations in his bones. Unlike his fire, hers didn't bend or sway. It stood ramrod straight, tall and bright. Her fingers fluttered around the fire, dancing.

"How do you do it?" Samson said, voice soft with wonder. "How do you call your Agni so easily?"

Without pain, he thought.

Elena played with the flame in her hand. "It's not easy," she said, and a tiny line appeared between her eyebrows. It was oddly endearing. "I've gotten better, but... it takes practice. Focus. Dance, at least for me." She glanced up at him, and he saw that the line between her brows had deepened like a mark, a scar, and he had a strange desire to take his blue flames and mend it away. She raised the flame higher. Her fire cast an orange glow on her face, making her features starker, harsher—frightful even—and he was reminded of the Sesharian stories of a queen so in love with infernos that she drove all those around her to ruin. His adoration withered a degree.

"How do you summon yours?" she asked.

The flame flickered, and for a moment, her eyes shifted from brown to a pale gold—like those of the man in his dreams. He froze. Fear, sudden and ancient, threaded down his spine. But then the fire steadied, and the shadows wavered, and Elena's eyes were the same warm brown, the same they had always been.

"What is it?" she asked, peering at him.

Samson blinked. Whatever he had seen, he must have imagined. *I am tired, that's all.*

"I dance too, but differently." He patted the urumi at his waist. "You use your body only. I use my body and a sword. I have more control then, and more power."

"So if I were to use an urumi, my Agni will become more…" She paused, as if tasting the word on her tongue. "Surgical."

He smiled, knifelike. "Precisely."

"But I prefer a slingsword. It's cleaner, better."

"You can learn."

Elena eyed his urumi, though he wondered, with distant amusement, if she was staring at his waist for other reasons. "If we want to learn about each other's Agni, then we learn them in their original states. Without weapons."

She watched him closely, and he realized this was a test. A challenge.

He opened his palm, and a blue flame burst to life without a sound. The effort sent a cold chill through his arm, but he ignored it. "You and I are made of the same thing."

He extended his hand.

"Show me your Agni, and I'll show you what I know of mine."

She stared at his hand and then, slowly, placed her own in his. Their flames intertwined. Not a kiss, not an embrace, but a trapping. A sizing up of sorts. Elena squeezed, and heat sizzled up his arm as their flames sparked and died between their palms.

"Leave your urumi, Prophet," she said, brushing past him. "You don't need it to dance."

CHAPTER 12

ELENA

I have tasted and seen the Prophet's hunger. Nothing can compare to its wretchedness.

—from the dairies of Priestess Nomu of the Fire Order

Samson was waiting for her the next day in the cool bowels of the canyons. He leaned against the wall, one foot raised, head bent in thought, his urumi belted silver around his waist.

How he did not cut himself was beyond her. She had heard from Black Scales that only those who had dedicated suns to learning the art of the urumi wore the sword like belts or sashes. *Warriors*, the soldiers called them, voices hushed with awe.

Fools was a better moniker.

As Samson turned to her, Elena wondered, not for the first time, if he was inured to death. That, by being the Prophet reborn, he thought himself above it. Even when it coiled around him in the form of a silver metal snake, he stood unperturbed, smiling at her.

"Ready?" he said.

"I told you that you won't need your urumi," she said.

"You don't need it, but I do," he said, and there was something in his voice that made her pause. Was it envy? Want? She studied him, but he was already unlooping the urumi, his long fingers deftly wrapping around the leather-bound hilt as the twin blades unfurled with a hiss.

He flicked his wrist, a movement so quick she almost didn't see it, and the blades ionized. The air tightened, charged. Elena took an involuntary step back as a blue flame rippled down his hand and split, spiraling down the blades of the urumi.

It had taken a matter of seconds, without warning.

Elena blinked, realizing only now how her heart jackhammered in short successive beats. *Leave. Run.*

Samson's eyes slid to hers. In the blue light of the flames, they almost seemed to glow.

"Your turn," he said.

Elena swallowed. She forced herself to inhale deeply, to still her yammering heart and push back the wave of dread that seemed to seize her bones the moment his inferno had taken its first breath.

She shifted her weight, raising her left heel ever so slightly. She felt Samson's eyes on her, tracking her every movement. It sent every breath a hot thrill down her spine, along with an instinctual fear, like the ancient preservation of self. The fight or flight. But Elena ground her teeth and turned her ankle, thrusting out her arms just as the heat in her gut flowed up, out, down her biceps, her elbows, her hands and blazed into a red flame so bright and fierce it towered over them. As she felt its power, its *presence*, ripple through her body, Elena almost forgot her fear.

Almost.

The blades flashed as Samson slashed, and the flames tore forth with an eager hunger that set her teeth on edge. The air thickened, so hot and claustrophobic that Elena struggled to breathe, but then Samson pulled his arm to his chest and the fire died at once. Black scorch marks were left in its wake.

He turned to her, lifting an eyebrow. *Well?*

Elena spun, splaying out her fingers to form lotuses, and then cut diagonally. While Samson's fire had been hungry, it had been controlled. Hers shot forth with a quickness that surprised her. Elena peeled back, but as she brought her palms together, she felt its resistance.

She could almost hear the whine of her Agni, its hurt in being denied, before she crushed palm to palm, and it dissipated into smoke.

Elena straightened with a shudder. It was happening more often now. Her Agni, resisting in small ways. Its hunger growing. When she had destroyed the mines, she had not wanted control. She wanted everything to *burn*. When she had summoned the flames during the attack, it was Samson who had taken it, addled it, and honed their infernos into a controlled blaze. She looked down at her hands, at the sparks just dying. Even now, she could feel her Agni rustle within her, its appetite indulged but not whetted. It wanted *more*.

She turned to Samson, who was watching her with close interest. Again, she wondered if this was a mistake. She was protective of her Agni, for no reason other than it was hers and hers alone. But Samson knew more. He could control his Agni with a precision that made her bristle, a ferocity that made her ache in want. And then there was the other part.

The healing.

She saw how his blue flames had enveloped the young girl, knitting back her skin and bones and the scars into his mark. Elena remembered how the mother had fallen reverently onto her knees, sobbing, and it had filled her with such bitterness she was surprised her stomach hadn't shriveled with the acidity. Word was spreading. The Prophet was here. Her people were beginning to look to Samson to lead them. Not her, the queen. But him, a butcher.

A butcher who could heal the burned in a land that knew too much of burning.

"Why are you holding back?" Samson said.

The question took her by surprise. "What?"

"Just now, when you wielded the flames, you were restrained. I could feel it," he said.

"I wasn't—" she began and stopped short. Did she dare tell him? The small bouts of resistance, the refusal of the inferno to disappear. She studied Samson, his tall, dark frame, legs spread wide, as if he was ready to leap, arms relaxed, as if he knew he was in charge.

"I didn't think there was a need to burn with…abandon," she said.

Samson laughed. "With abandon? That's what fire *is*. It is a wild, beautiful, and dangerous force. You're denying its true nature by repressing it."

"If that's so, then how do you control it?" she said.

"Simple," Samson said. "I understand it. By understanding it, I can control it."

"You need to be more specific," she said dryly.

"Agni is, by its nature, ravenous. It wants and takes and will not be appeased until it consumes everything. Until one day it consumes us." At this, he smiled, sharp and rueful. "As Fireblood, we are its instruments. Its…guardians. Like the Prophet." His smile deepened, carving into something more dangerous. "Agni flows through us into the world. But you cannot channel it well if you resist its hunger."

"I—I can manage it," she said with a scowl.

"And yet you're afraid of it consuming you," Samson said, and at this, she stilled.

With one smooth motion, Samson curled his urumi around his shoulder and strode toward her. It took her unawares, but Elena forced herself not to flinch.

Samson stopped before her, so close she had to look up to meet his eyes. He smelled of ash and musk, but below that, something fresh, pleasant even, like earth after the rain. He placed one hand below his belly button, the other on his chest.

"There are two places where Agni can reside. Your navel chakra"—he tapped his stomach—"or your heart." He patted his chest. "Prana, the life force that exists in all things, flows through ours nadis and powers our chakra centers. As guardians of the Agneepath, we can manipulate prana. Manifest it into flame, into infernos."

He slowly dropped his hands and took hers. She sucked in her breath as he placed her hands on his chest and stomach. His heart thrummed beneath her fingers. She tried not to stare at the scar peeking through his open collar, or how his chest trembled, ever so slightly, at her touch.

"But manipulating prana is tricky. If you overshoot, you can burn yourself from within. Or your Agni begins to eat itself and fade." He paused, his hands wavering over her own. "This is why you can't refuse the nature of Agni. You'll block prana and corrupt your chakras. You're essentially giving yourself a slow, gruesome death. We control Agni by *accepting its nature*. The inferno will respond to you if you understand that it wants to burn. We can't avoid its appetite because its appetite is *ours*. It is a part of you. It is you."

And she saw it then, in his eyes. The desire to burn, the want for *more*.

Always more. It was an ache she knew, a hunger she felt in her bones and was afraid to acknowledge. But he had accepted it, controlled it, and now he, a Prophet who could heal the burned, was a master of Agni.

But she had seen his rapacity. His hunger knew no bounds, had no qualms. After all, Samson had not even blinked when he learned of the crushed Ravani civilians under the wall. He had moved on to the next objective, the next mission, without so much as a guilty dream. Her estrangement from her own people was because of *him*. All of this was a result of him.

His want.

His desire.

Elena pulled her hands back.

"Maybe it is for you. But I don't want to burn without regret," she said.

He dropped her hands. "Who said there wasn't regret?"

She began to speak when Samson slipped the urumi down from his shoulder to his waist. Over the sounds of sliding metal, his voice was soft.

"I have regrets that will last more than a lifetime, Elena," he said. "But I also have a purpose that will outlast that—Seshar. Ravence, for you. What we pay now . . . does it matter? Will it matter, if it means freeing our homes?"

She said nothing to this, afraid her voice would betray her.

He pulled back, his smile grim. "If we must face consequences, let it be after the war. You and I can burn together then."

This time, when he unleashed his inferno, Elena felt her own Agni rise, as if in fear. As if in recognition.

They trained every dawn as they waited on the Cyleoni. The boulders bore the brunt of their attacks, their red faces slashed with scorch marks and blades. She began to understand the breadth of his power, the obsession of his control. Samson Kytuu wielded his Agni with the fervency of a thousand devotees clamoring up to the high temple. Every swing, every thrust, every twist—feverishly controlled.

Elena spun out of the Snake, arms twisting as a flame flowed down her shoulders to her hands and then lanced onto a boulder. The scorch mark was lighter than Samson's.

He paused, one hand on his hip, sweat dripping down his collar. For a second, she thought she saw him shudder as if in pain, but then he was striding toward her.

"You're still holding back," he said.

"I am not," she snapped. They had been at it since before dawn, and her arms felt hot and heavy, her feet sore. She had stayed up last night reading the scrolls, to no avail. She had found no evidence of the Phoenix's existence. Neither had she found proof of Her falsity, but her hope felt strained. Bitter.

"You are. That mark should have gone deeper. What are you so afraid of, Elena?"

That her kingdom was a lie. That her mother and father had died for nothing. That he would take it all away from her one day.

Samson sighed. "Let's try something else."

He returned with two chakrams. "Since you're not ready for the urumi yet, we'll use this. Channel your flames around the disc."

Unconvinced, Elena wrapped her hand around the hilt set within the circular weapon. Its disc was chiseled down to a sharp edge, with small patterns etched into the blade. Samson stood back, closing his eyes. Still as a dune. In one moment, she felt a pressure growing in her ears, as if the air had suddenly tightened and clamped down, like a hoverpod suddenly descending, so fierce she yearned for release. And then, within the space of a breath, she felt the air *flare*. Her Agni *tugged* and flames burst down and around Samson's chakram. The inferno spat sparks, hissing, but it traveled no farther down the blade, nor down his arm. It stayed corralled, immensely powerful and precise.

Samson swung. The disc soared through the air with a hiss and slashed deep into the boulder. The blue flames snapped, biting, tearing. When Samson pulled them back, there was one clean, deep incision. She raised her weapon as he neared.

"Your turn, Ravani."

Elena imagined the prana in her body racing down into the blade as Samson had taught her. The chakram was just an extension of her limb, a conduit for her body's heat.

Gradually, her Agni stirred. Sweat pooled in her armpits. Sparks flared around her wrist. Flames whipped out, bright, eager, and she pushed them onto the blade—but they did not stop. They pushed past her blade and leapt onto the ground. Fear, panic—icy hot and animallike—gripped her throat as her inferno barreled forward. *Magar.* All at once, she saw her inferno rushing down the canyon and into the city. She saw the Eternal Fire eating the mountain. She saw the landslides of her making crush civilians in that sleepy mountain town while Yassen was buried alive in the dirt.

Elena dropped her weapon and slammed her palms together to smother the flames. They hissed in displeasure. Again, she felt a bout of resistance—sharp, indignant—and then her hands closed, and the fire died.

She stood staring at the ash, feeling drained and as threadbare as wisps of smoke.

After a moment, Samson knelt, then stood, holding out the chakram.

"Again, but this time, imagine Yassen. Ferma. Leo. Imagine that if you can't—"

She whipped around, snarling in anger, at herself, at him, at this gift that felt more like a curse, her frustration bubbling up as she tried to wrench away the chakram—only to be stayed by Samson.

"Careful," he said as the disc hovered inches from his chest. "I'm fragile."

"I thought butchers liked knives," she spat.

His eyes raked over her, sending hot chills down to her stomach. Suddenly, he grabbed her wrist, and Elena froze as he stepped closer, the edge of the chakram pricking his skin. A bead of ruby bloomed outward.

"Only when I hold it."

Despite the bright morning, his eyes seemed to become darker, resembling pools of an inky, liquid black that rippled as he beheld her. Elena tried to pull away, but his grip was firm.

"Do you know what your problem is, my rani? You lack faith."

She laughed, high and dry. "Maybe it's because you said my god is a lie."

"No." His fingers curled around hers. "You lack faith in yourself."

It was her turn to hesitate.

I believe in myself, she wanted to say, but the words felt shallow. Did she, after all she had lost? After she could not stop the Jantari from taking her home? After she could not save her own people at the wall? Her sole duty, her *only* duty, was to protect Ravence. And she had failed, in every miserable and possible way.

Somewhere, between Jantar and Ravence, between the Agnee mountains and the Sona Range, she had lost something. For months, she had tried to find what it had been. It felt like trying to grab mist. She could feel its absence, like a dull, aching hollow in her chest. Now she understood it. It was a simple word, brief, powerful.

Faith.

Her faith in the Phoenix had always been precarious. But this faith was far more vulnerable, far more integral. She had thought she knew the nature of her Agni, but she did not know its basic components, unlike Samson. She felt jealousy, but it withered away quickly for something deeper.

Loss.

It rang through her bones like the fading clangs of the temple bells. She was lost, she had lost, and she did not know how to begin again.

She let go of the chakram.

"I need to return to the temple," she said.

"Elena," he called after her. She did not stop walking, but he continued, his words bouncing off the canyon walls. "So what if your god is a lie? Ravence isn't. *Make Ravence your god.*" She stopped, turning to meet his gaze. "Your country can become your faith. And that faith can become faith in yourself. But you must hunger for it. Crave it, with an appetite that knows no bounds."

He held out the chakram. A slick of blood wetted its edge.

"Try again. But this time, think of Ravence. Her dunes. Her freedom."

She closed the distance between them and took the chakram. Beside her, Samson watched, his expression hopeful and yet still somehow ravenous. Hope and hunger were the same for him. And she thought then of how that must be the same for Farin, for the Arohassin, for every enemy of Ravence that hoped and hungered for her dunes, her mountains, her riches. Elena balanced the chakram. This time, when she called her Agni, she did not think of her god, or her people, or her country. She thought of the predators lining up along her borders and the ones already nestled within. She thought of their gluttony. She thought of their greed. And then she thought of their deaths, and she *desired.*

Flames rushed down the chakram, hissing, tearing, but she curbed their movement, leashed them with the strength of her will. The flames stayed.

With a snap of her wrist, she hurled the chakram.

The cut was not deep. The flames died at once upon impact. But the smoke was sweet and substantial, and Elena inhaled deeply.

Behind her, Samson clapped. Elena turned to see him smiling.

"Tomorrow, we begin with the urumi."

CHAPTER 13

SAMSON

O Great Warrior, what is it you wield? A sword? A whip? For it sings like a snake, bites twice as fast, and still, I wish to hear its hiss.
    —from *The Odyssey of Goromount: A Play*

He arrived early the next day, when the shadows ran deep and the moons still reigned in the sky. The smell of smoke lingered within the boulders. The two incisions seemed to pulse like sweating wounds as he traced the marks of her Agni. Elena could barely dissect her flames into separate formations and control each individually. Her inferno was a great blaze. Unruly, overwhelming—powerful. Wondrous.

After she had left, he had taken her chakram. The blade had still been warm, and he heard an echo of her Agni then, like the last note of a fading song. He imagined that song reverberating through his bones once he opened the connection between their Agnis. He did not want to take hers—simply to savor it. To feel its heady potency and become *vital* again, his Agni boundless and full. It had been torture enough to simply stand there and not at least *taste* her Agni.

For a moment, Samson closed his eyes. He imagined the rush of warmth along his skin as Elena sent flames down the urumi. The pull of his Agni, responding to hers. By the time she arrived, he had checked the single-bladed urumi for the eleventh time.

"There you are!" He sprang forward, and perhaps something of his eagerness showed on his face, because Elena slowed. Her gaze flickered from his face to the suede bag in his hands.

She frowned. "What's that?"

"A gift." He forced himself to keep his anticipation from his voice. "I had this one made especially for you."

She made no move to take it. Did she know? Did she feel his Agni tremble in want? Samson schooled his expression, pretending to sound indifferent.

"Or you could refuse. I can give this to one of my followers. I'm sure they'd appreciate their Prophet's gifts."

Elena scowled. Carefully, she took the suede bag and withdrew the urumi. Even curled, the silver blade was stunning. The edges were thin and sharp, nearly invisible, while the long tongue of the blade shone with a vicious brilliance. Tiny birds—Akino, that cheeky bastard—rose up the spine of the blade. Some carried flowers in their beaks. Others, fragments of the moon and sun.

"It's beautiful," she said softly.

She gripped the leather hilt, and Samson's mouth ran dry. He needed only to make her rush the blade with fire, and then he would take it immediately after. With her flames still fresh, he could open their connection.

And then he would feed, slowly.

It took him a moment to realize Elena was watching him, eyes narrowed. "What's wrong with you?"

His eyes flicked to her hand, at the perfect, unblemished urumi. It seemed to taunt him: how close he was, how her fingers curled around its grip.

"N-nothing." He pulled out his own urumi. Sparks flared down his wrist. He did not want to wait. "Ready?"

Her frown deepened, and he felt her Agni twitch as if in aversion. Samson cursed himself. He was moving too quickly. He crushed the sparks, which sent a dull pang up his arm, but he ignored it.

"You taught me your dance, now let me teach you mine." He unlooped his sword, the twin blades whispering against the ground. "The trick with the urumi is to use momentum. As long as you keep moving, you'll build power."

He spun, whipping his arm overhead. The twin blades hissed as they whirred like the fins of a thopter, then slashed down. The earth cracked. Pebbles flew, but he did not stop. Turning, Samson drew his arm across his body, and the blades followed suit. They were a harmony. A blend of movement and power, flesh and steel, man and weapon.

He caught Elena staring, awe opening her expression as if she was drinking him in. He grinned. He swung his blade behind his back and then forward. He leapt to the right, then left, then swung down, leaving marks in his wake. With every step, he felt her eyes follow. And despite his earlier impatience, Samson relished this brief intermezzo. He realized he enjoyed her eyes on him.

Samson bent backward so deep that the crown of his head kissed the earth. His silver blades blazed above him, like wings. And then he was pulling up and up, his blade arcing through the air, hissing with power, and he etched a final groove in the ground.

When Elena drew up beside him, she gasped.

An image of the Serpent unfurled beneath them, slightly smoking.

"Show off," she muttered, but he heard the astonishment in her voice. A hot pleasure blossomed in the pit of his stomach.

He stepped back, holding out his urumi. This time, Elena followed suit.

"Just copy me."

He led her through the basics, from whipping out the urumi to hit an approaching target to reeling it in with a quick flick of the wrist. Advance and retreat. Elena grunted as she spun on her heel, slashing down.

"Again," Samson said.

Her urumi slapped dully against the ground.

"You have to swing your entire arm." He ran his hand lightly down from her shoulder to her wrist. She inhaled sharply. "Like this." He took her hand and mimicked the motion, their arms moving in unison. If Elena felt anything, she did not show it. Her hand stayed steady, her gaze pointedly set away from him. But she could not mask her Agni. He felt it judder, then pulse, and he knew without a shadow of doubt that if he felt for her pulse now, it would thud erratically.

He turned to face her, and Elena was forced to meet his eyes. He paused, struck by the heat of her gaze. They were close enough that he could see the slight sheen of sweat on her upper lip. He resisted the urge to wipe it away.

Agni, he thought. *I'm here for her Agni.*

Elena was the first to push away. A light hand on his chest, a firm shove. His skin blazed where she had touched him, and he watched as she rotated from her shoulder and slashed. This time, the urumi made a faint ring.

"Better?"

His throat was oddly dry. "Try with your fire."

Elena faltered. "Already?"

But he could still feel the heat of her touch and the torturous presence of her Agni. He could wait no longer. "Summon it."

Elena stepped back, and he involuntarily leaned forward. The air grew taut, charged, as she raised the blade. All his senses, all his muscles, tightened. Like a yeseri ready to pounce, he watched, his hand clenched around his urumi hilt. Any second now, he would feel her Agni unfurl. He would feel it call to his own through their urumis, the call a question, a search for something in kind.

Sparks fizzed from her wrists. He inched closer, ready to leap—

"I found it!"

Elena startled, turning.

He sprang forward, desperate to catch the sparks on her urumi. "Here, let me."

As soon as his fingers brushed hers around the hilt, Samson felt a jolt. A sudden heat flashed through the urumi, like an electric bolt, and for one excruciating moment, he saw the horrible, agonizing breadth of her Agni before Elena dropped the weapon. At once, the sensation disappeared. His heart thundered as Elena stared at her hand in confusion, in shock, but before he could say anything, Kruppa burst onto the grounds, waving a scroll.

"She exists!" she cried. "The Phoenix exists!"

CHAPTER 14

SAMSON

I believe the people who left the first continent brought their gods with them. This has led to the creation of a protomyth of the fire gods. The Phoenix, the Great Serpent, and the Yumi Goddess all exhibit similar origin stories and death cycles. However, the question of power remains. If all three gods stem from the same protomyth, who then is the most powerful?

—from *A Critique of the Ancient Gods*
(note: debunked by historians)

Elena hurried after Kruppa, Samson stumbling behind them as if in a daze. He had been so close. So *fucking close*. The shape of her Agni haunted him, wavering in his mind's eye as he remembered the excruciating flash of its power ricocheting through his body. If only he had had a moment longer... He sought Elena, but people clamored forward as they weaved their way toward the temple.

"Prophet!"

"Bless me, Prophet!"

"Look upon me!"

In the distance, Elena turned. No doubt she observed that all the onlookers were Ravani bearing his mark. No doubt she noticed how no one hailed her. All her people latched on to him with an intense fervor, their faces wide, desperate.

"Prophet!" they called as they jostled past Elena and rushed to Samson.

Dimly, Samson knew he should bless them, but he moved in a stupor, his body aching for the phantomlike presence of Elena's Agni that it had briefly tasted. A hand grabbed his arm. Another his shoulder. Samson jerked back, but no matter where he turned, people pressed forward, palms outstretched, faces upturned. *Prophet, Prophet, Prophet.* A panicked cry bubbled and died in his throat as he suddenly remembered the tunnels, the sweet, rotten aroma of sweat and blood and bodies too close. There were too many, coming at once—

Someone touched his chest, his scar, and he jolted back into himself, the memory sluicing through his limbs like black, brackish water.

"Space," he panted.

"Prophet, give me your mark—"

"SPACE!" he roared.

The followers recoiled, as if struck. Samson sucked in a fresh spurt of air. He knew, judging by the fear on their faces, that he'd been too brusque.

But he did not care. He could use fear, another day. Samson stumbled on, and the crowd parted for him like the sea before a relentless ship.

He found Elena and Kruppa already inside the temple. The inferno roiled at his approach. That was his first warning. When Samson reached for the fire, he could feel it resist his desire, and a quick, anxious alarm thumped through him. The flames rustled, but when he turned to listen, he found their song indecipherable, spoken in a low hissing language he did not understand.

Speak to me, he commanded.

The tiny inferno did not respond.

Samson swallowed back his panic, but his throat felt painfully dry. Kruppa was busy unfurling the scrolls, talking rapidly.

"—the diary entries make no sense. Nomu's timeline, her comments— gosh, even her *syntax*—it's a mess. She never names the inferno as the

Eternal Fire and seems to stop writing after the arrival of the Sixth Prophet. But then I started considering what your mother said, Elena, and I—"

"Kruppa, desert be blessed, slow down," Elena laughed, though Samson noted how her eyes darted about uneasily. Did she sense the fire's resistance too?

Behind his back, Samson curled his fingers. He imagined a flame darting out of the inferno—right into his hand. He concentrated on that image, the sensation of heat spidering down his palm, and pulled.

The inferno hissed and held. He glowered at it and commanded again. The fire only spat out sparks, as if cursing him.

A sick, cold sensation ran down his throat, like inhaling salt water in his dreams. Why was the inferno resisting him? No flame could ever deny him. He was a god of Agni, blessed by the Great Serpent. He was *the* wielder of the Eternal Fire and its pets, but the small temple fire remained in its hold, resolute. Samson wrestled back his dread, but it had threaded into his bones now and he could feel it throb through his veins in time with the inferno's crude, indecipherable song.

Great Serpent, what is happening?

"Don't you see, Blue Star? There are three."

Samson turned, broken from his thoughts, and found both Elena and Kruppa watching him.

"Three what?"

"Three manifestations of Agni." Kruppa held up a scroll. "'I have felt the deep grief of the inferno. It is dark and bottomless, but not because it suffers alone. The grief is made of three. Three powers who have loved and betrayed and lost each other. Three sisters. Our god is but one.'" She looked up at him, shaking the scroll. "This is proof! Our Phoenix does exist. She is one of the three powers."

"I would not call that proof," Samson began.

"What proof do you have of your own god other than faith?" Kruppa shot back.

"Your Eternal Fire bends to *me*," he snapped. "*I* wield it. *I* can control it because it was created by the Great Serpent. What more proof do you need?"

"But it's written here that one of the three—"

"Enough!" Elena cried.

They fell silent. Her face grew pinched, as if she were considering something, or *listening*. Samson watched her and the flames and wondered, with a sick jealousy, if the flames were only speaking to her.

He stepped forward. "Elena, what is the fire saying to you?"

Her mouth twisted. Her voice was flat, hard. "It tells me nothing. It has always told me *nothing*. The Eternal Fire barely ever speaks to me, unlike with you, Prophet." She spat out the last word. He did not know if he should feel relieved or infuriated at her response.

Elena took the scroll from Kruppa and read it again. "'Three powers who have loved and betrayed and lost each other. Three *sisters*.'" She looked between them both. "She must mean goddesses."

"Like the Phoenix!" Kruppa cried.

"Like the Great Serpent," he said.

"Like the Goddess Mother," Elena said softly, almost to herself. Her eyes met his. "The third Agni is the Yumi's Goddess."

"That's absurd," he said. "There are other goddesses throughout our world. Tsuana's horned shark, Nbru's great huntress—Ayona has two! People even worship the fucking moons. You can't just create gods out of nothing and claim them to be all-powerful."

"Nor can you claim someone's faith to be blasphemous," Elena said.

"Elena, we are gods of Agni," he said. "*We are real.* You can feel your fire running through your veins. How can you deny that?"

"And what if my Agni comes from a goddess, like yours?" she said.

Silence stretched between them. Samson held her gaze as his heart jackhammered hard enough to rattle his teeth. His throat bobbed, caught.

"You told me that your Agni came from the Great Serpent," Elena said. "What if mine is connected to the Yumi's Goddess? When I first learned how to wield the flames, it was Ferma who told me about the Mother. We should go to Moksh and seek out the Yumi—"

"No," Samson said, finally finding his voice.

The flames swelled, and he felt their heat prick his skin as if to bite. He stepped away from the inferno and into the cool shadows. They curled around him, his old friends.

"A trip to Moksh will take days, and we both need to be here. Syla could contact us at any moment. Jantar could launch a counterattack when we're gone. We could lose Magar, Elena." He broke off as a coughing fit overtook him. A dry ache rattled down his throat and chest. Silently, he cursed the Eternal Fire.

"But if we have the Yumi with us, then I can sway the council. No one would dare to cross the Yumi." Her mouth set. "I could go alone."

"The Yumi won't listen," he rasped.

"They will listen, especially when I show them my Agni."

He imagined it then: Elena standing on the shore of Moksh and turning the black sands to glass with her vicious, fervent desire. He saw her returning with the Yumi, a powerful army of rage and death sweeping through Ravence, through Jantar, forcing the world to bend. And he saw himself, faded, withered. His Agni so weak it emitted only one faint spark. He would be made to watch as Farin retreated from Ravence and tightened his hold on Seshar, as Elena celebrated her freedom while his continued to be a plaything of kings. Seshar would be forgotten, as always.

He stepped out of the shadows. The heat returned, but he ignored the fire's scathing sparks. He felt the flames twist, felt the Eternal Fire hum and the gods listen.

"We finish your training first. If you can wield the urumi with flames, then you will be ready to face the Yumi."

"But why would the Yumi care if I can—"

"You want to convince them with your Agni? Then hone it first."

The flames hissed in warning, but Elena could not hear them anyway. She nodded, once.

Kruppa clutched the scroll to her chest, watching them with uncertainty. "If you think you share the Goddess's Agni, then who shares the Phoenix's?"

Samson gave a wry smile. "No one alive, Priestess."

He held out Elena's urumi, but the queen crossed her arms. "You'll have to do one thing for me first."

He bit back his annoyance. "Do what?"

"Celebrate Laal Joon with me tomorrow afternoon. Magar never got the chance to honor the founding of Ravence. And now she can do so with her queen and Prophet."

She smiled, and it sent an uncomfortable, dangerous sensation through him, simultaneously provocative and miserably infuriating. He hated how much he *needed* her Agni. How much he craved it. Her Agni bloomed so painstakingly close, so tantalizingly within his reach.

"Tomorrow, then."

The temple fire crackled as if laughing, but whether in delight or cruelty, he could not tell.

CHAPTER 15

ELENA

Gods may change, names may die, but the fact of their essence remains:
The divine shall always betray, and the betrayed shall always pray.
—from *The Legends and Myths of Sayon*

Crimson powder speckled the late-afternoon air, brushing her cheeks, her hair. Elena turned in to the haze as a young girl laughed, red handprints dimpling her smile as she grabbed another fistful of color. She streaked past, quick as wildfire, shrieking as her friends gave chase. *Chim, chim, chim.* Anklets tinkling, braids flying. Elena caught a fleeting last look as the girls rounded the corner into the city square. She could still hear their laughter, bouncing off the sandstone walls, fading.

A sudden thickness clogged her throat. She used to race through the palace halls, sneaking up on Ferma, her mother, her father, to cover their cheeks with crimson powder. Ruby. Scarlet. Maroon. Endless shades of red. By sunset, she, her parents, and the palace staff had been transformed into flames of a great inferno, burning in a glorious blaze.

Laal Joon! she'd squeal.

How long, she wondered, until her palace on the hill rang with laughter once more? How long until her sands turned crimson from the blood of usurpers instead?

Elena checked her slingsword. Slowly, she ran her thumb along the grooves of the newly minted inscription.

Soon, she thought.

Soon, the usurpers both real and imagined would bend to her.

Powdered crimson plumed above the rooftops, flaring. Somewhere, she heard the quivering notes of a sarangi and the beating of dhols. The music and laughter grew louder as she neared the city square.

A Ravani soldier snapped to a salute. "Your Majesty."

"Are the men here?" she asked.

"As requested. Though, I get the feeling some are participating more than watching." He grinned, wiping a red streak from his cheek. "It feels like a lifetime ago since we've celebrated like this. And to have the Prophet with us too! Is it true? Can he really heal the burned?"

His look of reverence sent a dark, ugly sensation down her throat. She was not a jealous woman, and yet Elena felt the irrational urge to shake the soldier until the illusion of Samson shattered. Could he so easily command their love? Their belief? She remembered her Ravani flocking to Samson. The vicious bite of their casual indifference as they had rushed past her.

He is not the leader you want, she had wanted to shriek. *I am.*

But Elena only smiled, tight-lipped. "He is gifted like they say."

"Then we are truly blessed."

Blessed, or cursed?

She entered the square and was nearly bowled over by a trio of teens. They laughed, throwing apologies into the wind as they dashed off. Elena lost them in the crowd. A woman on her left shrieked as her friend doused her in crimson. On the far right, artisans ground stones from the canyons into a fine powder that merchants then bagged and sold. A sweets seller twisted sugar sheets into phoenixes and other animals for awaiting children. Dhols beat somewhere in the north. A couple danced, their heads thrown back. When the wife laughed, her husband touched the edge of her mouth, the gesture so tender that it reminded Elena of Yassen, and she was forced to turn away, her throat thick with longing.

What a fool she was, she thought later, for not noticing then. As Elena stumbled, she felt a deep thrum within her navel, like a chord plucked. Her head snapped up. She searched the crowd, but she need not have. Calls broke, gasps, then rushed prayers, shouts. People turned as if pulled by a magnetic force, yet she knew it was no force but a man.

A Prophet.

Samson entered the square. He wore a resplendent white kurta with heavy beadwork and crystals hemming the collar and sleeves. Even from this distance, they shone. A rich, embroidered scarf looped artfully over his shoulder and arm, the blue motifs sprawling across his body like waves. His urumi glinted around his waist, a vicious kamarbandh. Delighted cheers followed him. And though her Agni flared with a sudden heat, Elena felt a cold, visceral shock, as if someone had touched the back of her neck with an icy finger.

He did not look like a humble Prophet.

He looked like a king.

She cursed herself for her simple white-and-gold sari. Though this was not a battle, Elena had a strange sensation that she was already losing.

"Where is my rani?"

The call swelled through the crowd, built. People turned and seemed to recognize her as if for the first time. Elena was pushed forward until she found herself face-to-face with the Prophet.

"There's my girl. I was looking for you everywhere." Samson winked. He had lined his eyes with kohl as in the Ravani tradition, and though it had pleased her before, Elena now wanted to rub it away until his eyes turned red. "I have a gift for you."

Gift exchanges were traditional during Laal Joon, with the unsaid rule of each side subtly seeking to outdo the other. In the middle of the crowd, Elena felt the prick of stares. The charged weight of their questions, their expectations. She would play along, then, for them.

"As do I. Guests go first."

If Samson sensed the jab, he made no sign. Visha brought forward a small black case. People leaned forward, and despite herself, Elena leaned too as Samson slowly opened the case and withdrew a pair of long golden anklets. Polki diamonds, thick and heavy as tears, dripped down the first tier of intricate kundan metalwork like fresh raindrops caught in a web. On the second tier, rubies glistened, so rich and dark it was as if the embers of flames were caught inside. Samson held them up. In the crimson-coated air, they glowed. Glorious. Ethereal.

Elena carefully took the end of one of the anklets. "They are beautiful. Thank you . . . Prophet."

She began to turn when Samson tugged on the anklet. He pulled her forward, closer. So close she could feel the hot brush of his breath on her nose. Murmurs went through the crowd as he gently took her hand and peeled back her fingers, one by one.

"Let me put them on you," he whispered.

Before she could respond, he raised her leg and rested her foot on his knee. A man hooted, followed by a fit of laughter that was hurriedly hushed. Elena swallowed. Her cheeks burned. She felt exposed, embarrassed, and yet traitorously, her heart began to beat faster as Samson raised the hem of her sari. The cool air brushed the soft skin of her ankle. Slowly, he wrapped the anklet around her foot, his fingers deft and strong. He locked it into place, then tapped her other knee. Biting back a hot flush, Elena raised her leg. Samson locked the second anklet, but instead of dropping her foot, he looked up, his eyes dark and endless as if to drink her in.

Or drown her, as oceans do.

"Are you pleased, my rani?" he asked, his voice a low rasp.

Her heart thundered erratically as her people began to whisper, to point. One woman blushed heavily.

So this is his game. The anklets were not the gift meant to please her. It was the manner in which they were given. A warm rumble of approval swept through the crowd. She knew what they were thinking. It was a magnificent gift, fit for a queen. What could she possibly do to outcompete a gift so tenderly given?

But she had already known tenderness. And it had died with him. Elena had no want for another.

The anklets clung to her skin like heavy leeches. Slowly, she lowered her foot and straightened. When Samson caught her gaze again, she smiled—genuinely, for once.

"Not as pleased as you will be with my gift."

With that, she unsheathed her sword.

CHAPTER 16

SAMSON

There are silences that litter the heart, fill it with a longing that kills.
—from the dairies of Priestess Nomu of the Fire Order

At the ring of metal, his hand flew to his urumi. The people closest to them jerked back, and someone in the crowd shrieked.

But Elena held out the slingsword, palms up, and when her gaze met his, he saw the question in them.

The challenge.

"Do not be afraid, Prophet. It won't bite."

Around them, citizens chuckled. Samson cursed himself for being so reactionary. He was a Prophet, *their Prophet*, not some weak-bellied Jantari cadet.

But perhaps that was what she wanted him to seem. Fearful. Impulsive. He knew she still smarted from her people's growing disregard of her. Was this her way of rebalancing the power scale through optics? Or was this a part of the strange Ravani tradition of egotistical gift giving, like Chandi had explained?

If you want the people to love you, you need to make a grand gesture bigger than hers.

The Ravani loved beauty, but they treasured romance above all. The more adoring, the better. And what would make the people love him more than if he played the humble, tender Prophet sent to save them?

So what if Akiri had fashioned the anklets from stolen jewelry locked in the old Jantari safes? So what if Visha had hidden small trackers in them to monitor their queen's comings and goings? So what if, when he touched Elena's skin, his Agni flailed with such desperate vehemence that it ruined his voice to a rasp?

"Thank you, my rani," he said.

Elena's smile only deepened, and something sharp tugged in his chest. "Read the inscription."

Carefully, he took the slingsword. The blade gleamed with fresh oil, the trigger hilt cushioned in soft rubber that smelled faintly of a dying fire. It was light, balanced. He would have admired it, had he not seen the inscription. A Phoenix seal soared at the tip of the blade. Beneath it glared:

The queen is the protector of the flame, and I its servant.

The first line of the Desert Oath. He would recognize it anywhere. He had sworn it in that gleaming throne room with his friend and sealed their disastrous fate. But it was the very last word, etched deeper than the others, that made him want to smash the blade into pieces.

Servant.

He was no servant. He was a *free man*, a general with an army, a god of Agni. They bent to *him*.

Elena moved closer as he held the blade, the back of his knuckles brushing her chest. "A Prophet of Ravence deserves a slingsword gifted by his queen and protected by the Desert Oath. You have blessed so many of us. Let me bless you, on behalf of the Ravani."

Her smile was broad, warm, and more infuriatingly, he heard people murmur in agreement.

"Let us return the favor, Prophet."

"Yes, let us thank you."

Fear and annoyance sparked within him, but deeper still was the churning ocean of black rage; a wrath only born from a lifetime of bitter subjugation under a screaming zeemir and ruthless overlords; a mad, howling, frothing fury that flooded him until he tasted ash on his tongue.

He was no fucking servant.

His oath to Leo had been necessary and *temporary*. Oaths were made between people of different levels of power, a ruler and a servant, a superior and someone inherently inferior. *But I am equal to you now*, he thought viciously.

He would give her no oath.

"You forget, my rani, that I serve no one," he said, struggling to make his voice level, calm. The people *could not* see him break. "My only oath now is to my god. To our land."

"What greater thing to serve than Ravence itself?" she said. "You once told me to make Ravence my god. If you are Prophet of this land, is it not yours too? Surely, you will not rebuke this gift, for it is from the people as much as it is from me."

He could feel their stares, their whispered confusion, their growing doubts. Damn her. Elena had pinned him, trapped him so effortlessly that he could not help but feel a vague sense of respect beneath his resentment. Had he been her, he would have done the same.

"Besides," Elena said, dropping her voice so only he could hear, "you said you would do this if I trained with your urumi."

The strangled scream died in his chest. His Agni grew weaker while hers remained so temptingly strong. Even now, he could feel it. The damn fool still did not know how to hide it from him. It flickered within his mind's eye, a torrent of strength and *abundancy*. His Agni had been like that in the beginning, bright and vicious and plentiful, and he yearned to feel like that again. To fill the empty, aching parts of himself.

After all he had bled for, fought for, *sinned for*, he deserved it.

Because he was a god, and gods devoured one another.

And great skies above, he was tired of staving off his own hunger too.

Samson swallowed thickly. Then, before his army, his friends, and the people of Ravence, he bent to Elena.

"I will take this oath, then, my rani."

There were no white sands this time. No fire. Elena took the sword and tapped it on his shoulders and crown, her voice sonorous, his clipped and flat, as he repeated after her.

*"The queen is the protector of the flame, and I its servant.
Together, we shall give our blood to this land.
I swear it, or burn my name in the sand."*

Roars erupted around him, deafening. The Ravani flung their cursed powder and coated him with crimson as dark as blood. Elena returned the slingsword to him, smiling, laughing, and he hoped, for her sake and her people's, that she was innocent. That this was not a play meant to demean him, but a genuine effort to upraise the Ravani. He hoped.

It was a fragile, broken thing.

Visha tugged on his sleeve. "General, a tanker is approaching."

"Enemy tanker?" he rasped, watching Elena.

But Visha shook her head, her voice tight. "Cyleoni."

CHAPTER 17

ELENA

During the Five Desert Wars, Cyleon sent military aid to Ravence. Pundits have criticized the emerald kingdom for sending untrained men, but the combined force of Ravence and Cyleon turned the tide of battle against the Jantari in Rasbakan.
—from chapter 42 of The Great History of Sayon

The Cyleoni tanker perched on top of a boulder the size of seven grown men, a fly on the hide of a great red beast. That didn't prevent Black Scales from surrounding the ship. They crept forward with their guns balanced nervously in their hands. Five soldiers marched out of the tanker, armed with zingers and saber collars. Elena inhaled sharply. The Cyleoni had come in their battle gear.

Beside her, Samson stiffened. His hand fell to his waist, and for a wild, breathless heartbeat, she worried he would draw his urumi. Hurriedly, she stepped forward. At once, all heads swiveled to her—like birds of prey spotting a trapped rodent—when a thin, lank man walked down the ramp.

"Queen Elena," he said.

"Kirri," Elena gasped. "Phoenix Above, it has been so long."

She quickly embraced the Cyleoni ambassador, waving back the Black Scales. They eased, but she still sensed the churning energy of Samson's Agni nip at the back of her arms, unconvinced.

"It feels like an age since your coronation dance," Kirri said. He was of her height, with long snow-white hair and spidery fingers. He squeezed her hands. "Are you well? Have the Jantari hurt you?"

"I am better now seeing you." She smiled, though her eyes moved to the armed soldiers and the waiting tanker.

Kirri followed her gaze. "I'm here to escort you to our king. He is already waiting at the rendezvous point." He paused, looking behind her to Samson and his men. "He requests her alone."

"No," Samson said instantly. "We come together, all of us."

"Unfortunately, you all won't fit," Kirri said with an apologetic smile. "We managed to sneak a small tanker past Jantari radars in northern Ravence. I'm sorry, but we only have room for one more."

Elena glanced between him and the armed soldiers, her sudden relief slowly withering. "Your men, why are they in battle fatigues?"

"A precaution. Jantar has grown increasingly...ornery these days, even toward a fly," he said. "King Syla wanted to make sure you would be protected."

"Yours is quite the fly," she said as she studied the rough steel hide of the tanker. Armored plates beefed up its sides, and she saw the flicker of shields above the glass panes. The tanker was outfitted like a war machine, and she wondered if the guns the soldiers wore were the only ones they had brought. Her unease grew, and she stepped back.

"Please, Your Majesty," Kirri said, gesturing. "King Syla awaits."

"It's a trap, Elena," Samson said.

"I assure you, it is not." Kirri smiled, smooth and suave. "You requested a meeting. Now our king extends his hand. Are you really going to refuse, queen?"

Elena hesitated. Syla was an ally, her father's friend. Surely he did not mean to assassinate her. Surely these soldiers were just for her protection. Right? If they tried to attack her, she could burn them—if she was fast enough—but how then would she fly the tanker? She had the sudden horrible image of the ship bursting mid-flight and plummeting through the sky like a great wreathing ball of flame. The fall—not the fire—would kill her.

"Elena," Samson began.

She pulled on a practiced smile. "You've had a long, hard journey, Kirri," she said. "Stay and rest. My people will make sure all your needs are met. I'll go with your men, and by the time you've eaten all the sweets Magar has to offer, I'll be back."

"I would love to, Your Majesty, but my king needs me—"

"Nonsense." She linked her arm through his and gently tugged him back, toward Samson and his men. "You are now my guest. I insist you stay."

Kirri laughed nervously as Samson met her eyes, his expression a mix of doubt and surprise. He gave her a quick, furtive nod. Elena beckoned to Chandi.

"Meet Chandi, your personal secretary during your stay. She'll see to all your needs. Won't you, Chandi?"

Chandi bowed stiffly, her eyes screaming bloody murder. "Of course, Your Majesty. A friend of yours is always welcome."

"You hear that, Kirri?" Elena didn't let go of his arm as he tried to turn away. "You're a dear friend. Surely you won't offend my hospitality and my people by refusing, just as I won't offend your king by refusing his precious chariot."

Kirri glanced between her and his men, licking his lips. He was trapped, and he knew it. Refusing her offer would be seen as a slight—to her, to Ravence itself. If Cyleon truly was her ally and friend, he could not refuse—unless something had changed. Unless Syla had turned and this was indeed a trap. Elena watched Kirri carefully, assessing his silence. *How are you going to play this?* she thought. If he refused her now, he would reveal Cyleon's true intentions. But if he accepted, he would become a hostage, leverage she could use if Syla's soldiers were for more than just mere protection.

Finally, Kirri bowed deeply. This time, his smile lacked the smoothness from before.

"I would not dream of offending you, Your Majesty. I will h-happily stay." He turned to speak to his men, but Chandi stepped forward.

"Come, sir," she said. "Let's get you a nice warm meal, yes?"

The Cyleoni soldiers stiffened, one even curling his hand around his zinger, but Kirri shot him a glare. "See to it that the queen is treated well."

When he was gone, Elena turned to the soldiers. "Let's go."

"Wait, Elena, you can't—" Samson began.

"You're coming with me. It seems like a second seat is available now."

He paused, and then a slow smile spread across his face. "It seems there is."

They followed the soldiers into the tanker and settled into their seats. As the ramp closed, Elena leaned toward Samson.

"When we see Syla, let me lead," she whispered. "I'll broach the topic of calling for the council."

The smile on Samson's face faltered, a quick slip of his lips, but then he righted it. "Right. Of course."

"Samson—"

"You lead," he said as the tanker began to lift. "You're the queen. I'm but a humble servant, aren't I?"

The soldiers did not speak to them as the sky darkened, though Elena felt their careful eyes tracking her every movement. She glanced at Samson. He warily regarded the Cyleoni, his Agni flickering in errant jerks like a snake, twisting on itself. She could see it better now, feel its shape. With all those lessons, all that time training beside Samson, she had grown to almost anticipate the flare of his Agni. Electric and sulfuric, like lightning. The intense vehemency of his desire charged through his sword.

Samson turned to the soldier closest to them. "Your king—"

"Hush!" the soldier whispered fiercely. The others grew taut as they scanned the windows.

"What—" she began, but then she saw a shape darker than the night itself *move*.

Out of the corner of her eye, she saw the shimmer of their shields. The tanker dipped, gradually, carefully. It was then that Elena realized the shape was a *ship*, a thopter of some sort, long and missile-like with black wings that fluttered soundlessly. Liquid limbs grew out of its stomach like the legs of a bug, made of reflective panels that seemed to drink in and refract its surroundings.

The limbs flailed, tasting the night.

Her heart thundered as Elena focused her strength, her desire, her palms warming. She could feel Samson prepare too. If that thopter detected their tanker . . .

But then the legs curled back, finding nothing but empty air, and the ship flew on to resume its ghostly patrol.

When it was gone, the soldier beside her relaxed, wiping sweat from his brow.

"What was that?" she whispered, afraid to raise her voice.

"A Jantari phantom," he rasped. "They're geared to hear the vibration of voices. They usually patrol the airspace around Rani, but I haven't seen one this far east before."

"So the shields . . ." She glanced out the window, grateful to see their shimmer. "They're hiding us."

"Cloaks, not shields."

She regarded the soldiers anew, this time wondering if Kirri had been honest. Perhaps they were for her protection. This was the first time she had heard of or seen a Jantari phantom. What other ships had the Jantari created for their invasion? How many more weapons would she come across? With a sickening feeling, Elena realized the depth of her ill-preparedness. They had regained Magar but remained in the dark as the Jantari pillaged and razed her country.

Elena caught Samson's gaze. Slowly, he tapped his belted urumi. Then his lower stomach. His gaze was steady, assuring. They had their Agni. They had the power of the gods.

But hours later, when the tanker began to descend, she still could not shake off her sense of foreboding.

The pines rose to greet them like tall, silver ghosts. They were deep into the Agnee mountains, far more north than she had been in a long time. The tanker lowered into a small clearing. When she stepped outside, Elena caught a glimmer of dawn dusting the upper peaks of the trees.

The soldiers quickly covered the tanker with a tarp.

"This way," one said.

They followed him through the forest, up a dirt path that led to a hover-pod hidden between two thick pines, camouflaged with green paint and leafy canopies. The door opened as they approached, and Syla strode out.

The Cyleoni king was dressed in battle fatigues: dark black jacket with long trousers made specifically to hide knives. He looked older than what Elena remembered. More haggard. But his eyes still held the same sharpness she had seen since childhood.

Syla Cyleon had been a steady ally of her father. *The only decent man remaining*, Leo had said. She remembered how she had looked forward to his visits. He would bring bouquets of moonspun flowers for her mother, drinks for her father, and sugared sweets for her. When she had completed her registaan, Syla had sent her a wooden elephant, an animal once native to Cyleon. She had treasured it for many suns.

"Elena," he said. "Gods' Blood, is it good to see you."

He kissed three of his fingers and pressed them against her forehead.

"Syla," she said, breathless as a sudden vicious pang cramped her throat. She missed familiar faces from *before*, before the fall, before everything had greatly and irrefutably changed.

Syla squeezed her shoulder.

"You have been so strong, young queen," he said softly.

Elena took one shuddering breath and nodded. She drew herself together, swallowing the bittersweetness of tears. "A bit too strong. I'm afraid I forced Kirri to stay behind because I thought this was a trap."

Syla laughed, thick and booming, and it brought back those sweet, aching memories of warm nights sitting with him and her father in the courtyard, drinking wine and sharing stories.

"Leo taught you well," he began, but then his face sobered as he caught his words.

The cramp in her throat intensified. "I still have much to learn."

Samson cleared his throat, and she remembered his presence. She gestured to him.

"This is Samson Kytuu, general of the Black Scales. He helped me regain Magar and sent my message to you. He is"—her voice faltered as Samson stepped forward—"my fian—friend."

Syla's eyes coolly slid to Samson.

"I've heard the Jantari call you Butcher," he said. "They want to hang you for your crimes against the nation and personally against the king."

Samson smiled, quick and knifelike. "Well. I'm disappointed they didn't list more reasons."

Syla regarded him with a slow wariness. "Come," he said.

They ducked inside the hoverpod and entered a large landing. A stone table sat in the middle. Below, banks of holos hugged the dark windows. Two soldiers snapped to attention and drew chairs for Elena and Syla. Samson drew his own seat.

"Syla, I need—"

"How did you escape?" the king asked suddenly.

The question caught her off guard. "Escape?"

"I sent out messages to the palace. To you, your Astras, and even your generals. Then I learned the Arohassin had killed you and your father in the temple."

"Generals?" She sat upright. "Are they alive? Muftasa? Anyone?"

Syla shook his head. "None that I know. They were all gathered in Rani when the Arohassin attacked. They took out everyone."

Her hope, small and desperate like a match flame, died just as quick.

"The Arohassin weren't behind the attack," Samson said, and Syla turned to him. "It was Farin."

"How so?"

"He promised to help the Arohassin establish a new government in Ravence if they killed the royal family and gave him the mountains," he said. "But Farin broke that promise. As he always does."

"Why did Farin want the Agnee Range?"

"To mine for metal." Samson gestured to the windows, to the mountains beyond. "The Ravani haven't touched them because the mountains are sacred to their Phoenix and their temple. But to Farin, they're untapped potential."

The king settled back in his chair, a mildly curious expression flitting across his face. "So. The Butcher knows all things, then."

Elena looked at Samson in warning. *Let me lead*, she thought. He caught her gaze. Something passed in his eyes, dark and furtive, before he turned his attention back to the king.

"The Jantari blame the Arohassin for the attack on Rani, but in truth, the Arohassin are mere tools," Samson said.

"They also blame you," Syla said. "Farin was said to treat you like a son. He's been taking your . . . betrayal quite personally."

"I was going to be his puppet king," Samson said, and there was an edge to his voice, brittle and sharp.

Syla arched a brow. "So why play along until now?"

"Because now I—we," Samson corrected quickly, shooting her a glance. "We have the means to defeat Farin."

"The Council of the Second Continent," Elena said.

At this, Syla inhaled sharply. "You mean to call it."

"With your help." She leaned forward, resting her hands on the table. "Farin attempted to execute a living royal. Who is to say he won't try to execute another? You? King Bormani? Queen Risha? He's unstable, Syla. A threat to every royal family. We *must* call a council and move against him."

"The other rulers won't come," Syla said, matter of fact. "They are afraid. More importantly, they're beholden to him. Do you know how much the others rely on his metal? If they lose access to the trade, their coffers will dry up. Their cities will shrink. Every kingdom, every trade on this continent, is fueled by godforsaken Jantari metal. And with the loss of the Jantari southern mines in Sona, things are already tense."

Elena grimaced. She remembered the corrosive stench of burning metal. The roar of the landslides. The fading touch of Yassen's hand on hers.

"Your father was smart to never dip into the trade," Syla said ruefully. "He tried to tell me, but I was a fool to think my ore was safe from Farin. When the Jantari began mining their mountains along our shared borders, I was worried they would leech my ore supply. I dammed the river, so Farin had no water for his mines. I ordered my men to dig faster. But the bastard only chucked in more Sesharians and sucked *my* deposits dry. Then he went deeper into his own mountains to find more. There are rumors that he's creating an army of *men* made of steel. That is what you're going up against."

"We can help you," Samson said.

"With what?" Syla snapped. "Your little ragtag army of refugees? You don't understand. The Jantari have been mining and stocking up their steel for *years*. Who knows what monstrosities they've created."

"We are not a ragtag army of refugees," Elena said.

Syla checked himself. "Not you, Elena. Not the Ravani. I meant the Sesh—"

"I know what you meant," she said flatly.

They fell silent, an awkward impasse settling between them. Elena remembered the crying Ravani mother and the stalwart Sesharian father, and she felt a deep bitterness then, for herself, her predicament, her need to submit before those who saw her as nothing more than a leader of a forsaken land. But she swallowed it. It burned her throat, wounded her pride, but Elena pulled on a beseeching look as she touched Syla's arm.

"My people know how to fight," she said. "And I know someone even the Jantari fear. Someone all kingdoms fear."

Syla stilled. "Who?"

Samson shot her a look, but she ignored it as she leaned forward, her fingers pressing into his forearm. "The Yumi."

Syla stared at her, waiting for her to deliver the punch line, but when her face remained as serious as before, his mouth shuttered. "Surely you are jesting. The Yumi kingdom has not involved itself in second-continent politics for centuries."

"They will. And with you, me, and the Yumi calling, the other kingdoms will come to the council. Farin will be forced to attend too. If not out of fear, then out of curiosity. Imagine what a ruckus we'll cause when Moksh sails into the Tsuani harbor."

"But the Yumi—"

"—are the strongest, most lethal warriors of the land," Elena said. "Their hair can cut through Farin's metal. His army will stand no chance against the Mokshi."

"But how will you manage to convince the Yumi to come?"

With power.

With fire.

Her Agni thrummed. Elena glanced down the table, her gaze crashing into Samson's. Dark like the sea, entrenched with secrets. Ones they both shared.

But before she could speak, Samson slammed his fist onto the table, surprising her and Syla.

"We don't need the Yumi," he snarled. "All we need is the metal itself. And I can give you that—tenfold."

Elena stared, too taken aback by his sudden maneuver to interject. Syla recovered faster.

"You?" he scoffed. "And what can a Sesharian give me?"

Though his face was calm, Elena felt Samson's Agni quiver in rage at the slight. But he merely withdrew a holopod. It revealed a map of the mountains that bordered Cyleon and Jantar. "I have men already inside Farin's mines along your border. They know its tunnels, its loading bays, its secrets better than they know their homeland. Give me access through your mountains, and I will take them for you."

"Bullshit," Syla said softly, but he did not lean away.

"You want the kingdoms to come to the council? You attack what is most precious to them: the metal trade itself. Our queen has already destroyed three mines in southern Jantar," Samson said, and Syla turned to her in surprise. "The metal kingdom is suffering. If we take out ones along your border, then Farin will be bleeding to death. Jantar's industry will come to a grinding halt. Veran, Karven, Tsuana—all of them, stopped. We will have their attention then. And Farin will have to come to the table. Crawling. Begging. Then we make our demands."

"You destroyed those mines?" Syla asked her.

She nodded, and the awe in his eyes, the glorious vindication, twisted her stomach into a sticky entangle of guilt and discomfort.

"Yes," she said. *But the cost was too great. The loss too much.* In her dreams, she still saw Yassen, burning.

"It is *our* second plan," Samson said, though he did not meet her gaze. "Another option, should you not find the Yumi one…attractive."

Syla leaned forward, examining the maps with a renewed eagerness and intensity. "How soon can you execute?"

And just like that, he had chosen. Samson smiled, as if already expecting his answer. "Give us two weeks."

Syla was smart enough to pause then, glancing between her and Samson. "Of course, this is *Queen Elena's* plan at the end of the day, right? You agree with this, Elena?" And when his eyes slid to hers, coy, calculative, she heard the hidden question in his voice, the challenge. Was this really her call? Did she really have control?

Her hands prickled with a sudden heat as she glared at Samson. *You damn fool.* She had the rash urge to grab him by the throat and shake sense into him, but her hands remained still in her lap. Samson met her gaze calmly. He had forced her into a corner, but she, the bigger fool, had allowed herself to be pinned. And he knew it. Damn him, he knew.

Pushing back against *his* proposed plan now would show weakness. Syla would find them divided, and he would never help them if he sensed a rift. Who poured resources into a torn bucket? Elena cursed herself. She should have never brought him, never trusted him, never even allowed him into her court. She realized, with the cold clarity that comes to all who find themselves defeated, that Samson had never seen her as a partner or someone of equal power. She was a tool, a prisoner. He had made her dance to his whims, and she, the foolish queen, had never been the wiser.

Ravence was her home. The one she had lost, the one she hoped to win back. But it had become less than that. It was a land to be ravaged. Gutted. Pieced apart and given to petty victors. Suddenly, it wasn't a home anymore, but a prize.

Be ruthless. Become whatever Ravence demands, because without you, it will die, Leo had told her.

Bit by bit, her tired resentment crystallized into a rage that fit deep in the pockets between her bones. Every time she drew breath, Elena felt it. Like fire in a serpent's throat. Ever present, ever ready. A reminder of what she had lost, and the people who had stood by and allowed it.

She met Syla's gaze. "Send us the ships, and we will bring down those mines. You can get a quarter of the ore we recover."

"Half," Syla said immediately. He attempted to cover his eagerness by gesturing to the maps. "It's only fair. Farin has stolen my ore from me."

Fair. Fair was seeing Farin suffer the same destitute helplessness she had endured when her kingdom fell. Fair was his head at her feet. Fair was frankly a concept Cyleon had no idea of, but Elena kept this to herself. If power rather than loyalty moved Syla, so be it.

She plastered on a smile, as wide as she could, and grasped Syla's hand.

CHAPTER 18

ELENA

The Great Serpent is a wicked and benevolent god who descended from the kingdoms of the skies to the dark waters of the sea. To worship Her is to crave power itself. To demean Her is to damn oneself.
—from The Legends and Myths of Sayon

Sunlight pushed limply through the dark pines to outline Samson's shoulders with a cold, thin light. He strode slowly, purposefully—a man who'd already won. He slipped in and out of the shadows with an oily slickness, and a small, irrational part of Elena wondered if that was not from where he had come. He and his lies and that devilish fire. But when Samson turned, finally feeling the weight of her gaze, she kept her countenance hard and unreadable. She did not even acknowledge his questioning eyes as she faced Syla.

"I'll be sure to send Kirri back with Ravani sweets. I know a priestess who makes the best ladoos, far better than your favorites in the palace."

Syla laughed. "Send them with my men instead. I want Kirri to stay and help you with the plans."

And be your eyes and ears, she thought.

"Here." He gave her a holopod. "If you ever need to communicate with me directly, or need anything at all, you can reach me through this."

Elena turned it over and saw the Cyleoni black gada engraved on the back. A palace-grade pod. With a dull pang, she remembered the Phoenix engraved behind her and Leo's own pods.

"Thank you." She slipped it into her pocket. "I will see you soon, then, yes?"

Syla bowed. She bowed stiffly in return, and when the ramp of the tanker lifted, she found the king gazing up with the pinched, thoughtful expression of a man who had bartered his silver for gold and questioned its shine.

You will dance along with me, as long as I need.

They returned to Magar under a leaden sky. Dark, heavy clouds had crept down from the mountains, bringing the promise of a storm. Elena turned her face to the wind. In the desert, the aroma of dry stone and sand preceded the rain, but here in the canyons, an electric tang, rich and sharp, knifed down her throat, more taste than scent.

Visha, Chandi, Kruppa, and Akino waited for them, but she ignored their questions, striding past the cruisers. Samson called after her. But she only hurried down the canyon, and soon, his voice rang hollow within the boulders.

Heavens help me, Yassen. She gripped his holopod, her fingers trembling with rage. *I want to claw his face off.*

A light drizzle began to fall by the time she reached the temple. To her surprise, she found Samson already sitting on the steps.

"How—"

"I knew this would be the first place you would go." His urumi flashed around his waist as he rose to his feet. "So I took a cruiser, like a sane person."

He leaned one hand on a pillar, the other resting right above his blade. "Why are you running from me, Elena Aadya Ravence?"

Around them, passersby paused. A few hailed the Prophet, while others stopped to consider the scene: her, standing at the edge of the courtyard in the soft rain; him, waiting under the temple entrance with a weapon around his waist. Blocking her way. Elena considered turning away then and avoiding a spectacle. But she would be damned if she was going to allow *him* to bar her from her own temple.

"I am not running," she said, her voice thin with strain.

Samson stalked forward, each step slow and measured. "Then why are you avoiding me?"

I am avoiding an idiot who just bartered my country for fucking steel.

Gradually, with great effort, Elena forced her hands to uncurl. She counted to three, then to ten. Then, "Get out of my way, Samson."

Samson stopped just on the other side of the gate, but he did not move out of her path. "You might think I overstepped, but I am ensuring victory for *both* our countries. Ravence and Seshar."

The roar of cruisers made her turn, and she saw Kruppa and the others arrive. The priestess began to walk toward the temple and stopped, frowning as she saw Samson standing within the gates.

"Blue Star," she began.

He chuckled, his voice a low whisper so only Elena could hear. "See how even your own have come to regard me? Worship me? I am your Prophet and command your fires. I am not your enemy, Elena."

Her eyes slowly slid to Kruppa. "Leave," she growled.

"Your Majesty—"

But Elena's gaze did not falter, and the priestess shrank back. Out of the corner of her eye, Elena saw Chandi lean forward with a taut alertness, almost as if she feared that Elena would harm the precious Blue Star. The thought made her smile.

Samson clocked it. "Does that amuse you?"

"Your hypocrisy amuses me, O Prophet. You call yourself powerful when your very power comes from *my people*." Her eyes found his. "Your Eternal Fire is built upon the beliefs of the Ravani."

"You mean your false god?" He looked up at the Phoenix soaring upon the temple spire. "How many times do I have to explain? There is no Holy Bird. There never was. You have fallen for a lie, but just like Leo, you're too stubborn to see it."

"Do not say his name," she said.

At this, Samson's smile twisted into a vicious, vindictive sneer. "Do you know what he told me? That your people would never accept me. But *I* command your Eternal Fire. *I* heal your burned. *I* brought the army that freed this city."

It struck her then. Samson was right. He *did* control the Eternal Fire.

He had done so on the day it had tried to attack them, and he had done it on the day her father had burned. Samson had killed her father. Samson had unleashed the Eternal Fire upon them all.

She trembled with the realization, and when she met Samson's eyes, he flinched back from the fury in them.

"You *lied*," she said, her voice dark and terrible. "You unbound the Eternal Fire and set it upon my father. The guards, the priests, the officials— they died because of you."

"No," Samson snapped. "Leo died because he tried to harm me, and the Eternal Fire sought to protect its Prophet. It has a mind of its own. And Leo was a tyrant. A murderer. He killed those priests. He killed helpless people in his manhunt, and for what? To leave his kingdom ruined and burned? His daughter helpless and lost? Surely you can see that he was wrong, Elena. Even if you loved him, surely you must see that he could have done better by you."

"No," Elena choked out, even as something broke within her, revealing a pain so raw and acute that it felt as if he had reached out and wrenched her heart. Because he was right, again. Leo Malhari Ravence had been a cruel and cunning king—but he was also her father. She had seen him regret. Seen him sink under the weight of his sins.

She staggered forward. "You want to talk about a ruined kingdom? That is what you will bring on us with your Jantari steel obsession."

"We must attack the mines," Samson said. "We need to weaken Jantar from within. It's the only way Farin will even consider Sesharian and Ravani liberation—"

"We cannot do both," she cut in.

"We must." Samson's voice shook with such force that she felt its impact like a punch to her gut. The rain had quickened, but more people were beginning to gather, to listen.

"Ravence and Seshar," she began.

"You once said you understood my people. Then hear this. The only reason, the real reason, Leo allowed more Sesharian refugees into Ravence was because he wanted to use our hate for his own gain. We would willingly fight his war against Jantar. But what do you think would have happened once he beat out the metalheads?" Samson stalked forward, his eyes sharp as the twin blades of his urumi. "He would have packed up his armies and dismissed the Sesharians who had bled for him. He would have lounged on his throne, gloating in his victory, while those same Sesharian soldiers cried for their stolen homeland." He jabbed his finger to the north, to the horizon, toward Palace Hill. "He would have won on the back of Sesharians, but he wouldn't have given a shit about their own home. My home."

"And if the roles were reversed?" she said softly.

Samson frowned, his arm lowering a degree. "What?"

"If it had been Ravani refugees in Seshar, wouldn't you do the same?" She stepped forward, so close that he took a step back, his frown deepening into a scowl. She raised her hand, jabbing her finger into his chest. Once, twice, like twin pulse shots. "That's what you're doing now. Using refugees. Ravani, Sesharian, any poor fool who needs to believe in something. You take them and mold them to become your soldiers. Your weapons. To fight your. Fucking. War."

Samson stared, his mouth frozen. His throat bobbed, but no words came. He simply stared down at her, and in his widened eyes, she saw understanding flare and die, followed quickly by loathing. His expression changed then, the peaks and angles of his face sharpening into anger. It happened so fast, so viciously, as if lightning surged through him, threatening to snap and break everything around.

Elena retreated, but Samson did not move. When he finally spoke, his voice was strangely, frighteningly calm.

"Tell me. If Yassen hadn't been there, could you have taken down those mines? Could you have taken this city? Who even are you, alone?"

He leaned down, his breath hot against her nose. "A spoiled, privileged queen who doesn't know her friends from her enemies."

His words bored into her, opening a wound she had tried to ignore. *I am something*, she wanted to say. She was the queen of Ravence. She had an army, a kingdom, a throne. *Once.*

She had the power of Agni, a power that even the Jantari feared when she had burned down their mines. *With Yassen's help.*

She had broken through the gates of Magar and freed the city. *And crushed civilians.*

The voice, contrarian and wicked, whispered in her mind. It sounded like the rush of flames, their soft hiss and sharp pops.

Who even are you, alone?

Samson watched her, and for a moment, pity flashed in his eyes, and that made her feel even worse. She would not allow him to walk over her as if this wasn't her land, her people, her kingdom.

It was hers and hers alone.

"You are driving us to ruin," she said.

"I am saving us," he snapped, his voice cracking the air with a definitive, resounding slap.

Around them, the crowd stiffened. She could feel the prickle of heat of their collective gaze. Elena swallowed as a hiss thrummed through her body at the pull of Samson's Agni. He glowered, all spite, all fury, leveled into his cursed eyes.

Eyes too blue, she thought. *A cursed, dangerous man.*

"Do you want to know the truth, Elena?" Samson held up his hand, and a blue flame slowly emerged, winding down his wrist to his elbow. "You believe that only those like you deserve power. That the rest of us should be forced to kneel. To bend. But you forget one thing, queen. There are higher things than kings, and I am one of them."

Lightning split the heavens with a loud shriek that shook the valley. Its echo reverberated through her, building. And with every thunderous drum of the rain, Elena felt her control slipping, her anger swelling until all she could see, all she wanted, was him kneeling before her once more, face in the dirt, begging for her forgiveness.

"You are a butcher, not a Prophet," she snarled.

With a sudden hiss, blue flames surged down Samson's arms and legs, covering his body in a coat of flames that defied the rain and burned with an intense brilliance.

But Elena responded in turn. Heat rushed through her body, her heart pumping erratically as her Agni sensed its brethren awaken. A red flame looped around her wrist.

"Careful, queen," he said, eyeing her flame.

She slid out the slingsword from her waist. "Careful, Butcher."

With a violent, smooth motion, Samson whipped out his urumi and slashed downward. The tongues of the twin blades narrowly missed her shoulder as Elena jumped, but she did not expect the flames. They dashed forward, skipping along the length of the blades and singeing her cheekbone.

She stumbled back, cheek throbbing. The crowd started, some crying out for Samson, others for her. She barely had time to bring up her weapon before he charged, his blades slapping against her slingsword. Elena swatted away a parry, but his flames beat her face, and she was forced to retreat. She gasped, robbed of oxygen. Out of instinct, she ducked and rolled, red flames cloaking her like a blanket. Samson, propelled by his own momentum, missed her, and Elena took the opportunity to jump to her feet and pull the trigger of her slingsword. The blade slit the length of his back, ripping the cloth. She caught a glimpse of marred skin and dark scars, and then he was on her, relentless.

His urumi sang a high, vicious song as it sliced through her flames. There were yells and cries from the crowd, pleas to stop. She tried to pull back her blade, but he was too fast, too merciless. A force of pure power and fury. His flames leapt on top of hers, tearing, biting.

Elena drew up her flames to shield herself, but Samson parted the blaze as easily as a butcher cutting off the neck of a bird. His urumi flashed, and she ducked. The blade hissed over her head. Elena lunged to the side— and forgot the second blade. Its tongue grazed her stomach, and a stinging sensation exploded down her skin.

Elena roared in pain, but he easily snapped his blade, and her sword was torn from her grasp. She reeled back. Blood dripped down her wrist. In a desperate attempt, she fired a volley of flames, each seething and intense, snapping with sparks. His blue inferno merely swallowed them into its own.

She spun to avoid his next advance when his inferno broke through the defense of her fiery cocoon, and she saw Samson's face. His monstrous rage.

He was going to kill her.

"Sam—"

He grabbed her by the throat and slammed her against the wall. Her head banged against the stone. A buzz filled her ears. Gasping, Elena felt something thick and hot trail down her forehead and cheek. Dark spots danced in her vision. Her chest cramped, the pain intensifying with each second. She struggled—clawing, spitting, howling—but Samson did not even wince as he leaned in close.

"You are nothing without a butcher, queen," he snarled, his breath hot against her ear. "And I am far worse than that."

He let her go, and Elena crashed to her knees. She hacked out blood as the rain soaked her skin, her cuts. Her vision wavered, and she saw Samson's dirt-speckled boots, his silver blades. For a moment, she feared that he would raise his urumi and cut off her head, but he only took a step back, and then he was gone.

He left her like that—they all did. Even her own people. They eyed her with a mixture of horror and pity, and then followed their Prophet until she was left cold and alone, wheezing in the rain.

CHAPTER 19

SAMSON

*Y*ou *are driving us to ruin.*

Samson looked down at his trembling hands, which were slick with rain. With her blood.

Carefully, he took a rag and dabbed away the specks from his hands and forearms. Then, piece by piece, he undressed. His wet shirt sucked against his skin as he stripped it off, and he turned in the mirror.

A red gash, about five inches long, razored across his back. The brightness of his new wound glared against the faded scars already littered along his spine.

He touched the cut, winced. A single ruby bead slipped down his finger and wrist.

Butcher, butcher, butcher, the fire sang.

Samson clenched his hands, but they continued to tremble.

What did Elena know of the things he had seen, the things he had done, the things—and people—he had sacrificed? She did not know what it meant to live in a home stolen from beneath you. She had never felt the brutal sting of a zeemir or the contemptuous gazes of the Jantari. She hadn't experienced the cold, sickly feeling of being *less* than even the dirt on their boots.

How could he tell her what it felt like to grow up with pale-eyed foreigners judging his every move? To live his life according to their terms? To camouflage himself in their ways and customs if only to carve a living for himself?

The Jantari had not just taken away his home. They had taken his dignity. His personhood. Because the man he was today, the *butcher* she so easily called him, was not a true reflection of himself, but a creature forged to survive under their rule. How different would he be, Samson wondered as he stared at his bloody reflection, if he had lived in a free land? What would he have been like? Would he carry the same caustic rage he carried now?

The fire hissed, as if it could sense his warring emotions.

"You know nothing," he whispered, but even when he closed his eyes, he saw her. The fear twisting her lips, the desperate bent of her scream. He splashed his face, and the water slowly spiraled down the sink in one long, red stream.

He shouldn't have attacked her so horribly. But the things she had said…And the contempt in her eyes. They dug into his old wounds in ways he did not quite comprehend, but nonetheless had pulled out something raw and all too painful. What right did she have to question him?

She had so easily branded him a monster, as if she did not recognize her own monstrous self. As if his rage wasn't hers.

He had wanted her on his side. *Needed* her to understand, to see him. They were gods, couldn't she tell? Forged from the same fire, bearing the same burning burden. The same terrible purpose. But she, his only kin, detested him. In a way, her flames had been a more vicious attack than a Jantari zeemir. She did not even need to touch him to land a blow.

He swallowed, fighting back his bitterness.

It was better this way, he reasoned. Better if he held her at a distance.

Better if he did not build something deeper, more integral. He had, in a moment of weakness, entertained the thought of *fellowship*. Like a lone traveler who had finally seen a fellow countryman in a foreign land, he had hoped that they shared the same kindred spirit. But their only commonality began and ended with their fire. He needed her for only one reason.

There could be no *more*.

The inferno swelled, singing.

Butcher, butcher, butcher.

Samson stood abruptly, pushing away from the sink. He shoved on trousers and a shirt, and was reaching for his coat when the door flew open and Chandi strode in.

Samson steeled himself. "I know, I know. That was a fucking mess. H-how is she?"

He turned to face Chandi and started. A quiet smile tugged her lips, one he had never seen before. She crossed her arms and leaned against the doorframe, and he thought, with a wretched certainty, that had Chandi been fighting, Elena would not be breathing.

"You were brilliant," she said.

Samson eyed her. "Did Visha slip you one of her poisons?"

"Everyone—Ravani, Sesharians, even the priestess—they all saw, Samson. They saw *you*. The Prophet, righteous and powerful, conquering the queen. They— Oh, just come look."

He followed her outside into the rain. Along the steps of the city hall, people were gathered. Ravani, Sesharian, heads bowed under hoods and umbrellas, but as he stepped onto the landing, they looked up to him. He saw the mother and her child standing with the Sesharians she had once cursed. He saw the thin man who had once spat at his feet watching him with a fierce devotion that made Samson feel both repulsed and invincible.

"There are those who still don't believe," Chandi whispered at his side, "but they fear you now. They saw you defeat Elena and her inferno. See how you do not need her influence. You *are* their god. And our Blue Star."

Samson wavered, wary of her words, wary of the naked fervor in their eyes, but a sound made him turn.

"Prophet, Prophet, Prophet."

Not Butcher. Not a monster who drove them to ruin.

Their voices rustled forward, awed and timid within the rain, but they swept him up, lifting him from his quagmire of guilt. He turned to face them—her people turned his.

There were about two hundred of them, but Samson knew more would come. Already, his followers had grown since his healing of the burned. They were old and young, Sesharian and Ravani, workers, medics, soldiers, mothers, fathers, daughters, and sons—the faithful who had finally found someone worthy of their belief.

Vindication, blistering and acute, surged through him as the rain kissed his scars. And yet, Samson held back. It was too much—they wanted too much of him, *saw* too much. He stumbled, overwhelmed, and then Chandi touched his shoulder. He was not sure if it had been a push or a squeeze as she said, "Go."

And then he was moving, or they were reaching, but he found himself among them with hands touching his face, his arms, his body.

The mother kissed his hand. The thin man bent so low his nose nearly touched the ground. Everywhere he turned, people offered themselves up. They held prayer beads and trinkets and palms out for his blessings. He was in a sea of believers, held aloft by their prayers and worship.

"Bless me, Prophet."

"Look upon my child, Prophet, and give him your sign."

"Lead me to the sands of prophecy."

Once, their calls, their *demands*, had made him feel cramped, squeezed underneath the relentless weight of their belief, but now, now Samson bore their summons. Now, he let them lift him, his body at once weightless and buoyant.

This was what it meant to be a god.

So when they carried him to the front of the temple, underneath the glare of the false deity, Samson cared not for his promise. He pointed, and his people followed. They struck down the walls. Smashed icons. Broke the stones. They heaved ropes around the spire and tore it down with a tremendous crack that echoed through the street and the city beyond.

And then he summoned his Agni, even if it sent a cold pain through his chest. He inked his sin. He drew it delicately, with care. Upon upturned cheeks and arms, within the crevices of necks, and on the soft skin of palms.

He met each of them. Exchanged their wishes with his mark, and after what seemed like hours, he came before the ruins of the temple, his flames swelling, his followers crouched in the rain.

"Tell us." The mother knelt before him, hands splayed. "Tell us what is to come, Prophet."

They watched him, cold and hungry, and he recognized their appetite as worthy of his.

He looked out across the dark horizon, beyond the canyons and the desert, to the cold tunnels of the mountains where Farin's most precious metal lay.

"Vengeance," he said.

CHAPTER 20

ELENA

Hate endures what love cannot.

—a Ravani proverb

Elena did not remember how she made it back to her rooms that night. When she woke in the morning, she had only brief recollections, like the flighty vestiges of a dream. She remembered the cold rain, her chattering teeth. Dark eyes watching as she walked. Hands, warm and firm; a stern but not unkind voice, speaking.

Elena rose carefully. She still wore her clothes from last night, her sari sticking to her skin like a leech. When she glimpsed her image in the cracked mirror, she froze, breath caught in her chest like a shard lodged between her bones.

Blood crusted her swollen right cheek. The pallu of her sari was tattered, her arms littered with scratches and tiny marks. It was as if she had been attacked by an animal. Torn and ripped apart, left for dead.

For a moment, she did not understand. Pain clouded her thoughts, her memory, but when she saw the lines of red, thin and long, stretching across her neck like a horrid necklace, she remembered.

Samson's wild, ferocious eyes, the rough crush of his hands on her throat.

You are nothing without a butcher, queen. And I am far worse than that.

A white-hot horror flashed through her body, followed swiftly by anger so intense that her fingers trembled as she touched her neck.

She was going to kill him.

She was going *to fucking kill him.*

Elena began to reach for her coat, already picturing how she would rip her sword through his neck again and again until the blue leached from his eyes, when the door drew back, and Kruppa entered, breaking her out of her fury.

"You're awake," Kruppa said, but Elena heard the unspoken words beneath. *You're alive.*

"Where is he?" Elena asked, her voice strained.

"I do not know." Kruppa sighed. "But word has spread that the Ravani queen has fallen out of favor with the Prophet."

Elena stilled. Her rage wavered, tamped down now by a slow, marching trepidation. "What do you mean, fallen out of favor?"

Kruppa looked at her, deep lines fanning along her eyes. "It means you are not fit to lead."

"Me?" Indignation clawed up her throat, nearly choking her. "Me?! He is the monster. *He* is unfit."

But Kruppa kept quiet, and Elena slowly felt her anger wither away in the woman's stoic silence until she felt dizzy, her knees weak. She crashed into a seat.

"Me," she whispered. Her fingers curled around the wooden frame of the bed as grief and resentment coiled within her into a black, throbbing ball of pain. "Me."

Kruppa finally spoke. "We saw how he beat back your fire with his own. His holy rage."

At this, her stomach churned. What had been holy about that fight? What had been *right*?

"He is a god, greater than you, greater than us. Even those who did not believe in the gods are now clutching their prayer beads. And his followers, they…" She faltered, an anguish so deep wrenching her face. "They destroyed the temple."

"The bastard," Elena seethed. She began to rise, but Kruppa shook her head, and Elena found her fury an insubstantial speck compared with the priestess's sorrow.

"The people would rather align themselves with him than..." She paused, looking away, as if the words caused her pain. Then, in a softer voice, "I am sorry, Your Majesty. Truly. But you have lost."

Lost.

What a simple word. So quick on Kruppa's tongue, so quick to ensure Elena's defeat.

She had lost in a simple skirmish that had evolved into something more, something she could not control. Why had she reached for her sword? Why had she not left, when she had had the chance?

Elena blinked hot tears from her eyes and hurriedly wiped them away in disgust. She should not be crying. She should be raging. Marching through the city, straight toward Samson, and taking his head for all to see. But even as she thought it, Elena remembered how easily his flames had cut through hers, how viciously his urumi sang through the air. His utter, complete control. She knew that if she went now, she would not defeat Samson. She would lose, again. The people would see her fall, again. What little trust and loyalty she had gained would quickly vanish like landmarks in a sandstorm.

But I cannot stay still.

The thought, only half-formed, quickly solidified and sank into her bones as if she was buried deep in sand.

She could not stay within the clutches of a monster who called himself a prophet and further jeopardize her standing with the Ravani. If she did, she would have to live according to his terms. Make herself smaller, lesser. Elena could already see the confines of her cage, feel the rough scratch of a noose around her neck.

No.

Elena rose with a borrowed strength. Heat thrummed in her veins, her Agni stirring. She was Elena Aadya Ravence. The queen of Ravence.

She was not meant to be caged.

Elena met Kruppa's eyes and saw the older woman shrink back. "Where is my sword?"

Elena ignored the whispers as she strode toward the command center. People stared or reeled back as she neared them. One woman signed across herself, while an older man clutched his prayer beads and averted his eyes—as if merely catching her gaze was considered sacrilegious. Not long ago they had showered her with flower garlands and praise as she had stood on the hall steps. That day, she had wanted to fling off their love and wallow in her self-misery. What she wouldn't do to feel that devotion again. *Kruppa was right*, she thought bitterly. *I am carrying the black plague of the godless.* She drew her scarf tighter and bounded up the stairs. Guards at the door started at her appearance, but she swept through and pushed back the doors with a loud boom.

Chandi looked up from the holopanel. Akino froze at his worktable littered with urumis. Visha lowered a metal contraption and gave her a cold, hard smile. But Elena gazed past them all as Samson slowly swiveled in his chair and met her eyes.

"Elena."

"Samson."

She sauntered forward and winced inwardly as her wounds smarted, as if a reminder of being so close to his Agni. Samson rose, his face stoic and cold.

"You've recovered," he said.

"You'll have to try harder to put me down."

His mask did not slip, but she caught the small twitch of his lips.

"Undoubtedly so." He paused, and in the awkward silence that followed, Elena felt for his Agni. She searched for that familiar presence of heat, so ruthless and self-assured, and found it *less*. It was as if his Agni was . . . tempered. Like a shobu made to heel, it felt contained. No bracelets of fire adorned his wrists.

"I—I wanted to apol—" he began and frowned. "I . . . Well, I wanted to check on you. Kruppa, Visha"—at this Visha gave a snort—"the others were worried. The people were worried. Yesterday went too far."

Elena smiled at him, thinking, *What utter bullshit, you snakeskinned bastard.*

She dropped her hand to her waist and drew her sword. Akino gasped. Visha sprang to her feet. Chandi loosed her urumi, and the metal sound of it scraping against the floor filled the space. Only Samson remained still, his eyes narrowed.

"Have you come to lose again?" he said.

"No," she said. And then Elena Aadya Ravence did something she had sworn never to do.

She knelt.

She knelt before the Prophet and laid down her sword.

"I have come to apologize." Her voice, strong and reverberant, rang through the hall. "I doubted your legitimacy. But I was wrong. Yesterday, you proved to me and everyone who you really are."

She raised her eyes.

A butcher.

"A Prophet," she said. "Our Prophet."

At this, everyone stilled. Even Samson's mask had fallen, his face stricken and confused, his mouth slightly agape.

"You are no monster, Samson," she said, and she saw him tremble, a quick movement across his chest and shoulders. He closed his eyes. Swallowed. And she knew then what he felt because she had seen that movement before. When she had forgiven her father, he had shown a similar release. To be forgiven was to be freed. Absolved of whatever sins you had inflicted on the other. But Leo had deserved her forgiveness.

A butcher like Samson did not.

Elena swallowed her shame and fury and softened her voice. "I—*we*— are of Agni. And it was foolish of me to think of you as my enemy when you and I are the same. I—I am sorry." She dropped her head. "Forgive me."

Silence stretched heavily through the hall. She felt the weight of their gazes, but Elena did not look up. She stared hard at the floor, and when she finally heard movement, when she finally saw his boots fill up her vision, she allowed herself a small, private smile.

Slowly, she raised her head and met his dark eyes. Samson watched her with something akin to wary pleasure, like a man who had found his lost falcon back on its perch, deadly and beautiful and perfect.

"Why should I trust you?"

"Because you once asked me how far I would go to save Ravence, and I told you I would go far enough." She immersed herself in the memory, of the spinning roses and Farin's calculating gaze and Samson's fierce voice. She allowed her promise to show on her face. "If saving Ravence means swallowing my pride and working with you, I will do it. I am not above my country, Sam. Just as I know you are not above yours."

This time, the smile she gave, tight and full of hurt, felt true.

"People like us do not regret," she said quietly so that only they could hear. "We only move forward to take what is ours. And if that means being roughed up now and then, so be it. Besides. I got you too, didn't I?"

Samson laughed softly. "Yes, you did."

"Then let's put this behind us," she said. "We have two weeks. In two weeks, let's change the power play. Let's make Farin crawl to us, begging on his knees. Let's show Syla what a refugee army can do."

Slowly, Samson grabbed her shoulders and raised her to her feet. Around them, the others stirred, not sure what to make of this sudden reconciliation. Samson held her a second longer, his calloused fingers warm against her shoulders, and then broke away.

"Come. We're already drafting the plans. Chandi can fill you in." He drew a chair up to the table and looked back her. "I could use your firepower."

And at this, he smiled shrewdly. She returned it as her blood drummed in her ears, and she thought, clear and fierce and full of fury:

I will be your ruin, Samson Kytuu.

CHAPTER 21

SAMSON

Where are our sons and daughters? Where are the young children who sacrificed their lives to fight against tyranny? Their lives belong to the sea.

—from *The Lament of Seshar: A People's History*

It had been a week since Elena had knelt in front of him, but he had been watching her carefully. It was not that he didn't believe her. He believed she would do anything to save Ravence—even if that meant working with him. She had remained mostly the same, still rising to Visha's quips, meeting Chandi's silent stares, and catching his gaze from time to time. He just didn't trust her.

He had expected her to retaliate by now. He had expected to wake up in the dark of the night and feel her dagger against his throat. Of all things, Elena Aadya Ravence was not a patient and docile woman. But she had done nothing, and it was this that flummoxed him the most.

"You can't possibly trust her," Chandi said, echoing his thoughts as they left the command center.

"No, but I want to," he replied, surprised by the depth of his own desire. If he and Elena could truly work together, if their Agni could meld... The possibilities were staggering. He could almost see it. And he tried to stop himself from dreaming, but his dreams had always been powerful. He saw Ravence, freed; Seshar, freed; and Jantar, burning.

The vision was so clear, the path stark and righteous. Before, their alliance had felt like a necessity. Even when Elena had given her hand in front of the ruined high temple, he had seen bitterness in the turn of her mouth. But since she had swallowed her pride and knelt before him, he had noticed a softening. An opening. Could this be the start of a true, sincere alliance?

But he pushed the thought away, stamped it down into the cold reaches of his heart. *There can be no more*, he reminded himself.

"Do *you* trust her?" he asked.

Chandi shrugged as they passed over rubble. They were making their way toward the wall, where the Jantari prisoners were kept. The Cyleoni ambassador had wished to see them, and Samson spotted the man in the distance, surrounded by his contingent of soldiers who had stayed behind with their tanker.

"I am cautious," Chandi said finally. "It takes a great deal to make someone as proud as Elena bend. Either she has finally come to her senses, or she has lost them altogether."

Samson laughed, and Chandi shared a conspiratorial smirk.

"General," the ambassador called as they neared. His eyes fell to the urumi around Samson's waist. "What a beautiful blade."

"It's a family heirloom," Samson said. He turned at the sound of footsteps and found Elena approaching them.

"The Jantari might tear off your head if you stand too close, Kirri," she said.

Kirri glanced nervously at the metal fence erected along the wall. Prisoners sat in the sparse shade or shuffled listlessly, dispirited. Still, Samson recalled the angry soldier who had attacked him. His men had strengthened the posts and fence with hardy cement and steel, but even he took a cautionary step back.

"Oh, I'm kidding. These poor men can barely save themselves." Elena smiled, though there was something pained and sorrowful in her eyes, as if the sun had briefly passed behind a cloud and stoppered the light. Within the next moment, it was gone. He wondered what it meant. Did she sympathize with the prisoners? *How* did she still have compassion left for them? That ability to see the enemy and still find someone worth saving—was that what she saw in him, then? A man worthy of being redeemed? At once, he felt clammy and uncomfortable, like wool scratching against his skin. He turned away, averting his gaze.

He did not need her compassion—only her Agni. She was working with him to save Ravence—nothing more. *There is no more*, he told himself again.

"How many are there?" Kirri asked.

"Six hundred and fifty-nine," Chandi replied. "They're spread out along other parts of the wall. We lost a few prisoners who tried to bolt."

Kirri raised a brow. "Bolt? Have there been many revolts?"

"None that we couldn't handle," Samson said.

Kirri glanced at him, his gaze flicking back to the urumi around his waist. "I trust you've been treating them well. War or not, enemy prisoners are given rights."

Samson had half a mind to tell the politician that if enemy prisoners truly had rights, then his people wouldn't be mining Jantar's steel until their hands bled, but he kept his tongue.

"They will be sent back to Jantar as soon as Farin comes to the table," Elena said. "You have my word, Kirri."

"Yes, concerning that..." the ambassador said as Elena adjusted her scarf. Though her scarf hid it well, Samson knew his handprints still ringed her neck, and a sudden, terrible guilt slipped through him.

She had started the fight. She had apologized for it. It was done. And yet, he could not stop staring at her throat and feeling the hot flush of shame.

"We would like to start the exchange of prisoners soon after the mission," Kirri said. "You cut off communications when you invaded, so Farin still believes Magar is under Jantari control, but once we take his mines, he will suspect. We should act while he still plots his next move. Ask for Ravani and Cyleoni prisoners in exchange for his Jantari."

"What about Sesharians?" Chandi asked sharply. "The miners. The servants forced to serve Jantari lords. They should be freed too."

"Well, they aren't technically prisoners now, are they?" Kirri said in an almost apologetic tone. "It's just not the same."

"Not the same—" Chandi started, but a look from Samson silenced her.

"You're forgetting, Ambassador, that Sesharians in Jantar are not free," he said lightly. "They are not even proper citizens. We should exchange the Jantari soldiers for miners as well as Ravani and Cyleoni prisoners."

Kirri gave a perfect, sympathetic smile. "I see your case, General, but Farin would never consider us if we ask for any kind of Sesharian freedom. It simply will not do." He gave a small, careless shrug. "We must work with the means we have. Perhaps once Ravence is free and peace restored, we can reconsider Seshar. Yes?"

If he weren't the ambassador, if Cyleon wasn't supplying the tankers and entry points for their mission, Samson would have drawn his urumi then and there.

Elena suddenly brushed his elbow, and he froze. Her touch was hot, seething, but not painful.

"Kirri," she said, her voice dangerously flat, "have you no shame?"

The ambassador blinked, taken aback. "Your Majesty—"

"It is Samson and his *Sesharian* men who helped me free this city. It is Samson and his *Sesharian* army that will take those mines and deliver its steel to your king. If you are to use them and give them no freedom, how are you any better than the Jantari?"

Silence coiled like a noose around them. Kirri stared, shock written clearly over his face. Slowly, Samson turned to her as Elena dropped her hand and pointed to the horizon beyond.

"We all have one common enemy, and I will be damned if we turn into someone like him," she said. "When we take the mines, we will ask for the exchange of all prisoners, including Sesharians, or we will not take the mines at all."

Kirri seemed to find himself, because he sputtered, walking forward. "Your Majesty. Forgive me, I spoke out of turn. It—it is not my place to decide the fate of these prisoners. I will leave that up to you and our king."

A smart countermove, to lay the blame on your king and not yourself, Samson thought darkly.

"Of course you must." Elena smiled, her eyes clouded and unreadable. "Come. Let us walk the wall, alone."

Kirri nodded quickly, as if grateful to be removed from the situation. Elena waited until he was out of earshot and turned to Samson.

"I was afraid you were going to cut his head off," she said.

"I had half a mind to," he said. "Chicken-livered jackass."

"You can say that again," Chandi muttered.

"Chicken-livered jackass."

Elena laughed, and the sound of it, short and quick and airy, fastened something in his chest in a way he did not understand.

"Just let me handle him."

As Samson watched her go, her Agni and its warmth fading, he had the sudden, wild urge to rush after.

"Wait!" he called. He jogged to meet her. "You..." he began and found the words disappearing from his tongue as she half turned to face him.

"Yes?" she said.

"Don't scare him off" was all he could manage. Her gaze met his, and for a moment, there was something akin to regret there, so quick he could have imagined it, but then Elena dipped her head.

"I'll see you later tonight, Prophet," she said and left.

CHAPTER 22

ELENA

She found the Cyleoni ambassador walking the northern wall, his soldiers and a group of Black Scales standing watch.

"Your Majesty." He bowed as she neared, but she caught how his eyes skittered past her. "I truly do apologize. I spoke out of turn."

"It is nothing, Kirri," she said hastily. She dismissed the guards, save the Cyleoni.

"I heard your trip to King Syla was successful."

"I'm sure you've heard many things. Walk with me."

The early-winter sun perched precariously above the canyons, washing out the deep reds and carving shadowed faces into the rocks. A wind nipped at her scarf. Elena wound it tighter, hiding her swollen cheek, as Kirri watched her with a wary alertness.

"The general. I fear I've upset him."

"Samson has thicker skin than you think. Though, it would be better if you didn't insult Sesharians in his presence."

"I hear his wrath is monstrous," Kirri said, studying her cheek.

Elena inhaled sharply, her mind caught on the word *monstrous*, and she thought of the vicious, seething Agni thrumming within Samson's veins, the sudden crush of his hands on her throat. But she quickly pushed the sensation away.

"What do you think of Magar, Ambassador?" Elena asked, recovering.

"It is…remarkable in its strength," Kirri said. "Your people have endured so much and yet retain their spirit."

"Quite remarkable for refugees, no?" Her eyes slid coolly to him, and to his credit, Kirri gave her a plain, bland smile.

"Your people have always been proud warriors, Your Majesty. Both those born of the desert and the ones who found refuge in it after." They came to the parapets, and Kirri paused to observe the canyons and the mountains beyond. "Though I wonder, when the council negotiations begin, whose freedom will you fight for: Ravani, or Sesharian?"

Elena considered how to play this. She could not have Kirri signaling to Samson or the Black Scales that her fight, her only fight, was for Ravani freedom. She could not send her army, whatever remained of it, to a foreign island when her own home lay broken. But the Sesharians were her people too, in a way. "My loyalty is to my people. They can come from all walks of life: Ravani, Sesharian, Cyleoni. I will protect and defend them, as long as they wish to call the desert their home."

Kirri studied her, his face revealing nothing. "Are they your men, Your Majesty? Are they under your control?" he asked, his voice slow and calculative as he watched the shifting shadows. When she did not respond, he trailed his finger over the stone, flicking away dried flakes of blood. "I heard you were badly injured recently, and yet here you are, entertaining an old man. I would fear to think what would happen to Ravence if something were to befall you in this city."

"I am among friends, Kirri," she said. "Sometimes, we bicker, but there is great love among us. Rest assured. My people's spirit and regard for me shall never waver."

Kirri's eyes flicked to her cheek. "Unless, of course, they found someone just as worthy of their love."

Her smile faltered. Elena thought of the old man who had averted his eyes from her, of Kruppa's pained voice.

I am sorry, Your Majesty. But you have lost.

She had the horrid, half-formed image of standing in the glittering palace hall as another man sat on her throne. For a moment, Elena could say nothing. A deep, bottomless fear slowly bore a hole in her stomach. Ghostlike fingers fluttered across her throat.

"Your Majesty?"

Elena blinked, and the fingers released. She drew in a shaky breath, cool air rushing into her chest as she drew on a smile and faced Kirri.

"I believe your fear is unfounded, Ambassador. Syla could never replace me."

"I did not mean him but Sa—" Kirri caught himself, just in time. He drew back his hand to hide his blunder, but he had only affirmed what she had feared—that he had heard of her fight with Samson.

She could feel his belief, like the others, slowly slipping from her grasp.

"I apologize, Your Majesty," he muttered.

"Oh, I don't blame you. Samson is quite dashing and pretty to look at." She laughed, and she saw how Kirri eased, his shoulders dropping from his ears. "I admit the people love him. But Samson and his army serve me, Ambassador. And I come on behalf of all of us with a request for you."

"What kind of request?"

"It's come to my attention that the Yumi of Moksh have asked for an audience with me, but alas, I do not have the means to go. Could I—with your permission, of course—take the tanker across the Ahi Sea?"

"Moksh seeks an audience?" This time, Kirri did not hide his incredulity. "Is their request founded?"

"It came the morning of my coronation day," Elena said. "You remember my Spear, the Yumi Ferma?"

He nodded. "Yes. Wasn't she killed in the Arohassin attack prior to your coronation?"

Elena nodded mutely as she remembered building the funeral pyre and talking to the wind. She remembered Ferma's body, cold and lifeless, and the fire she had lit. *Forgive me, dear Ferma.*

"Ferma was the estranged granddaughter of the current queen of Moksh," she said. "Moksh requests that I—*we*—bring her ashes to her family so that she can be laid to rest with her ancestors." The first part was true, the second a lie, and yet it was the latter that came easily to Elena. A small part of her marveled at it. How quickly it slipped off her tongue, how quickly it had come to her mind when she had asked Kruppa for her sword. Guilt pinched her throat, but Elena rubbed her skin as she adjusted her scarf. "Now, I must admit, I do have an ulterior motive to see the Yumi, one I've already shared with Syla."

Kirri eyed her, the smile gone from his face. "Let me guess: You wish for them to fight in this war."

"Clever as always, Kirri," she said. "Request clearance from your king. We must leave tonight. I will have the ashes prepared by then."

"But the mines—"

"Samson will take care of them," Elena said. "You will find that he has no qualms pursuing the Jantari on his own."

Kirri rubbed his chin. "Forgive me, Your Majesty, but I don't believe it's prudent to fly all the way to Moksh during a time like this. How will you even convince the Yumi?"

"I'm sure you've heard the rumors of a . . . brawl between me and Samson," she said suddenly.

The ambassador fell quiet. He regarded her carefully, his eyes wandering back to her cheek.

"Yes," he said after a pause. "I have."

"Then you may have heard of a great inferno enveloping us." She stepped back, her palms beginning to warm. "The Yumi, I believe, will be interested in how I summoned that inferno."

"You? The rumors say that it was only Samson."

As he looked at her, caught between curiosity and unease, his eyes going from her cheek to her hands, Elena thought how easy it was to ensnare and twist someone's belief. Samson had done it. He had taken their god, pronounced Her a lie, and replaced Her with himself. He had healed the burned and said to all naysayers *See*. He had made the gods tangible, and her people had fallen for it.

But Elena understood the pain of Agni.

For every person he healed, Samson burned down another. For every belief he sowed, he destroyed a thousand more. A god like him could not proclaim himself all-mighty and all-powerful.

Not when someone like her existed.

Not when their Agni was made of three.

So Elena met Kirri's gaze and *desired*. A pinpoint of heat glowed in the middle of her palms, and then two flames flared up. Kirri gasped and stumbled back.

"I believe," she said over the hiss of the flames, "the queen of Moksh will want to see how I can call her Goddess's inferno."

She twisted her hand, and the flames curled down her wrist, spiraling up her arms like twisting vines.

Kirri stared, his mouth agape. "H-how?"

"The Yumi can answer why I have such powers," she said. Her voice barely faltered over the next lie. "I have seen visions of their Goddess, calling me. And I have seen you in them too, Kirri." She offered a soft, secretive smile. "I've seen you bring great prosperity to Cyleon with the Yumi. Imagine it. Your name will go down in history, not as a simple ambassador to Ravence, but as the man who changed Cyleon's fate."

Kirri watched the flames with a mixture of fascination and horror, but she saw the hunger in his eyes too. Politicians like him always craved more. Legacy meant more than honor, and power, the great force that supplemented it all, was king. She needed only to show a glimpse of it.

Elena closed her palms, and the flames slowly disappeared with a whispered hiss. Her voice was soft. "What say you, Kirri?"

He rubbed his eyes, and when he withdrew his hands, he looked beyond the canyons again, to the mountains beyond.

"If I get you clearance, you must show your fire to Syla. Immediately after visiting Moksh."

Elena nodded. "Done."

He sighed and finally met her eyes. "Tonight, then."

"Tonight."

CHAPTER 23

SAMSON

A wise man seeks fortitude. A fool craves happiness.

—a Sesharian proverb

Samson's hands trembled as he raised his smoking pipe to his lips. A single flame flared from his finger, bright and vicious, but then his chest spasmed, and pain nipped along his sword arm like a pup desperate for attention. Desperately, he inhaled. The sweet and slightly earthy smoke of ganja rolled through him, dampening the pain.

The sun glimmered low on the horizon, sinking between two pointed rocks in the distance. The pale shadows of the moons began to appear over the canyons.

The Ravani knelt wherever he walked. As he turned down a street, heading back to the command center, their whispers followed, and Samson welcomed it. He touched the head of a child who gazed up at him with big, curious eyes. Beckoning to the child, he blew out a smoke ring and shot a single flame through it, much to the delight of the child's friends. Their awe sent a hot rush of satisfaction through him, even as his bones ached.

It was all a show. That was what the others—Elena, Farin, the great royal families—did not understand. They had been born into their power and their performance had become their truth. They believed their sovereignty was not an act, but a god-given right. But prophets and kings were shallow, hollow titles. Samson knew that once that illusion was broken, once the promise of safety and control was reneged, they would tear him apart as quickly as they kissed his feet.

The Ravani bowed to him now, but they were a fierce people. Proud, unwilling to lose. In a way, they reminded him of Sesharians.

They all relied on him. The Sesharian puppet turned into a general. They had come to him because, somehow, he had made them believe he was the right man to forge a new history. A world where every man was free.

But was he? Samson looked down at his hands as his body throbbed, the pain a restless visitor beneath the sweet narcotics. Was he strong enough to withstand the madness? Sparks blazed between his fingers. He drew on his pipe and let out a shaky breath as he ascended the hall steps. Even now, he could feel the inferno's hunger. It was an insidious sensation, nibbling his stomach with soft kisses.

"There you are."

He looked up to see Visha standing in the entrance. She had switched out her black gloves for long crimson ones, creating the illusion of being soaked in blood, wrist to elbow. The image fit her.

"Which poor soul did you gut out today?" he asked.

"Well, it would have been the ambassador, but our fair queen has whisked him away for a tour of the city."

I'll see you later tonight, Prophet, Elena had told him. Secretly, he looked forward to it.

Visha nodded to his pipe. "Can I?"

He took one last pull, and then breathed smoke out his nostrils. Visha retrieved the pipe and had a long draw.

She exhaled slowly, and for a moment, the smoke curled around her cheeks. It reminded him of when he had found her burning poisonous incense outside a Jantari officer's quarters. She closed her eyes, nodded once.

"Right." She handed the pipe back to him. "Finish it before you come inside. You'll need it."

He eyed her warily. "What kind of battle strategy did you draft this time?"

She gave her thin, vicious grin, the same one that had compelled him to join her and smoke out the officer. "The best you've ever seen."

"That is the stupidest idea I've ever heard," Chandi said.

Visha scowled. "It's ballsy, but it'll work."

"It exposes us to the Jantari," Akino said. "We're primed to get fucked."

"You would know."

Akino gave her a scathing look. "I swear, the Jantari and I were drunk—"

"Enough, you two." Chandi scowled, turning to Samson. "This is too much, General."

"Are you all right?" Akino asked, peering at Samson. "You look pale."

"It's nothing." Samson sat forward, though sweat broke down his spine. "Start from the top again, Visha."

Visha winked at Chandi and pointed at a mountain passage that began along the Cyleoni border. It began to glow in red. "The only way into Jantar is this mountain pass from Cyleon. The Jantari will be patrolling their side of the valley, but according to our intel from miners, there's an underground tunnel entrance hidden within this bluff."

She zoomed in on the holomap, indicating a tall, carved mountain wall. "We don't know what the entrance looks like—"

"And you still think this is a good plan?" Chandi asked Samson.

"—but at least we know where it is," Visha continued, glaring at Chandi. "This tunnel creeps under the mountain pass and leads to the northwestern forest surrounding Mine One."

"The Jantari will have that tunnel covered," Chandi said. "We'll be crawling toward a trap."

"Not if we spring a trap on them," Visha said.

"What do you mean?" Samson asked.

Visha nodded toward the three glowing dots that indicated the mines. "What do you see there?"

"The Jantari mines," Samson said.

"I know that, but where are they exactly?"

"On the mountainside," Akino said slowly.

Visha nodded expectantly, waiting for him to continue, but Akino only stared at her. He shrugged.

Visha sighed and touched the mountain, her finger slicing through the holo and tapping the table. "They're all downslope."

They stared at her in silence.

"Honestly, guys, this isn't alchemy."

"Just get to the point," Samson said.

"The ore deposit beneath the northern mines is just one fat lump. It's deep but concentrated. The Jantari planted three mines to pump all that shit out. They're distanced for safety, but they didn't count the mountain grade. If one mine collapses, the others risk falling too because they're all downhill."

"But that doesn't make any sense," Akino rebutted. "Why would the Jantari make such a stupid mistake?"

"Greed," Samson said. He saw it now. How had he not seen it before? Farin had built these mines to reap the land, damn the consequences. If there were landslides caused by the nearby drilling, he didn't care. After all, Sesharians were working those mines. Sesharians and lowborn Jantari soldiers. They were all expendable to him.

"It works in our favor," Visha said. "General, you and Elena can burn through the tunnels as our first offense. We and the Cyleoni soldiers can follow as the second wave. Once we take out Mine One, the others will topple like dominoes."

He hesitated. He remembered his weakness after capturing Magar, the waning of his Agni. He had already given too much. Even he knew he could not lead another attack like Magar, at least not for a while.

But there was something else. He tried not to recall the memory, but it came anyway, sticky and vile. The closed walls, the stale, fetid smell of sweat and blood. Screams echoing beneath the earth. Him, frozen in the dark tunnel, palms sweaty around his pulse gun.

How could he tell them? These men who fought and bled for him, these men who would follow him blindly into battle. How could he tell them that their Blue Star, their infallible Prophet, was afraid of the dark?

Before his ascent, before he had become a war hero for Jantar, he had become a traitor to his own people. He had joined the Jantari army after he had fled the Arohassin, thinking he could sell his secrets for safety. But he had been foolish. With one look, a Jantari officer had sent him to serve in the mines. Not as a miner. He hadn't been that merciful.

The officer had made him an overseer of the Sesharians.

He wore the garb of a Jantari soldier, armed with a zeemir and a pulse gun, and patrolled the underground tunnels while his people toiled. He had hated the cramped walls. The dark, wet scent of the earth. His Jantari counterparts snickered whenever he passed. *Coward*, they had called him. Some even went as far as to ridicule him, stealing his clothes from their shared lockers, jumping him in dark tunnels. On one occasion, he had wet himself. They had lorded that over him for the rest of his service.

But their taunts hadn't really bothered Samson. It was the miners' whispers that had threatened to undo him. On his patrols, the Sesharians had glanced at him with disgust. *Rustblood*, they spat as he passed. *Traitor*.

He had wanted to tell them that he was one of them. Couldn't they see?

But they only saw the gleam of his zeemir and the glare of the winged bull on his chest.

Beneath the table, Samson gripped his knees. That had been long ago. The officer who had assigned him that station was long dead now. The soldiers who had taunted him were buried deep within the earth. He had made sure of it. The same Sesharians who had worked in those mines were now free men, serving him. He was the redeemer. The ember that had sprung from the ashes. He would lead them to glory and free their home from the silver shackles of the Jantari.

And he was afraid.

Visha and Akino looked at him, expectant, but only Chandi met his gaze. Only she recognized his hesitation as fear.

"No," she said, and silently, Samson thanked her.

"What?" Visha turned to Chandi.

"Exposing Samson and Elena is too risky. Especially in enemy territory."

"But we did the same in Magar," Visha began, but Chandi held up her hand. She pointed at Mine One.

"The tunnels won't work, Visha, because it traps us all. If we get caught during the landslides, we won't be able to escape. And not just us, but also the Sesharians working the mines. We can't just leave them."

Visha rubbed the back of her neck. She stared at the map, her eyebrows knitting together.

"Wait," she said suddenly. "What if—"

She was interrupted by a loud bang at the front of the hall. They sprang up at once. Samson pulled out his urumi as Chandi shouted for the men in the armory to guard the doors. But it was only Akiri. The twin weapons master called them to come out, quick, look, look!

Samson was already midway down the stairs when he heard it. The roar of engines. His heart stuttered and dropped. Had the Jantari launched a counterattack? Was Farin finally making his move?

But Akiri pointed north, to the Agnee mountains, and in the fading dusk, Samson saw the shape of a tanker lift into the air.

"What?" he began.

"Did the Cyleoni fucking abandon us?" Visha said.

"They're gone," Chandi said, looking at her holopod. "Both of them."

"Sir!" A soldier jogged up the steps, saluted, and handed him three things: *her* urumi and anklets.

"General," Visha said.

Samson took them with shaking fingers. A message was crudely etched on the urumi, and he raised the blade to read it.

The Yumi never liked urumis. I'm leaving it with you.

"General."

She knew about the trackers in the anklets. She knew, and she had left him. *She had fucking abandoned him.* Samson searched the sky, but the tanker was already fading into the distance. The urumi and anklets hung limply in his hands.

"General!"

He turned, a snarl on his lips, when Visha pointed behind them and into the hall. On the table beside the holopanel, the metal lotus began to glow a deep incarnadine. Then it began to vibrate.

Suddenly, alarms blared. Samson whipped around to see pulse fire coming from the walls as the tiny shapes of his soldiers ran up and down the ramparts.

"The Arohassin are here."

THE VILLAIN

CHAPTER 24

ELENA

Every great man must know how to betray.

—a Sesharian proverb

The Ahi Sea glimmered beneath her like a liquid sheet of black glass, trapping starlight within its dark and unknowable depths. It was as if she were staring into a void. A deep, unsettling feeling limned the bottom of her chest, and Elena looked away. The sea always frightened her. She had only traveled across it once, on a state visit to Nbru with her father back when he still took trips to the first continent. Then, and even now, she had retreated.

"Nervous?" Kirri asked.

"Is it that obvious?"

Before Kirri could answer, the panel chimed, and a holo of Syla appeared before them.

"Elena," he cried, "you are either mad or a genius for a maneuver like this."

"Some say there's a fine line between the two," she said.

"Spoken like your father," he grumbled, though a smile tugged at his mouth. "When Kirri first told me of your plan, I had half a mind to call back my men. But he was right. We can cut two stalks with one sword. I just hope that at least one of you succeeds."

It will be me, she thought suddenly, with more vehemence than she expected. When she returned to Magar with the Yumi in tow, the people would flock to her, and she would accept them despite their betrayals and show them the power of a true leader. A queen, not a butcher.

"I will see you in Goldor, then, with the Yumi," she said.

When the line cut, Elena turned back to the dark sea. Kirri sat beside her, and after some time, he spoke, the edges of his reflection furring within the glass.

"There's a strange thing about this sea." He sounded almost wistful. "It will hide nearly everything and everyone. A man could disappear out here, and no one would know it."

Elena blinked as a cold shock washed through her. She had the sudden memory of standing on top of the dunes with Yassen as he gazed out over the desert. *All the quiet, with no one to judge your shortcomings. A man could disappear out here, and no one would know it.* Kirri must have noticed the alarm in her reflection, because his smile faltered.

"Oh—I—I don't mean that I have something to hide—"

"I know what you mean," she said in a hushed voice, thinking of Yassen in the moonlight and his simple wish to be free. Her heart ached. "It's the illusion that enchants us. Here, we can forget ourselves and our duties and just *be*."

She was quiet after that, and Kirri had the good sense to leave her alone. She thought of Samson and his bitter rage, Chandi and her calculating patience, Visha and her subtle poisons—and her own withering pride. They were caught in a torturous dance to hurt and make others hurt worse than they had. She could not escape it. And she did not have the heart to tell Kirri that people like her, people like them, could never afford true freedom. There were worse ways to live and die than bleeding for one's own home, but the thought of freedom—from it all—immobilized her.

Why are you running, Elena? Yassen whispered. His murky reflection flickered in the dark window. *What shriveled version of freedom are you fighting for?*

She turned, but there was no one beside her. Elena shuddered.

It took them over a day to fly across the Ahi Sea as they painstakingly avoided Ayoni airspace, so by the time Kirri shook her gently awake, Elena longed for the sight of land.

The mountains came first.

They broke the blue horizon like blackened knuckles. Bruised and vast. Deep red veins of cooling magma trickled down their southern faces. As they flew closer, she saw the infamous black beaches of the Mokshi coast where, centuries ago, a foolish Paguan king had waged an invasion, only to be sent back a boat full of his sons' severed heads.

"Hailing Moksh," the pilot called.

Elena only half listened to the pilot as she drank in the towering cliffs of the western coast and the great statues of the first queens carved within. Yamni and Yamsiya, the twin regents. The priestess and the warrior. Their large stone eyes seemed to follow her, and deep within her gut, Elena felt a strange warmth blooming.

"Tower, come in," the pilot repeated. "Requesting clearance for landing."

Silence.

Elena frowned, turning to the pilot, when she saw movement flicker in the south. Just there, beyond the cliffs, toward the famed capital of Azadi. She had never been to the Yumi city, but now she tasted its name on her tongue, pressing it against the back curve of her teeth for the last syllable. *Azadi.* It was a Yumi word, a word of power and consequence. The same cry the Sixth Prophet had taken as she burned down armies and kingdoms, singing her vicious call for freedom.

Azadi, azadi, azadi.

The ancient name, the ancient call of *freedom*, plucked something within her. She had heard of the city's glorious black marble and silver-veined spires and its floating universities dedicated to the ancient teachings of the Great Goddess. And then there was the infamous palace, thin and long like a shard. But when they finally cleared the cliffs, it was not the palace, or towers, or universities that she noticed but a kingdom—burning.

Faint fingers of smoke writhed between the broken spires. Scorch marks marred the faces of some buildings, while rubble dotted the streets. She saw no armies, no pulse fire, no encroaching enemies, but she saw the evidence of an attack in the city.

"Shit," Kirri said. "Shit, shit, shit."

"Pilot," Elena called, but the soldier was already pulling away from the burning city.

"What is happening?" Kirri cried. "I thought you said Moksh called for you—"

"Pilot!"

"Your Majesty, no one is answering our hails. We must turn—"

A garbled voice broke through the static. "Reroute westward, Cyleoni."

Elena grabbed the pilot's comms. "Who is this? What happened in Azadi? Has there been an invasion?"

The static thinned, then doubled. "The general—" The voice broke, then chimed again. "—sister queen. We've sent the coordinates."

"What about the queen? What has happened to her?"

But there was no answer. On the panel, a new pair of coordinates flickered, and the pilot banked toward the western mountains. Elena twisted just as the burning city slipped out of her view, and then all she saw were the black clouds of smoke slowly rising to meet the dawn.

They dove through the cliffs, hurtling past the twin queens, and up the western coastline. Elena frantically scanned the forests for smoke, but they remained untouched by fire. Had the fighting only been in the capital, then? She hailed the comms again, but no Yumi answered.

Suddenly, Elena felt a low pull in her stomach, a quickening in her blood not unlike when she summoned her Agni. As they descended, Elena caught glimpses of a river, the water so pure, so bright, it burned silver. The Yumi temple sat on its banks. It was greater than any Ravani temple, older, prouder, and looking upon it, Elena felt a finger curl underneath the base of her skull and *tug*.

She was out of the tanker the moment they landed, her heart thumping wildly, her blood a raucous call that seemed to answer the river's song. The temple was made of two large pyramids stacked upon each other, one below, the other floating upside down above, their peaks meeting in a sliver through which only sunlight could pass. Four waterfalls fell between the corners of the pyramids in a never-ending stream. Elena stumbled, overwhelmed by the vastness of the two structures, the way the dark walls seemed to drink in the light and reflect it with a slight green iridescence.

Kirri called to her as the temple doors opened. Two Yumi descended the great steps. Twins, joined at the hip. They walked in perfect unison, their orange robes and black hair unfurling like flickering flames. They wore no jewelry, no ornaments, no weapons twined in their hair. Their robes were plain, spun of smooth silk. At first glance, there was nothing extraordinary about the priestesses.

But then Elena saw their eyes.

Heat seeped out of her bones.

They were black on black, so dark that it seemed shadows themselves lived within. The Yumi regarded her, unblinking.

Elena took a step back. "Who are you? Where is your queen?"

"There has been a glorious revolution," they said, their voices lilting, echoing. "The queen is dead."

"Dead?" Terror, anger, confusion rose and swept through her in rapid succession, followed swiftly by a cold and heavy dread. "At whose hand?"

"At our own." Their lips twisted into a serene smile. "Welcome, Elena Aadya Ravence. Queen of Fire. Blood of Alabore. The Divine Grace of Desert and Sky. We have been expecting you."

CHAPTER 25

SAMSON

It is foolish to believe that I am now among friends. The world has changed around me, and I find myself irrefutably altered with it.
—from the diaries of Priestess Nomu of the Fire Order

Samson stood between the open gates and waited for the enemy to appear. Ahead of him, alone in the wide entrance, leaned a limp white flag. He knew who would come. He had known as soon as Visha had uttered those godforsaken words: *The Arohassin are here.*

But still. It did not dampen the blow.

A tall man appeared behind the flag. In the low light, his face was smooth, serene. Beautiful even, with dark eyes and soft, polished curls that fell too neatly across his forehead. A trim beard hid the burn on his cheek, but Samson remembered its shape—curved, sallow, like a dying moon. He smiled, revealing teeth too perfect, too white.

"Hello, Sam."

The same voice from the metal lotus, the same one that had haunted him from the Arohassin to the dark, miserable depths of the mines. A wild roaring built in his ears as he felt something ancient and rotten stir within his chest like a slumbering beast awakened.

"Akaros."

Akaros folded himself into one of the chairs beside the flag and gestured to the other. "Sit."

Stiffly, Samson sat. He dared not speak again, afraid that whatever would come out would somehow be radioactive, horrid. Akaros watched him closely. A light smile ghosted his long lips, his eyes still and yet always moving, always observing, always, *always*, finding his faults.

"So your little bird has gone and fled the coop?"

Samson bit back his reply. Elena's sudden departure and her message had thrown him, but he'd barely had the time to process before finding himself here in this sham of a parley. So he said nothing.

Akaros sighed. "That's the thing with these royals, Sam. Try as hard as you can, coerce them, break them, shame them—love them—and they'll still choose themselves. Yassen learned that lesson. I'm surprised you haven't sooner. You've worked with rulers longer than he worked with them."

Carefully, Samson dug his forefinger into his palm, focusing on the sharp, uncomfortable pinprick of pain rather than the sudden vision of Yassen dying on the mountain, abandoned by Elena. Or of himself, watching the tanker disappear into the night.

"Hmm. Well. You boys were both self-sacrificial to a fault. Suppose she doesn't come back. What are you going to do? What are you going to tell her people?" Akaros paused, his eyes sliding coolly to him. "How will you ever take those mines without her Agni?"

Samson's throat ran dry. In the time between Elena's departure and the Arohassin's arrival, he hadn't the time to consider that question. His confusion must have shown, because Akaros leaned back in his seat and smiled, and that alone destroyed Samson's resolve.

"She's coming back," he said hotly. *She is, I know she is.* "She wouldn't leave Ravence alone to me. She's going to raise an army, to help us in our war against Farin—"

Akaros barked a laugh. "Listen to yourself. 'Raise an army to help.' *Help?* Help who, Sam, you or her? Your men answer to you. They're devoted to you. If she marches in with her own army, you think they'll lie down and swear fealty to your sword? Gods above, I didn't realize time in the desert has made you so . . . desperate."

The word ripped into him deeper than Samson anticipated, and he smarted. "Desperate? You're the one who has come to *my* door, seeking my help."

"Oh no, Sam," Akaros said in a chillingly soft voice. "We were invited."

At this, Samson stilled. He thought back to when they had discovered the man of sand, of how Chandi had insisted they at least consider the offer. *Don't you see? We can use them.*

A bitterness festered within him, a ripening fruit growing on a gnarled and twisted plant.

"Don't blame your commander," Akaros said, watching his face. "She made the right decision. Now that your greatest ally has left you, I have become your greatest friend." He leaned forward. "Without Elena's Agni, you can't take Farin's mines. But we know how to destroy them without her. All I ask in return is amrithi."

"But I do not have it."

"Yet we both know only you can activate it."

Samson inhaled sharply. "What do you know of amrithi?"

" 'A metal so fine it can cut through steel.' A metal that can only be harvested by the god's cursed son. You."

"I am not giving you amrithi," he growled. "Who knows what you intend to use it for—"

Akaros spread out his arms. "I don't see anyone else coming to your aid. It's a fair deal, Sam. Take it, or lose the mines. Take it, or watch Elena come back the conquering hero. Take it, and *win*."

Samson felt a hundred things at once, all of it dark, all of it hateful, burning into a black ball that lodged between his lungs and his throat. He wished he could think of something clever, something that could push him out of this corner where, deprived of friends, he was forced to make do with his enemy. But only Akaros sat before him. Only his old tormentor offered him a hand.

When he spoke, Samson's voice was dry, weak. "How?"

Akaros grew still, eyes unmoving, perfect as a statue, and Samson had the feeling that if he somehow touched him, he would have felt rigid as stone. Then, slowly, he unfolded from his chair, all angles and long limbs separating and opening like the elegant legs of a spider.

"Look," he said simply.

So Samson stood and watched. There, beyond the wall, multiple men crawled down the canyons. *No, not men*, Samson thought. *Things.* It was as if someone had dissembled the man of sand, then put him back together—but with none of the grace or heed of the natural order. There were arms. There were heads. They were people—of a sort. But they were *wrong.* Made of limbs that bent unnaturally and moved too fast. A great swath of darkness multiplying and building while the eerie susurration of sand filled the air. And they kept coming. Soon, they filled the gates and the canyons beyond, watching him with eyeless sockets.

Samson stared out at the unnatural army and thought, distantly, that if they succeeded, then a new kind of warfare would begin. One of fire and sand and nothing of mercy. He stood at the precipice of this distant future, and he could not see its end.

"We can send this army to overwhelm the Jantari while we take the tunnels," Akaros said.

"When?"

"Whenever you need."

Samson turned to him, remembering his promise to Yassen all those suns ago. *I'm going to kill him*, he had rasped. Akaros watched him, his face purposefully blank.

"How do we control them?"

Akaros turned, and a shape detached from the wall. At first, Samson thought it was one of those unnatural men, but as it came closer, he realized with a start that it was a woman. No, not a woman. A Yumi, with eyes of gold and hair so long and lethal he took an involuntary step back as she neared.

"Samson, meet our chief gamemaster, Jaya."

CHAPTER 26

JAYA

*After the fracturing of the great Yumi family, a Yumi must swear fealty
to either the Yamni or Yamsiya sect. To choose something outside either
is to choose death and abandonment.*
—from chapter 16 of The Great History of Sayon

When they pulled her from the warm, dark embrace of her mother, the Yumi solpriest dangled her by the ends of her hair and slapped her. She did not react. At least, not in the way they wanted. She let out a pitiful cry, and her hair remained limp.

The solpriest grimaced and dropped her as if she were something infectious.

"She is clipped," she said. Her withering gaze fell on the mother. "See what you have done?"

But her mother gathered her in her arms, hair sharpening and curling around her protectively. "Her name is Jaya."

The solpriest gave them no blessings, no warnings. She stood impassively in the doorway with her face drawn and heavy with things Jaya could not have understood then.

But she would see that look, again and again, all her life.

It was always the Yumi adults. Like her mother, they served either as soldiers or as guards or, the rarer sort, in the palace. When invited to her home, they greeted her with pleasantries and comments about her beautiful hair. But as the compass turned to the blessed north, the conversation arrived at her truth. And one by one, she saw that same terrible look the solpriest wore, all those suns ago.

She was clipped. A Yumi without the power of her hair. A Yumi not worthy of their Great Mother.

Their disappointment irritated her, but it was their fear, laced in their hushed voices, in their reproachful gazes, that wounded Jaya. No one ever said it directly to *her*. To comment on her fate was to welcome the evil eye upon themselves. But over the suns, naturally, like a herd slowly outpacing the lame, they distanced themselves, creating a berth so wide that Jaya could hear its excruciating echo in her bones. She did not chase them. Her pride denied her, though at night she would stare up at the ceiling of her room, listening to sand rattle against her windowpane, and wonder about that terrible *if*.

What if she had been born worthy? What if she had not been born half-Yumi at all but as a normal Yumi girl with normal Yumi parents whose hair was a weapon?

Div laughed at her. He was always laughing, her younger brother. "You care too much what others think." And when she would protest, he'd tease and tease until she found herself smiling with him.

Her brother fought anyone who sneered at her. Her mother braided her hair with gentle fingers. Her father smiled apologetically, for he was a man who had dared to love a Yumi, and unlike the stories of the twin moons, no gods had come to save them. No gods had delivered them from their collective unhappiness.

Not until she had met the gamemaster.

They were sitting at a bar, Jaya holding a cold beer to Div's split lip (the latest of his chivalry) while he shouted at the game playing on the holos.

"Hold still," she snapped.

"Come on—Jaya—look, look, man! He's right behind you!"

The fighter stepped from behind a sand pillar, lancing his blade into the back of his confused opponent. His suit blinked red, and the Jantari fighter received another point.

"Fucking Jantari, always stabbing you in the back," Div said. Jaya flicked beer into his face, and he yelped.

"It was a trap set up by the gamemaster and they both walked into it," she said. "See how the pillars are formed? They force the fighters in. Close off the escape. If our fighter was smart, she would have remained along the perimeter, circling around like a vulture until she spotted the Jantari."

"Then she would have gone in for the kill."

They turned to the man beside them at the bar. He was tall, too thin, with a burn on his cheek that reminded her of a dying moon.

"Exactly," Jaya said, eyeing Div as he sized up the stranger. She placed a hand on his elbow to calm him. There was no need to explain another black eye to their parents.

"Are you a game novice?" the stranger said.

"Who's asking?" Div said.

The man laughed and extended his hand. "Akaros."

She proved a quick study, taking to gameplanning with as natural a talent as Yumi took to the slingsword. She spent suns studying, enacting strategies, drafting gameplays, casting her favorite fighters for all-star matches. At night, she could barely hear the painful echo of the berth within her, her head filled with so many game designs that her heart, lonely as it was, gave in.

The day she was crowned a gamemaster was the day the gold caps had come for her parents.

"Rebel sympathizers," the mob had shouted as they raised the fires.

She screamed for Div, her mother, and her father, all trapped within the house as the gold caps dragged her out of her home by her hair. Her useless, weaponless hair. She had never wished more desperately than at that moment to have been a true Yumi, one who could shred the hands grabbing her with the simple swipe of her locks.

Akaros found her rotting in a jail. He bailed her out and told her the news that she had already known, already feared.

Her parents had died, choking. Div was alive, barely, his body a ruin. He would be bedridden for the rest of his life. Investigations had begun, for her mother had been an army commander and women of her rank did not die quietly.

Jaya did not have the courage to tell the investigators that her mother spat on the name of Ravence. That she had called the king a liar, a fraud. She was a Yumi, proud and unflinching, left to serve a king who could not protect his own woman. *It is shameful*, she had said.

"I can't stay here," she whispered to Div when he awoke.

"There's nowhere else to go," he said. "You have to find those bastards."

"Div—"

"No, Jaya! Ma and Papa deserved more. Where is your honor? Where is your *anger*?" And on the last word, his voice broke, hot and fierce and hurt.

"Where is it?" he said, softer now.

She clutched his hand as Akaros watched. "It's here. I'm sorry, Div."

When Div slipped back into sleep, Jaya turned to Akaros. She did not see disappointment in his eyes, like in the others'. There was only an emboldened recognition, wordless and powerful. She felt struck, as if seized by lightning, her senses sharpening to a singular point, a shared understanding of like meeting like. A feeling of weightlessness tickled her stomach.

He held out his hand.

"Let us help you."

She took it, anchoring herself. The loneliness within her awakened into something wolfish and wicked, all angles and teeth and hunger. Never mind the community that shunned her. Here was someone who knew of her hunger and had his own to share.

"We start with the one who struck the match."

Jaya entered the Black Scales' makeshift command center and found her toy immediately.

"What did you think of it?" she asked as she ran a finger over the metal lotus.

"Unnatural yet brilliant," Chandi replied, not meeting her eyes. She was looking past them to the Butcher, who stood to the side of the room with a stunned expression, as if he could not yet believe what had happened. Akaros was directing Arohassin agents into the room, telling them to place this machine here, that panel there, no, you idiot, *there*.

Jaya watched Chandi, Chandi watched Samson, and Samson watched them all, unseeing.

"Did you not tell him?" Jaya asked.

Chandi did not reply.

If Chandi felt guilty, Jaya had no sympathy for her. They had spoken earlier through encrypted messages. It was the commander who had accepted their invite. Their arrival was not a surprise, and yet Chandi wore guilt in the softness of her jaw, in the way her eyes darted from Akaros to Samson. She called to a Black Scale, the master of arms, but he ignored her as he whispered in Samson's ear. Chandi rocked back on her heels, quiet.

"There's a saying among us gamemasters," Jaya said. "'Every move is binding until the sands stop churning. But the gamemaster sees all and finds the path unwinding.'"

Chandi's eyes slid to her. "Are you telling me that I need to accept the bed I've made?"

"You saw the path through the sands, Chandi. Surely your general won't punish you too long for it."

Chandi laughed, short and brusque, like a dull hammer striking a metal bowl. "You don't know Samson Kytuu, then."

The Butcher detached from the wall and marched to the center panel. His stride was efficient, exact. All his focus, all his energy, wired into precise movements that could, at any moment, transform into a strike. *He's a fighter all right*, she thought with a sudden, breathless giddiness. Gods, it had been so long since she had spun up a game with proper challengers. She wondered how quickly he'd adapt to her rules. How soon he'd break beneath them.

Akaros was already sitting, waiting. Jaya smoothly folded into a seat beside him.

"So, you're the gamemaster."

Jaya turned to the speaker, a raven-haired woman with leather gloves and henna tattoos spiraling down her arms. She tapped a metal lotus. "And I'm guessing this is part of your gameplay."

Leather gloves, vine henna tattoos, Sesharian hair streak—her heart stuttered a beat as Jaya recognized the woman. "And you must be the vishkanya. I've heard about you and your sisters. There were fifteen of you, weren't there, hand selected by Jantari intelligence to become assassins? Tell me, is it true you must drink poison and an antidote every day to keep your touch deadly?"

"An old wives' tale." Visha's lips twisted as if she tasted something foul. "The poison the Jantari forced me to digest will last me a lifetime."

"How does it work?"

She met her gaze. "Would you like me to demonstrate, gamemaster?"

Jaya eyed her gloves, then the shape of her arms, then the sharp slope of her jaw and found, disconcertingly, that she was beautiful. She looked away quickly. Visha did too, although Jaya felt the prick of her stare on the back of her neck, and she felt herself go hot all over again.

Samson finally sat at the head of the panel, and Chandi sat beside her, the bridge between their side of the table and the Black Scales.

"Gamemaster," he called. "How many of your . . . *sand creatures* can you conjure?"

"They're not *creatures*. They're called the Sandsworn," Jaya said, indignant. "And I don't *conjure* them like some sort of wizard. It is a science. I create them using magnetic black sands and signals sent via my metal lotuses—"

"I don't care how they work," Samson cut in. "I want to know how many you can create."

Jaya had half a mind to tell him about the sanctity of the gameplay process, but Akaros cast her a sidelong glance, and she bit back her retort.

"I can bring five hundred Sandsworn. That should be more than enough to distract the Jantari overseers aboveground while you attack through the tunnels."

Though Samson did not wince, she saw his shoulders stiffen like a fighter who sensed danger in the field but could not find where.

He's traumatized, Akaros had told her. *Even in training, he hated small spaces. He almost blew another kid's head off because he panicked during a recon.*

"The tunnels—" Samson began.

"You led the assault in Magar and took back the city from an even stronger Jantari force. Surely, this is nothing you can't handle." Jaya met his gaze then, waiting, because she knew as well as he that he would not admit to his fear, not in front of his men, and certainly not in front of the Arohassin.

Samson's mouth tightened. When he spoke, there was an acidity in his voice, as if he was now realizing how terribly he had underestimated her.

"You're right. Nothing I can't handle."

Chandi looked to him in alarm. "General, you don't need to be on the front lines for this one. It might be wiser if you stayed back—"

"Noted, Commander," Samson said, his voice like the sound of cold meat slapping on a butcher's block.

Chandi stiffened. She looked to her fellow men, but no one else dared to speak. Jaya plucked up the metal lotus and held it out to Samson.

"I'll need you to carry this with you during the attack."

"Absolutely not," Samson growled.

"Don't tell me you're afraid of a little flower, Sam," Akaros said.

"And let a sand creature jump me in the tunnels? How do I know this isn't some part of your ulterior motive to harm me or my men?"

"If I wanted to harm you with the Sandsworn, I would have done so already," Jaya said flatly.

She activated the lotus, and it began to rise. The sound of rushing sand whispered through the room as black kernels slowly spilled out of its closed petals.

"This will protect you. You can mold any form, whether it's a shield"— she waved her arm, and the sand solidified into a shield the length of her arm—"screen"—it lengthened into a tall screen—"or sword."

The sand formed an urumi, *his* urumi to be exact. The twin blades dark and long instead of silver. The urumi slowly unspooled, the tongues tasting the air as if to strike. She heard the others gasp. Visha grinned, and Akaros and Chandi looked to Samson, but the Butcher was not watching the blade. He was watching her.

Too much water. Men of blue are made of greed, she thought involuntarily as she met his gaze. Then she chided herself for giving in to such superstitions.

Her Butcher—she was already thinking of him as *her* fighter—observed her with a coiled alertness that made her palms itch for her stylus. She sketched the field. *Tiered stepwells, four sides, two fighters across a faulty bridge that cascades minute by minute into the quicksand below. He will be armed with an urumi.*

Slowly, Samson placed his hands on the table. "Can I wield my Agni through it?"

Jaya hesitated. "I haven't experimented, but you are welcome to try—"

That was when the fire began.

It sparked from his palms. Two bright white flares that made her jerk back and cover her face. There were cries around the room, startled shouts. Then the light darkened. Slitting her fingers, Jaya saw that the flares had coiled into two blue flames that slowly twined around the sand. It was working. *It was working.* The flames grew in length around the blades, swelling, hissing, and Samson leaned forward just as she did—breaths caught—and then the urumi collapsed.

The metal lotus hit the table with a clang that echoed through the room.

The others were silent, stunned. But the Butcher rose slowly, and she could see the quick movement behind his eyes, the strategies weaving and unspooling, his hunger growing. He recalled the sand urumi and swung.

"General," Chandi began.

The blades rent two deep dents in an adjoining table. He swung again and again. By the time he was done, the table lay crumpled and bent.

Samson stepped back, panting. "You have a deal, gamemaster. Go and gather your Sandsworn."

But she watched the flames around his wrists. All the secrets of Agni, its nature, its power, were but five feet away from her. Div's cure was within her grasp. She had the urge to take his Agni and pry open its mystery, to see the truth of its being. To re-create it for herself.

With great effort, Jaya tore away to raise her army.

CHAPTER 27

ELENA

I can give my flesh for my people to eat, and still, they will ask for my bones.

—from the diaries of Priestess Nomu of the Fire Order

Elena followed the priestesses into the temple, alone. The Yamni did not allow the Cyleoni into their sacred home, and Kirri, seeing the priestesses' twitching hair, had not protested. She supposed she should feel afraid. The stairway was steep and dark, the priestesses strange, quiet, but Elena found herself climbing the steps two at a time. There was something *here*. Her Agni hissed, and the dull roar in her ears only strengthened as they entered the temple hall.

The hall was a deep, cavernous chamber with sloped, latticed ceilings that met at a hidden point. Sunlight bounced off two long silver pools that ran alongside the walkway, their waters so still, so clear, they might as well have been mirrors. But as Elena neared the end of the path, her gaze pulled from the pools to the icon above. The Goddess towered over them. Tall, monstrous—beautiful. She held two weapons, a slingsword in

188

Her upper left, a spear of fire in Her lower right, Her other hands splayed in perfect halves of a lotus. Made of the same obsidian as the temple, She commanded an unspeakable gravity that plucked invisible strings within Elena and yanked her forward.

"Our Goddess welcomes you, little queen."

A priestess walked from behind the silver altar. Unlike the other Yamni, she was of Elena's height with golden irises, as if the Goddess had taken a kernel of fire and set it within her eyes. Scriptures were inked across her face, and when she dropped her hood—Elena inhaled sharply—she saw that the priestess was completely bald.

Clipped.

She knew enough from Ferma's stories to understand that a clipped Yumi was an abomination. A shame. And yet the twin priestesses bowed low to her, the ends of their hair sweeping across the floor. "High Sister."

The high sister turned to Elena. The sleeves of her robe inched back as she raised her arms, revealing red tattoos swirling down her brown skin. She opened her palms for Elena to take.

"I have waited a long time to meet you, Elena."

Elena made no move to take her hands. Though her Agni still hummed with a beating desperation, though she knew something in this room called to her, Elena retreated. "Why?"

The high sister smiled gently, lowering her hands. "Because your mother said you would come."

Elena felt something sharp and small still in her heart. *"What?"*

"A few weeks before the queen's death, Ferma sent us a message saying your mother was not well. That she was prone to hallucinations and long silences. That when she did speak, she spoke of three fires. Your Spear begged me to help. So I met your mother. I journeyed into your dunes, and we met under the shared gaze of the moons, and she told me of you. She told me that I would one day see visions of a woman so broken and embittered by her own grief that she could not connect with the Goddess's fire. At first, I did not understand. But then I saw you in our temple fire, and I knew." She touched Elena's elbow, her voice strong and warm with conviction. "I could not help your mother. But I can help you, Elena. Trust your Ferma, if not us."

Elena trembled. She remembered their glittering, broken reflections as

Ferma said, *Maybe the dance in the scroll isn't one dedicated to the Phoenix. Maybe it's of the Goddess.*

What was it about this place that made her memories so fresh, her grief so raw?

"H-help?" Elena said. Her mother had been mad. She was not. "I—I do not need your help. I would like to meet your next-in-line regent—"

The high sister rested her hand on Elena's arm to stop her from shaking. "You struggle to hear the flames. And I know your Agni could not withstand the Prophet's attack. But I can help you."

Elena tensed at the mention of Samson, and she had to stop herself from touching the marks on her neck.

She swallowed, hard. "Show me, then."

An altar stretched beneath the Goddess's feet. Four Yumi held up the base, each with a different emotion. One bridled with anger; the other hid in fear; another smiled with joy; and the last wept, her tears eternal.

A silver bowl, as wide and long as Elena's torso, perched within their hands. White sand filled its depths. Elena stilled. She remembered her father sitting on his throne, Samson and Yassen taking the Desert Oath and reaching into the fire. Their imprints in the sand. How young they were. How naive.

"Do you remember the fire dance?"

Elena blinked. "Of course. You know it?"

And at this, the high sister laughed. "We Yamni made the dance. Let us do it together."

Before the Goddess, Elena and the priestess sank into the Warrior. Heat flared up Elena's spine, her Agni awake, ready. She spun, and so did the Yamni, their movements mirrored like two perfect halves, like the twin pools running through the temple. Elena startled. The priestess smiled at her surprise, and despite herself, Elena returned it.

The Desert Sparrow, the Lotus, the Spider, the Tree, the Snake, they flowed through the positions, their arms strong and fluid, their feet skipping over the black floor. The twins began to sing, and the sand rose. It leapt from the bowl and swirled around them, guided by their dance.

"Listen," the priestess said.

Elena felt the pull in her gut, the call of the land. It was the song of the river, the roar of the waterfalls, the steady pulsing beat of the sleeping volcano, everywhere, all at once.

So she listened.

Elena could have sworn the sand was *talking* as it swept around her, whispering a secret she could not understand. She tried to focus on its susurration, but the sand swirled, faster and faster, singing, laughing, purring, grains skating across her cheeks, marking her skin, filling her nostrils. She gasped. She could no longer see the high sister or hear her voice.

She was back in the sandstorms of Ravence, lost in the fray of the desert's anger. Somehow, she knew in her bones it was angry at *her*. For losing her kingdom, for failing to protect her lands.

For not being enough, alone.

Who even are you, alone?

It was a question she could not answer, and caught in the storm, Elena felt herself failing once more. Her Agni flickered, buffeted down by a wind.

"There are three types of fire, little queen." The high sister's voice rang around her, though Elena still could not see her. "That of the Phoenix—a wild, vengeful power. That of the Serpent—a cold, haughty power. And that of the Goddess—a power that nourishes, provides. To find yours, you must first let go of your grief."

But the sand came on, thicker, gaining weight, gaining speed. Burying her.

Elena tried to fight, but her limbs grew heavy, slow. Maybe she deserved this. Maybe, after all the things she had done, the people she had so recklessly buried alive, she deserved a fate like theirs too. Samson was wrong. They could never absolve themselves of their guilt or of their regret.

Elena sank to her knees and raised her head, her gaze wandering to the heavens—

The eyes of the Goddess seared into her.

Suddenly, the walls bled out. The voices of the priestesses faded. She was drifting alone in an endless expanse with no beginning, no end, an abyss that felt as alive and hungry as her.

You must first let go of your grief.

Her body thrummed, and she knew at once that she was here looking for someone. She began to run. To call. The abyss trembled, awake to her voice, swallowing it in and sending it—where, she could not tell. Only that she could not stop calling, could not stop running. And as time passed in this strange place, she came to the slow realization that she was searching for him. That this abyss was the cathedral of her grief.

"Yassen!"

She ached for him. The abyss ached for him. She and the abyss were one, overwhelmed by the cavernous quality of a grief unburied. He had become a physical reminder, a tightness in her chest, the gritty, popping sensation in her throat. She had tried to ignore it. Tried to push on, to bury her anguish. Even when she had thought she was safe, caught in the immediacy of the present, he still came to her. The smell of wet jasmine reminded her of when they had stood in the garden; a fallen eyelash of when he had touched her cheek and told her, *Make a wish*.

There were others. Her father, her mother, Ferma, Eshaant, Diya, the ones crushed by the wall, the ones buried in the ruins of Rani. Their faces blurred in the dark until they were a bleating ruinous mass crushing her chest.

Perhaps this was the true nature of her sorrow: to be withered and beaten down to the husk until she was a shell. Empty, like the abyss.

You must let go of your grief.

She felt herself slowing. Her throat cracked and her voice came out in a dry croak.

You must let go.

The darkness sucked at her limbs, and she sank into its grasp.

Let go—

The darkness swallowed her. *Let me drown*, she thought gently. *Let me sleep.*

But then she saw it.

A light flaring at the far end.

With the guttural instinct of those prone to surviving, she knew she needed to climb. To grasp the light that now sparked into a flame. Her body felt clumsy, awkward. She focused on the fire and its warmth. She had known a fire like this, she remembered. She had felt it coursing through her veins once, melded it into her bones, spun it into a spear.

And these people, they had seen it too. They had taught her of love, and family, and home.

Who even are you, alone?

"I am them," Elena told the abyss. "I am nothing without them."

And so from deep within, beneath her grief, her anger, her loneliness, Elena called her Agni.

It came roaring. Skating up her spine, zipping through her veins as Elena found herself looking up at the Goddess. It clicked then. The inexplicable pull since stepping onto this land, since wielding Agni itself. It came from here.

From Her.

"Do you see now?" the high sister said as the inferno spun around them. "You were always one of the three."

How had she not seen it before?

Elena fell into the final form of the dance, the Goddess, and the inferno sighed as if it had been waiting all this time. It enveloped her, gently. Colors burst and flared, brilliant and vivid and unlike anything she had ever seen, shades and hues she could not name. She heard the flames clearly for the first time. They told her about the fire thrumming through the temple, and the small, distant ones flaring through the capital. They told her of hunger, and anger, and loss, but beauty too.

The Goddess's inferno sang to her with a song as familiar to her as her own heartbeat. Was this what Samson heard when he commanded the Eternal Fire? A song of his own being? Elena swayed, overcome.

The high sister steadied her and gestured to the Goddess above.

"The Goddess, the Serpent, the Phoenix, their power is everywhere. It is the prana of the universe. The Triagni can bend it to their will. They can even take it."

Elena touched her navel chakra, feeling, for the first time, its power. "What is the Triagni?"

"The three wielders of Agni. The three manifestations of the fire goddesses. You, the one they call Prophet, and the third. You are all connected. Created from the same ancient spark of the universe. The core spark spoiled when the Great Serpent betrayed Her sisters. She imprisoned the Phoenix and put our Goddess into a deep sleep. But there was a consequence. The Great Serpent was imprisoned in a cage of Her own making. You must break that cage for the third to rise and the Triagni to be complete."

Elena turned to the priestess, and as she did so, her vision split. It was as if she was looking at the priestess from two views: through her own eyes, and that of her Agni. She saw the heat centers in her body, the warmth in her veins. Her chakras and nadis were a glowing map. Elena wondered if she could pluck…

The high sister clapped her hands, and the inferno returned to the bowl, morphing back into white sand. Elena blinked as her vision centered. There were no scorch marks on the floor, no ash, no sign of an inferno. It was as if it had never existed.

"Not yet, little queen," the priestess said firmly. "You have only just opened your chakras. Taking prana now will hurt your Agni, but give it time. You will learn."

Her body felt raw and aching, as if she had run for several days and had only now come to a standstill. But even through the fog of her exhaustion, Elena desired the inferno and its luscious power. She wanted it back. "Tell me how."

The Yamni withdrew a shard of obsidian. Frozen within the rock lay a feather as thin as her fingernail and no taller than her pinkie.

"We start with this. Give it to the one they call Prophet, and his Agni can be yours for the taking."

"Wh-what do you mean?"

The priestess smiled, though Elena could see a tinge of sorrow in it. "The Phoenix gifted this feather to our Goddess. It was once a token of friendship, but it will be a weapon for you now. Give it to the Prophet, and you will open a connection between your Agnis. Then you can start to siphon his power."

Elena thought of Samson standing in the rain with her blood on his boots, and she imagined her Agni overwhelming his, suffocating the flames one by one.

"Not siphon," Elena said. "Devour."

The high sister met her gaze then, but at the sound of footsteps, she hurriedly pulled away. A figure stood in the doorway, and the priestesses shrank back at her approach.

"Sura, you did not tell me that we had such an esteemed guest in our midst," the Yumi said. She was tall and limber, with a hooked nose and broad shoulders that made her seem like an eagle perched on a branch, ready to soar. Her hair twisted into a three-layered braid that ended at her feet. She gestured, and it was then that Elena saw the golden talons welded around her fingers. "How ever did you find her?"

Sura, the high sister, did not balk. Her expression remained serene, though her eyes narrowed, and her voice was devoid of its melody from before.

"She is our guest and shall not be harmed, Rhumia."

"I did not plan on it," Rhumia said dourly. "I have merely come to fetch her for the general. Come, little queen."

"General—?" Elena began and stopped. "Was he the one who killed your queen?"

Rhumia studied her, and a small smile tugged at her lips. "No, little queen. I did. He merely provided the blade."

CHAPTER 28

SAMSON

Once more into the storm.
Fight, fight, for the lives of the sea depend on you now.
>   —from a Sesharian poem

Samson sat alone on the canyons overlooking the ruined wall. Below, white-clad figures picked their way over the debris. A wind stirred within the valley, carrying the sickening scent of copper and sweet perfumes. The Ravani were burning their dead again.

Some of the funeral pyres had been burning for hours, but the mourners did not leave until the body had been burned down to the bone. Even then, Samson knew bits of the poor soul would remain behind. Pieces of the skull. Chipped flakes from the femur. When he had worked the Jantari mines, overworked Sesharians would often tip over in exhaustion. Most would not wake up. He had to drag them out of the tunnels and, at the end of the day, burn the bodies.

The Sesharians buried their dead, but the Jantari did not even grant them that solace.

His thoughts, like a wheel journeying down a well-trodden path, returned to Elena. Had she rallied the Yumi troops? Were they flying over the Ahi Sea right now? Was she—and the question surprised him—safe?

He remembered the bruise on her cheek, her blood on his hands. Hot shame flooded him, followed swiftly by anger. She did not deserve his regret. Elena Aadya Ravence had scurried off like a thief in the night after he had given her his forgiveness. He wanted to hate her. But even as he searched the depths of his own spite, Samson found it lacking.

He blamed himself. His misery curdled into a self-loathing that hurt so close to pleasure that he relished it. *Let me hurt,* he thought. He had been weak. Complacent. He had underestimated Elena. The Ravani queen was proud, vain too, but she was not stupid. He should have recognized the distrust in her dark eyes, the distance she had put between them. And now she had soared beyond his reach.

The Burning Queen, alone in her power.

Alone in her misery.

He would not punish Elena. Punishment would only stoke the fire of her rage.

No, he would wait. Like a serpent in the shadows, like the tide waiting for the moon, he would bide his time. And then he would play his hand, as surely as the sea raked the shore.

Samson turned and boarded the waiting tanker.

They followed the Cyleoni guide through the mountain pass. The cold air dug into his lungs, rattling between his ribs like a solid chip. Behind him, Black Scale, Arohassin, and Cyleoni soldiers brought up the rear.

Samson counted silently: They had ninety men to bring down Jantar's treasured northern mines. He tried not to think of the awaiting dark tunnels and their cramped walls ready to close in and suck him down to its bottomless hell.

Ninety men. Three mines. One fire. He whispered it to himself until it became a chant, a melody that mixed with their footfalls and the charged silence of the mountains; until it was all he could think, all that he knew.

Ninety men.

Three mines.

And one fire.

"We're here."

Samson stopped, and the sound of 180 boots stopped with him.

They stood on a ridge that looked down into a snow-carpeted valley. An eerie stillness swallowed all sound. There was neither the whispered scuttle of animals nor the sweet lilt of birdsong.

"I'm detecting no movements." A Cyleoni soldier peered into the valley with his radar. "No heat signatures either. This is it. The tunnel entrance is just below this ridge."

Samson turned to Jaya as she began to set up her board. It had taken three soldiers to haul up her panel, another ten to guide the hovercrates of metal lotuses. As soon as they lined up her crates, she flew forward, a flurry of hums and chirps as she deactivated the hover sensors and began to magnetize the sand.

"How long do you need?"

"Seven hours." She did not look up as she warmed up her panel. "You should get moving. No, put that *there*, you idiot. And you, get your grimy little hands off the lotuses. They're fragile. Mother's Gold. *What did I just say—*"

Akaros drew up beside him as the soldiers scuttled under Jaya's instructions. "Time to get moving, Haku."

Samson froze. He had not heard that name in a long time, and hearing it now brought back memories of the Arohassin, the few joyous ones with Yassen as they discarded their old identities for something stronger, meaner— but mostly, he remembered the pain. Akaros smiled, and Samson hated how his old master could still conjure fear within him, all these suns after.

He brushed past Akaros to gather his soldiers. He saw his own exhaustion reflected in their faces. They had marched for two days now, camping during the day and moving in the night, guided only by a partial moon and their headgear lights, eating stale rotis and hard strips of salted meat.

Once more into the storm, he thought. It was a part of a Sesharian poem, one whose name he could not remember. He gripped the hilt of his urumi and called to his men.

Fight, fight, for the lives of the sea depend on you now.

The entrance led them to old, abandoned tunnels of a pit that had run dry. Patrols rarely ventured down here, but even so, Samson rested his finger on the trigger. Tremors vibrated through the tunnels, shaking loose dirt. With each one, his shoulders tightened, his heart ratcheting up a degree. Even now, in the cold dead of winter, the Jantari were mining. The hours inched by, torturous, as they neared the main chamber that adjoined the old tunnels to the new pit. The air grew thick, musty. Despite his mouth filter, Samson could taste its rank staleness in the back of his throat. He crept forward, pulse gun raised, silencer on, as Chandi brought up his right. Their squads followed.

"Approaching Mine One," Jaya said, her voice tinny and warped in his comms unit. "Arrival in thirty minutes."

"We'll be in position by then," Samson said as they finally reached the fork.

He nodded at Chandi. She paused for a beat, and he felt the unsaid desperation in her stare, the awkward tension between them both, before she rapped her chest in salute. Stiffly, she broke off toward the right with her squad. The rustle of their footsteps soon disappeared.

Akino crept forward, taking the lead with his two men. They ventured down the left tunnel, and after a few moments, Samson and the remaining men followed.

The tunnel began to squeeze in toward the end, the walls crushing down with the weight of the mountains above. Samson swallowed. His arm brushed against the wall, and he jerked away. The wall gave a wet pop, as if the earth wanted to suck him in.

"You all right?" Akino called.

Samson nodded fiercely, blinking sweat from his eyes. *Like clockwork*, he thought. *In and out. In and out.*

After what felt like hours, but was only twenty minutes, they reached a turn. The tunnel forked into three separate chambers. Akino consulted the holomap, its pale blue light washing out his features.

"This is it," he said.

Quickly, quietly, they pressed the explosives against the walls, tucking them in the depressions of shadows. Samson took a step back, assessing. Heat teased down his chest to his fingertips as his Agni stirred with his intent.

Burn, it crooned.

"Go," he commanded. His men hurried down the second tunnel as he stood in the entrance. On his right, he could see the slot where the fire wall lay hidden. The explosives blinked to life.

"Thirty seconds," Akino warbled through the comms.

Samson took a steadying breath, exhaling his vicious tangle of fear and dread. He thought not of the closed, cramped walls of the tunnel, or of the tons of earth bearing down above his head, but of his Agni. It lay waiting, simmering, a blue warmth that bloomed through his nadis and up into his chest and throat. He opened his eyes just a fraction before the explosives were set off.

Flames roared forward, a growling, thunderous force. Samson whipped his urumi and captured that percussive power into a fiery ball. The explosion rippled, trapped, and he trembled as its strength surged through his bones. It wanted to burn. Great Serpent, it wanted to *feed*. Samson felt himself bending to that intense hunger, and a whip of flame flared out, hitting the wall. He grunted and flattened it back into place.

The ball quivered, straining against his hold. Sweat beaded down his forehead as Samson carefully guided the ball and placed it right between the three tunnels. With a snarl, he snapped his urumi, and the ball cleaved in two, rushing down the adjacent tunnels in giddy laughter.

"Now!"

He released his hold and stepped back as Akino activated the fire wall. The fire howled, but then the wall slammed into place, cutting them off from the explosion. Samson stared, his breath loud and deafening in the sudden onslaught of silence. He could feel the flames rushing down the other tunnels, gaining speed, power. By the time the fire reached the main chambers, the Jantari would be powerless to stop it.

"The tinmen are out," Jaya cracked in his ear. "Move your asses."

Alarms began to blare, but all Samson could hear was the wicked, bloody cackle of the inferno and its desire beating through him with a terrible, glorious peal. Despite his fear, he grinned. His men watched, transfixed.

"It's time to hunt," he said.

CHAPTER 29

ELENA

*She is a being of destruction, and the liberator of death. From the dark-
ness she will rise, and to darkness she will descend.*
           —from *Hymns of the Goddess of the Yamuna*

The palace smelled faintly of smoke when she stumbled into the throne
room. Outside, soldiers quickly put out fires in the west wing, but Elena
could feel their presence in her mind's eye now, and she heard their song
of betrayal and destruction as she raised her eyes to the figure on the dais.

She had expected a squarish brute, like the late General Rohtak, or
someone polished and sinister, like Samson, but General Daz of the Moksh
was neither brutish nor menacing nor cruel. He was frail and lank, with
the spindly hands of a scholar. Grey strands glimmered in curly hair that
would have looked unkempt on another man but, on him, looked rather
charming, if not affectionately scruffy.

But his eyes gave him away. Amber colored, with a quick, discerning
intelligence. When she met his gaze, Elena felt herself involuntarily tense
as Daz beckoned her forward.

"Queen Elena, welcome."

She approached cautiously. Behind her, Rhumia and her sister Afira, a Yumi with soft, kind eyes that seemed unfit for a place like this, snapped to a salute.

"At ease, grandnieces," he said.

"The queen," Elena began as she searched the throne room for signs of a struggle. Of course, the queen could have been killed anywhere in the palace. Her courtyards. Her gardens. Her bedroom. Elena shuddered at the thought of waking up in her bed to find her own family looming above, blades ready.

Daz studied her intently. "You disapprove of my methods."

Elena snapped her mouth shut. A part of her screamed to leave this room full of traitors and return to the safety of her desert. But her home wasn't safe either. It was torn into strips governed by petty men, and she would be a fool to leave without fulfilling her promise of raising an army that would make Farin bend.

Elena hesitated, her mind still reeling. "Why have you done this? Why stage a coup?"

"Not a coup. A revolution." He surveyed her. "Are you not trying to lead one yourself, in Ravence and Seshar?"

"I expected to meet a queen. Not her usurper of a brother."

Daz chuckled, though pain skittered across his tired face. "I did not expect you either, little queen, but I can guess why you're here. You seek Moksh's aid in your war. Does it matter if it comes from a queen or a usurper?"

It mattered. It mattered because she was a queen who had lost her throne. It mattered because as she stood here now, another man sought her power, her throne, her people, and they, unwittingly, were already beginning to give what had been hers. But Elena did not say this.

She straightened, feeling the heat of her Agni rush through her nadis.

"What can a usurper offer me? All I see is a burning kingdom."

"You of all people, Elena, know that fire is nothing against a people used to burning." Daz descended from the dais. "You think I killed my sister. You think that I moved for selfish notions of power. No, little queen." He began to circle her, and Elena fought down the urge to flinch. "A week ago, the Yumi of Moksh deposed a ruler who was too proud, too vain, to see the dangers posed against our kingdom."

He gestured out the windows, toward the east. "For a long time, our intelligence has gathered reports of a brewing alliance between Jantar and our pleasant neighbor Mandur. Farin wants to expand Mandur's mining operations and take a share of the ore. In exchange, he will supply naval ships. Ships that Mandur will eventually use in a war against us."

Elena froze. "Are you sure?"

His smile was cutting, sardonic. "My sister asked the same. She believed that Mandur would not turn against us. She insisted we do nothing. She reminded me that it is our history to never draw the first blade. That it is below us. Dishonorable. But I know Mandur. They may not sail tomorrow, or in the next few months, but they will sail within a sun. I do not want a long, tiresome war any more than you do, Elena."

"Then what do you want from me?" she said carefully.

"What you want: Peace. Good fortune. A kingdom that is whole and healthy and strong." He stopped in front of her then, his tawny eyes bright in the dark room. "And that comes with a seat at your council. You can get that for me."

She had come prepared to ask the Yumi for their sword, not to be asked to perform as an administrative liaison. *The Yumi is far too clever for his own good.* "Why do you care about a foreign council?"

"For too long, Moksh has remained removed from the politics of the second continent, and it has hurt us. So I want a say. It is by the Great Mother's grace that She delivered you to my doorstep. You and King Syla will work together to vote to add a new council seat, and you will give it to me. With our shared strength, our combined *threat*, Farin will not dare to send those ships."

His eyes blazed with such fervor, such conviction, that for a moment, Elena saw herself and her own hatred of Farin. But then the moment passed, and she was forced to face the truth. If she appeared before the council with a usurper, what would that make her? She, who had lost her throne to one. She, who struggled to wrest back control of her country. If it was not the hypocrisy that threatened to overwhelm her, it was the depth of her own shame. Her throat burned with it.

Elena looked away. "I—I cannot promise it."

"Just consider—"

"I cannot!" she snapped.

Rhumia bristled, but Daz stayed her with a hand. "Do you and your Prophet not wish Ravence and Seshar freed?"

"What does Samson have to do with this?"

"Surely, you cannot expect freedom without his help."

Elena laughed then.

Loud, unbidden, uncontrollable.

The irony was astounding. She had come to free herself of Samson, to help her kingdom, and yet the Yumi sought only to bring him closer.

Daz stared at her, his confidence slowly fading.

"All of you," she said in between gasps. "All of you think Ravence is gone. Beyond help." She swallowed her laughter, letting it burn down her throat and pool in her stomach until her voice was as acidic and powerful as the vicious Agni thrumming through her veins. "Seshar means *nothing* to me. Ravence is my home. And it does not need a warmongering Prophet to win back its freedom. It needs a queen. *It needs me.*"

Daz said nothing. He seemed to soak in her words, watching her with something akin to uncertainty and disappointment.

"Ravence and Seshar are the same, little queen," he said finally. "You help one, and you'll save the other."

He had not seen her scars. He had not felt the cold rain slicking down her spine as she watched Samson's boots fade away. She thought of Samson, standing there alone in the canyons, the vengeance on his lips.

"I'll believe you when it's true."

CHAPTER 30

SAMSON

Son born of a sorceress, destined for the sea, who will come to save thee?
—from the hymns of the Great Serpent

Alarms wailed through the mines as they raced toward the offload site. Samson lurched flames in front of heat sensors, triggering fire walls to close behind them and cut off the path to the docks. He glanced at his pod. They had less than thirty minutes until his inferno reached the main chambers of the mine, twenty before the Jantari regained control of the safety system. They were running out of time.

"I'm at the transport bay," Chandi said in his ear. "Where the hell are you?"

"We're coming. Ten minutes, max."

Short, percussive sounds shot through their comms, and Samson flinched.

"Was that pulse fire?" He tapped his comms. "What is that? Skeleton? Skeleton? Fuck, Chandi, can you hear me?"

Static noise blared through his ears, then, "We—we've been hit. Seven of them came out of nowhere. One of the transports—"

Her voice cut off again.

Samson swore as something tightened in his chest, fear, worry, desperation bleeding together until he couldn't tell where one ended and the other began. He ran faster.

They raced down the bend, and through the opening at the end, Samson saw pulse fire ricocheting within the transport bay.

"Fan out! Akino, on me!"

He and Akino shot through the opening, diving to the side and hiding behind a deactivated hovercart while his men ran up to the right. Across the floor, Chandi and her squad crouched behind two transport luggers, taking heavy fire.

"Why isn't Chandi shooting back?" Akino said.

"Because of that." Samson pointed at the ore pails at the opposite end of the docking bay. "They don't want to damage the payloads."

Seven Jantari soldiers guarded the ore, shouting commands, razing the wings of the luggers with pulse fire. Chandi hid beside the left engine. *Move*, he thought desperately as the soldiers advanced. *Get out of there.*

But there was nowhere she could escape to. Samson cursed. His mind raced, anguish clawing at his throat like some wild, cornered beast, as he watched one soldier reach for their belt, for something silver and rigid, and he thought, *Slab grenade*, just as he shouted, "Chandi!"

The soldier turned. Chandi cried out. And then Akino fired, a clean shot that cleaved through the soldier's chest. He toppled, the slab grenade bouncing, blinking, and the Jantari ran, shouting "Take cover!" not one thinking to throw himself on the explosive when the grenade detonated.

A searing white light ripped through the bay. Samson felt its heat a moment before it blew, and he called to it, his Agni churning, seeking, borne on the ancient instinct of finding the familiar, and he met the grenade's fire with his own. Blue flames swarmed the shape of the explosion. Curbed it. Samson snapped his urumi, forcing it to become smaller, imposing his will on its hunger. Pain ripped up his bicep, needling into his chest with a sudden abrasiveness that made him gasp. His arm trembled. The explosion wobbled. But his flames held, lengthening into tongues that finally swallowed the grenade's inferno into his own.

Samson collapsed, and the flames dissipated into smoke. His vision swam as Akino barked a command, and the Black Scales who had been sneaking up the end of the bay charged forward, tackling the Jantari. There were cries, blood-soaked moans. *Chandi.* His fear snapped him back, and he forgot his pain, his exhaustion, even his own tired anger against her as he pushed himself to his feet.

"Chandi!" He dodged through the crates and staggered up the ramp, calling her name. "Chandi!"

There was no answer.

Worry, fresh and fetid, churned his chest. *Great Serpent, if she's hurt—*

He staggered toward the lugger, crying himself hoarse. "Chandi!"

"Sam!"

She appeared behind the tail of the lugger, blood leaking from her shoulder, and it took all his strength not to grab her.

"You—you're hit—"

"Get down!"

They slammed to the ground just as a shot skipped off the hull. Akino slashed his urumi through the shooter, ripping off his arm. The man toppled, and Akino made quick work of him after. Only three Jantari remained. Samson's Black Scales pressed forward, and they raised their arms in surrender.

"Smartest thing they've done yet," Chandi said with a grimace.

Her shoulder wept openly, and Samson tore out the bandages from his kit. "Sit still."

"General—"

"Sit still, damn it, or can you no longer take orders from me?" he said, his voice cracking. Chandi fell silent, her eyes flicking across his face as he hurriedly wrapped the cloth around her shoulder.

"General," she began again.

"Chandi, I swear—"

"*Sam.*" Her eyes met his. "The miners. We still need to get them out."

His hands trembled as he knotted the wrap. Below them, Akino activated the hovercarts and guided the pallets into the luggers as Chandi's men, the two who remained, kept watch over the Jantari.

With every second, Samson felt the press of time against his neck.

"Go," Chandi said as the bay doors opened, revealing the purpling dawn. Her bloodstained hand wrapped around his wrist. "Take Akino. He's a better shot than you. And don't take too long. Don't push yourself too hard, too quick. Promise me, Sam." And in that moment, as she looked at him with wide, imploring eyes, her voice a plea, a command, the bitter knot in his chest loosened. Chandi, his fearless commander. The one who knew his fears better than he did and lent him her strength. He nodded, overwhelmed. She let him go and he rushed into the tunnel without looking back, Akino on his heels.

They sprinted to the bunker as the ground started to rumble.

"The mine's collapsing," Samson said, panic spearing down his throat.

He called for his flames and heard in the music of their voices the intoxicating glow of the ore, slowly growing brighter. He could not pull them back now even if he tried.

They descended the tunnel and finally found the metal door of the barracks, the guards gone, their posts abandoned. More concerned about their own lives than the Sesharian ones that lay beyond this door.

"Open the door, Akino," Samson said.

But as seconds slipped away and Akino cursed, floundering with his pod, Samson felt time tighten its noose around his neck. "Akino."

"I can't!" he said. "The Jantari have taken control of the system."

Fists slammed against the door. Muffled shouts, pleas. Samson felt each snip the threads of his heart until he felt frayed, beaten.

"Akino," he pleaded.

But the master of arms was shaking his head, his mouth pinched, eyes red.

Samson swore and tore out his urumi. He'd burn down the door if he had to. He swung the blades, but then pain, sharp and acute, splintered down his arm and he cried out, dropping his urumi. He stared at his hand. Tiny blood spots began to appear. It took him a moment to realize his nose was bleeding, and then, that the cold had returned, that insidious, cruel reminder of his own limitations. He tried to summon a flame, found he could not.

"General," Akino said as the pounding increased.

"Help!" a voice keened behind the door. "Let us out!"

Suddenly, a squeal pierced the air, like metal grating against metal. They whirled around. Two metal gates, one at the entrance of the tunnel from where they entered, the other at the adjoining corridor, slowly began to slide out.

The Jantari were closing off the mines.

"Mother's Gold," Akino swore. He threw himself against the silver door with a roar. Again and again, each attempt as futile as the one before.

Samson could only stare, listening to Akino's choked curses and the muffled cries beyond the door. He could not leave his people trapped. He could not let them die as caged animals. What kind of Prophet would that make him? But he knew, as deeply as he knew his own Agni, that he needed to leave. They had the ore. Their work was done.

The gates groaned. His victory slipping by, second by second.

Samson clenched his urumi, his knuckles turning white. Before he could stop himself, he stepped back. He pushed himself away from the silver door before Akino realized what he was doing. But his officer saw him.

"General," he began. Samson could not meet his eyes.

Every step broke him. The glint of the silver door blinded him. But he could not stay. Freedom for Seshar did not lie within these tunnels; it lay above, in the luggers Chandi kept in wait.

"I'm sorry," he said, his voice full of grief. "We have to go."

Rocks tumbled from the ceiling. One as big as Samson's head slammed between them and split apart.

"I'm not leaving," Akino said.

"We must."

"Look me in the eyes and say that."

But Samson was already turning around, already striding toward the achingly slow door. Perhaps if it closed faster, it would save him the misery of hearing the biting accusation in Akino's voice.

"Samson!"

As he stepped through, a pulse blazed by his head. Samson whirled around in surprise. Akino held the pulse gun, his arm trembling, tears dripping down his chin. Samson should have felt guilt then. He should have felt thick, bitter shame burning down his throat.

But when he finally met Akino's eyes, he found only pity. He could see a sliver of Akino's bloodied cheek, the terror on his face.

"I hope you live," he said.

And then the door rolled shut between them, damning him and those he left behind.

CHAPTER 31

ELENA

Villain, hero, and conqueror is our Great Mother. To behold her is to behold the truth.

—from Hymns of the Goddess of the Yamuna

The Yumi took her back to the Cyleoni tanker, but when their crawler came to a stop, Elena made no move to leave.

She stared out at Kirri waiting alone on the ramp, the temple rising behind him, and felt a sense of deep, utter loss. Humiliation, bare and cruel in its learned normality, lined her bones as if melded to her body. She thought of Samson gloating upon her return, the haughty purr of his blue inferno. She did not have it within her to bend to him again.

"I hope you will consider my offer," Daz said.

She said nothing to this, trapped by her own frayed pride. She could only imagine what Samson would say.

Seeking out rebels and usurpers? Elena Aadya Ravence, you wicked girl. See how you are nothing without us?

She swallowed her anger. "I appreciate your hospitality, General."

She began to reach for the door when Daz, quietly, said, "I loved my sister, but her pride was her undoing. It has been the downfall of many great rulers. But hatred to the point of obsession? It has led to the death of countries, little queen."

Elena stilled. She could feel his keen gaze prickle the back of her head, discerning her base desires. "May the Goddess's Light guide you."

She jumped out before he could say anything more. She boarded the tanker with Kirri, and soon, they rose into the night sky. Elena turned to watch the red glow of the mountains fade into the horizon until the waves swallowed the coast, and Moksh disappeared beyond the sea.

"You do not look happy," Kirri said as he set down a cup of tea. "Did the queen agree?"

Elena looked away, unable to bear the weight of his gaze. "No."

"But your fire. You had visions sent by their Goddess. How could she disagree?"

"Because she is dead."

"*What?*"

Elena told him then of Daz, the coup, the Yamni, and the high sister. She left out her visions of the abyss, the insatiable inferno she had briefly controlled, and the third Agni. By the time she finished, the tea had long gone cold. A pale, grey dawn washed the horizon. In the window, she saw the wavering outline of Yassen's ghost. Before, she would have been alarmed by such visions, thinking herself mad, but now . . . now she gazed at Yassen's watery reflection with a resigned acceptance. Of course ghosts plagued her now.

Kirri sat back in his seat, chewing his lip.

When he finally spoke, his voice was quiet, pensive. "It makes me uneasy to take aid from a usurper. But we will need the Yumi. To attend the council, to end the war, to stop Farin." He sighed. "I'll set our coordinates for Goldor and inform King Syla. Let us discuss General Daz's proposal together."

Elena nodded, when a thought struck her. She reached into her pocket and pulled out the high sister's gift.

"What is that?" Kirri asked.

"I have no idea," Elena said.

It *felt* familiar, like a detail of a childhood story, long forgotten. She could almost taste the memory on her tongue. But when she turned over the disc and saw the inscription on the back, she let out an involuntary gasp.

A. M.

She would recognize those initials anywhere, the tiny loop curling from the foot of the *A*, the slanted lines of the *M*. Her mother had always inscribed her initials on the things she read, the objects she studied.

Aahnah Madhani had held this feather. Had she given it to Sura? Or was it Sura who had first given it to her, then taken it back upon her death?

"Your Majesty, what is it?" Kirri searched her face. "Are you well?"

"This—this…" She set down the feather with trembling fingers. A question, pellucid and sharp, cut through the terrible roar of her heart.

Why did my mother study this feather?

There are stories of the Phoenix giving Her feathers to men, Aahnah had told her. *Tokens that brought much fortune and power to the holder. But a god's gift is a strange thing. It always demands a price, at the end.*

Had her mother paid that price? Was that why she had jumped to her death?

"I—I need air," Elena said, rising, when a soldier appeared at the doorway.

"We just received word from the Sesharians. They've taken the mines."

Kirri asked, "And the ore?"

"They secured fifty payloads, sir."

He sucked in his breath. "Fifty?"

"Fifty." The soldier smiled. "Looks like the Butcher is useful after all."

Elena rocked a little, stunned, as Kirri clucked in approval. So Samson had succeeded in the end. They would hail him a conquering hero and call her a contemptuous queen who would not ally with a usurper. They would crown him, glorify him, all because she would not sell her kingdom. It was horribly, brutally *unfair*. She had the wild, irrational urge then to return to her desert and be alone in her dunes, away from these men.

To be free—like Yassen had wished. Of kingdoms and gods and dreams of power. She closed her eyes, hoping to find a sliver of that peace, but Elena only found her burgeoning longing to hurt. She only wanted to shake these men and wreak the same misery they had inflicted on her and her kingdom.

She could not leave. Queens did not have that luxury. Ravence demanded her to remain, to stand there with resentment barely hidden behind her face, as Kirri asked for their arrival time in Cyleon.

In the curved glass of the tanker, Yassen's ghost smiled sorrowfully.

CHAPTER 32

SAMSON

Gods breed guilty heroes.

—a Sesharian proverb

Samson stood underneath the darkened eaves of the palace courtyards as Syla spoke with his advisors. They had counted the ore. Fifty payloads. *Fifty.* Months' worth of work, of blood and sweat and prayers. He should have felt vindicated—victorious—seeing the respect in Syla's eyes and the quiet unease in his advisors'. They feared him, as they should. But his pleasure was short-lived, his pride blunted by the thick shame that roped his stomach and left burns on his skin.

He could still hear their screams.

Four hundred miners. Four hundred of his own kin, trapped by his own hand. Samson looked up at the bright, clear sky and wished the heavens could reflect at least some of his inner turmoil, but the gods were infinite in their cruelty.

The blue hills of Goldor rolled sleepily into the distance, the emerald palace glimmering in the sunlight with a radiance that made his eyes hurt.

Clouds pillowed the hills. Above them, the infamous shards of Nymia's heart rose into the sky, floating islands of trees so verdant, so lush, it felt as if the earth meant to swallow the sky.

There was an unusual warmth hovering over the palace, trapped in by the sensors above, but Samson found it too moist, too sticky. His eyelids were hot and feverish. He wondered if it was illness—or guilt. Perhaps both.

Syla dismissed the advisors and motioned Samson forward. He came, though much to his chagrin. He felt like a summoned show dog, made to run and hunt and come limping back to parade his kill.

I have enough deaths for the both of us, he thought. An involuntary, high laugh escaped his lips.

Syla gave him a strange look. "Are you well?"

I am mad, Samson thought. *I am the god reborn.*

"I'm all right," he said dryly.

Syla studied him a moment longer before continuing. "I have received word from Kirri. He and Queen Elena are on their way to Goldor."

Samson nodded, though his chest heaved. The very mention of her name brought back a flood of bitterness. She would see past his victory and attack him for leaving the miners, for abandoning his people. *Butcher, butcher, butcher.* If she called him that, Samson did not know what he would do, and the thought frightened him. He pulled at his collar, swallowing his irritation. Skies above, it was too damn hot.

"Have you heard from Farin?" he said, changing the subject, as Chandi and Jaya entered the courtyard. Akaros took his time, his movements slow, relaxed, no doubt already making note of the guards along the hall. Samson felt a cold heat lick the back of his throat as they came.

He searched Chandi's face, but she had said nothing about Akino's disappearance, or the lack of miners, as they flew back to Cyleon. She had merely asked for his urumi. She held it now, the steel pristine and spotless, almost blue in the sunlight.

"Ah, there you are." Akaros stooped into a low, mocking bow. "Your Majesty."

"I never imagined an Arohassin to break his back before a king." Syla regarded him stiffly, his lips thin. "Have you brought your chief architect?"

"Gamemaster." Jaya spoke up. "Though, I haven't officially received my certification from the boards."

"No, I imagine your superiors delayed that when you destroyed Rani."

Jaya fell silent as Akaros heaved a long, dramatic sigh. "Sordid bureaucratic entities hardly deserve to be saved, Your Majesty. They're just buildings, taking up space. Not actual men and women trapped within."

Samson stiffened as Akaros's eyes slid to him. Syla cast him a look, as did the servant boy, as did the others, the guards, the heavens, and Samson felt the invisible ropes tighten around his chest, biting into his skin. He wanted them to stop looking. To stop judging. They hadn't been there, they did not know, could not even begin to understand—

Chandi's hand brushed against his. "Here."

Samson took his urumi, wrapping his fingers around the hilt, and the familiar weight of his sword comforted him. In the twin blades, he caught his reflection: high forehead and sharp cheeks, eyes too blue.

You were born a god, he reminded himself. So why, then, did he feel such pain?

"Have you heard from Farin?" he asked again.

Syla hesitated. His face darkened.

"You have," Samson said. "Tell me what he said."

"Farin asks to bargain," Syla said.

"So then why don't you look happy?"

Syla paused. He glanced at his advisor, who opened another holo. "It's best you see for yourself."

Samson stared in horror as he saw the reports, the images, the fires.

Soldiers raided Sesharian homes on the islands. They flung out clothes, knick-knacks, priceless family heirlooms. A man screamed as a soldier grabbed his child and threw him across the threshold. The child tried to get up, but he wasn't fast enough. The Jantari yanked him by the hair and pulled him away from his family.

They boarded them on trucks. Children only. Wide-eyed and soft-cheeked, many who had only heard of the cruelty of the mines but never seen it for themselves.

"These children must be protected. Shielded from the evils of terrorist influences," Farin said in a news comm. *"It starts from their own homes, from their parents who have been poisoned by such ideologies. Effective immediately, all Sesharian children aged between five and eighteen will be given admittance to mining colonies here in Jantar. They will be given an education in trade and commerce. They will be kept safe. These terrorists believe we are hurting Sesharians, when they themselves killed*

over four hundred brave men and women in the mine attacks. These children are at risk, and it is our responsibility to see to their welfare."

Soldiers marched the streets, keeping back the wailing parents. Some charged the lines, yelling, cursing, and a zeemir flashed, grey and bright in the sun. It came singing down. A woman screamed as it cut into her hip, down her thigh, out her leg. She tumbled, wailing.

Her blood was the same crimson red as the fires.

Samson dropped the pod and stumbled back. He blinked rapidly but the images would not go away. The boy with eyes wide like the twin moons, holding the guardrails of a tanker. The father screaming himself hoarse.

He looked to Chandi, who had gone pale.

"What have we done?" she whispered.

"He cannot do this," Samson said. When the king did not respond, Samson charged forward and gripped his collar. "How can you just stand there!"

The advisor shouted for the guards, but Syla merely met his eyes with a chilled disgust.

"If I recall, Butcher," Syla said, "it was you who left those men and women behind."

Samson staggered as if struck. Syla smoothed his collar, his voice maddeningly calm.

"We have gotten the attention of Farin and the other kingdoms. They will attend the council now. But do you understand Farin's intent? He is coming to the table with blood. And he knows you will react accordingly. You will go blood for blood, but you will lose, Butcher. Because that is what Farin wants. You will only prove that you are the villain he warns us against."

Samson swallowed. "You think I shouldn't react."

"You should," Jaya said.

"You shouldn't," Syla answered.

They stopped and glared at each other, the old king frowning, the gamemaster narrowing her eyes shrewdly, but it was Akaros who spoke first.

"You can't run away from this, Sam. Not this time. Even gods have to fall on their own swords."

Samson knew that look in his eyes, that astute calculation and withered pragmatism, and suddenly he felt like a boy again. Lost and angry. Willing to do anything if only to stop hurting.

"I think it's time we focus on amrithi," Akaros said.

"Akaros," Jaya warned.

"Amrithi?" Syla asked.

"Sam," Chandi called.

But all he could hear were the miners' desperate pleas for help and Akino's cry of anger. Guilt, black and shameful, furred his throat like a parasite.

Samson swallowed. "No. Not yet. We haven't exhausted all our options."

At this, Akaros smiled, slow and cold. "You have, Haku. And one of them was Yassen. Why do you think I sent him to you?"

They sat in a courtyard underneath stars that shone like uncut gems. Yassen remained silent and still as Samson asked him about the special steel, but when he spoke, his voice came out rushed.

"No," he said. "My father never knew anything about the steel."

He was lying, but Samson loved him enough to accept it.

Samson knew Akaros loved to play mind games, and he remembered the torture he had endured at the cost of his shrewdness. The cost Yassen had ultimately paid.

"Yassen's father never found the amrithi. Yassen didn't know where it was either," Samson said, his voice tight, but the look on Akaros's face made him stop.

He thought then of Elena escaping through the tunnels, of the presence she had felt. His Agni always grew more aware whenever he traveled into the heart of the Sona Range. *A metal so fine it could cut through steel.*

He had spent suns trying to find it. Building paths underneath Chand Mahal, sending free Sesharians to work his tunnels and reassuring himself that it was better than the mines. That when they returned, they were still free men. And once it was done, he would journey through the dark, because if they found it, when they found his godhood...well.

Then the world would fear Seshar.

"Farin is getting closer every day," Akaros said. "Better we find it first than him."

"How close are they?" Samson said.

Akaros smiled at his eagerness.

His anger came, lightning fast, and when it struck, its sheer power frightened even him. Samson tucked his trembling hands behind his back and forced himself to remain calm before his old master.

"How close are they?" he repeated.

"What is amrithi?" Syla demanded.

"A legend," Chandi said, a warning in her eyes. "There's nothing there, right, Sam?"

"Oh, give up the hoax, Commander," Akaros said.

"You never told me about this," Syla said, turning to Samson.

"I wouldn't trust anything that comes out of the Arohassin's mouth," Chandi spat.

Akaros laughed. "Would you rather waltz into a death trap of a council? Farin won't let you out of there alive. Not unless you go with a royal. But yours is missing, isn't she?"

"Farin could not lock me up if he tried."

Samson froze at that voice. He turned, heart rushing to his throat, to see Elena striding toward him.

CHAPTER 33

ELENA

Never trust the happy hero. They are a myth.
—a Sesharian proverb

Samson was staring at her, his face haggard, his mouth slightly agape as if he had come up for air and sucked in water. Inwardly, Elena smiled. She relished his displeasure, though something chafed within her ribs. It hurt to see his surprise.

I would never abandon my people to you, she thought. Had he underestimated her so poorly?

"Syla." She turned away from Samson with more force than she intended. "Could you tell me why we're discussing bargains with Farin?"

"Farin wants to call the council," Syla said.

Elena stilled. Her heart, which had already begun to double its pace at the sight of Samson, now thundered. "It's a trick."

"I assure you, Elena, it is not," Syla said with a bitter smile. "Your men succeeded in destroying the mines, and we've forced Farin to come to the table—in a way. Farin comes with his own . . . terms."

"What are they?" When no one answered, Elena found her gaze returning to Samson. He avoided her eyes. "What did you do?"

He said nothing for a long moment. She could sense his Agni fidgeting, as if it was crumbling within itself. Elena saw now the deep shadows that carved hollows beneath his eyes and cheekbones. The sallowness of his skin. There was almost something *insubstantial* about him—like a great oak withered down to a stalk, shaking in the wind. She almost reached out to touch him, but then Samson met her gaze, and she stopped.

"We couldn't save the miners," Samson said. His voice was barren. "We had to escape ourselves, so we left them. Four hundred of them. They died from either the fire or the quakes. Now Farin's rounding up Sesharian children into camps as punishment."

Elena stared at him, horror, black and thick, pressing her voice into a whisper. "Why couldn't you stop the fires?"

Samson flinched. His lower lip trembled, whether in anger or sorrow, she could not tell.

"You don't think I tried?" he said, and she heard the familiar sting of his words, the sharp edge of his ire that she had come to know intimately. She rose to it. At least this she knew, not the broken, haunted man he pretended to be. Violence and pain fed his Agni, as much as grief fed hers.

"You can control the Eternal Fire, but you can't stop infernos of your own making? Mother's Gold, Sam! What were you thinking? They were people, your people! And you buried them." She had hoped that the tragedy would happen only once, that they would learn—amend—but her failure in Magar had only been doubled. Warped into something more sinister, more treacherous. She whipped around to Chandi, who stood with a stiff chin, her eyes narrowed. "Where is Visha? What happened to having the most cunning strategist in the world?"

"It is a tragedy all around, Elena, and we are all sorry for it," Syla cut in. "But Farin is on the move, and it would be a disservice to those men and women if we stand around bickering and pointing out each other's faults. However deep they run." He cast a glance at Samson. Elena found her gaze wandering past Samson, to the man and woman who stood like shadowed wings.

"And who are you?"

The bearded man smiled. "Well, we're the Arohassin, darling."

Instantly, she dropped her hand to her waist, her palm warming, heat razoring up her spine as she called for the guards, for Syla to step back, but the old king shouted and Chandi yelled at her to stop.

Samson stood, watching her. And then he laughed.

High and thin, like a madman.

His laughter cut through the courtyard with the force of an arrow splitting through the unexpecting throat of a hare.

Elena froze. They all did, save for the bearded man and the woman. The man smiled with a degree of self-pleasure that made her skin crawl. The woman watched Samson with a crude fascination as if he were a specimen to be analyzed. She did not know who to fear more.

"Gods, Elena, you have missed so much." Samson grinned, his eyes dead like stagnant pools of festering waters. "Thanks to your little rendez-vous with the Yumi, I had to seek help from them. Speaking of. Where are your feared warriors?" He turned, calling. "Oh great madams, where are you? Come quick! Our queen is afraid of our visitors."

Elena straightened, hands curling into fists. "That's enough."

"Come, come! We need your help. Apparently, we're shit at protecting our own."

"I said that's enough!" she snarled.

Samson whipped around, lightning quick, and she flinched at the sudden movement, hands rising in defense. His eyes fell to her palms. Guilt flickered across his face before he killed it like an ember smothered. "So you failed too."

She bristled at his tone. "Not quite."

"Did the Yumi agree to show for the council? Did they pledge help?" Syla asked. The Arohassin woman perked up at this, though she remained quiet.

Elena hesitated. Samson was watching her with a new alertness, and she wondered if he felt it too. The feather warming in her pocket. She withdrew it and held it up.

"Their high priestess gave me this."

"What is that?" Syla drew closer. "A feather?"

"I believe it's a powerful token," she said and remembered the high sister's instructions.

Give it to the one they call Prophet, and his Agni can be yours for the taking.

Slowly, she held it out to Samson. The feather grew warmer as he approached, and at the same time, she felt her Agni snap alert. A sudden hum thrilled through her bones, as if her blood had awakened, heightened. And with it, an irritational fear. It spidered down her spine, hooking its long legs into her ribs, and pulled slowly. She ignored it.

"Take a look," she said.

Samson reached for the feather.

CHAPTER 34

SAMSON

Such is the tragedy of gods. They are not aware of their own mortality.
—from the diaries of Priestess Nomu of the Fire Order

This was a kind of pain that had no name.

Samson's chest heaved, fire lacerating down his ribs. He crashed to the ground, writhing, screaming, clutching his chest as the token slipped from his hand.

The others were shouting, but Samson could not hear, a roar rising in his ears as something cold and sharp slid between the notches in his spine. *Not again.*

Panic closed his throat. He had the sensation of being squeezed, like a lemon, wrung and wrung until he had no more juice to give.

Fire, he tried to say, but no sound came out of his mouth. He needed fire. Warmth. Couldn't they hear?

His vision swam. He was no longer in the courtyard of the king, but back in the dark, dank tunnels, the walls wet and alive around him.

The darkness laughed in a voice painfully familiar. He cried, kicked, and then he was hurtling through nothingness, the wind tearing at his face, the laughter rising—only to smash into the ground.

Around him, ore glittered like the stars untouched. A long and silver object snaked across the chamber. At its center, a fire burned.

Black.

Smokeless.

He tried to run. Instinct told him that if he looked into the black fire, if he so much as saw the face that lay ruined within, it would ruin *him*.

The stones and gems around him trembled as the great silver snake reared its head, and the Great Serpent looked upon him.

"Son of sea," She sang.

The fire, he wanted to warn Her. *Look out for the fire!*

But it was rising, forming into a figure with unnaturally long, terrible black limbs. It struck the side of the god. The Great Serpent hissed, roiling back, and the figure was not a figure, but a bird, a Phoenix, and it gave a great cry worth eons of grief and rage as it dove for the Serpent's throat.

Stop! he cried. *Stop!*

But the gods would not listen, and the shadows did not care. They rose around him. Swallowed him, and he was drowning again. Hands clutched his throat and gold eyes laughed above him.

For a moment, he could see nothing. Then the lights rushed back, and he felt arms pulling him up and up. A familiar face.

Elena shook him, and he could see her lips shape his name, but he couldn't hear her voice. *Help me*, he pleaded. A bone-deep chill slithered through his body. *Help me, please!* But his voice caught in his throat. He clawed his neck, his torso, wishing for heat, for warmth, but his Agni would not come. There was only the piercing cold. Only a wide, gaping hole, and the waiting darkness beyond.

CHAPTER 35

ELENA

The Phoenix, the Goddess, and the Serpent. All bound by the same fire. All damned by it.

—from *A Critique of the Ancient Gods*
(note: debunked by historians)

Ravence and Seshar are the same, little queen.

Samson sagged in her arms, his face sweaty and grey as his body grew alarmingly cold.

You help one, and you'll save the other.

Around her, Syla called for the medics as Chandi shouted for them all to step back, give him air, let him breathe. But Elena could tell he was not breathing, that touching the feather had snapped something within him.

"Sam," she whispered.

Hands pulled at her. Chandi, barking at her to get up and make way for the medics. Elena was pushed away. She had never seen the commander so panicked, her eyes wide with violent desperation as she grabbed Samson's hand and begged him to hold on, to fight.

226

Fight what? she wanted to ask, but her question caught in the frays of her chest as medics rushed past her. Syla stood to the side, his mouth slack. Even the Arohassin woman looked alarmed, her knuckles white around her stylus. Only the bearded man seemed untouched by the chaos. He stood still with the gravitational quality of a boulder in a sandstorm. His dark eyes met hers.

Fire, he mouthed.

Elena blinked, and then she understood. She pushed through the guards and medics.

"Get away," Chandi snarled.

"I can help him," Elena said, though she did not know how, not really, only that something within her too had shifted when he took the feather from her palm.

"He needs fire, Chandi," she said, pitching her voice low to calm the commander. "Let me help him."

Chandi hesitated, but then Samson let out a soft gasp, and she shuddered. She closed her eyes. Her face rippled with emotions Elena could not read, but when she opened her eyes, there was a steeliness there that made Elena balk.

"If you kill him, I swear I'll cut you down right here."

Chandi unspooled her urumi with a hiss. She moved aside, hovering close so that when Elena stepped forward, she could still see the malicious glint of her blade.

On the hover stretcher, Samson shivered violently. His eyes fluttered, unseeing.

Too much water, Elena thought.

Too much greed, too much ambition. Samson Kytuu was a man of war, and he had already razed the earth with his merciless inferno. How many more would die? How many more would he bury?

Slowly, Elena placed her hands on his chest.

She still remembered the cruel heat of his fire. The cold touch of the rain as he pressed his hands around her throat and told her that she was nothing without him.

Who even are you, alone?

Her fingers trembled.

Better to let him die now. Better to stop him before all her people fell to his sordid prophecies and his bloodletting. Would it not be a mercy to kill a man before he became a monster?

His Agni can be yours for the taking.

Her own Agni trembled. It felt like a fissure had run through her body, and she could still feel the afterquakes vibrate through her bones. Of course she wanted to stop him, but—but Elena had not expected this. She had only wanted his fire, and though she did not know what exactly *that* entailed, she had not wished this. As Samson wheezed, as his face greyed and his spittle dripped down his lips, something raw and hurt twisted within her. She thought of the burned girl and how Samson had healed her wounds. She remembered how her people had bowed to him and forgotten their squabbles if only to gaze upon his fire. Though she saw Samson Kytuu as the Butcher, they saw him as their Blue Star. The man whom they loved, if not feared, for his terrible power. Allowing him to die now would only make him a martyr. And what then would happen to Ravence? To Seshar? If she killed hope, was she not as monstrous as him?

Elena did not know if they could truly achieve peace for Ravence and Seshar. Only that the man who could possibly help save them both was now dying in her arms.

She pressed her palm against his chest, heat fanning from her hand. Her flames spread across Samson's body, wrapping around his arms, torso, and legs. Elena closed her eyes and sought his Agni, following its plea deep down to the spark. To the hidden place the high sister had shown her. She felt the ghost of it, like shadows thrown on the wall by firelight, and heard its alarmed hiss, but she could not find it.

Beneath her touch, Samson trembled. A groan escaped his lips. Chandi shouted something again, but her voice seemed to come from far away as Elena's world contracted and sound seeped out. His Agni evaded her. She could feel its vibrations, the resonance of its power shrinking beneath her touch, but as she chased it to its source, she found only darkness. And the cold.

It came at her with claws.

A chill crept up from where her palms touched his skin, up her wrists, her elbows, biting into the warm vibrance of her own Agni. Elena gasped. The cold reared up her spine, into the base of her neck. She felt her throat close, her concentration break.

Samson moaned, and her flames flickered.

"Come on, you brute," she hissed beneath her breath. Her nails dug into his chest, hard enough to leave marks. "Work with me."

Her flames waned, weakening as fatigue washed over her, but she pressed on, her hands shaking with effort.

"Sam," she pleaded.

The name, soft like a prayer, escaped her lips without thought. And his Agni heard.

She felt it flail, and she surged her Agni forward, fueled it with heat, with desire, with the one desperation they both knew too well.

Endure.

Her Agni rolled into his, and she felt it then: the clear life force of it, irradiant and extant. Suddenly, Samson gasped. His body knifed up, and before Elena could react, his hands closed around her throat, his blue fire searing her face.

She cried out, falling on her back as Samson pinned her down.

His eyes were wild and crazed, his face twisted into a snarl. Her vision split then. She saw Samson above her, choking her, and she saw him as her Agni did. A deep, beating radix of power so bright, so vicious, his chakras and nadis glowed with the terrible force of it. But there was a darkness at the root of him. A toxic waste, slowly feeding. And when she peered, it looked back with golden eyes of reckoning. *Goddess*, it whispered. *I will hurt you for what you took from me.* And then she was back in the courtyard, pinned beneath him. Helplessly, Elena beat against his hands. Someone yanked Samson by the shoulders, but he still would not budge. With one last effort, Elena reached up and slapped him, hard.

Samson gasped, head whipping to the side. Whatever had taken over him passed as he fell back and met her gaze, recognition and alarm flashing across his face.

They stared at each other for a moment, drenched in sweat and horror, before she rasped, "What. The. Hell?"

"I—I'm sorry," Samson said. His eyes were wide and filled with a terror Elena had never seen him wear before. "I felt—I thought—you were trying to kill me."

The bearded man wiped blood from his mouth where Samson's shoulder had connected with his chin. "She's the reason you're still alive."

Samson blinked, as if only now realizing the people around them, the chaos that had ensued. He touched his chest, then his lower belly. When he opened his hand, a blue flame curled up, and he stared at it, amazed.

"How——" he began.

Chandi helped him up, her voice small and strained. "That's enough now. You need to rest."

But Samson turned to Elena, reaching out to help her stand.

"Get away from me," she spat. Her throat throbbed. It hurt to speak. She scrambled back as Samson watched her with something akin to heartbreak.

This too felt familiar, this hurt too much.

"I didn't mean to, Elena, *please*, let me help," he said.

Syla stepped between them. "Your commander is right, Butcher. You need rest. All of us do. Come."

He offered his arm to Elena, and she took it. Samson did not try to stop her, though she felt his eyes and the weight of his guilt. When they began to leave, he called out to her.

"Thank you," he said.

She ventured one glance back.

Too blue, she thought. *A curse. A curse that is now mine.*

"It's too late to go back now," she said and turned away. It was an insufficient reply, but it was the only one Elena could give. Because she did not know if, by saving Samson and the darkness within him, she had now damned the world.

CHAPTER 36

SAMSON

*There comes a time when a man must fold his morals into the pockets of
his heart and forget its existence.*
        —from the diaries of Priestess Nomu of the Fire Order

He swam through the hellscape of dreams. They morphed without
pattern, without reason. He saw his mother and sister calling for him on
the beach. Shadows waned around his feet. One rose with eyes of gold,
and he screamed for them to run when hands pulled him into the dark
waters of the sea. Salt water rushed up his nostrils and into his mouth,
stinging his throat.

He coughed out sand.

The desert stretched before him in its cold austerity. Dunes upon dunes
that seemed to grow toward the heavens. They moved with the awful
gradual force of plates shifting beneath the earth's skin, bearing toward a
collision that could not be stopped. And there in the bowl of the dunes,
the black figure stood. White fire wreathed its arms like armor and formed
a crown upon its head.

At the sound of his gasp, it began to turn, and Samson felt the awful, crushing certainty that if he saw its face, the dunes would swallow the moons.

He scrambled back, and out of the corner of his eye, he detected movement. Another figure. Another shadow barely real. But he knew that flickering face. He had seen it before in his memories, in the chambers of his heart he dare not enter. Samson called to it, and it turned to him with eyes of gold.

He snapped awake. Someone startled beside him, and in the irritational dregs of his dream, Samson thought it was the black figure. He yelled, reaching for his urumi, but his waist lay bare.

"Easy!" Chandi said.

"I—I thought—" he gasped. Visions swam before him. The figure stood behind Chandi and smiled at him, but then he blinked, and it was gone. Samson sagged into his bed.

"Water," he rasped.

Chandi poured from a pitcher, and he accepted the glass with a trembling hand. She watched, quiet, but he could feel the weight of her thoughts, see the tension laced in her shoulders, and he remembered his cold indifference toward her. It seemed so worthless now.

"I'm sorry, Chandi," he said.

She started, surprised. "Wh-what do you mean?"

"When you went behind my back with the Arohassin, I couldn't stand to look you in the face, but...I—I was wrong. You've only ever done what's best for us. For Seshar. For me, and I have treated you unkindly for it." He met her eyes. "I was blind, Chandi. I've been blind to many things, and I—I..." He trailed off, looking away. When he spoke again, his voice was choked. "I'm sorry."

"Oh, you fool." She hit his arm, her eyes wet. "I know I'm a better fighter than you."

He laughed, a crushed, choking sound. "They will need you. After what I've done...I don't know how to face them. Akino, he—he shot me when I left. When I saw his eyes, there was so much betrayal. So much disappointment. I—I have never hated myself more than in that moment. And now Farin, those children." He stopped, his chest twisting into an excruciating tangle of shame. "I tried to protect us all, and I have only damned us more."

"Then defeat Farin and earn your forgiveness." Her voice was hard, and he winced at the harsh truth of it. "You cannot wallow, Samson. You have not earned that pleasure. *We* cannot afford it. For better or for worse, the Great Serpent chose you to see through Her purpose. So fight until we are free, and maybe then you'll earn forgiveness from the dead. We must go to the council. *You* must face Farin and kill him."

He chuckled humorlessly. "You would have made a ruthless Prophet."

"I know. Perhaps that is why I was not chosen," Chandi said dryly, but then her face softened. "Do you remember the day you saved me?"

How can I forget? He remembered the damp smell of the sea as he had stood at the docks of Rysanti and watched the new islanders be brought in. One lagged. Dragged behind, really. Chandi had hissed and screamed and punched the overseers. He, the lone Sesharian officer, had been called in to calm her. "You spat at my feet as soon as you saw me."

"You were dressed in Jantari grey, what else did you expect?" she said, smiling. "I thought you were a rustblood. But then when that Jantari began to drown me, you pulled him off. You took his blows." She touched his right arm where the zeemir had cut into his bicep. "You spilled your own blood in the sea for me, Samson, and that's when I knew. That's when I recognized the fire in your eyes. You suffered that day and suffer today because you will do anything to see us all free. Your life is not your own, but ours."

She cupped the nape of his neck and brought their foreheads together in a traditional Sesharian salute.

"Do not question who you are or why you are here. You are our Blue Star. You are the one they call Butcher. Make them fear, and then bring us home."

Samson swallowed. He did not deserve such loyalty. But he loved her all the more for it.

Slowly, he reached for his urumi curled by his bedside. Chandi helped him stand, and he looped it around his waist. Its weight anchored him. Chandi was right. He could not wallow. Self-pity was a luxury for those who knew nothing of endurance. And he had endured worse horrors than most kings, seen the black face of death far more than most soldiers, been given a curse and turned it into power.

"There's someone I need to see," he said.

"Elena."

He nodded. "Do you think she will forgive me?"

Chandi sighed. "The queen is wary, but she is not a fool. She saved you for a reason. Maybe that is worth something."

"Well, I haven't made things easier for her," he muttered bitterly. *What a fool I have been.* They were on the same side, fighting for the same hope. No matter their differences, in this he and Elena were the same.

They would do anything to see their homes freed.

"Where is she?"

He found her among the floating shards. Great cathedrals were carved into the floating formations, each symbolizing an aspect of Nymia's heart. Beneath the golden arch of Nymia's Righteousness, Elena spoke with Syla. An ancient tree with face-shaped leaves shook at his approach, and the rulers turned.

He had prepared his remarks, ran through them multiple times, but standing before her now, underneath her scrutiny, Samson flailed for the words.

"Hello," he said weakly.

Elena looked to Syla, who departed without a word or so much as a look at him.

"How are you?" he ventured once they were alone.

"Alive." She cocked her head. "And, oh look, so are you. I wonder why."

"Elena." He started forward, then stopped. He held her urumi in his hands, the same one she had left behind before her journey to Moksh. She noticed but made no move to retrieve it. They stood there for a moment, entombed in their own silences, her blade in his hands and his mark on her throat. It had been easier to talk to Chandi; why not her, then?

Samson looked away. He still remembered the bitter acidity of her betrayal. It had struck him deeper than most, and it maddened him, for he knew not why.

"Th-this is yours," he said finally.

Elena stared at the urumi, and he could not tell if she regarded the blade as a hissing snake or a peace offering. She took it carefully, examining the silver tongue, the horned hilt.

"You know, I never understood why you preferred the urumi above all else," she said as she ran a finger delicately along its spine. "But when I was with the Yumi, I learned that sometimes it's not the blade, it's the symbol. The fight it represents. You could just as easily summon flames with a slingsword as with an urumi, but you chose the urumi because it hisses like your Great Serpent. Strikes twice as fast." Her hand curled around the hilt. "Do you think those miners found comfort, then, that their death came from an urumi rather than a zeemir?"

He absorbed her jab, found himself deserving of it. "Better to not have died at all," he whispered.

Her eyes searched his face. Did she see his remorse? His shame?

"Yes," she said softly after a moment. She hesitated, and something quick and sharp flickered in her eyes before her mouth twisted and she looked away. "But someone once told me that there is no room for regret, or those who feel it. So, tell me, Butcher. Do you still want vengeance, or will I have to leave you behind?"

He blinked in surprise to hear his own words repeated back to him. *Skies above, did I really say that?* It felt like a lifetime ago. But then, they had lost Ravani that day, not Sesharians, and he chided himself for caring about the distinction.

"I'm a fool," he blurted. "I—I did not mean—"

Elena gave him a pitiless smile. "Oh, I think I know what you meant."

She looped her urumi and hung it on her shoulder.

"Wear it like a belt," he said suddenly.

Elena paused, her hand on the hilt.

"May I?" He stepped closer and unhooked the urumi from her shoulder. Carefully, he wound his arms around her, his hands brushing against the curves of her waist and then back around, sliding the blade into the hilt. His eyes met hers. She was so close that he could see the gold flecks in her irises. The small birthmark hidden within the arch of her right brow. *Funny,* he thought. He had never noticed it before.

"Your hands," she said slowly, "are on top of my crotch."

Samson jerked away, heat rising to his cheeks as he quickly clasped his hands behind his back. "N-now you look like a proper warrior."

Elena looked down at the urumi wound around her hips. "I think I'll cut myself if I move."

"Ah, but that's the beauty of it." He patted his waist. " 'A beltless warrior is a blind warrior.' You can't relax when you wear an urumi like this. It keeps you alert. Whether for an enemy or—" He hesitated, then rushed her. Elena immediately snapped back, her urumi slashing upward to fend off his advance. The cut was slow, lazy. She still had a lot to learn. Samson sidestepped and whirled around, catching her from behind, his hand pressing into the small of her back. "—a friend."

But then she did something unexpected. She fell into his instep, her elbow lancing into his side as a red flame curled up from her shoulder and launched into his face. Samson cried out. He grasped the flame and spun on his toe, using momentum to throw the flame against the arch. It hit the stone and hissed. Samson steeled himself, his blue flames crackling, black spots already creeping into the edges of his vision. He still wasn't strong enough to conjure his Agni fully. But then the red flame sputtered and died with an undignified gasp.

"You have your urumi, I have my dance," Elena said. Samson turned to face her. The urumi coiled around her feet like a silver serpent. "To each their own."

He sensed the flare of her inferno before it appeared. Elena called her Agni, and as flames darted down the blade, he felt his Agni *soar*.

It was as if he had been plodding through his life in a dream and only now, with her flames rushing down his urumi's twin, did he know the true feeling of being *alive*. For a brief, aching moment, his Agni flared, brilliant and awake. In his mind's eye, he saw their connection. And he followed it to the life force of her inferno, the bloodied radiance of crimson and the heat of sand. The taste of salt and earth. It ran deep, deeper than he had thought, into the very soil of this land and ones beyond, in the hidden volcanoes of the sea to the mountains kissing the skies. His heart quickened as the potency of her Agni licked up his spine. His jaw hurt. He felt a giddiness and an ancient terror, one laid into the very marrow of his bones, and he thought, with an awful clarity, *I have done it*.

He had linked his Agni to hers.

Unknowingly, she had given a spark of her own Agni to his, which meant...

Amrithi.

Samson wobbled. Elena turned to him with a smile as she gazed at the urumi, but her smile quickly fell.

"Your eyes," she gasped.

He touched his face. "Wh-what?"

"They're blue on blue."

Your eyes are too blue, his mother had said. *It is a curse, and a god-given gift. A death wish, Ruru.*

His name used to be Ruru. Little Ruru. Prince Ruru. Little Prince Ruru. His mother had different variations, plucking the name from the air with a smile as white as the beaches beyond their home.

"Samson," his father had said, "is more suitable. He won't be singled out by the older Jantari boys."

And so he became Samson. Studious Samson. Careful Samson. Don't-Push-Back-Against-the-Jantari Samson.

But to his mother, he was always Ruru. Mischievous Ruru. Brave Ruru. My sweet, beautiful Ruru.

He treasured that name. Kept it close to his heart, like the lion-heart seashell his father had found for him.

"Ruru," he'd whisper into the shell.

"Ruru," it would sing back.

At the state-sponsored school, he went by his Jantari name. His official government name, according to the records. The Jantari preferred rigidity and tradition, and Samson, his father had said, was a name that met their demands.

Samson was not the only one with two names. In school, he rubbed shoulders with other well-off Sesharian boys who had replaced their family names with a Jantari one. Parsho, Jai, and Ramora became Parson, Jayson, and Ramson. Son of the father, so it was easier to trace their lineage and their chains. Their Jantari teachers pattered off their names while the boys struggled with the harsh consonants, the strange letters, the crude signals of a language that, merely decades ago, had lived in a different country, across the sea.

"I don't like my name," Samson had told his father one day.

"It's a fine name, Sam." His father hated abbreviations but, for Samson's sake, allowed it. "See, this is how you spell it. S-A-M. Easy."

"But Ruru is better," he protested.

"But Ruru is different." His father's hand lay heavy on his shoulder.

"And we need to fit in right now, Samson. We can't afford to look foreign. Do you understand?"

Samson nodded, though he did not understand, not really. When his father had left to meet with the Jantari official who, once again, offered to buy their home, his mother slipped him her white smile.

"My little Ruru, how was your day?"

And he'd answer in a conspiratorial whisper: "As fresh as the sea."

When his eyes had first turned completely blue, his mother took him to the temple. She made him sit before the dais as she lit incense and placed offerings at the feet of the serpent god.

"Great Serpent," she sang, "have you come to free us?"

She consulted the scrolls. As the high nagini, his mother had access to all the temple vaults—the same ones the Jantari pleasantly but firmly offered to watch for her.

She flipped through scrolls, books, maps, and pictures while he sat, nursing a headache and a terrible itch on his back that would not go away, no matter how hard he scratched.

When she finally found her answer, she descended into an uncharacteristic silence.

"What's wrong, Mama?" he asked.

She turned to him, her eyes wide, reverent, her face pale with fear.

"My sweet Ruru," she said. Her hands shook as she touched his shoulders, his cheeks. "My little warrior. One day, you will set the Great Serpent free." She pressed her forehead against his, her voice dropping to their familiar conspiratorial whisper. "But you must keep this a secret. A secret between us. Do you understand?"

Samson touched his eyes and then pressed his fingers against her brows in a solemn promise.

"I swear by the Great Sea," he answered.

"Good." She smiled, wide and bright. "Now, let me show you how to hide them."

"It'll go away," he said.

Samson leaned his face into the fire. The flames curled up, kissing his jaw, his cheeks, his lips. The heat brushed against his face, gentle like a lover, but he needed it to be a monster.

"More wood," he instructed.

Elena threw more wood into the pit, stoking the flames. They jumped onto the dry branches instantly, spitting and hissing. The heat intensified, but Samson did not pull away. He leaned into the fire, the heat pressing against his face and, like his mother had said, chasing away the blue.

Fire and water create the most beautiful dance, she had said. *But they will always devour each other in the end.*

He sat like that for a long time, letting the flames erase the blue, the curse, until his sclera were white once more.

Elena watched as he palmed a red flame. It curled around his wrist and then stretched to embrace his individual fingers. He tried to change it. To make it blue, more like him, foreign and strange, a drop of the sea in the ocean of this greenery, but the flame merely pulsed. It did not shed its likeness.

"What was that?" she asked.

He hesitated. He still did not know where he stood with her, if she forgave him or trusted him. Samson curled his hand and killed the inferno.

"You saved me, Elena, when you could have easily left me for dead. Why?"

Her mouth tightened, but her eyes gave her away. Desperation and pain. The same as him.

"Because I need you to save Ravence," she said.

"And I need you to save Seshar," he said.

Silence descended upon them, heavy with the weight of truth. They regarded one another, stunned by each other's honesty, wary of the secrets they still held. Finally, Samson found the strength to break the stillness.

"Elena," he said, his voice a plea.

She met his gaze.

"I'm tired of fighting you," he said.

"Me too," she whispered.

"So fight with me," he said. Blue flames fanned from his fingers, wrapping around his wrists like bracelets. Like shackles. "Tell me how I can make things right."

Elena turned away, and he made no further move to persuade her. The choice was hers and hers alone. He wanted her to know that. Their alliance could be either a blessing or a death sentence, but she would decide its outcome. It had taken dying in her arms for him to understand that he could not force Elena to do anything; that her friendship, her Agni, came only when she could control it.

Freedom for Ravence, freedom for Seshar, was one and the same. It was the same azadi. The word sent a shiver through him. It was a song his soul ached for. The song he wished for all his countrymen to sing. Azadi, azadi, azadi.

Finally, Elena answered, her voice tired and quiet. "First we go home. We see to our people. Then we go to the council and make our demands."

You must face Farin and kill him.

He hesitated. Elena turned to him, and he thought, *But I must avenge the dead.*

"Are you with me?"

Flames licked down her fingers, and he met Elena's gaze over the fiery light of their inferno: red and blue, fire and water, the desert and the sea.

He could do both. Seek vengeance and peace. Bring freedom and horror.

He grasped her hands, his flames lacing around her wrists, joining them.

"I'm with you," he said.

CHAPTER 37

ELENA

The destruction of the Five Desert Wars between Ravence and Jantar became so great that the council finally moved into action. The Treaty of Borders is perhaps its greatest achievement, second only to its execution of the traitorous Karven king. The treaty states no ruler shall invade another's borders without consequence. But King Harrow of Jantar shrewdly found a loophole. Seshar was not a kingdom. It had no such protection. So Seshar fell, thanks to the shrewdness of a king and the cowardice of others.

—from chapter 43 of The Great History of Sayon

With trembling hands, Elena loosened her scarf. Faded bruises braided her neck, though the ointment had lessened the pain, and the operation had bleached the color.

"It will disappear in two days," the medic said.

Elena touched the skin where, the day before, the medic had used a laser to lighten the marks. Now she skinned an aloe vera leaf and scooped out the gel. Elena watched as she ground dry sage and lionweed, then mixed it with the aloe and topped it off with fresh lavender buds. The sounds soothed her. Elena closed her eyes, drifting, when she felt hands at her throat.

"No—" she gasped.

The medic stopped. She gave a soft, understanding smile and gently placed the jar in Elena's hands.

"Apply it twice a day, for the next three days," she said.

Elena nodded, weariness creeping into her bones. "I'm sorry. I did not mean to startle like that."

The medic drew a slow breath. "Make him pay for it."

The comment, meant to strengthen her, only made her remember his hands on her neck, his wild, naked terror after. Twice, he had attacked her. And she had rescued him nonetheless. Why?

Because I had no other choice. She had accepted his horrors because of his power, because of what he represented: freedom, bloody and vicious. Yet a freedom all the same.

"I wish I could," she said and left.

The floating islands of Nymia towered above her. They were great behemoths of stone and rich, dense forests. Clouds wrapped around their deeply grooved cliffs like beards of old men. Waterfalls, purple as the blood of Nymia, fell into the sky, and Elena wondered, Had the men who raised their faces to purple rain understood that a god bled above them?

There were seven temples erected upon the floating islands, just like there had been seven petals of the Phoenix's temple. On the shard named Nymia's Righteousness, she met Syla.

The king kissed her hand, his eyes lingering on her scarf.

"How are you now?"

Confused. Bitter. Afraid, she thought.

"Tired," she said.

"I could have him executed for what he did."

"And let my efforts go in vain?" She meant to sound lighthearted, but sounded bitter instead. "You can't simply kill a prophet, especially not one as loved as him."

Syla snorted. "Would they love him if they knew how he attacked their queen?"

She thought of herself lying cold in the rain, alone.

"They prefer the strong. Even at death's door, Samson Kytuu proved to be deadly. No, they will not abandon him."

"So what do you want to do with him?"

She avoided the question, turning instead to the pillars. Fourteen pillars and seven arches circled a stone ground. At the center, a tall, lone tree grew with eyeless faces in its leaves and tongues upon its bark. The Seeing Tree. It was a mark of the Cyleoni goddess who valued information and knowledge above all else. Perhaps that was why Cyleon was heralded for its universities and libraries, its markets of flying books and endless mazes that led scholars to even more mysteries and fewer answers. A wind sighed through the eaves, and Elena strained to listen.

"What have you heard from your spies, Syla?"

"Spies?"

She fixed him with a crooked grin. "The very ones who informed you of Farin's edict before it transpired."

"Perhaps you can tell me first of this amrithi."

"I know nothing, same as you. But I know it's something Samson and the Arohassin value greatly."

"When the Arohassin spoke of it, the Butcher froze like a scholar who found his theory copied by another." Syla sighed. "I fear they are playing behind our backs."

"The Arohassin hiding secrets? Is that all your spies have found?" She laughed, harsh and short. "Perhaps you should fire your spies and replace them with Arohassin assassins."

Syla frowned, quiet.

"I'm sorry. I'm just..." She waved her hand.

"Tired?"

"Exhausted, more like. The Yumi barely gave me anything to eat."

"They aren't exactly used to hosting," Syla said, his mouth quirking. "I'll have my chefs cook something Ravani. Do you still enjoy bhindi masala?"

She started. "You remember?"

"Remember? The last time I had it, I nearly burned my tongue. Your chef does not understand the meaning of *mild*."

Elena laughed, and this time, it felt genuine. "And I'm sure yours doesn't understand the meaning of *spicy*."

Syla grinned, though after a moment, his smile shrank into a pensive line and his voice softened.

"My spies did learn something. They confirmed that Jantar means to send a fleet to Mandur. The Yumi general was right. I fear Farin's ambition knows no limits."

"The Jantari never do," she said sourly.

"Have you heard from the general?"

"He's waiting for my answer."

Syla sighed. "I do not like the idea of colluding with a usurper. And a Yumi usurper, of all things. But Jantar and the other kingdoms are crying for blood. They believe the Black Scales are behind the attacks and blame them for disturbing their metal trade. It's a small miracle he hasn't sniffed you out yet. Or me. But Farin will want to root out the rebel Sesharians. He might even give up his fight with the Arohassin in Rani and move south to your stronghold. If we had the Yumi, he'd think twice."

"I know," she whispered.

"So what answer will you give General Daz?"

"Not him." She looked up at the Seeing Tree and its many tongues. "Farin."

She had thought it over the last two days, chewing the idea until it had hardened into a nugget, then grew into a burden. Meaty and heavy. Fed by the rage that never seemed to leave her bones, the pain she was forced to endure, again and again, by a man who had claimed himself king.

"We give him Samson and the Black Scales."

Syla started. "Why?"

"Samson thought that by destroying their mines, he could stop Farin. But it only hurt the ones most vulnerable. No, the metal king is not a man. He is a beast, so we will hunt him like one."

Elena turned to him, her words born like a phoenix rising, hot and vengeful. "You will propose a deal. Tell Farin that at the council, he will have the opportunity to capture his most coveted enemy. When he asks who, be aloof. You are the master of spies. Tell him it's someone of the sea. He will come. And I will surprise him there. Chandi told me that the Jantari do not know I'm still alive. When I finally show my face, when the others finally learn of his breach of the Treaty of Borders, when..." And here she paused, gritting her teeth. She had mulled over this for some time, trying to find sweetness within its misery. It was what she had to do. Still, it hurt. "When I bring the Yumi with me, he will have no choice but to withdraw from Ravence."

"So you intend to accept General Daz's offer?"

She swallowed. "Yes. Together, you and I can motion for him to get a seat at the council."

"You're sure of this?" Syla eyed her. "Farin is never one to act according to our expectations."

"Do you know why Farin is targeting the Sesharians?" Her smile was thin, sharp. "It's because Samson betrayed him. Samson was meant to be his puppet, ready to offer Ravence on a platter once he came calling. But the Butcher turned against him. The metal king burns with jealousy and bitter pride. Bait him with only the idea of Samson's head, and Farin will come."

Syla stared at her quietly, and she saw his trepidation, his slow horror. He seemed not to recognize her. Her reflection, caught in the wild green of his eyes, was morphed and foreign even to her, and Elena found not fear in this discovery, but a delayed mourning, like soreness creeping into the body.

She mourned the woman she could have been.

She mourned the queen she was to become.

Perhaps this was regret. Perhaps this was retribution from the gods for her lack of faith, for her inability to protect her home. Or perhaps this was her own selfish desire to look fate in the eyes and scratch her fucking eyes out.

"I saved Samson because he serves a purpose. Nothing more," she said.

"So you would offer him as your sacrificial lamb?"

"Once I am before Farin, I do not care about Samson's fate or the Black Scales. I want them out of my kingdom. His death will be of his own making, not mine," Elena said, each word striking like flint. "I bring him only like a butcher before the ox he cannot kill. It is up to him to save his people, or himself."

The sound of a hoverpod made them turn, and she recognized Samson's Agni drawing close. A roar began to build in her ears.

Syla watched her, his eyes sad. "Do not become like him in your anger, Elena."

"I am nothing like Samson Kytuu."

"I do not mean Samson. I mean your father."

Elena turned away before her face crumpled, her heart quickening with a sudden, shooting pain. She reached for her Agni, for the wrath inlaid in her bones. She wanted to drown the ache. But it hooked into her ribs, and when she looked up again, she saw her father falling into the Eternal Fire. In the near distance, Samson climbed the path toward them.

"I won't," she said. "I'll be better."

CHAPTER 38

JAYA

A Sesharian is a hard worker, but they are not honest. The ones with a higher pedigree must be watched closely, for they have tasted freedom and power, and they will not so easily give them up.
—from *A Manual on Employing a Sesharian for Jantari Gentlefolk*

Jaya surveyed the holos of Samson's Agni in the darkness of their make-shift encampment. All Arohassin operatives were housed in the western district of the city, close to the command center—close enough for Chandi to keep an eye on them. But Jaya had taken great care with her holos. If someone were to glance at her panel, they would only see battle schematics and gameplans of their last mission. Not the terrible truth of Samson's fire.

Jaya cast a glance at Akaros as he paced.

"See this?" She pointed to a holo full of temperature readings. "See how it flares when he summons his urumi. How quickly it rises, then drops. His urumi is his channel. That is how he controls his Agni."

Akaros chewed on his lip. "And what of Elena?"

"I've heard rumors that when she and Samson fought, she needed no weapon to call her fire. She twirled, or spun, or made signals with her hands—"

"She dances," Akaros said. "The Goddess's Dance. Of course."

"So Elena's channel is dance. Samson's is his urumi. I wonder, then, what the third's will be," she mused.

Akaros pointed. "What about that? Did you get a reading?"

Jaya brought up a holo of a video recording of the Cyleoni courtyard, where she and the others had watched Elena kneel above Samson and raise him from near death. Samson still had the metal lotus in his pocket then.

"There was an alteration. His temperature was dropping rapidly, but at the exact moment Elena summoned her flames, it went haywire. Spiked beyond what I could measure." She remembered the blue brilliance of Samson's fire, the red earthiness of Elena's. How, for a beat, they had twined together when she healed him.

She sighed. "Something happened there. I *felt* it—didn't you? Like lightning in the air, except there was no storm. And the way he revived…" She trailed off, thinking hard. "You don't suppose she did something to his Agni?"

Akaros deftly slipped a coin in and out of his fingers. It was a nervous tic. His only tell, or the only one she had found. "If she did, then she can endanger the third."

She thought of Div. The burns lacing his throat, the quiet rattle of his lungs as he lay trapped in a coma on borrowed time. The night before she had left for Magar, she had sat with him in his ghostly chamber and whispered her promise against the glass.

I will revive you, come what may.

"I will not allow it," she growled.

"So why haven't you given Elena a metal lotus yet?"

He finally met her gaze. Before, long ago, Akaros had frightened her in the way he so easily cut his mark to the bone. He was always watching. It had intimidated her, his casual hunting. But now Jaya chided herself for not picking up on the details he had seen, for ignoring what had been before them all along. If she meant to fulfill her purpose, how could she be so ignorant?

"I will," she said hotly. "I just haven't had the chance—"

"The longer we wait, Elena becomes stronger. The third grows more unstable. Div gets weaker."

It was not a provocation. Not a threat. She knew Akaros well enough now to understand how he delicately manipulated others to his bidding. She knew his tricks. And yet, Div's name sent a searing, blearing hurt through her.

"I'm not hesitating. You know that. I just—I'm not—"

"You're not a fighter, I know." Akaros slid his coin back into his pocket. "And I know you'd rather hide behind a panel, safe with your bank of holos. But you need to grow a fucking spine, Jaya. Elena won't bite your head off." He rapped his knuckles on her panel. "I won't let her."

Jaya stared at him, then the holos, and then the second metal lotus, a perfect mirror of the one she had given Samson. It was not that she feared Elena any more or less than Samson. They were both so laughably transparent in their obsession with each other, she almost felt pity for their stubborn blindness. But Jaya had not forgotten who had burned down her house. The gold caps had sworn fealty to Leo, to *Elena*, and had erected a gold statue brazenly in the heart of Rani to declare, *Look how she is one of us.*

Jaya feared that if she faced Elena, she would lose her objectivity in the face of her own hatred, and it would lead to a fatal mistake.

Jaya carefully picked up the lotus. "I don't know if I can pretend in front of her."

Akaros gripped her shoulder. "You will. *You must.*"

Jaya threaded through a throng of people crowding the street. Taller than most, she spotted the ruined spire of the temple in the distance, and the retinue of guards standing outside its walls.

She stopped on the corner of the street, observing the guards. There were seven Black Scales in total, three posted by the entrance, the others along the wall. She noticed how some passersby cast quick glances in their direction and hurried past the temple. Others knelt or lay prostrate, kissing the ground and showering it with rose petals. There were Ravani and Sesharian devotees, all of them marked with a black serpent on their cheeks.

"Why are there guards by the temple?" she asked a Sesharian woman carrying a thali of offerings.

The woman gave her an odd look. "Have you not heard? The Prophet nearly killed the queen here. He enacted his deliverance, and this is now a holy site."

Jaya frowned. She saw no sign of battle, no evidence of a scuffle. "When?"

"Weeks ago. Are you daft, girl? Were you living out in the rocks?"

In a tunnel in the desert, so about the same. Jaya watched as one unmarked Ravani man knelt with hands clasped around a rosary. Trinkets of the Phoenix and the Serpent dangled on its end. "Look, he's praying to both. I thought the Prophet ended the worship of the Phoenix goddess."

The woman spat and made a quick sign. "Blasphemous. He's afraid to let go of his old god."

"Why isn't anyone stopping him?"

"And risk a riot? Not everyone is willing to give up their Phoenix icons, even if our Blue Star burns Her down in front of them." The woman snorted. "Some are just too stuck in their old ways."

As the woman hurried to the temple gates, Jaya sat down on the ruined steps of what had once been an old sari shop. She noted how the guard on the far right favored his left leg, how the one in the middle kept tapping her finger against the butt of her pulse gun. The ones by the temple doors looked bored. Odd. This square had been the sight of a bloody, sacred battle, and the guards looked indifferent. Jaya chewed on a nail, thinking, when she caught a whiff of a conversation in Ambari.

"—buried, every last one of them."

She stood, tracking the speaker. It was a Sesharian talking to another, and though they spoke in the old Sesharian tongue, Jaya had spent suns learning it under Maya's tutelage. She followed the pair as they carefully avoided the prayer circle.

"—he could destroy the mines, but he couldn't save his own."

"Hush, Bemon," his companion said, a small woman with narrow shoulders. She glanced around them, and Jaya quickly hid behind the side of a building. "His followers are everywhere."

"And? They will do nothing. Ours are too weak to call him out, the Ravani too stupid. How can he free us if he is killing us in turn?"

"This is war, Bemon. We are lucky to even live. Let's go back to the temple, pray for the dead." She tugged on his arm, but the man shook himself free.

"I'm not setting foot in that temple," he snarled. "Prophet or not, he's still a rustblood. His father bent the knee to the Jantari. And now he sold our brothers and sisters for a little piece of their cursed metal."

Jaya followed them at a distance as they traveled deeper into the Sesharian quarters. Here, the buildings cramped in, as if to shield themselves and others. Mothers sat on the thresholds, peeling vegetables, while their children dashed through the alleys, laughing. Neighbors called to one another in Ambari. Conversation flowed loosely, addled by drink, by song. There was an ease here, a slow breath released. No doubt, a Sesharian Prophet added a sense of security. They all bore his mark. They all lit a diya in his name before their doorsteps.

But as Jaya slipped through the shops, the children, the gossiping fathers and tired mothers, she sensed something else too. A quiet turmoil. She heard it in the quick way conversations dropped into whispers when discussing a delicate subject. She saw it in the stiff, mechanical movements of a mother relighting her diya, as if the task was a burden she must bear, rather than a prayer to a savior.

Jaya stopped, uncertain. Were the Sesharians losing faith in Samson? The couple slipped down an alleyway, and Jaya followed when the wall on her right caught her attention.

On the side of a building, she saw it. A simple number.

400.

Four hundred Sesharians lost in the mines. Four hundred of their own, buried by their Prophet. A sick sense of satisfaction settled in her stomach then, and Jaya turned back. She needed to tell Akaros. If the Sesharians were losing faith in their leader, then the Arohassin could use that to their advantage. And if Samson could be removed, then Elena—

She stopped short of the temple courtyard as the guards snapped to a salute. People suddenly shoved one another, craning their necks, whispering. Even the pilgrims had abandoned their supplications to raise their thalis. Jaya elbowed past one, earning her a glare, but once he saw her eyes, her hair, he fell back.

"Yumi," he gasped.

Others began to turn to her.

Their curiosity sent an ugly pang of disgust and jealousy through Jaya. She remembered others touching her hair as a child. *But look, her hair is soft! She is not one.* Their frowns, the confusion in their eyes, the simple

What are you? closing her throat in a panic. She had to get out. Jaya pushed past them, ignoring the curses, the questions, when suddenly the crowd opened, and she was spit in front of the temple gates.

Behind them.

Samson and Elena turned at her sudden appearance.

"Gamemaster?" Samson said.

Elena studied her with distrust, and Jaya felt the prick of her old hatred, like a sleeping fire stirred. *You will find a way. You must.*

"Prophet. Queen." Jaya instinctively began to bow, then stopped short. She no longer bowed to queens or kings. "Have you come to bless us?"

She tried to hide the sneer in her voice, but Elena caught it.

"Stay out of the way, gamemaster," she said.

Jaya held, defiant. For a moment, she forgot Akaros's warnings, Div's coma, the Prophet, and the crowd. She saw only the fires and the gold caps and Elena's and Leo's statues, rising above it all. But then ululations started through the crowd as Samson stepped forward, and Jaya ducked back, swallowing her burning pride.

"The queen and I have come here today to usher in a new era of peace. Forget what transpired here a few weeks ago. We hold no animosity for each other. And as proof," he said, raising his urumi, "we will create a new temple fire. One made by us both."

Elena raised her hand, her fingers quickly tapping out signs Jaya could not read. Without warning, an inferno blazed down her arm. Its light blinded Jaya, and she staggered back as the crowd gasped. With a crack of his urumi, Samson summoned his flame, and together, they lit the torches on top of the gates.

"Before you all, we promise, as queen and Prophet, to bring freedom to Ravence," Elena called.

"Ravence *and* Seshar," Samson said.

To this, Elena nodded, and perhaps it signified nothing. Perhaps, as the queen quickly pulled on a smile, as the gatherers caught their bearings, as loud prayers, roars of approval, and desperate pleas to be blessed thundered through the street, there was nothing to read. But Jaya had spent suns studying fighters. Their strengths and weaknesses. Their tells. And when Elena faced the crowd, away from Samson so that he could not notice, Jaya saw the slight quiver in her throat.

She felt a breathless thrill in the pit of her stomach, an exhilaration similar to finding a fighter who fought in ways she had not anticipated in her designs. Jaya gripped her lotus and followed the Firebloods into the temple.

"Are you tracking us now, gamemaster?" Elena asked.

Jaya shrugged. "Is that a crime?"

Elena scowled. Jaya noted the practiced violence in the way she stood, how she held her head and arms slightly forward, as if ready to leap. *Charged violence*, Jaya amended. Elena's eyes, dark and calculating, swept over her, and Jaya felt her skin prickle as the queen took her in. She was taller than Elena, leaner too, but where Jaya was wiry, Elena was sharper. They were mirrors. Broken apart and put back together in the memory of resemblance.

Samson moved forward, breaking Jaya from her study. He looked gaunter than before, his cheeks pallid and sunken. "Have you come to pray, gamemaster?"

She had not prayed in many suns. But she nodded and knelt with them. The ceremony was short. The priestess, a Ravani woman, stumbled her way through Sesharian litanies of the Serpent. Her icon had been erected on top of the Phoenix, but bits of the bird still flared through. A feather there. A talon here. The Firebloods barely uttered their prayers, Samson's eyes always roaming, Elena silent and still.

This is a performance, Jaya thought.

She could hear the crowd outside, waiting. How many hoped to be blessed by these two? How many believed them to be their saviors?

She stood when the others rose.

"May I speak with you?" she said to Elena.

Elena shared a glance with Samson, then nodded. They were left alone, the temple fire crackling softly in the near dark.

"What is it you need with me, Arohassin?" Elena said. She did not try to hide the derision dripping from her voice.

Believe me, I despise your presence too, Jaya thought acidly. For a moment, she considered leaving.

But she had heard the whispers, seen the nervous glances. More so, she noticed how the Prophet had thinned into a husk of a man. If she had all the time in the world, then maybe she would wait. Create a game to flawless execution. But no challenger won a game without a risk. No gamemaster outsmarted the players without inviting danger.

"The Sesharians are losing faith in the Prophet," she said. To her credit, Elena fought down her shock. Jaya then told her about the whispers, the pilgrims, the unrest. So what if she exaggerated? Div was running out of time.

When she was done, the queen said slowly, "They are wrong. He deserves their faith."

"Wh-what? I thought…Didn't he…?" She shook her head. "I'm sorry. Are you defending him? Because I heard he nearly killed you."

"And I should use the Arohassin to kill him? The same people who killed my father and my Yassen?" Elena's voice hardened. "Be grateful, gamemaster, that I'm not telling of your transgression to the Black Scales. This is your warning. If you speak of this with me again, you and your like will be driven into the earth."

Jaya snorted. "So, you're protecting him."

Something cold and sharp flickered across Elena's face. Her mouth twisted into a half snarl, half smile. "He is my Prophet."

She turned to go, and Jaya licked her lips, thinking, *Just say it.*

"Your Agni is stronger than his."

Elena stopped short. "What?"

"I—I have been studying Agni. For suns now. The nature of its heat, its burning point, the life force it demands. How one can differ from another."

"How?"

"From scrolls. Some from the black market, others stolen from the Royal Library." Elena scowled at that, and Jaya shrugged. "What else can you expect? You royals keep all the knowledge to yourselves and, even then, fail to learn it."

Elena's voice was a low growl. "And what did you learn?"

"Agni is a force. One rooted in elemental nature, powered by the gods themselves. And the gods are not equal. They are jealous and vicious and fight each other for more. There are even rumors of gods learning to devour and steal each other's power." She held out the metal lotus. "This will help prevent Samson from taking your power. See, it can form any weapon." She demonstrated, the black sand hissing into a slingsword, then a chakram, then an urumi. "It might come to your aid, if he turns against you. Again."

Elena studied her for a long moment, her body completely still. Then she drew in a deep breath and left.

Jaya stood alone, the sand gently susurrating around her. *Damn it.* She had been sure Elena would take the bait. But something nagged at her. For as much as Elena had claimed her allegiance to the Prophet, Jaya had noticed her gaze slide past her to the broken vestiges of the Phoenix. And the look in her eyes wasn't one of piety.

It had been of pain.

This would be a slow game, then. No matter.

Those were her favorite.

CHAPTER 39

SAMSON

I have seen too much pain, too much sorrow. Take this from me, O Great Serpent. Allow me the mercy of your waters.
—from *The Lament of Seshar: A People's History*

He abandoned them beneath the earth.
Turned against his own men.
What else can you expect from a rustblood?

He had heard them. Ravani and Sesharian alike, whispering of his shortcomings, his sin. He had hoped his appearance with Elena would help to show that the Prophet and the queen were one. *Something to bridge the gap,* he had said. Something to show he was not afraid of their judgment. But he still heard their voices over the roar of the flames. He still heard them crying for help.

Samson hugged his jacket tighter as he slowly climbed the high temple steps. A chill lingered in his bones, threading through his veins with ghostlike fingers and disappearing as soon as he tried to pin it down. He had tried everything. Coals on his naked skin, layers of sweaters until he sweated underneath the winter sun. Still, the chill persisted. Short of siphoning Elena's Agni, only the Eternal Fire remained, and he could hear it rumbling just over the landing, calling him home.

Saayna bowed at his approach. "Prophet."

"Saayna. How have you kept?"

Her eyes skittered over his sunken cheeks, his pale lips, and he thought he saw a flicker of worry—or was it doubt?—cross her face before she bowed once more.

"Well, now that we have been honored by your Divine Presence."

Divine Presence. His stomach curdled. *Would the divine leave his people like so?*

"Prophet?"

She stared up at him, and Samson realized he had been standing still for too long. He kissed three of his fingers and placed them on Saayna's head to bless her.

"We have brought provisions for you and your order. My men will bring them up, but they will need your direction."

It was only after a beat that he noticed his fingers were trembling against her skin. He tucked his hand back into his coat. "Go."

Saayna hesitated. Her brows pinched, and there was something furtive about her gaze, as if she was trying to piece him together without his noticing. But then she scurried off, and he was alone with the Eternal Fire.

It roiled at his approach, though no flames rushed to meet him. He watched them split, separate tongues twisting away while others twined together. Vicious red bled to burnt orange to cool blue and then the slight bite of green. It was as if all the colors in the world could be found in the heart of a flame. He stood, hypnotized by the conflagration. Pity, how something so beautiful could wreak so much destruction.

He began to reach for a flame. Better to heal himself now before the priests came back. He imagined the fire looping around his body, sinking into his skin, his bones, chasing away the chill and filling him with a peace he no longer recognized. But even as he reached forward and curled his fingers, Samson felt resistance, as if someone was pushing against his hand and trying to pry it open.

"Come here," he commanded.

At last, a tiny flame wrenched away from the inferno with a squawk.

It danced within his palm, jittery and erratic, as if looking for an escape. Samson frowned.

In his mind's eye, he followed the flames down to their roots as he had done before, in search of its savage song that spoke of the delicious tang of the earth and the clear notes of the wind. A song of old when the desert was a forest, and the forest had been an ocean filled with creatures deep. It had been thunderous, thrumming with power and a vicious vitality. He searched and heard…nothing.

Only the crackle of the flames, their whispers unknown to him.

Samson stumbled back, his heart thumping wildly.

He could taste it. Something foreign, a spice that salted the air with its tangy smoke. He whipped around, scanning his surroundings, but he saw no priest, no soldier, not even a curious bird pecking at the debris. Only the Eternal Fire remained. Only the flames stretched before him, crackling in a language he could no longer hear, and he did not know whether it was its silence or its refusal to greet him that hurt him more.

"Great Serpent," he said.

And then it began to laugh.

Samson gasped as the Eternal Fire charged, biting his feet with soft pops, its laughter buzzing through his bones. He tried to push away the flames, but they merely toyed with him, snapping at his wrist, his knee, his neck.

"Listen to me!" he cried.

He attempted to fling off a flame that cracked his cheek, but it zipped away quickly in a laughter of sparks. The Eternal Fire swept in, trapping him. The air thickened with heat. *Just walk through*, he thought. *I won't burn.*

A flame smacked his tricep, and Samson hissed in pain. He raised his bruised arm. A welt, black as tar, curdled his skin and just as quickly disappeared. The Eternal Fire attacked again. Samson fell to his knees, crying out as flames bit into his flesh, tearing away as he healed only to latch on again.

"Stop!" he commanded.

The inferno only roared in response, and it was then that he realized he could not feel the vigor of its vicious hunger or the heat of its power sizzle through his veins. All he felt was the sting of sudden betrayal.

The Eternal Fire was no longer his.

Get up, he thought. *Get up, up, UP!*

He crawled forward, gritting his teeth as the flames rained down their punishment. It was as if he was swimming against the current, each flame a wave beating against him. At long last, he reached the threshold, and the Eternal Fire roiled back.

Samson lay there, stunned. After a few minutes, sensation came back into his toes, his fingers, then the rest of his body. But he felt something different in his navel chakra: a cold so intense it bowled him over. His Agni shriveled, distant, weak.

You did not heal me, he thought.

The Eternal Fire yawned, the silence of its absent song roaring in his ears.

Samson pushed himself to his feet and ran down the landing, down the steps, down the burnt vestiges of the broken temple. He did not stop running until he saw the gleam of the tanker, and only when he was under the shadow of its wings did he finally collapse.

A soldier cried out in alarm. Others began to rush toward him.

I look feeble, he thought first. And then, *I look mad.*

Someone touched his arm. Saayna. Worry ringed her eyes as she sat him up and smoothed back his sweaty hair.

"Prophet?" she asked.

And in his delirium, he began to laugh. Saayna froze, watching him with an expression stuck between horror and confusion. But he could not stop. Could not bottle the feeling of panic as he thought, with awful clarity, *Your Prophet is dying.*

Samson ordered no one to disturb him once he returned to Magar. He knew his men would say nothing, but if people saw him like this, they would begin to wonder, and he could not hear more whispers of his shortcomings. Most of all, he could not bear Elena's judgment. His supporters may desert him. People were slow to accept gods, but quick to destroy them. But if Elena forsook him . . . He shuddered at the thought.

Samson peeled off his clothes until he was bare chested. Gooseflesh prickled up his skin. *Damn this cold.*

He splashed water on his face when he heard a sound. Turning, he saw Elena in the doorway.

"Oh."

Water dripped down his neck, his chest. She stared openly. Was that a smile flickering on her face? No, he must have imagined it, because when she met his eyes, her gaze was cool, controlled.

"We've got a comms channel open with the Yumi."

"What?" He stared at her. "When?"

She handed him a towel, her eyes lingering on the scar on his chest. The weight of her gaze sent a strange fire down his spine. "Get dressed. We're needed in the war room."

"Why did you come yourself to tell me? You could have sent a soldier."

"I wanted to spare someone else of your narcissism," she said. "Coming?"

He laughed, surprised he still remembered how. "I am not a narcissist."

"That's what they all say."

"And you know many?"

"Just one. But he's enough for me to make sense of them all."

He wagged a finger. "You have barely scratched the surface of Samson Kytuu."

"See. He even refers to himself in the third person."

Samson smiled as he toweled off and grabbed a sweater. He walked slowly in controlled strides to hide his limp when Elena stopped. She offered an arm.

"Chivalry isn't dead, you know," she said.

"I'm fine." He pushed past her, and after a moment, Elena followed.

"What happened at the high temple?" she asked.

"Nothing. I said I'm fine."

"You're limping."

"I am just tired, Elena."

He could feel her staring, tasting the lie, but instead of responding with a quip, she rested her arm on his and squeezed.

"You don't need to pretend with me," she said quietly.

His heart flailed, ringing inside his chest. "I am not pretending."

"All right," she said, but her arm remained on his, steady and sure, and he leaned into her as they walked, his chest quickening and tightening with nameless, breathless sensation.

It looked as if they were walking arm in arm, the Prophet and the queen, but Samson could feel the weight of accusatory glares as they passed through the streets. Out of the corner of his eye, he saw a Sesharian boy glowering, the serpent on his cheek curling inward as if to mock him. An older man stood behind, his cheek a bloated red mess, as he had peeled off the skin to remove the mark. Fear skittered down Samson's spine, and he leaned closer to Elena.

A few stopped to bow. Many stared, and he caught the snatches of whispers, the offhand glares, the rippling agitation as the people looked upon their Prophet and found him wanting.

Elena gripped his arm. "Just stay with me."

They finally ducked inside the army headquarters. The war room was cold and cramped, each seat filled with either a Black Scale or an Aro-hassin. The soldiers stopped talking when they entered, and the sudden silence felt nauseating, as if someone had stretched plastic over his face and pulled.

"We have guests," Chandi said in greeting.

"Who?"

"Ah, the Butcher," said a voice in an accent he knew at once to be Mokshi.

"I hailed General Daz," Elena said as she slipped her arm from his and took a seat. "To discuss the recent calling of the council."

In the projection before him, a Yumi man with curly hair and slight shoulders watched him with bright, calculative eyes.

"I've heard many things about you, General Kytuu," Daz said. "But namely your hatred of Farin."

"In this, we're all aligned," Elena said, casting a glance down the table to Akaros and Jaya. His former mentor winked.

"Oh, we are, Your Majesty," Akaros purred. His eyes met Samson's. "In more ways than one."

"The council meets at the end of this week. Which means we only have a few days to prepare," Elena said.

"Less," Daz cut in. "I've received word that Farin means to sail two fully manned killdoms stationed in Rysanti toward Tsuana."

"Why would he send military ships to the council?" Chandi said.

"To show force," Jaya answered. "Obviously."

Chandi stared at the girl, and he knew her well enough to know that Jaya's quick, haughty confidence had taken his commander off guard. *Don't underestimate Jaya,* Akaros had once warned him.

"It's *obvious* political suicide," Chandi retorted. "The council is a neutral ground. The other kingdoms won't stand for it."

"Unless Farin means to keep his ships just at the edge of international waters where it's still legal to sail," Jaya said. "Far enough to not be a threat, but close enough to remind the kingdoms who they're bargaining with."

"Farin isn't stupid enough to attack the council," Elena said. "The other kingdoms would wage war immediately, and he can't fight alone on multiple fronts. No. He's being provocative, per usual."

"What are the names of the ships?" Samson asked Daz.

"*Lord of Sea* and *Relentless Destiny*," Daz said.

Samson stiffened. Around the table, every Black Scale, Chandi, Visha, Akiri, stilled. Akiri quickly drew the sign of the Great Serpent across herself as Chandi stared into some distant space, her face closed. He felt it too. An ancient resentment, beaten into his bones like every Sesharian child who had stood on the shores of his home and found it not his to own.

"You mean the flesh crawlers," Visha spat.

The *Lord of Sea* and the *Relentless Destiny* were old ships, grand ships, and the first ships that had sailed into Sesharian harbors those seventy suns ago with armed Jantari. They were the same ships that had taken the first Sesharians to a life of indentured labor and a death in a dark, windless grave. How many stories had he heard of those behemoths? Fifty? A hundred? How many times had he fantasized standing on their decks and ripping them apart seam by seam as his fire burned through the steel with a slow, agonizing relish?

"That son of a bitch," he snarled.

"What?" Elena said, looking at the Sesharians. "What's so important about those ships?"

It was Jaya who answered.

"It's the symbolism," she said in a condescending tone, as if Elena was slow for not making the connection herself. "The flesh crawlers are the epitome of Jantari dominance. Of course he's sending them to Tsuana. He wants to remind every king of what he has conquered—"

"—and to warn that he can conquer more," Elena finished, glaring at the gamemaster. "I get it." She rested her chin on her fist, her brows furrowing, and Samson found, even in the bleakness of his anger, a strange fondness for that gesture.

"He's spitting on everyone's face, General," Visha growled.

"Let him," Jaya said. "Last time I checked, we don't have ships."

"But you do," Elena said, looking to Daz.

They all turned to his projection, and the Yumi smiled.

"And why would I send my ships to you?" he asked.

Elena's eyes shuttered, her lips thin and tight. She seemed to gather herself. Then, "Because I accept your proposal."

"What proposal?" Samson asked.

"You will give me a seat at your council?" Daz said.

Elena nodded. "Syla and I will start the motion. Tsuana will likely agree, and Veran will fall in line simply because the king is afraid of angering Tsuana."

Tsuana? Veran? Samson's mind whirled. The politics and games of monarchs were not foreign to him, but this had unfolded so fast that he was not sure where to start.

"Elena, wait, let's consider this together," he urged.

But she ignored him. "I want those flesh crawlers destroyed on their way to Tsuana. Let Farin see his ships burn on the eve of the council. How is that for symbolism?"

"The Ayoni have built two new bounders in an older contract with my sister," Daz said. "Meet us in Ayona. You will be granted safe passage there."

"Hold on. Just—wait. Elena," Samson said, and he stood, motioning for her.

She hesitated, then followed him outside, where the pale winter sun grazed the top of the canyons. Beyond the courtyard, he could hear the warbling call for rations. He had forgotten today was rations day. The Cyleoni had sent food along with medicine, and he wondered if it would be enough. If any of this would be enough so long as Farin reigned and hatred bloomed in the gnawing hunger of those without. He thought of the children, torn from the islands. The miners, buried in the earth. All that death, all that loss. How much longer would it take until they were freed?

"I don't trust Daz," Samson said.

Elena sat back against a pillar. "I don't either. But what else can we do?"

"What if he plans to strong-arm the council into his own private demands? Or to prevent Seshar from gaining a council seat too?"

Elena looked up, her expression wary, guarded. "We will deal with it when the time comes."

He sighed and sat down beside her. "The council kingdoms think we Sesharians are helpless. We couldn't protect our own home. Couldn't stop the Jantari from taking us to theirs. So they gave up on Seshar. But…" And here he faltered.

"But…?" Elena asked.

He blew air from his cheeks. "But if we take those killdoms, if we sail in bearing my flag, bearing your flag, then the world will see that both you and I and any other country taken for granted will not die in our own helplessness. That we can fight. And, more importantly, *win*."

Elena said nothing for a long time. She stared across the courtyard, arms wrapped around her knees as if to hug herself and trap her thoughts. But even if he could not read her face, he felt her Agni. Sensed its seething spark, its voracious bitterness that mirrored his own.

They were the same, the Butcher and the Burning Queen.

Hungry to win, even in defeat.

"I'm afraid of the sea," she said finally, softly, her admittance a quick, flighty thing. But he caught it and rested his arm on hers, as she had for him, and squeezed.

"There's no need to be afraid. You have me. You have your Agni. Together, we are enough."

"Are we?" she asked.

He met her eyes. For once, he found no trace of that relentless cold razoring down his spine. Only a calm, warm assurance of her Agni, and their connection between.

"We are gods. A thousand kingdoms could not make us bend, Elena Aadya Ravence. What is one king?"

CHAPTER 40

SAMSON

The Ayoni have kept their nation and its secrets to themselves. Perhaps that is why they endure today. Whatever darkness they hold, it is theirs and theirs alone.

—from chapter 30 of *The Great History of Sayon*

Ayona emerged from beneath a grey lumbering mass of storm clouds that rippled with distant lightning. Even within the tanker, Samson could taste the metallic bite of the storm. The singed charge in the air. When they docked upon the pier with their Yumi call signs, he half imagined the fearsome warriors coming out, lightning burning through the sky with every step. He knew the stories.

"When a female sorceress seethes, all the world shakes," his mother had said as she delicately plucked a crystal from a smoking pit. The crystal had shattered upon her tongue with blue mist, and the Jantari soldier kneeling before them had cried out as a cut slowly opened along his neck. "See?"

He cast a glance at Elena. Was she one of them? A female sorceress who would make the world shatter?

She must have felt him staring, because without turning, she said, "Are you afraid?"

He watched as the ramp lowered and Ayona appeared before them in its violent shades of purple. "Of who?"

She turned to him with a teasing smile that disarmed him more than he liked to admit. "The Yumi. This is your first time meeting one of the Mokshi."

"No," he said, not quite a lie, not quite the truth. He wasn't afraid of the Yumi, but he was apprehensive about *her*. *Her* power. *Her* sway.

But she's on your side. And you have her Agni, he reminded himself. He probed their connection and felt her Agni flutter at his touch. If he wanted, he could push further, tap into her nadis and pull what he needed.

He offered his arm. "Ready?"

They disembarked along with Chandi and Jaya. They were each allowed to bring only one companion, and he had elected Chandi, while Elena had chosen the gamemaster. *She's too smart and notices everything*, she had told him. *We'll need that when we meet the Ayoni.*

A Yumi came forward, along with a short man. *The dockmaster.* The Ayoni wore a thick leather coat that fastened at the collar and carried the scent of something sweet, like licorice. He had thin features and a bleak nose. Small holos hovered around his eyes, but he waved them away and slipped off his clear visor in a manner that reminded Samson of a raven plucking at its feathers. His lips were painted black, his long hair pulled tight into a low bun and fastened with silver coins shaped like crescent moons.

He said something in his jabbering Ayini and then looked to the Yumi beside him to translate.

"He welcomes you," the Yumi said in smooth Hind.

"We're grateful he allowed us to land. It is an honor to be granted passage into your country."

The Yumi spoke softly, and the man chortled. He looked at them with slight derision, though Samson felt as if the dockmaster was examining him, his eyes sweeping over his shoulders, his legs, his hands. When the man met his eyes, he scowled and looked back at the Yumi.

"He says you are welcome guests, as long as you stay within the set bounds," the Yumi said.

"And what are these boundaries?" Samson asked, eyeing their surroundings.

They stood on an empty dock, though the port around them bustled with activity. He could see the glittering hulls of the ships docked at other points and men moving in between, hauling crates, switching tools, mending ships. They worked with a mechanical efficiency, each movement precise, nothing wasted. But Samson could not hear them.

Beyond the port, the sharp, crystallized buildings of the city sprouted between the violet trees, shining with a vibrancy that made the back of his eyes slightly sore. A thopter flew from the city and landed on a far dock, and he did not hear it. In fact, Samson heard nothing. No hum of ships. No grunts of men at work. Not even the slight vibration of the air as the thopter launched back into the sky. It was as if silence had unhinged its mighty jaw and swallowed the people before him, shaving them down into pantomimes of movement.

"To speak only when spoken to, to stay with your Yumi hosts, and to leave in three hours." The man spoke again, and the Yumi hummed. "Oh, and that you all wear this. To show that you are with us."

She presented armbands that locked around the bicep and whirred softly. A blue light warmed his skin. *A tracker.* Warily, Samson scanned their surroundings again, but the Yumi did not seem alarmed by the strange quiet. And the dockmaster respected them, enough. So long as he stayed with the warriors, he was safe.

Chandi fell into step with him.

"Is it just me, or is there something strange about this place?" she murmured.

"I've been trying to figure it out myself." He watched the workers. None had stopped to take a breath or to even look their way. They wore helmet visors that covered their faces, so he could not tell one from another, and he had the strange, disembodied sensation of watching cogs in a machine, each as unremarkable as the last. "Why is it so quiet here?"

Out of the corner of his eye, he saw Jaya stop to peer at something beneath the dock. She clucked her tongue. "Those are black-market propulsion sensors."

"Why would they have that?" Chandi asked.

"Keeps the docks afloat. See?" She pointed to the silver metal disc peeking between the planks as they walked across. "I bet it's underneath all of them. But why is this dock empty?"

"They must have cleared it out for our arrival," Elena said, her voice low.

But Samson saw no scratches or footmarks on the planks, no scuffs from boots or stalls or shipment unloaded from vessels. The wood panels glistened, as if brand-new. It was as if they had arrived in a ghost port devoid of history, of memory. He wondered if this port ever saw trade, and remembered the Ayoni rarely fraternized with the other nations. Was that why they had resigned themselves to black-market sensors? Where had they even gotten them from?

"Here we are," the Yumi said as they arrived at a low building built on the edge of the pier.

"Are we not going into the city?" Elena asked.

"No time. The bounders will be here soon," the Yumi said. The short man stood aside to let them in. Was it Samson's imagination, or did his eyes linger on him and Chandi?

"What a peculiar little man," Jaya mumbled.

"Quiet now," the Yumi warned. "They may be cold, but they have good ears. Don't disgrace our host."

She opened the door, and they ducked inside. Three Yumi dressed in battle gear stood around a gamepanel, a mock-up battle already unfolding across the table. Samson spotted the two Jantari killdoms sailing from Rysanti and into the open sea while two smaller ships snuck along the far edge of Seshar.

"General Daz," Elena said.

A tall Yumi man turned from the projection and looked between her and Samson. "Little queen. I see you've finally taken my advice."

Elena tensed, color warming her cheeks. "The Prophet and I are one. You've taught me that, Daz."

A thrill ran through Samson, quick and electric. His Agni pulsed, and he felt the shiver of hers. *We are connected*, he thought with satisfaction. How long had he yearned for such a companion? Elena turned to him and offered a quick smile before she approached the panel. "Afira. Rhumia."

The two other Yumi nodded courteously.

The Ayoni muttered something to Daz, which made the Yumi look up and scrutinize him and Chandi. Gooseflesh prickled down Samson's neck as the Ayoni continued speaking. Continued watching. Was the dockmaster noticing them simply because they were newcomers, or because they were Sesharians? He was used to such stares, though it had been a long time since someone so small could make him nervous. Daz made a noncommittal noise and shook his head. The Ayoni's scowl deepened, but he sat back.

Carefully, Samson ignored his glare and turned to the panel as Jaya examined the design.

"This is your gameplan?" she scoffed.

"It is incomplete," Rhumia said.

"It's total shit, that's what it is. You'll never catch up to the killdoms at this rate."

Over the table, he and Elena shared a look. She arched a brow. *See?*

"Ignore her," Chandi said.

"Not if you want to actually win this fight and stick one up Farin's ass."

Daz chuckled as Rhumia scowled, her long hair rippling behind her. "And what does a clipped foreigner know about Yumi warships?"

For a moment, Jaya stilled, and Samson saw something hurt and raw cross her face before her lips curled into a sneer. "This *clipped foreigner* knows that your ships will deplete their fuel before they even set sight on Sesharian harbors. You'll lose the game before you begin the fight."

Afira clucked her tongue. "She's right. And she's rude. I like the little one. She could be good for you, Rhumia."

Rhumia snorted. "Your calculations are incorrect, gamemaster. Our bounders are lighter and face less resistance. We'll still have plenty of fuel by the time we reach the Jantari killdoms."

"So you intend to sail through the Black Pit?" Jaya tapped the middle of the sea, the cursed area where sensors jammed and ships infamously disappeared. "That's the only way you can conserve fuel."

"She *is* right. You didn't account for the pit, Rhumia," Daz said softly.

"I'm sorry, General." Rhumia glared at Jaya. "I'll rectify the mistake."

Daz slowly rose from his chair and regarded the small gamemaster with amusement. He then turned to Samson, and his expression withered into something more solemn.

"Prophet," he said, gaze lingering on Samson's glowing armband. "What do you think? You know the seas better than all of us."

"I have not sailed past the pit," Samson said as the Ayoni rose and began to walk around the panel.

"But you have been in it, yes?"

"I have," Samson said, remembering the lone lantern fighting against the suffocating darkness as his mother guided their boat. He had been seized with terror as he thought about the bottomless pit yawning beneath, and the thin wood separating him from its maw. "The rumors are true. All sensors and lights fail within the pit. Except for fire."

"It's like in the stories," Chandi said. "'Sorceress of the water, son of the sea. Give up your fire, and the pit responds to thee.'"

"Old wives' tales," Rhumia snorted.

"Most ships skirt around it, but we don't have time. We need to cut through," Daz said, throwing his grandniece a look. "Do you know a way?"

"Sorceress of the water, son of the sea." His mother tipped the dead Jantari soldier overboard, and Samson recoiled as he heard the body slam into the water. Their boat shook upon its impact, and then began to vibrate as the sea heard their call. "Feast upon the enemies of thee."

"Fire can help guide you, along with the stars," he said. It was not a lie, but neither was it the whole truth. The sea was always hungry. The Great Serpent desired Her sacrifices, and he did not have the heart to give one. But fire? He glanced at Elena. The Great Serpent would allow them passage if a fire bound their ships. It would require him to summon for a prolonged period, but he was still too weak to wield. Unless he drew on Elena's own Agni.

Samson vacillated, looking between Elena and the blue holo of the pit. If he siphoned her Agni, he'd reveal their connection. She could just as easily draw on him then—if she knew how. But he could not give her this power over him. Even if she gave him soft smiles. Even if his name on her lips sounded like an utterance of faith, borne on the truths they had surrendered to each other.

The Ayoni slipped behind him. It was only then that Samson noticed that his and Chandi's bands were glowing, but not Elena's or Jaya's. He began to question their host when Jaya threw up her hands with a cry.

"I know!"

She quickly tuned the panel in a flurry of limbs and curses. Samson watched, transfixed, as the holomaps blurred, Jaya's voice quickening.

"The killdoms won't sail straight from Rysanti to Tsuana like we think. If they head straight east, they'll inevitably run into the merchant and carrier ships sailing north of Seshar. Everyone will see them. Sesharians will gossip about the infamous flesh crawlers seen heading east of Seshar. Word will spread to Tsuana of foreign ships bearing down upon her waters. Farin can't risk that."

"So they head south," Samson mused, tracing a finger along the map. "Curving along the islands and out back, where no one can see."

"Exactly."

He saw it now, clear as day. "So we ambush—"

"Exactly," Jaya chattered excitedly.

"—before they turn around the islands—"

"Yes. It's a straight shot. If we sail through the pit, we'll cut right through their path. Take the battle on open seas."

"'Everything is settled on the open waters,'" he intoned. "'If it is not, then laugh, son of sea. For you have died and your enemy has lived longer than thee.'"

The Ayoni spoke up then. He approached the panel, pointing to the two Yumi ships and making pincer cuts with two fingers.

"He says that with Sesharians on board, we'll win on the open sea, so long as—" Afira halted then as the Ayoni continued. He finally stopped and looked at Afira, but she stood stiffly, eyes skittering away. Her sister fidgeted. Even Daz looked uncomfortable as he suddenly focused on the edge of the panel. Samson had the distinct sensation that whatever else the Ayoni had said was something caustic, an insult directed toward Seshar. He knew as soon as the Ayoni glanced at him. There was derision in his eyes, tinged with distrust. He knew the Ayoni were often unfriendly hosts, but he had not known of their prejudice against Sesharians. His skin crawled, and had he had the strength, he would have summoned an inferno so hot it would have dried the insults on the small man's tongue. The Ayoni spoke again, and this time, Daz recovered quickly.

"Apologies, friend." He rose, beckoning the Ayoni to take a seat again. "Our host cautions us to be careful about...treacherous force waves. There have been more winter storms around Seshar than we've seen before. Please, continue."

Samson slowly turned back to the panel. "I can lead a ship," he began.

The Ayoni sneered, and suddenly, he was a young boy again, filled with the gnawing desire to prove himself and rub his victories in all the naysayers' faces. They could not disrespect him once they feared him. "I know this part of the sea better than *anyone* here. Elena, once we're in the open sea, you peel off to trap in the first killdom."

She nodded, though he noticed panic creasing the corners of her eyes. *I'm afraid of the sea.* He touched her hand and bent close so that only she could hear.

"I'm with you, remember?"

She was so close that he could see her top lip quiver as her eyes caught his. A flash again, that fleeting emotion he could not name, before she nodded.

"I'll do it," she murmured.

He did not notice that the others were staring until he turned. Jaya looked amused, Chandi as if she was ready to berate him, and the Yumi indifferent, except for Daz. The general smiled, though it was cold and devoid of kindness.

"How brave of the two of you," he said.

The door slid open, and their Yumi escort stepped through.

"The ships are ready," she said.

Two black Ayoni ships floated at the end of the dock. Their hulls curved elegantly, each plank perfectly melded into the other so that there seemed to be no seams but a collective whole. Even the guns outfitted along the sides had an organic quality, as if they were living, breathing beasts. Samson had not heard the ships approach. They made no sounds as they floated, a marvel in itself. Elena drew up beside him, eyes wide.

"Have you ever seen anything like this?" she asked, her voice soft with awe.

He shook his head mutely.

"They'll do," Jaya said.

Rhumia started. "*They'll do?* The bounders aren't styluses you swap in and out like in one of your games."

"Everything is a game, dear Rhumia," Jaya said as she walked the length of the boat. "Everything."

"Let's load in now," Daz said.

Samson nodded, unable to tear his eyes away. "Yes. Chandi, bring in the men from the tankers. It's time we set sail."

As his soldiers filed onto the docks, Samson watched them take in this strange, silent port. Like him, they observed the workers in the distance and the glass city they could not touch. They watched the lone Ayoni, who stood in his rigid black coat and counted off on his holopod, his eyes sweeping over them.

"There's something odd about that man," he whispered to Elena.

"The quicker we get everyone in, the faster we can get out of here," she said.

Suddenly, a whirring started beneath their feet. Samson startled as the dock *shifted*. Elena cried out in alarm, and he grabbed her hand, pulling her to him, as the dock where she had stood turned inward, blocking off the first boat. His men shouted, pinned against the trapped ship. On the other side, the adjacent dock blocked the second bounder, and the workers in their helmets marched onto the platform.

Armed with guns.

"Fuck," he said.

"Sam." Her hand was warm against his chest, her voice urgent. "Sam, *look*."

Behind them, Daz shouted in Ayini. The Yumi were cornered on one end, and then Samson noticed the dockmaster standing on the only stable part of the dock, a stylus glinting in his hand.

"I knew it! You fucking chicken-livered sandbag!" Jaya screamed. She was balanced on two planks that precariously floated before the ship engines. "You took my design!"

And then Samson saw that she was right, that the docks hedging in the two boats was like the gameplan Jaya had made earlier of the bounders trapping in the killdoms.

"What's happening?" Chandi called. She stood on the other end of the plank with Jaya. "Daz, tell us!"

"I'll tell you," the Ayoni said in perfect Hind. "We have been awaiting payment for three days now, and here you are speaking of setting sail. That will not do, friends. General Daz must pay."

"Then make him pay up and stop fooling with us," Jaya shot back.

"I'm afraid you are a part of the payment," he said.

Elena whipped to Daz. "What kind of payment?"

"This was not a part of our agreement," Daz snapped. "Bresingi, we already paid our fare with contracts pledged to your empress. You are breaking the good faith between our—"

"You came with Sesharians," Bresingi said coldly, and the look he gave to Samson then made his skin curdle. "Our empress asks for fifty hail Sesharian sailors to work and sail the ships you've contracted to us. I believe there are over fifty who came with your guests."

"No," Samson spat.

The Ayoni ignored him, speaking only to Daz. "Fifty for your guests' fare."

"These are free men, not Jantari servants," Daz said.

"And they will be free after their contracts."

"Keep your horrid ships," Samson said. He wished he had never set his eyes upon them. "We don't need your help. We're leaving."

"But you do need these ships, little Sesharian," Bresingi mused. "How else will you enact your *great revenge*? How else will you make the great metal king bend?" He smiled. "All I require are fifty men."

"Bresingi," Daz implored. "Let us talk this through, eh? Surely your empress does not want tired, malnourished soldiers. They will be useless to you."

"Remember your place, Mokshi," Bresingi said, and there was something hidden in his voice, the soft whisperings of warning, because Daz fell back, his face shuttered with regret and helplessness.

Anger spiked down Samson's throat. *You fool.* How could he have not seen it before? The black-market sensors. Bresingi's slow, unpeeling examination. The Ayoni were traders, forcing free men into servitude behind their iron curtain of self-solitude. He should have never come. He should have never trusted the Yumi.

"Done."

His heart plummeted as Chandi called to the Ayoni. "I will pay their debt."

"Chandi, *no*," he said.

"You need to stop those killdoms and make it to Tsuana," she said to him. "Remember your promise."

She looked at him, her face resolute, and if he had not known her better, he would have thought her brave. But he saw fear in the quiver below her cheek. "Chandi—"

"I will pay the debt too," said another Black Scale, stepping forward.

"As will I."

"As will I."

Samson watched, helplessly, as his men followed their commander to their own ruin.

"Black Scales," he called. "I demand—I order—*take up your arms*—"

With a wave of his stylus, Bresingi pulled Chandi's plank in, and Samson's commander stood face-to-face with the Ayoni. He examined her slowly, and Samson felt bile rise in his throat as Bresingi made a soft, satisfactory cluck.

"This one will do," he said.

Immediately, the docks opened beneath Chandi, and she dropped.

"CHANDI!"

The force field cut her scream short. But Samson heard it, and he clawed forward, only to be repelled as the planks shifted. He howled in frustration.

"Careful, Sesharian, or else I'll drift you and her out to sea," Bresingi said.

It was only then Samson noticed that Elena had been separated too. She was on her hands and knees on tiny planks, shaking violently, and he thought, with a sudden malignant venom, of how she had not spoken up when Bresingi told them the price, how she had remained silent in this exchange, but then she looked up, and he saw her white-lipped fear.

I'm afraid of the sea.

"You fucking purple-brained brute—" he began.

Bresingi twirled his stylus, and a sudden force field ensconced Samson. He screamed, shouted, yelled—but he could not hear his own voice, and they could not hear him.

"Much better," Bresingi said as he turned to a pale-faced Daz. "Pleasure doing business, General. Now get off my docks."

CHAPTER 41

ELENA

Mourn not the hero, the villain, or the god. Mourn the woman she could not become.
— from the diaries of Priestess Nomu of the Fire Order

Elena watched Samson's sleeping form as her pale fire cast shadows across his face. His Agni twinged. And then his eyes shot open, and he sat up with a gasp.

"Chandi," he cried.

Slowly, she closed her fists, smothering the flames. "Hey, Sam."

He looked at her blearily, and for a beat, hope brightened his eyes. But then recognition shuttered his expression, and something small and crude bit into her chest. It hurt. And it bothered Elena even more because she did not know why it did, to see hope flee his eyes when he looked upon her.

"How—how are you feeling?" she asked, more roughly than she intended.

"Like I'm still waking from a dream." He ran a hand through his hair. "Chandi, the others, wh-where are they?"

"In Ayoni," she said. "Daz is furious. Says the Ayoni broke their trust. He's going to make sure they're freed as soon as possible." But even as she said it, the words felt rote, hollow.

She could not shake the terrible memory of traps opening beneath the docks and swallowing the Sesharian soldiers. Could not unhear Chandi's scream. She had been overcome by a dizzying sense of helplessness as the masked workers had filed onto the docks. She realized then that they wore not masks, but visors. Faded bulls dotted their hands. Their lips had been sewn shut, and she was not sure what was more horrifying: that the dock-workers were Sesharians forced into silence, or that they were forced to imprison their own under the brutal orders of Bresingi.

Their ships, which were meant to be full of fighting men, ran empty. They had only a few Black Scales left, and then Daz's men. They were sailing into a losing fight, and she did not know how to make it right. The same crushing helplessness clawed her throat again, and she looked away.

"How many of us are left?" Samson asked.

"Forty. Seventy, if you count Jaya's Sandsworn."

"Skies above." He hung his head, crushing the heels of his hands into his eyes. "Serpent forgive me."

"Sam—"

"I swore to protect them," he said, his voice strangled. "I promised, Elena. And I—I've failed. First the miners, now my men. Chandi." His voice broke under the weight of her name. "We're cursed gods, Elena. All we bring is ruin."

Reassure him, she thought remotely. *Make him think I'm on his side.* This was the game, wasn't it? To win his trust until she drove the blade between his ribs. But Elena could not summon the strength. Looking at him now, alone, withered, she felt the ire of her hate waver. This was the man she meant to destroy. This broken, bleeding boy without a home.

He reminded her so much of herself in that moment. They were both lost and forsaken, trapped in a vicious hunt for freedom when it remained the most elusive victory of all. She knew of his self-hatred: of not being enough, of not doing enough, of losing the ones closest no matter how hard you tried to keep them safe. They were one and the same. The Burning Queen and the Butcher. And this recognition almost felt like surrender, like a truce.

But Samson Kytuu did not deserve it.

Elena swallowed the quiet ache gnawing at her throat, and it felt like burying a knife within her own ribs. To acknowledge their similarities was to then open the floodgates of their shared monstrosity, of their own wicked selfishness, and Elena knew that if she were to do so, if she were to even give an inch, Samson would take two. And then another. Until she was back in the rain, abandoned and bleeding.

No. Samson was a monster.

She just had to be so much worse.

"Where are you going?" Samson asked as she rose.

"I—I need air," she said and stumbled out of the room.

She went to the upper deck and heaved herself onto the guardrails, gasping. She needed only a moment. Just a few minutes for the world to stop reeling. Just some air to beat out the hollow thumping of guilt building in her chest.

We're cursed gods, Elena. All we bring is ruin.

Everyone she loved had burned to ash, and Elena could blame only herself. The destruction she had once chastised Samson for had become her legacy. All these deaths were a part of her legacy too.

"You all right?" Daz asked.

Elena startled. "Y-yes."

"Don't worry, you'll get your sea legs soon enough." He drew up beside her, already dressed in his battle gear. "How is Samson?"

Devastated, she thought.

"Recovering," she said. "How far are we from the pit?"

"Two days' sailing," Daz said. "I should warn you, the pit is a strange and horrible place. It plays tricks on you. Makes you see things, hear things—"

"I'll be fine."

Daz studied her quietly and then, in a gentle voice, said, "It is okay to grieve, little queen."

She snapped back, as if hit. "I—I know."

"The Sesharians will forgive you. Once you free them, once Seshar is its own nation again, they will welcome you with open arms."

But his assurances felt like stones, each hitting their mark. How could she tell him her only objective, her *only* kingdom, was—could only be—Ravence? She could not stand to owe Samson and therefore Seshar anything.

But she had heard their screams. She had seen the wild horror in their eyes as the Black Scales fell into the traps and were carted off like cattle for slaughter. They were not her people, not truly, but she felt the grave injustice of it as if they were her own. And the thought of Chandi, of Akiri, of all the others trapped without escape, without hope, brought a fire into her ribs that hurt more than her guilt. And yet.

"I—" she began. She almost wanted to tell him the truth. That she couldn't fight two wars. That Seshar needed Samson, and that by killing him, she would be responsible for its destruction. It sat there, heavy on her tongue, and Daz waited patiently. But Elena swallowed it, just as she had swallowed her ache, her shame, and gripped the rails tighter. "I think Seshar will endure. They—they're a brave people."

"I will fight to get your soldiers freed."

Elena nodded, trying not to wince when he said they were *her* soldiers. "When Bresingi said 'Remember your place,' what did he mean?"

Daz winced. "The Ayoni made these ships only because they were contracted under my sister's rule. They do not…approve of my revolution. But they will come around, in time." His voice hardened. "They will learn to answer to me."

Elena watched him warily, struck by the sudden darkness in his expression. He would make a terrible enemy, if he were not on her side. Perhaps it was a play of the starlight, or the churning of the waves, but she felt a sickness worming up her stomach. *They will learn to answer to me.* She was surrounded by tyrants. Each as selfish and greedy as the last, each vying for power. She needed only to prove that her hunger ran deeper, crueler, and more vicious, and perhaps she and Ravence would survive.

"They all will," she whispered. "Even Farin."

His eyes narrowed into a slow smile. "Let us hunt well, then, little queen."

CHAPTER 42

SAMSON

Do not grieve, my son. It does not do well to dwell on the past when the sea is ever-changing. Endure. The Great Serpent waits for us to bring justice in tow.

—from The Lament of Seshar: A People's History

The night bled into the dark sea so that Samson could not tell where the sky ended and the sea began. Before him, the world lay thick and opaque. Full of unknowing. The abyss stared, but Samson could feel it already gnawing its way within him, carving a hole full of—nothing.

Samson Ruru Kytuu, for once, felt nothing.

He had already swallowed his tears until they burned to numbness. He listened to the susurration of the sea until he could no longer hear Chandi's scream. His grief, which had felt so enormous, so overwhelming, was now a cold, wet thing.

He stared bleakly at his reflection and the black waves beyond. Within the hour, they would arrive at the pit. He knew he should get up. He knew he had to leave this room, but all Samson could see was the pit

280

waiting, ready to unhinge its jaw and swallow him whole should he fail. He reached for his Agni and felt its small, uneven edges.

Was this what his mother had warned him of? That his fire, his curse, would eat him up until he was an empty husk of a man, powerful and brutal, yet withered and hollow? Alone in his power. Alone in his misery.

Someone touched his shoulder. Samson turned.

Elena stood behind his chair, her hands pressing into his shoulders, holding him down, holding him in place. Her hands were firm. *Full.* She was not empty like him. Her Agni, so bright and sharp, flickered in his mind's eye, beating back the abyss.

I am here, it said. *I exist.*

Before, he had been jealous of her Agni's abundance, but now he latched on to it with tired relief, leaning into her hands and basking in her warmth.

She stared out the window, and Samson watched their reflections on the glass.

"When this is over, what's the first thing you'd like to do?"

He was startled by the stark normality of the question. *What's the first thing you'd like to do?* As if they were discussing their plans for an ordinary day. As if, when this was over, they would survive. Walk out, hand in hand, the Butcher and the Burning Queen.

"I..." The words danced in his mind. The traitors. Slippery whenever he needed them. "I—I..."

I don't deserve an ordinary, mundane day. Men—monsters—like him were the reason days twisted into horrors. So he relied on memory, on the past. It was only there he could find refuge.

"I would like a plate of cloud cookies," he answered finally. "Raspberry and black currant flavored."

He thought of Yassen, how they had shared tea on a balcony overlooking a garden. His bright eyes underneath the midsummer sun. The cool wind against their cheeks. If Samson had known that would be his last unremarkable day, maybe he would have held on to it longer.

"And some tea," he added. He disliked tea, but it fit. "Vermilion. With a dab of honey."

In her reflection, Elena's lips trembled. "That was Yassen's favorite."

"I know."

She began to pull away, when he asked, "What about you?"

"The same," she said, her voice breaking. "But with two dollops of honey. It's better that way."

"Is it?"

She searched his reflection in the window, and for a moment, he saw her. He saw the same grief in her eyes, the exhaustion pulling down her mouth, the ache quivering in the soft muscles of her throat.

He stood to face her.

"Elena—" he began.

"Don't fling yourself into the sea." Her voice thickened. "I can't swim. I won't be able to save you. But when this is all over, we're going to have tea. Vermilion. With lots of honey. And then—and then…"

He made a choked sound, between a gasp and a laugh. She nodded, beginning to turn, but slowly, slowly, he raised his hand, the back of his fingers lightly brushing her cheek.

"Don't," she whispered.

He stopped. But she did not leave. His hand hovered along her cheek, barely touching, and she did not push him away. Her dark eyes fixed on him, and he saw that strange light flicker in their depths.

He had fought hard for her friendship, and he knew he should be happy with it. He knew he did not deserve her love. Even if she had any left to give, he would only receive scraps of it. But he had always been a hungry man. He stood rooted. Unable to find the words, unwilling to relent. And in the silence, the weight of the unspoken bore down until Elena finally freed them.

"The men are ready for you."

She left then, and he watched her go, his hand still hovering in the air.

Samson clicked his armor into place and wrapped his urumi around his waist. On the deck below, his few Black Scales and the Yumi stood at attention. The rest listened, the comms sharing his message to the other ship. But what would be his message?

Fight for Seshar? Fight for azadi?

What was the use of freedom when the men beside him may not live to see it?

His soldiers gazed up at him. There were ten of them, ten of the sixty that had left Magar, but he saw their ghostly faces in the spots where they would have stood. Chandi, Akiri, Akino, the rest.

Of his officers, only Visha stood before him now, her face stony if not for the muscle fluttering in her jaw. She and the others were all dressed in black, their eyes rimmed with kohl and urumis laced in their hands. His angels of death. Samson felt a sudden, fierce pride for their composure. He knew they were hurt, mourning, and angry, but they remained stalwart like the soldiers he had trained them to be. Visha stood at the front, expectant. His gaze fell on her.

"When I was a boy, my mother told me that Seshar had been made by the Great Serpent." His voice slipped underneath the hiss of the waves, reverberating across the deck. "She said the Serpent descended from the sky and made a resting place where She could sleep. And that when She left, She anointed warriors to protect Her home. Warriors made of the sky and sea. My mother told me that one day, the Great Serpent would return. But what will She find there now?"

He looked beyond the horizon where Seshar, in all her beauty, in all her misery, awaited. He saw Chandi plunging into the water chamber. He heard Akino and the trapped miners screaming his name. And he saw the Jantari zeemir above it all, hanging like a guillotine over their necks. His voice hardened.

"You will find murderers in Seshar. Men with pale eyes and awful zeemirs. They slaughtered our warriors. Our families. And, to rub salt in the wound, they took us, young and helpless, to make into their work mules.

"But we will change how they perceive us. We will capture and slaughter those Jantari thieves and spike their heads on our flag. We will enter Tsuana's waters with their killdoms in tow, soaked in their blood. And then the world will forever know our names, but not because we are fighting for our freedom." He laughed, high and caustic. "No matter our loss, no matter the wrongs done upon us, they will always see us as filthy Sesharians, fanatical Ravani, and paganist Yumi out for blood and revenge. They will see us as villains."

A ripple among his soldiers. A shifting of shoulders, quiet glances, soft murmurs. He let it pass and then continued.

"But we must become what we have to be. Make no mistake. We are bringing a war. A great war. One that will forever change the face of this world. Some of us may not live to see its future, its end. But…" He gripped the railing, leaning forward. "We do it in the name of our families. Our fathers. Mothers. Brothers and sisters who were so carelessly slaughtered. We do it"—he glanced at Daz—"to protect our home from invaders, and"—his gaze went to Elena—"to save the home we once lost."

Samson unwrapped his urumi, the blade slithering against the floor.

"I will not ask you to fight for me. I will not ask you to fight for your god or against the villains who destroyed your temples. Because our fight, *your* fight, is much greater than that. Your fight today is for *you*.

"For the future you. The one who, in a far gentler world, gets to put your daughter and son to bed. Who enjoys a late-night drink and watches the twin moons rise among the stars. Who falls asleep in your chair and wakes up the next day to do it again. The one who gets to live a full life.

"So fight for that version of you. The non-warrior. The ordinary man or woman who would rather spend a night watching their children sleep than seeing them murdered. Go. For they have always been waiting for you."

Samson raised his urumi, and like a beautiful melody, all forty men and women answered his call with a roar that reverberated through the ship and the sea and the sky beyond, where even the gods were compelled to listen.

CHAPTER 43

ELENA

There are no records of what resides in the pit. There are no photos,
no scans, no logical explanations for the things we have seen. But it is
there. Whatever it is, it waits in hunger.
            —from *The Legends and Myths of Sayon*

The roar of the men had not yet faded when the lights shuddered and
the sea moaned. Elena froze. The low moan quickly churned into the
growl of a storm. A gale whipped across the deck, and Elena barely had
time to grab for a railing when the ship suddenly heaved to the side.

Soldiers slipped, yelling. Rain slashed them with vicious white teeth,
and the waves ripped forward, snapping at the railings.

"To your stations, now!" Daz shouted.

Shapes, shooting in the dark. It took her a moment to realize it was the
Yumi, their hair piercing into the deck and gaining purchase. Out of the
corner of her eye, Elena saw the dark mass of their second ship. *Agni.* They
needed to summon their Agni and guide the ships—

"Incoming!" someone yelled.

She turned to see a black wave unhinge its mighty jaw before it swallowed the deck. The ship dropped like a stone. She was flung into the air, the sea and the sky spinning into one black blur—and then she slammed down.

White-hot pain razored through her shoulder. Elena groaned, trying to stand.

"Get up!" Jaya cried.

She grasped Elena's arm, pulling her to her feet. Something hard pressed into her palm. Elena saw the glint of the metal lotus as Jaya passed it into her hand, shouting something about using the sand as a shield, when the ship heaved and Elena was thrown to the side. She twisted, clutching the lotus.

"Jaya!"

But the ship bucked wildly, and she was flung against the railing. Elena scrambled for a hold, calling out for Jaya, for Daz, when a wave pushed her overboard and she spun, flailing, the sea swelling forward to swallow her whole.

She screamed.

A hand suddenly grabbed her by the elbow, and Elena gasped, pain ripping down her side. Below, the waves frothed at her dangling feet. Samson leaned over the railing, his knuckles white around her arm, and she was struck by the delayed thought that Samson—cunning, selfish, monstrous—had saved her.

"Hold on!"

She grabbed his arm with her other hand, and Samson pulled her up and over until they both toppled back onto the deck.

She landed on top of him, shuddering. They lay still for a moment, breathing hard, the rain pelting their skin. She was overcome by a breath-less sensation, the sudden exhausted euphoria of finding oneself impossi-bly alive when they should be dead. It was only later that she noticed the warmth of his skin. The thunderous rattle of his heart, beating against her chest. Samson looked up into her eyes with an odd, wondrous look, and he seemed about to say something, when her stomach twisted.

"I think—" she began.

She hurled herself over, vomiting violently.

"It's okay, you're okay." Samson rubbed her back, his voice gentle, soothing. "You're okay."

Elena wiped her lips with trembling fingers. Distantly, she could hear shouts. She tried to rise but her knees wobbled, and she crashed back down, hissing in pain.

"Easy, easy," Samson said. He wrapped his arm around her shoulders, his body warm and comforting, his voice a low pull. "I got you."

Blearily, Elena looked up at him. His wet hair stuck to his face and his lips were thin and pale, but his eyes were vivid and bright, his voice strong as he held her, and for a moment, Elena forgot her pain, her fear, clutching him as he whispered in her ear and rubbed her back until the shuddering passed and she felt like she could rise again.

"Can you stand?"

She nodded, and Samson helped her up. Wind whipped their faces as the storm grew in its rage. Elena could barely see the bow up ahead.

"We need to get up there and summon our Agni," he said.

The ship tilted, and they instinctively grabbed the railing. Samson locked his arm over hers, and they held on for dear life as the waves tossed them as if they were a toy in the hands of a child.

"We can't make it!" she shouted.

"We can! Just hold on to me!" He wrapped himself around so that her back pressed into his torso, his hands braced on both sides of her body, shielding her. His warm breath tickled her ear. "Move with me, rani."

Despite herself, Elena fought back another kind of shudder. Together, they followed the railing until they made it to the bow of the ship.

Sea-foam sprayed onto her face, stinging her cheeks. Below, she could see the sea chomping at the hull of the ship, trying to break it in two. Fear seized her. She imagined the ship snapping, saw herself plunging into the dark depths, water crushing her lungs, beating out her breath—

"Focus!" Samson shook her shoulder. "Focus on your Agni!"

She felt for her fire, envisioned heat lighting up her veins, her skin, until a flame flared to life around her wrist. Its sudden brightness beat back the dark. Like a beacon, it burned the night with a vicious defiance. But rain slithered down her neck. The waves shot up, brushing the back of her hands, and she hissed at its cold bite.

"Focus!"

"I—I can't!" she cried. She tried to splay her trembling fingers into the form of the Lotus, but she could not hold it. Her flame gasped, dissipating into steam. "The dance, I—I need space. I—" The ship heaved, and Elena clung to the railing, barely keeping her balance. She could not dance on such a raging sea.

"We'll hit a break soon!"

Samson stepped back and unspooled his urumi. Blue flames ripped down the blades as he whipped it into an arc, moving faster and faster— and then he staggered in pain. He was too weak. His flames too small, too dull. His fire juddered against the cold, stinging rain.

The ship began to nose-dive.

"Elena," he cried, his voice a plea, "now!"

She pushed herself back from the railing, sliding, fighting for purchase, before she finally slammed her weight into her heels and brought up her arms and shoved her fist forward, her Agni ripping up her stomach to her chest and down her arm, roaring to life with red, vicious tongues.

Their flames hissed in unison.

Samson spun around, and they stood back-to-back, braced, when the ship careened down, and the sea surged up.

Water flooded the deck. But Samson whipped his flames forward, and she followed in step, and their inferno ballooned into a ball that burned back the sea. Inch by inch, the waves receded. For a wild, breathless beat, Elena thought they had done it. But then an eerie sound called through the pit, building in volume, until it seemed like the very night reverberated with its mournful cry. It came from the depths of the sea, in the darkness that had no name. And as Elena stared past the protective glow of their flames, she saw a shape expanding in the distance, beyond their reach.

She froze as Samson let out a curse. She could smell his fear, the sudden staleness of it. The way his Agni quivered like a bow strung by an invisible hand.

"Wh-what is that?" she asked.

He did not respond. The shape grew taller, larger. Her heart seized as it filled the horizon, growing impossibly vast, bleeding into the edges of the darkness she could not see through.

"Sam!"

His voice was quiet. "Do you trust me?"

The ship groaned, the deck beneath her vibrating as the waves rumbled with the call of the sea. It sounded wrong. Unnatural. Deep in her bones, Elena knew a sound like this could not exist, that the pit was merely a deep chasm made of earth and stone and water, not filled with wrathful creatures, but she could not ignore what she heard. Her knees buckled—and Samson caught her. In the glow of the flames, he held her close, his voice fervent, desperate.

"Do you trust me?"

No.

She did not trust a monster like him. She *could* not trust a monster like him. But he had grabbed her hand when he could have easily let her slip into the sea. He was the only thing standing before her and the vivid dark with his lonely, dying fire. And Elena realized there were two ways this nightmare could end: one, where they drowned in darkness; or two, where they survived, hearts in their throats, forsaken but alive.

"Samson," she said, and if her voice trembled, she was sure it was because of her fear, not because of the way he looked at her now, full of a quiet hope she did not deserve, "I do."

He took her hand, his touch achingly gentle, his eyes ardently bright, as his flames twined around hers and she felt a white-hot cold begin at the seat of her spine.

Then as his flames grew, as pain built through her body and Elena felt her veins burn with a heat she could not contain, he held her fixed, his voice low, lush. "Then lend your Agni to me."

CHAPTER 44

SAMSON

Only fire can banish the shadows. Only love can unburden grief. The Great Serpent is made of both, so take care of Her dualities, and you will fare through the deep.

—from the hymns of the Great Serpent

Her Agni hit him with such force that Samson did not know whether to laugh or to scream. Heat surged through his veins, ignited his nerves, filled him with a luscious, vicious intensity. This wasn't just power. It was *life*, a puissance so ripe he could feel every sinew and cell of his body thrum in wonder. What an irony, then, that he, the Prophet who could heal burns, could only heal himself by being burned by another.

For so long, he had lived in the absence of such power and called it normal. He had almost forgotten what it felt to live wholly. But now...

He wanted it all.

Samson looked down, a grin spreading across his face, and was struck by the bright, acute fear in Elena's eyes. It slammed him back. His ravenous desire juddered like the body of an arrow vibrating upon impact. His hold faltered, and her Agni began to slip. He could still take it. She did not know how to close the connection and guard her spark from him. He could *see* the map of her: the beacons of her chakras, the glowing channels of her nadis. He could devour it all.

But Samson hesitated.

His own desire would destroy her. And for some reason, that knowledge and the thought of holding her cold, lifeless corpse in his arms, of feeling her stolen fire buzz through his veins as hers went dark, seized him with a terror like no other.

Elena wheezed, her grip on him slackening. She gritted her teeth and closed her fist, and he watched, a bit in horror, a bit in awe, as a flame bent to twist around his. *Impossible.* That she could still control her Agni even as he diverted her prana from her nadis. That she could still stand, her eyes burnished with fear and stubborn strength, as she raised a shaking finger and pointed behind him.

"Sam," she said. "It's...getting...closer."

He turned and saw waves bend around the beast. If he took all of her Agni now, he could banish the monster himself. He could cut back time. Free Seshar, win back the years its freedom had cost him. But at the cost of her death?

No.

The answer struck clear in his mind, like a singular note. And as it grew, he found his resolve emboldened, strengthened.

He released her hand, retreating from her chakras, and tamped down his hunger.

"Move with me," he said.

She grunted but raised herself to mirror his movements. He whipped his urumi and called their Agni. He felt a slight, instinctive resistance from her, but with a gentle tug, it gave way, and their Agni surged forth, blue and red flames licking down his twin blades.

In his mother's stories, the Great Serpent was betrayed by Her sister. Hollowed by grief, She had splintered into shadows. Ravenous, wraithlike beings that had grown twisted and wrong in their anger. The pit became their home. Their prison. And the monster before him now howled with a mad, frothing fury that made him feel the weight of its grief, of its bitter sense of injustice.

He had no gems. No lives to sacrifice. But he had Agni, and Agni always found its path.

He surged to the right and Elena followed in step, their arms rising in unison as he thrust his blades and she extended her arms. Their inferno roared forward like a bolt of lightning hurled from the hands of a god. It struck the dark shape. A high, uneven keen cut through the storm, ripping his eardrums.

Samson gasped, staggering back. Pain sliced up his sword arm, and he would have dropped his weapon if not for Elena as she stepped forward, wrapping her hand around his, and raised the urumi.

"Together," she said.

Elena swung back his arm, and he followed, their bodies fluid and smooth, their Agni bright and seething, and hurled another volley of flames toward the shadow.

It screeched. An awful, racking crack. The shadow flailed, its edges shriveling back to its mutilated core.

"We have it!" he cried.

He raised his urumi once more when the shape snapped.

It split in two, and he saw the dark tendrils of the monster lancing through the air before their ship tilted, and the sea rushed to meet them.

"Sam!"

Her hold on him loosened, dropped. He twisted to catch her, her name ripping through his throat as their fingers brushed. And for a moment, just for a cruel, singular heartbeat, he thought he had caught her, her hand warm and sure in his. But then her fingers slipped.

Elena Aadya Ravence plummeted into the dark sea, and he could only hang there, heart heaving, screaming her name.

"ELENA!"

The ship pitched wildly. The waves swirled, faster and faster, tossing their ship. With a sudden, vicious rage, Samson surged forward. He slung his urumi and sent a flare of charged flames. They bolted through the air, a brilliance of light, and slammed right into the being's core.

It crashed into the sea with a howl. Waves swelled, and Samson had one last glimpse of the dark tendrils flailing at the edges of the ship before something hard smacked into his head and he toppled to the deck.

CHAPTER 45

ELENA

There are three main ways to employ the Sesharian laborer: one, as an industrious miner; two, as a duteous servant; and three, as an unerring soldier. Rustbloods, they call themselves. An unruly term, but then again, they are an unruly people. That is why it is integral to rule them with an iron hand.

—from A Manual on Employing a Sesharian for Jantari Gentlefolk

She woke to the smell of grease. Elena turned, vomiting into a bucket. An older, grey-uniformed woman watched her dispassionately and, when she was done, handed her a wilted rag.

"No sea legs," she muttered.

"Wh–where am I?" Elena said. She tried to sit up and knocked her head against the bottom of a bunk. "Ow!"

"You would have been better off drifting out at sea," the woman said.

It was only then that Elena noticed the bull inked on her hand. The blue streak in her hair. Someone pounded on the door, and without waiting for an answer, a Jantari officer sauntered in. At the sight of vomit, he wrinkled his nose.

"Well, good, at least she's awake." He turned to the woman. "Can she work?"

"She's got no broken limbs that I can see," she said. "Just a tattered soul."

"Quit complaining. Get her proper clothes and send her to the line. You. What's your name?"

"El—" she began, and stopped.

"Hmm? What was it?"

"Wh-where am I?"

"On the *Lord of Sea*. We found you drifting on a broken…mass when we found you." The officer studied her. "Where are you from?"

"I—I don't re-remember," she lied. "I was on a ship, and then there was a storm—"

"An islander, then, though your accent is strange." The officer nodded, pleased with himself. "Yes, well, looks like you're not being shipped off to the mainland. You'll work this ship. Now get her dressed, Maya."

He left, and Maya handed her folded clothes, rough to the touch. "What is your name?"

As the woman's fingers brushed hers, Elena startled. An electric shock, white-hot in its intensity, blazed up her arm, and she turned, half-confused, half-alarmed, to Maya. Her vision split. She saw the healer through not only her eyes, but her *Agni's*. She saw the woman's seven chakras lined up her spine, the rivers of energy flowing through her nadis like tributaries toward a sea. *She saw the map of her.*

"You look like you're going to faint."

As she spoke, Elena felt a deep and sudden compulsion to reach forward with her Agni and simply *tap* into Maya, to bend those streams of heat to her and—

"Hello?" Maya waved a hand in front of her face. "Girl. Where is your mind?"

"A-Aadya," she stuttered. "M-my name is Aadya."

"And where are you from, Aadya?"

"I—I don't remember."

Maya sniffed. "Well, you're not an islander. I can smell it on you. But he can't. So keep your head down and just follow everyone else, and maybe you'll survive the passage."

"Where are we going?"

"Tsuana," Maya said.

Elena froze. Tsuana? And the ship was named *Lord of Sea…Phoenix Above! I'm on one of the killdoms.* But how had she washed up here, this far out? The last thing she remembered was the cold impact of the waves, Samson's distant scream. She had tried to kick to the surface, but then a shadowy tendril had grasped her ankle, and everything went dark.

She glanced down at her ankle, and sure enough, a purple gash marred her skin. Fresh stitches held the wound together. Gingerly, she peeled off her clothes and put on the rough uniform, trying not to wince as the pant leg scratched against her welt. Instinctively, she reached inside her pocket, and when she felt nothing, a cold realization hit her at once.

"My holopod," she said, turning out the pockets. Yassen's pod. The only memory she had left of him. She whirled around, searching the small room. "Where is it?"

Maya scowled and held up the silver disc, along with a small lotus. *Jaya.* Elena snatched both. She tapped the pod's center, but no holos sprouted.

"It's dead," Maya said.

"No—no, it can't— There must be a way to fix it—" Her fingers trembled as she clutched the pod. Distantly, she knew the pod was nothing but an array of holos and codes and maps, that it could not replace the living memory of Yassen himself, but something wild and ferocious beat against her chest. She felt as if she had lost Yassen all over again.

Maya placed her hand on top of Elena's, her voice oddly gentle. "You can try to have it repaired once we land."

Numbly, Elena slid the pod and lotus into her pocket. A dirty mirror hung along the far wall. She caught sight of her hair, a tangled mess, but what stopped her was the unfamiliar streak of blue.

She touched her hair. "Did you—"

"Blending in as an islander will make things easier. Now hurry."

Elena nodded, her throat suddenly thick. She did not know if she should be appreciative of the woman's resourcefulness or horrified by what it meant—that she was a prisoner on this ship.

Inwardly, she reached for her Agni. It throbbed at her attention, warm, sure. When Samson had tapped into her chakras, she had been overcome by the sudden uncomfortable sensation of being *less*. It was as if he had taken all the bright, essential parts of herself, fused them to his Agni, and lobbed it at the beast. And even as it writhed and screamed, Elena felt as if she had been listening from afar. With ears that were not hers, with a body that felt strange and foreign, as if she had diminished into a shade of herself she did not want to meet.

Maya tutted. "If you move any slower, they'll chuck you back into the sea."

Elena rose carefully. "How long have you been on this ship?"

"We've only been half a day sailing."

Half a day, which means the bounders still have time to catch up. A frantic, furious hope fluttered in her stomach, fragile as moth wings. If only she could send them a signal. Let them know where she was . . .

Maya nudged her. "Did you hear me?"

"Huh?"

"Skies above, you're deaf and slow." Maya shook her head and opened the door. "Come, snail legs."

Elena followed her out into the passageway. Soldiers—Sesharian recruits—walked stiffly by, their zeemirs strapped high upon their shoulders. Maya glowered as they passed.

"Rustbloods," she said, loud enough for them to hear.

A soldier at the end picked up his pace, avoiding Maya's glare.

Elena glanced at Maya's uniform. *Strange.* Hers was the same dark slate grey as the Sesharian officers, but Maya regarded the others with derision, and they regarded her with fear.

Jantari officers passed then, nodding to Maya, who saluted stiffly. They barely gave her a second glance. Faintly, Elena could hear the bustle of a ship at work: the rumble of orders, the drum of boots, the quick staccato of guns firing during a weapons check. But the Sesharians were quiet. And she could feel their tensely corded anxiety as they followed the officers down an adjoining hall. One woman passed something into Maya's hand. She pocketed it quickly.

They went above to the quarterdeck where two Jantari officers, including the captain, oversaw Sesharians scrubbing grime from the deck. Dark liquid sluiced across the floor. Elena realized a moment too late that it was blood, and she let out a small yelp. The captain turned.

"Ah. So our mysterious passenger survived. Did you manage to stop the bleeding, healer?"

"Yes, sir," Maya said. "She's good as new. Name's Aadya."

"Good." The captain assessed her, his eyes scanning her hair, her face, her arms and legs. "And what is she trained in?"

"She can shadow me, sir," Maya said quickly. "Get her familiar with the ship."

"No, I don't need you babysitting. Put her in the laundry. The least she can do is clean out her blood from these rags." He nodded to one of the Sesharians. "You. Give her yours."

Elena accepted the rag, thin rivulets of rust-colored water beading down her fingers.

"Clean," the captain commanded.

Elena did not move. She stared at the rag in her hand, and then at Maya. Her face was carefully neutral, though Elena could see the warning in her eyes.

"Are you deaf, islander?" the captain said.

Elena slowly lowered onto her hands and knees and began to rub at the dried blood. There was so much. Surely this could not all be hers. And then Elena looked up and saw the Sesharians strung along the upper railing. Her heart stuttered to a halt. There were three, their arms and legs pinned up, their heads bare to the sun, blood caked on their faces.

The captain and his first officer stood nonchalantly underneath the hanged men, their white, crisp uniforms garishly bright in contrast. Elena could not tell how long the dead men had been up there, but she noticed how the deckhands did not dare look up. Did not dare stop. Did not dare show their grief, or their anger.

There was a charged quiet in the air, filled with the overzealous sound of brushes scraping against the deck. Them, scrubbing their frustration away. The Sesharian beside her caught her gaze. He was a young boy, no more than fifteen, with thick black curls pulled back in a low bun. When the captain turned to consult his officer, the boy leaned closer.

"They said you were screaming about monsters when they pulled you in," he whispered.

"Was I?"

He nodded. "It's got everyone on the ship talking about the Serpent's shadows. That nasty cut on your leg—" He stopped abruptly when the first officer glanced back. It was the same man from before, the one with an upturned nose and dirty ashen hair.

"What was that, boy?"

"N-nothing, sir," he said quickly.

"Come here."

The color drained from the boy's face. He stood obediently. Elena had the sudden urge to pull him back, to pull him down, but the boy moved forward, his movements stiff and stilted. He came to a salute before the officer.

"Now tell me what you just said to her."

The boy said nothing, his head bowed.

The officer glared at her. "You, girl, up."

Elena stood slowly, fisting the rag to stop her hand from shaking.

"What did he say to you?"

"Nothing," she said.

The officer frowned. The captain yawned, waving his hand. "Let it go, Kilith."

But this seemed to spur Kilith even more. He turned to the boy and, without warning, slapped him with his open hand.

The boy fell to his knees, gasping. The others froze. Kilith snarled and kicked the boy down. He was too slow to protect himself as the officer stomped on his hand. A wet, sickening crunch resounded through the deck. Without thinking, Elena threw herself onto the boy. Kilith's boot rammed into her side, white spots bursting before her eyes as she gasped, short of breath.

"Fucking Sesharian scum," Kilith spat.

"Enough, Kilith," the captain said, sounding bored.

But Kilith raised his foot again, and Elena whipped around, half snarling, to catch his boot with her hand. It glanced off her fingers, knocking her chin.

Pain blazed down her jaw. She coughed, hacking out blood, as the officer sniffed. He kicked over her rag.

"Clean it up," he said.

Elena did not know what possessed her then. Only that, as pain thundered through her skull, as the boy lay quivering on his side and Maya looked down, her shoulders stiff with rage, some bitter fury snapped her up and she flung the rag at the officer.

It hit him on the side, smearing blood on his white uniform.

Everyone went still.

And then the captain began to laugh.

CHAPTER 46

JAYA

*A short-lived game is the fault of only, and solely, the gamemaster. It is
a reflection of poor planning, poor execution, and—most importantly—
a weaker mind.*

> —from *The Gamemaster Manual*

Jaya slowly slackened her grip as the ship stilled. She glanced at the sensor
boards. Their radars were still off, but their comms flared back. One by
one, the alarms cut.

"Phoenix Above," she whispered. "It's gone."

She rushed to the window. The storm had finally cleared, and the sea
stretched around them, dark and opaque. She did not know how long
they had been caught in it. Only that the waves had risen impossibly high
to reveal a beast—an incongruous amalgamation of unnatural angles and
sharp teeth. It had struck. And then she remembered a cold, strange feeling, like a wet blanket wrapped around her bare skin, pulling tight.

"What happened?" Rhumia croaked.

Her hair released from the floor, softened into locks. Jaya eyed the indentions she had made but decided against complaining.

"I'm not sure," she said instead.

Daz rubbed his head, blinking blearily, but then he started. "Elena. Samson!"

He bolted outside. Jaya ran after him, Rhumia bringing up the rear. They found Samson standing at the bow. He did not turn at their approach.

He simply stood there, rooted to the spot, his eyes fixed on the sea as if it held all his secrets, all his guilt.

"She's gone," he said in a voice so bare, so empty, Jaya wondered how the wind had not taken him.

"Elena?" Daz prodded. He turned to the other Yumi. "Were any of you able to bring her inside?"

As Daz spoke to the Yumi, Jaya crept toward Samson. There was a dark bruise creeping underneath his hairline. His shoulders hunched forward as if he were tensing for an attack.

"Are you all right?" she asked softly to not spook him.

His eyes were vacant, forlorn. When he finally turned to her, Jaya saw that they were also wet, his cheeks already streaked with the passage of tears. How long had he been standing here, weeping?

"I lost her to the sea," he said.

"Great Mother." Daz ran a hand through his hair. "Fuck. *Fuck.*"

"How will we appear before the council without her?" Rhumia said.

"The council is the least of our worries," Jaya said. "What about the kill-doms? How are we going to take them?" They had already lost half their manpower. And now without Elena, they had lost half their firepower too.

She turned to Samson. "Can you still . . . wield?"

When he did not respond, she dropped her voice. Prodded him gently. "Sam? How long have you been standing here?"

"Hours." His voice cricked like a rusted saw. "It's been hours since it took her."

Jaya remembered the beast in the storm . . . *No.* She shook her head. There had been no beasts. It had been a figment of her delirium, her fear, and she must have hit her head when the ship tilted. She was a woman of logic, of strategy. There was no evidence of beasts in the pit, only fierce winds and undersea volcanoes that blocked their sensors and scrambled their data. Hence, the pit. There were no monsters.

There are no monsters, she thought. She clutched the stylus in her pocket. *Only the monsters men make.*

"Sam, listen to me carefully," she began. "I need you to come inside. You need to rest. We'll be out of the pit soon and on the killdoms. And when we find them, I need you to be ready. Okay? Sam?" She looked him in the eye. "*Focus.* Don't let Chandi's sacrifice be in vain."

He stared at her, and slowly, slowly, she saw him remember. The glazed look faded from his eyes, and his mouth quirked down into a frown. He really would be a handsome devil, if he weren't such a tool.

"Good." She smacked him on the shoulder. "Now move."

Back on the bridge, Jaya surveyed the field. A comms light blinked, and after making sure she was alone, she opened the line. Akaros's voice broke through the static.

"What the *fuck* was that?" he said.

"I don't know," Jaya said, gazing out the window to the other ship as she flicked her stylus. "How are things on your end?"

"Dead as Leo. We lost three men to the storm, two Black Scales and a Yumi. We need more men on this ship. Where's Elena?"

"Akaros, they wielded. Together."

She heard him inhale sharply. For a while, he said nothing, and then, "Were you able to get a read?"

Jaya hesitated. Her stylus flickered in and out of her hand, a blur.

"Jaya?"

"No." It took an enormous effort to push out that word. She stopped whirling her stylus and set it down. "I—I wasn't on the deck when they melded."

Silence. And in that silence, Jaya tried not to fixate on the past, on her shortcomings, but it was like picking at a festering pimple. Perverse, and borderline obsessive. While the Yumi were able to latch down with their hair and escape indoors, she had clutched the railing for dear life, her useless hair flapping in the wind. Never more had she wished to be born a full Yumi. Never more had she wished to be born braver, like Div, or more fearless, like her mother, or more clever, like her father. They wouldn't have failed. They would have turned and forced their way to the bow. They would have activated the metal lotus and taken a reading of the intertwined flames. Instead, she had cried like a child. And when Rhumia grabbed her, pulling them both inside, she had clung to her like a wet rag doll, eager to be saved.

"So." Akaros's voice could cut through flesh. "We'll never learn how to tap into the third, then."

"I gave her the lotus," Jaya said hurriedly. "If she's still alive—"

"Alive? What happened to her?"

Jaya glanced up as Samson entered. "Elena went overboard. Isn't that right, Sam?"

He flinched. Silence on the line, and then, "Did he throw her over?"

Samson reared, anger rippling across his face. "Did I *what*?"

"I'll take that as a no."

"You fucking bastard. How could you even imply—"

Jaya slowly closed her eyes. She knew what Akaros was doing—his subtle provocations to reveal information. Samson had fallen into it so easily, so quickly, she had the urge to rescue him from his own demise, but she had already erred herself. So she stayed quiet. Forced herself to listen. She thought of home. Of Div.

"—that I would toss her over?!" Samson gripped the edge of the panel, blue sparks snapping precariously. "She was of Agni. *She was my rani.* I would never betray her."

Akaros laughed, cold and slow. "Did you siphon her Agni?"

"She gave it to me," Samson said, and Jaya snapped up.

"I'm sorry. She *gave it to you*?"

"So her Agni is yours, then?" Akaros said.

"No, no," Samson said, dropping his head into his hands. He tugged on his locks. "I—I took too much—at first, I couldn't help it—but then I tried to stop. I withdrew so she could have control, but then the ship pitched and she—she..."

"But you connected." Jaya tried to hold back the eagerness in her voice, but something, hope perhaps, delirium even, rustled in her chest. Maybe she *could* get a reading. Maybe she could save Div after all. "What was it like? For how long? Did you feel the third, out there somewhere? Did you overpower her, or did she—"

"Jaya." Akaros's voice was edged with warning.

But Samson had stilled. Something *shifted*. It was as if every part of him had sharpened, and the desperation in his eyes, the sorrow heavy on his shoulders, had ground into a weapon. Even his band of fire had silvered, and Jaya tasted the slight metallic charge of electricity in the air.

"What do you mean about the third?"

Ice pricked her ribs as she realized her mistake. Jaya took a step back.

Daz entered then and stopped short when he saw Samson with fire on his wrists. "Prophet—"

"What about the third Agni?" Samson repeated, his eyes on hers.

"You said it yourself, Sam. There is no third," Akaros chimed in.

"I never told you that," he snapped.

Daz looked at her. "There's a third Agni?"

"It's nothing," she said quickly, but Samson slammed his hand against the table, and she jumped.

"What. Third."

He rounded the table toward her, but Daz blocked his way. "Samson, enough," he said. "We need to find the killdoms—"

"Elena is gone," Samson snarled, but his voice broke under the weight of her name, under the unsaid. He pushed Daz away and stood before Jaya. His flaming hand a fingerbreadth from her own on the panel. "How do you know about the third?"

Her pulse hitched. She looked to Daz for help, but the Yumi watched her with a keen vigilance, as if prepared for her to bolt. She thought quickly—perhaps a white lie? Subterfuge? A gentle touch, like arranging the pillars in the field just so, so that the players were forced to close upon each other—but all strategies fled her mind as she watched Samson's flame lengthen, barely kissing her knuckles. Jaya trembled but stayed her hand. She could not show weakness to the players, or else they would turn against her.

She forced herself to look Samson in the eye. "There is a third Agni. And we think it's here. In our world, hidden somewhere. And I— I thought that, if only, well, if you and Elena…" She trailed off, blood pounding in her ears. *Thought what?* She could not give him the truth, the whole truth. It would ruin all that they had built, all that *she* had built. It would end Div.

Suddenly, the flame launched forward and bit her flesh. Jaya yelped, yanking back her hand. Ash ringed her skin, and a welt was already rising. But Samson had not moved. Had not even blinked. He stood still and alert, and there was something uncanny about his stillness, in the way his eyes tracked her. Like a butcher, studying a cornered animal.

"Lie to me again, and it'll be your whole arm," he said.

Daz fidgeted but said nothing.

For the first time, Jaya felt dread, cold and thick, wrap around her spine. She cradled her hand to her chest and thought, *This is why the gods took away Agni.*

"You and Elena can awaken it. If your Agnis are strong enough, melded enough, it'll call to the third."

Samson's hand trembled. "Who is the third?"

"I—I don't know."

The flame flashed, and heat seared her face. White-hot pain exploded down her neck. Jaya cried out, stumbling back, as a burn lacerated her skin in thick, heavy ropes.

"I DON'T KNOW."

She felt her skin tightening, twisting, and she bit back a scream as her burns cooled. When it was done, she raised a trembling hand to her neck and found it smooth, unblemished.

"Well." Samson winced as he pulled back the flame, but if he felt any remorse, she did not hear it. "I suppose your third will remain hidden forever, then."

Jaya lowered her hand. Tears pooled in the corners of her eyes, and she rubbed them furiously, fighting to calm her trembling breath.

"You—you had no right to burn me," she said.

Samson said nothing for a long moment. He stared at the red light of the comms line, and then, in a soft voice, said, "We are not friends, Jaya. You are here because I had no other option. You'd do well to remember that."

He turned to go.

"But I am of worth to you," she said, and he stopped.

She did not want to help him. Let Samson suffer. Let him waste. She regretted ever feeling pity for the Butcher, but Jaya thought of Div, lying in his metal coffin, breathing on borrowed breath, and she thought of the glorious, vicious justice she'd have watching the Butcher sail to his doom.

"You lost your men, but I still have my Sandsworn. You lost your queen, but I still have a battle strategy that will help us win despite that.

You don't get to walk away from me, Samson Kytuu, because we are not *friends*. You stay, because you need me." She flicked her stylus, opening the comms. "And because my operative Maya is already on the *Lord of Sea*."

Samson blanched, and Jaya felt a cold, petty vindication in seeing unease creep across his face.

"How—"

"We'll be on them in half an hour. So brace yourself, Butcher. We have Jantari to hunt."

CHAPTER 47

ELENA

Our bodies are maps of the divine that flows within us. Fear, then, the man who uses it against his friend. Pity, then, the man who uses it against himself.

—from the diaries of Priestess Nomu of the Fire Order

Elena tried to wrench off the ropes on her hands, but the more she resisted, the tighter they dug into her skin. They had tied her to one of the killdom's long-range pulsers, her arms bent back and around the smooth neck of the cannon, her legs bound below. The mouth of the pulser vibrated slightly behind her back.

"Careful," the captain called. "If you move more, you might set it off."

Her chest tightened, panic limning her ribs. Kilith slammed his hand against the hull of the pulser, and Elena jumped. She could not see him, but she heard his laugh, somewhere below on her right.

"It's been a while since we've had some fun." Footsteps, drawing closer. A hand trailed up her leg, and Elena shuddered, whimpering as the head of the gun bit into her back. Kilith grinned from behind his visor.

"Now, where to begin."

"Kilith," the captain called, "arm the pulser."

Elena squirmed as his grin lengthened. "With pleasure, sir."

His hand slipped down her calf, her ankle, sending goose bumps up her leg. Kilith spoke into his pod, ordering for the weapons to arm. The pulser turned, and Elena yelped as she swung with it. Her feet dangled over the waves. Along the horizon, she saw the black mists of the pit coiling like writhing snakes. She wondered if Samson and the others were still trapped in its depths. There was a shimmer in the air, as if the sky itself was vibrating. Or perhaps it was her. Elena did not realize she was shaking, only that she could not stop. The pulser swerved right, and she spun, back to the deck. Below, the captain chuckled. Maya stood beside him, her jaw tight, as the other Sesharians dared not look up.

"Please—"

The pulser jerked left, and she spun back out to sea. It swung again, and again, her body like a rag doll, lurching with the gun as it whipped back and forth, back and forth, the sea and the ship blurring into splotches of grey. Elena had no time to think. The wind roared in her ears, and she could hear their laughter rising. The pulser finally stopped and turned inward. Elena snapped her mouth shut, but her stomach twisted, and she vomited, dry heaves racking her body.

"Tell me. Aadya, is it? How long was your contract?"

Tears and snot ran down her cheeks. The world was still spinning, and she squeezed her eyes shut. Still, the low sun spiked off the Jantari metal, and she could feel its merciless glare sear through her eyelids.

"C-contract?" she whispered.

"I believe twelve more years, sir," Maya said.

"Twelve," the captain mused, and blearily, Elena understood. Her contract to Jantar. He assumed she had one like every other Sesharian laborer.

Behind her, the barrel of the pulser whined to life. She could almost feel it. The heat building. She could not burn. But a pulse ripping through her stomach, shredding her lungs? Even Samson's fire could not heal her from that. Elena tried to call her Agni. If only she could wield, spark a flame from between her fingers, but her mind whirled. They had bound her hands so tightly that she could not even feel her fingers, let alone form the Lotus.

"Twelve years, and for it to end like this. What a waste."

The captain raised an yron to his lips, considering the hunched laborers before him.

"You." The unlit yron bobbed from his lips as he pointed to a Sesharian, a man with long hair tied back, his neck bare to the sun. "And you." He pointed to a small woman who froze as his accusing finger found her. "Six years will be added to each of your contracts. Someone must make up for her belligerence."

"No," Elena gasped.

"But, sir, she is not—" the woman began.

"I will make sure that it is done," Maya cut in.

The woman glared at her, and then looked at Elena with such anger, such loathing, Elena wanted to whittle into a ball. The man looked up, and she expected the same fury, but it was the look of defeat in his eyes, the tired acceptance carving the lines of his face, that cut her deeper than the ropes biting into her flesh.

"Please," she begged. "They are not responsible."

"Not responsible?" Kilith laughed. "You are one and the same. Remember that. And if any one of you wants to play the stupid hero, remember her."

Elena felt the pulser engage. She heard the deep internal thrum of its sensors zap to life, creating a charge. A strangled scream escaped her throat. Agni. She needed her Agni. She wrenched her hands, trying with all her might to snap the ropes as the captain calmly reached into his breast pocket.

The pulser thrummed louder.

Focus! Her fingers clawed the air helplessly as a roar built in her ears. *Focus.*

Kilith turned to his superior, waiting for his signal. The captain withdrew his lighter and flicked it open. A tiny flame bloomed to life. Small, inconsequential. But Elena heard it draw in its first breath of life, a thunderous clap in the quagmire of her panic. And like a starving man who sucked water from a rock, she pushed her mind forth, latching on to it.

The lighter's heat flared in her mind's eye. She reached, fingers flexing as if she could grasp that tiny flame. The captain raised the lighter to his lips, and her focus slid from the flame to his mouth. To the heat of his breath. To the warmth that pulsated through his veins, his bones, his nadis. It was like a channel, running from head to toe, and the fire was her boat through it. She saw him as her Agni did. A collection of chakras and nadis, a glowing, beating mass of prana, flowing throughout. *She saw the map of him.*

When Samson had fused with her Agni, it was as if an invisible force had latched on to all the bright and essential parts of her, and slowly throttled them. If he had continued, she was not sure what would have remained of *her.* But as she looked at the tiny flame and the heat nodes of the captain, Elena did not care.

She drove forth her mind, grasping on to the captain's chakras as Samson had done to her.

And she tore.

The captain let out a strangled cry. His hand seized. She felt the temperature of his body rise, tasted his bitter panic as she swam through his nadis, twisting, clawing.

He gasped. Blood beat behind his forehead, his pale skin turning a deep crimson red. She could see his veins straining against his temples. All that heat, trapped beneath his skin. She spiked it up. Like a dial, she turned up his temperature, and the captain screamed. She took control of his body then. Jerked him left and right like he had done to her. She rushed her Agni's awareness to his legs, and his feet skittered over the deck, then his arms, flapping them like a bird. He tried to scream, and she clamped his throat. His eyes bulged, the whites straining in their sockets.

Kilith rushed to him, trying to make him stop, screaming for help, screaming that she was a witch, a sorceress, but all she could hear was the rabbitlike beating of the captain's heart.

Blood poured from her nose. Distantly, Elena noticed the drumbeat of her heart quake with warning, but she did not stop. Their eyes were wide with terror, and she relished it. And as that power flooded her veins, as her own Agni flared with a vicious, delicious force of another, she forgot how Samson had made her less. She forgot her fear. She was burning from the inside out, and it was agonizing.

It was glorious.

So Elena reached. She dug into the deep waters of the captain, wrested into his prana, and burned.

He exploded in a flash of blood and flame.

They tore from *inside* his chest, eating into his flesh. Kilith screamed. Maya swore. The Sesharians bolted away as the captain's body toppled. The flames leapt out, rushing the deck. They climbed the gun and burned her bonds, and then Elena dropped to the deck with a solid, heavy *thump*.

Kilith stared at her in horror as she rose slowly. Her flames wreathed around her, curling around her legs, her arms, her chest and face. A glowing, fervent inferno.

"Please—" he said.

"The next time you want to play the villain, remember me."

Her inferno drowned his screams.

Boots thundered up the stairs. Elena turned to find Sesharian officers storming the deck, but when they saw her, when they saw what she had done, they froze.

Maya intercepted them, holding Kilith's pod. She did not look scared. In fact, she looked rather pleased.

"Lower your guns, rustbloods, or Great Serpent preserve me, we'll burn you down too."

One fool stepped forward and removed his visor. Elena gasped as she recognized his thick jaw, his dark eyes, the cut in his brow that had come from a mining accident.

"Akino." She swayed. "I—I thought you were dead."

"And I never thought I'd see you again," Akino said.

Maya held up the pod, a bright blue light blinking on its screen. "We need to take the bridge so I can contact Jaya."

Elena reexamined the healer carefully. "Who are you, really?"

Maya pocketed the pod. "Arohassin. But more importantly, who are *you*? Witch? Sorceress?" She paused. "Ravani?"

Elena considered, and as she did, she heard the song of her inferno, the intoxicating hiss of her flames as they chanted her one true name. She said, "I am Elena, queen of Ravence."

CHAPTER 48

ELENA

Godhood is not a blessing. It is a sickness that feeds on your hatred and withers all the bright and essential parts of you. I want it more every day.

—from the diaries of Priestess Nomu of the Fire Order

Alarms blared as she, Maya, and three rebels sprinted down the passage.

"The bridge is this way!" Maya shouted.

Sesharians ran past, some to the armory, others to the weapons deck. They seemed to have anticipated this rebellion, as Maya shouted orders, directing a contingent to the mess, another onto the bridge. Elena was struck with the fleeting sensation of being thrust into machinations beyond her control, but she had no time to consider as pulse fire echoed ahead of them.

Maya winged left, pressing her pod against a sensor, and a door swung open.

"Hurry! In here!"

Elena rushed through. They were in a supply room with hefty boxes floating between shelves. Maya called one down.

"Wear this." She handed them dark slate uniforms. "Seems like being a rustblood can do some good."

Elena pulled the uniform on, wincing as the collar brushed her bruised chin. Once they changed, Maya led them out of the storeroom, past the stateroom with its tipped chairs and half-finished drinks, and to a passage.

"The bridge is just there on the right. Now, when we get in there, let me do the talking—"

"Healer!"

Elena whipped around and saw an officer, followed by three others, gaining on them. Soon, they filled the small hall. This close, even her flames wouldn't be fast enough to catch the pulses. But if they drew nearer... She began to summon when Maya held out a hand.

"Sir." She saluted. "We were just reporting to the bridge. The sensors cut off. There's a fire spreading on deck—"

"Why are you armed, healer?" The officer drew closer, but he did not lower his gun.

Elena itched to burn. Heat thrummed up her veins, ash in her throat. Closer now...

"I had to apprehend a rebel. He's back there, outside the officers' quarters. Tried to ram his way in—"

He pushed the barrel into her mouth. "Shut. Up."

Maya froze. She looked out of the corner of her eye, met Elena's gaze.

The officer caught it. "Hey, what are you—"

Elena jabbed her arm forward, spearing a flame through his throat. He crumpled without a scream. The others reacted—too slow. Maya lunged, grabbing one officer while Ajira and Nurra took another, Tanmay the third.

Ajira wrested a gun, but Tanmay's officer fired, the pulse ripping through the ceiling. Someone shouted from inside the bridge.

"Shit," Maya said.

Elena growled and grabbed the gun, and together, she and Tanmay finally wrenched it away when an officer ran out.

"Rusting hells, what is going on—"

Elena pressed the gun into the new officer's head, pushing him forward. "Not another step, or I'll melt his brains."

The officer halted as the others followed her lead.

"Back," she said. "Go on."

He retreated, and they marched into the bridge, hostages held before them.

The officer on watch looked up from the three-dimensional holo of the killdom and froze.

"Healer, why do you have a gun on my quartermaster?" he said.

"Step away from the panel," Elena said.

He did not move. So she shot. He jumped back with a yelp as the pulse ripped through the panel's edge where his hand had been.

"I said: Step. Away."

Glowering, he slowly retreated. They corralled him and the others into the corner, Tanmay keeping watch as Elena and Maya rushed to the panel.

"Ajira, Nurra, contact Akino," Maya barked. "See if he got to the armory. Elena, how far and fast can your inferno spread? Elena? Elena!"

Elena turned from the sensors. She pointed to the two red dots. "What are those?" The question was directed to the officer on watch. When he did not respond, she strode over and yanked him up, pressing a flaming hand close to his face.

"How long have we been trailing them? Who are they?" she demanded.

He said nothing. Elena pressed closer, and he jerked his head, trying to pull away from the snapping flames on her wrist.

"I'm not going to repeat myself twice."

"They're Yumi ships," he said finally. Sweat beaded down his forehead. "They just sailed out of the pit."

The ship suddenly juddered. Elena glanced back to see the force field around the killdom disappear.

"Cloak is down," Maya said. "No distress signals were sent to our friends on the *Relentless Destiny*. I'll send word—"

Elena sensed movement. She turned—too late. The officer on watch grabbed her gun and shot, the pulse ripping past her and into Maya's hand.

She howled. Blood spurted from her missing finger as the pod clanged to the floor, melted and warped.

Elena tackled the officer, and he landed a knee in her stomach. She gasped. Black circles danced in her vision, but she clung on, grabbing the butt of his gun.

"You fucking bitch!" The officer tried to fling her off, but Elena held tight. He backpedaled and slammed into the wall, crushing her against it.

Elena choked, the air rushing out of her chest. Her hold slackened, and she slid down. He rammed the butt of the gun into her face. Pain exploded in her cheek and neck. Elena tasted blood as she bit into the soft skin of her mouth. Stars, searing and bright before her eyes. The officer swung, but she caught his blow this time, arms straining. He growled, bearing down, his sweat dripping onto her. This close, she could see the whites of his eyes, smell the stink of his fetid breath. His gun inched closer, and she felt her muscles scream, white-hot agony pulsing in her cheek, her jaw.

Suddenly, a hiss filled the air. She recognized it a beat before the slingsword blade slid cleanly through the Jantari's chest, the tip stopping inches from her own. The officer gasped, in panic, shock. Blood dribbled from his lips, onto her face, her chin. Elena gagged. She finally shoved him off and sat up, gasping.

Akino stood in the doorway with a slingsword. The other officers were dead, including one of their own, Nurra. Maya held her bleeding hand to her chest while Tanmay wrapped an arm around Ajira's shaking shoulders.

Red, everywhere. In the blood pooling across the floor; in the sensors floating before them, the two dots bright and crimson like pomegranate seeds.

Elena rose unsteadily to her feet. She had the urge to strip off her clothes, to clean all the blood and grime from her skin. The rush of battle, now that it was over, had left her cold and somewhat sick.

Akino reeled back the blade with a wet plop. He wiped the sword, then held out the hilt to Elena.

"For you."

Carefully, she accepted the blade. And then she swallowed her disgust. They still had a ship to take, a king who needed to be brought to heel. She pointed to the two blinking dots of the bounders.

"Take me to them."

CHAPTER 49

JAYA

If the gamemaster loses control, then the field becomes a bloodbath.
—from *The Gamemaster Manual*

The sensors flared to life as they cleared the mists of the pit and saw the killdoms racing through the night.

Jaya swallowed her victorious cry, saying only, "I told you so."

Rhumia scowled. "Lucky guess."

She rushed to the comms panel as Daz ordered his men to man their stations, arm their long-range pulsers. The bridge was a flurry of activity, and despite the danger lurking beyond, she could not help but feel a thrill of exhilaration, the anxious, breathless excitement that came before a game, when the field was set, the fighters ready to charge.

"Akaros, are you in position?" she said.

"We are," he replied through the comms. "Do we know which one is Maya's killdom?"

At his question, her excitement tamped down a degree. She scrambled through the comms units, heart climbing up her throat, but—no. There was no signal from Maya. "Something's gone wrong."

Rhumia heard. "This has been a suicide mission from the start—"

"Enough." Daz watched the second killdom, the *Relentless Destiny*, as it sailed out with the *Lord of Sea*, no doubt meaning to pincer them. "We go for both."

"But Maya is on one of those ships," Jaya said. "She's been gathering intelligence on the Jantari navy movements. If she's harmed, we would lose all that data."

"Tough," Rhumia said.

Jaya turned to her, a curse on her tongue, but Daz held up his hand. "Didn't I say *enough*? If you two continue to argue, I will relieve both of you of your duties."

Jaya wrenched her mouth shut, though she itched to drive her stylus through Rhumia's smirk. If only they were in the field. She would have had control, a gameplan—harmony.

"We're moving in," Akaros said. "The *Relentless Destiny* is mine."

"Left full rudder to ninety," Daz called.

Afira turned the model, and the ship groaned, slicing through the waves as they turned sharply. Akaros moved off their port stern, cutting out to the west to draw out the *Relentless*.

"Increase speed, hold steady."

"Increasing," Afira called.

Jaya grasped the panel edge as their ship bounded forth. But the killdoms did not split and take Akaros's bait. Instead, the *Relentless Destiny* kept its path behind the *Lord of Sea*, the two bearing toward them, much too fast.

"They're going to pincer us. Daz, please," she said. "At least send a signal to the ships. Something Maya knows. Then we'll know which one she's on."

"Shoot them down," Samson said, his voice edged with something that sounded like pain, felt more like spite. "We'll have them in range."

"*Lord* bearing two-ten, contact in ten minutes. *Relentless* in fifteen," Rhumia said.

"Port ninety," Daz said. "Afira, arm the pulsers."

The killdoms were armed with sparkbombs, old and heavy, but the bounders were too light, too fast, to hold any. And they did not mean to destroy the killdoms. They were to capture and sail them into Tsuana as victors. Jaya gripped the panel, her stomach twisting as Afira pressed the model for charges, and the holo flashed red, indicating that the pulsers were armed.

Suddenly, there came shouts from outside the bridge, up at the pilot's nest. Jaya rushed out just as she heard a hiss, then a loud sizzle. Visha held up a flare, and in the night, it seemed to throb, a panicking heart.

"Port stern!" she cried. "Turn! Turn!"

"Right full rudder!" Jaya shouted back to the bridge.

Rhumia seized the model, jerking them to the right. Jaya was flung onto the railings, and she gasped as the metal collided with her spine and sent shock waves down her back. She moaned, trying to rise to her feet.

And then she heard it.

How could she ever forget that sound?

Staccato noises, like fire spitting, logs cracking. The sound her mother's and father's pyres made as she lit the bases and offered their souls to whatever cruel gods lay beyond.

And then it flared on their screens: a bright white dot hurtling toward them. Yet it was Visha's cry, loud and terrified in the night, that made it all too real.

"Sparker! Sparker! It's coming right at us!"

CHAPTER 50

ELENA

*The goddesses are similar, but their followers ignorant. Little do they
know there is a being just like her, just as hungry, just as monstrous.*
—from *A Critique of the Ancient Gods*
(note: debunked by historians)

Elena sensed the sudden flare of a foreign fire racing through the sea.
She whirled around, searching the screens. There! The white sparker, racing from the *Relentless* toward the Yumi ship.

"Fuck. Fuck!"

"Jaya and Akaros could be on that ship," Maya said.

And Samson, she thought, surprised by the depth of her concern, her
sudden desperate ache to *know*.

She pushed it back. In moments, the sparker would pass parallel to
them in its warpath to the bounder. Daz, the Yumi, everyone would be
lost. Perhaps that was why the idea came to her. Not out of her regard
for Samson and his well-being, but for the Yumi. After all, if she lost
Daz now, who would represent Moksh at the council? How would she

intimidate the kings and queens if not with the Yumi? It was the logic she could accept, the reasoning she sold to herself, even if it tasted gently of a lie.

"Increase speed," she said to Maya. "We're going to intercept it."

Maya balked. "We have rebels on board. Free Sesharians—"

"Mother's Gold, increase speed!" she snapped. She reached for the projection, but Maya pushed her back.

"You don't know how to operate it," she hissed.

"Put us in the path. Now, Maya! We'll take the hit."

Her eyes widened. "Who knows how many will survive. Who knows if *we* will survive."

"This ship can take the strike! They can't! And I can control fire, remember?" A flame snaked down her arm. "I'll protect us. Trust me."

The comms suddenly blinked, and the warbled voice of the captain of *Relentless* drifted through.

"Captain Risith. XO Kilith. We're seeing pulse fire on your deck. Who has command of the ship? Who is the officer on watch?"

Elena thought fast. If the *Relentless* thought the *Lord* had been overtaken, they would turn their guns on them. "This is Officer Narian, sir," she said, reading the name tag of the fallen officer. "Captain Risith and XO Kilith were called to quash a Sesharian scuffle. A little noise, that's all."

"Are you a blockhead? We're engaged with the enemy. Call him back!"

"I'll send a—"

"Now!"

Elena cut the line, whirling toward Maya. "Please, Maya," she begged. "Turn us."

Maya stared at her, unwilling, but then she moved forward, and the engines clanged. They turned hard just as the sparker neared. And then Elena felt it.

The heat signature of the sparker. Bright and staccato, like spitting flames. They swerved into its path, and it exploded along their starboard.

The ship shuddered, and Elena lost her footing. Maya was flung over the panel. The world tilted, slingswords, pulsers, bodies, and men tumbling around her. And then the ship snapped still, alarms blaring.

She heard the hiss of the flames scratch the back of her mind.

Elena threw her Agni forward, searching, feeling, and found the new inferno. It shied from her touch, but she pursued it. Snagged into its essence. Slowly, Elena quelled it, forcing the flames to turn inward, to contract. Blood dripped from her nose again, and her arms trembled, a vein straining in her forehead. Pops of resistance, like tiny headaches jabbing in her mind. The inferno lashed back, pushing its will on her. But her will was stronger. It always had been. With sheer stubbornness, with a strangled cry, Elena sucked the inferno until she felt its will bleed—and then the flames were hers.

"I have it," she said weakly.

She collapsed onto her knees.

Distantly, Elena heard Maya cry out in warning. She turned—and saw it out the window. It appeared like a wraith, surreal and unbecoming. Black hull as dark as oil, bones painted down the side, the red of its pulsers whining to life.

The *Relentless* had turned their guns on them.

CHAPTER 51

SAMSON

I cannot bear to find your mad heart silenced, your inner comet stilled.
There is music for us still to hear, my love. So why are you not near?
—from *The Odyssey of Goromount: A Play*

The *Lord* exploded in a sheath of flames running down its sides, but that was not the inferno that called to Samson. It first came with a bloom. Soft and warm, beneath the cage of his chest. Even as his own exhaustion subdued the edges of the world, he felt something sharp and vicious, awakening. He turned, half-afraid, half-hoping. *Could it be?* The sensation intensified into a calcified, white-hot heat that snagged the corner of his heart and tugged. He almost cried out in pain and relief. It was her. He knew the shape of her desire, the fury of her wanting. He knew it as well as he knew the curves of Seshar's moonlit bays, or the song of the wind as it rattled through the mangrove leaves, soft and low like a murmur. He tried to call to her. To catch the indefinite ribbons of her prana, but when he tried to grasp them, they fizzled through his mind.

Samson stumbled back into the bridge, Jaya on his heels.

"It's Elena," he gasped. "She's alive."

"What? How?" Daz whirled, searching the sensors. "Did she send a signal?"

"Her Agni, I can feel it. She's on the *Lord of Sea*."

Pity flickered in her eyes as Rhumia turned to him. "She's gone to the sea, islander."

"She is not! Why else did the *Lord* take the hit? She screened us."

"He has a point," Jaya said. "I saw the flames on the *Lord*. They moved like hers."

Daz shook his head. "Forget the killdoms. We can't win. We must make for Tsuana in haste. Rhumia, set a course for the south to outrun these bastards, then send a distress signal to—"

"But Elena needs us!" Samson interjected. "It is her! I know it. She is on that ship."

"Our priority now is getting to Tsuana, safe and sound. Elena may be gone, but I can still push our cause when I take my seat at the council—"

Daz yelped in alarm as a blue flame snapped forth, biting his wrist. Rhumia whipped around, her hair rippling, hardening, as Afira lunged for him.

Samson dodged her, his urumi singing as he snapped it forward. Flames roared down the blade.

"Daz," he called over the inferno. "I don't want to harm you. Turn us toward the *Relentless* or give me command of the ship."

Rhumia swiped, and the edge of her hair caught his forearm, cutting through his skin. Samson hissed in pain. He brought up a flame, forcing her back.

"Daz! Turn back or surrender this ship."

But then Afira struck, swift and silent. He had not heard her creep behind him, but he felt her now as her hair dug into his shoulders. Samson cried out, his sword falling. She slammed him into the wall, and he crumpled to the floor.

Shadows ringed his vision. Faintly, he heard Jaya screaming, and then a wet, gurgling sound.

"I'm sorry, Sam," Daz said, his voice pinched. "But we must sail straight to Tsuana now."

CHAPTER 52

JAYA

A fight is won not by the strongest fighter, but the cleverest one. Think like your enemy, and you will defeat him long before he tastes the sword.
—from *The Gamemaster Manual*

You asshole," Jaya said, wincing against her bleeding tongue. It had swelled in minutes. Blood dripped down her chin, her hands bound behind her back.

Daz said nothing. But Rhumia smirked as she guided their ship forward, her hands floating above the panel, palms limned blue. Flecks of red still dotted her hair.

"Save your tongue, girl, and I might spare you once we reach Tsuana."

Jaya began to speak again, but Samson nudged her with his knee. His hands were tied painfully tight, skin already turning blue. Afira kept watch, his urumi in her lap, and would not meet Jaya's gaze.

Coward.

What Yumi ever ran from battle? Abandoned their friends? *Proud warriors my ass.* She had seen the ghostly glow of the fires on the *Lord*. She had studied Elena's Agni well enough to know it was hers. The queen was alive. And that meant she hadn't failed.

She could still measure their Agni. Div could still live.

Jaya studied the sensors. They only had the two, their comms dead. She wished she could hail Akaros's ship, let him know of the Yumi's change in course. She glanced at the locked door of the bridge. Maybe she could call for Visha. Or—her eyes cut to Rhumia—anger the warrior into moving toward her, striking her. Maybe then Samson could rush forward. Tackle Afira, grab his urumi, call his Agni, or—

Jaya stilled. Her gaze landed on Daz, who stood with his back to her.

"Are you king of the Yumi?"

Daz jerked back, as if slapped. Rhumia and Afira stiffened, eyes wide, incredulous.

"We do not speak such blasphemy," Afira said.

"I'm going to cut off that tongue," Rhumia snarled.

"But you are, aren't you?" Jaya continued. "I mean, you killed your sister. Took her throne. You are king."

Rhumia stepped toward her, voice dripping with derision. "Only a clipped foreigner would think the Yumi had kings. Your mother may have knelt to one, but we don't. So shut up. Or I *will* cut out your tongue."

Jaya glanced at Samson. He watched her intently, and her eyes darted to Afira. To his urumi.

"My mother said successions were always bloody," she said to Daz. She eyed the sensors, saw the *Relentless* turning on the *Lord*. "Especially between Yamni and Yamsiya. But you were both Yamsiya. So, what did others think of you killing your own?"

Rhumia snarled, "Not another word."

"She is goading us, Rhumia," Daz said tiredly. "Let it go."

"But, General—"

"Let. It. Go. That is an order."

Jaya smiled with bloody teeth. "Did you clip her?"

Such a notion was not just offensive; it was forsaken. Foreigners may clip a Yumi, but for a Yumi to do it to one of their own...It was unthinkable. Punishable by death. But when Daz snapped, when anger sundered his face and split his self-control, Jaya knew she had hit her mark.

She smiled wider—then cried out. Rhumia had slammed into her. She felt ribs breaking, blood leaking from her mouth, as the Yumi hit her with her hair.

Daz shouted. Samson dashed forward—Afira lunged—but he swiped his urumi and, with a snarl, summoned his Agni. Flames burst down the blades, burned his bonds. Samson spun on the balls of his feet, all momentum, all fury, his sword and inferno ringing high, and slashed down.

The two tongues cut cleanly through Afira. She whimpered. Rhumia whirled, crying out for her sister, and Jaya used the opportunity to kick her in the stomach. It felt like kicking stone.

The Yumi flung her off like a flea.

Jaya crashed to the floor, gasping as agony exploded through her body. She blacked out…and woke up to find Daz unconscious, Samson and Rhumia locked in battle, his flaming urumi trapped in her hair. Jaya smelled it burning, but the Yumi did not yield. With a roar, she yanked Samson up and clobbered him against the wall.

He howled. Rhumia jerked back, hair sharpening and shooting toward his chest, but then Jaya threw herself forward. She aimed low. Like Div had taught her, like Akaros had trained her. *If you cannot be a fighter, then be cleverer*, Akaros had said. *Use their bodies against them*.

She tackled Rhumia below the waist, pushing all her weight into it. The force of the impact rippled down her arms, her ribs, and Jaya muffled a scream even as Rhumia stumbled back. She did not fall.

But that was enough.

Samson whipped his urumi, flames zipping down the blade, down Rhumia's hair, onto her head and neck.

She shrieked.

The doors slid open as Visha entered, asking, "What's going on?" only to fling back as Rhumia barreled out, aflame. Jaya heard her screaming. She heard soldiers shouting, and then she heard a loud splash. Then silence.

Samson slid down the wall. Blood dripped down the side of his head, his shoulder. His flames flickered, slowed. Jaya slowly crawled up onto her hands and knees as he met her gaze.

They stayed like that for a moment, breathless. Exhausted. Finally, Samson held out a hand.

"I'm sorry for burning you earlier," he said.

Jaya took his hand. "And I for not trusting you."

He pulled her up, and Jaya staggered to the panel. Daz moaned softly, unconscious. As for Afira...Jaya avoided looking at that corner of the room, instead focusing on the holos as she sank into the captain's chair.

"The *Relentless* is turning on the *Lord*," she said.

"They know something's gone wrong," Samson said. He clutched his bloody urumi, flames reemerging from his wrists. "It's her. I can feel her wielding."

"Then let's get you back to your queen."

And with a flick of her stylus Jaya turned their ship back into battle.

CHAPTER 53

ELENA

Rise, sweet avenger! Rise, Lady Death! Rise, O Mother, and bequeath us your wrath!

        —from *Hymns of the Goddess of the Yamuna*

Elena stumbled across the deck, beating back flames. She moved as if in a stupor. Her nerves were frayed, yet with every inferno she put out, her Agni grew, ebullient, powerful. She could not feel the blood dripping from her nose, nor the pain that echoed down her jaw. There was no time to take stock of bodily damage. She knew only that the *Relentless* was off their starboard stern, giving chase. Bearing closer.

"Slow us down, Maya," she called. The *Relentless* had not sent another sparker, only because she knew they meant to recapture their ship. "Draw them in."

"Elena—"

She held up her slingsword, curled her finger around the trigger.

"Wait, you don't mean—" Maya began, then stopped as Elena turned to her.

"Do you trust me?"

Maya hesitated. "This is crazy. We should continue running—"

"Do you trust me?"

Maya looked at her companions. Tanmay unsheathed his sword. Ajira nodded, her face resolute. Slowly, finally, Maya raised her own sword. "This is madness."

Elena gave her a bloody smile. "Madness is just brilliance by another name."

They slowed. Three thousand yards, two thousand five hundred, two thousand. The *Relentless* grew in size, its bow glinting in the low light, its pulsers glowing like the maws of frothing beasts come to feed. *Closer.* It began to turn to draw up along their starboard. Multiple soldiers lined the deck, armed with pulse guns and zeemirs. All of them ready. All of them hungry.

Fear touched her then, a grey, smoky tendril, but Elena swallowed it. They had their anger, their bloodthirst, their weapons. But she had it too.

She had it *more*.

"On me," she whispered as the *Relentless* drew in. "Ready. One, two—"

She and the others fired their slingsword blades, cutting into the hull of the killdom. The lines caught, tightened. There were shouts, cries of alarm from the Jantari, but she pulled the trigger and flew forward.

Elena slammed onto the deck of the *Relentless* with the Sesharians. Crewmen shouted. Pulse fire shredded the air, but she stomped her feet, building her Agni, and thrust her fists. The inferno roared to life. High and bright, with a heat that dried her eyes and singed her hair. Someone screamed. There were howls, panicked orders, but the inferno's song swallowed them. She heard only its desire, and hers within it.

Snarling, Elena cut her arm through, and the inferno split.

Two flames whipped forward like the tongues of laughing beasts. One caught the leg of a fleeing Jantari. The other razored down an officer's spine, snapping each vertebra like twigs on a pyre.

Ahead of her, Tanmay whipped his urumi and cut the ankles of a running soldier. Maya knocked another's zeemir to the ground and rushed him, but he swerved, slamming his armored gauntlet into her face. She staggered back, nose spraying blood like a spigot. Elena saw it only a second before. The flash of steel. The quick shift in footwork. She screamed

"Knife! Knife!" as the Jantari raised his arm, dagger streaking red in the firelight like the tail of a burning star, and buried it in Maya's side.

The Sesharian laughed.

She *leaned* into the knife, her smile bloody and bright, and rammed her urumi up into the cave of his chest. He let out a wet, confused gurgle. Maya yanked out her blade, and he toppled face-first onto the deck.

"Fucking metalmen," she spat.

Something silver glinted from beneath her clothes. Before Elena could ask, Ajira let out a cry.

"Watch your left!"

Elena dodged as pulse fire ripped into the deck. She caught sight of a soldier at the helm of a pulser, turning the weapon toward her. A crimson light flared at its mouth. She flung her mind forth and snagged into the heat of the pulse. It tasted coppery, rusted. She imagined it flaring, melting, like iron on a forge. The pulser quivered, heating. The soldier shrieked and jumped off, waving his hands, burns bubbling down his skin. Elena did not hesitate, and neither did her fire.

A flame leapt onto him and swallowed his screams.

Her inferno beat onward, raucous, ravenous. The Sesharians pushed forward, and the Jantari peeled back, their pale eyes wide with fright, their skin singed by her fire. They cried for mercy, for aid. And for a moment, Elena thought the *Relentless* was theirs. But there were just *so many*.

For every Jantari soldier that fell, another took his place. Tanmay stumbled as a pulse grazed his shoulder. Elena flung her Agni toward him, to act as a shield of flame, but she was too slow. Another pulse hit him in the chest, and he toppled.

Ajira cried out, rushing to his side.

"Ajira, no!"

A pulse cleaved her leg, and she went down with a shriek.

Fury, immeasurable, immense, flared down Elena's spine. They were picking off her friends one by one, knowing they could not hit her. The cowards. *The fiends—*

"Elena!" Maya cried in between swipes. A Jantari fell down, but two more pressed forward. "A little help!"

Elena rushed across the deck, swiping one soldier with her sword. He dodged, but the tip of her blade nicked his thigh. He wobbled then, off-balance, and Elena pounced. Her blade cut through him. So quick, so clean. She yanked out her sword and turned to the other before he had even fallen.

She pressed her awareness onto the remaining soldier, observing the map of his body, the flow of his prana. She reached—

Pain, white-hot, impossibly sharp, ripped up her leg with such intensity that Elena gasped, staggering. Her mind flailed. She could not comprehend— had not seen—where—

The fallen soldier's dagger had cut her calf. Elena swallowed a scream, failed. She stumbled, crashing to her knees. Maya called out to her. More Jantari swarmed forward, this time without their pulse guns. This time with only daggers and swords she could not manipulate, could not bend. Elena hauled herself to her feet with snarl, and they leapt onto her.

CHAPTER 54

SAMSON

I have not forgotten the sting of the inferno, but I have come to long for its bitter wrath. Perhaps that is love. Perhaps this is my undoing.
—from the diaries of Priestess Nomu of the Fire Order

Samson slammed onto the deck of the *Relentless* with the Sandsworn. The sandmen swept forward, taking the Jantari by surprise. They tried to shoot them down, but the holes they made only closed again with a hiss of sand. Never had he been more grateful for these hideous creatures.

He whipped his urumi, twin blades singing. A maelstrom of metal and fire and fury. At the other side of the deck, he heard Elena scream, and it rent something dark and terrible within him, an awful burning desire to hurt and keep hurting until the ones who had made her scream no longer breathed.

He bounded forward, cutting the ones who tried to stop him. There were so many Jantari—but there were even more Sandsworn. They bolstered his advance, covering his blind sides, and Samson sent a silent thanks to Jaya, who controlled them using the sensor in his metal lotus.

I gave one to Elena too, Jaya had said as she pulled their bounder alongside the *Relentless. They'll find and protect her, like they will with you.*

Indeed, the Sandsword swept forward, barreling through squawking Jantari who barely had a chance to register what hit them before sand rushed down their throats.

His Agni twinged, seeking.

"Elena!"

He saw her then—a radiant, burning beacon amid the swarm of Jantari and Sandsworn—and his heart clamored with a deep, furious keen.

Stay alive, he thought. *I'm coming.*

He tore his way. He had no care for it, no elegant design, no grace. He slashed and cut, whirled and lunged, parrying and swinging, his twin blades alive with flame, crackling with malice.

"Sam," she cried as he was halfway across the deck.

Blood ran freely from her nose. Her eyes were bloodshot, inhuman. Through his mind's eye, he could see the prana sparking from her skin, as if she were an explosion waiting to be set off. It frightened him.

Thrilled him.

A line of Jantari stood between him and his queen. Some wheeled to face him, others charged toward Elena. Across the bloody deck of the ship, his eyes met hers.

"Together," he called.

At once, he swung his urumi, and Elena spun into her dance. A great inferno ripped forth, red and blue, the desert and the sea, growing, melding. Across the space, they reached for each other. In between, the Jantari screamed, but the roar of the inferno drowned them out, and then, there was nothing else but their conflagration. An Agni that swelled not from tapping into each other's power, but from simply *being.*

When the flames finally dissipated, Samson crashed to his knees. An awful, racking pain thrummed down his sword arm. He saw chips of bone. A smoking mound of flesh. It was like the Ravani funeral pyres, except there were no prayers to follow these men.

He felt sick.

He felt disgusted.

He felt like his namesake, the Butcher, full of power, full of shame.

But then he found her in the ash. Grasped her reaching hands. And despite his self-contempt, Samson felt better knowing that at least someone just as powerful, just as horrible, shared his abasement.

"Sam," Elena gasped.

He pulled on his best smile. "I believe I'm late for our appointment to tea."

CHAPTER 55

SAMSON

We are not good people, my love, but we have suffered enough.
　　　　　—from *The Odyssey of Goromount: A Play*

Samson clambered onto the *Lord of Sea* after the others. Suns ago, he had once stepped onto this deck in the grey cage of a Jantari uniform and been hailed a traitor. But now cheers greeted him. Sesharians, laughing as free men, called to him, and their joy brought a raw, fierce swell of pride in his chest. This was the victory he had dreamed of. This was the destiny he had been born to.

He accepted a beer. It was warm, far too old, but he savored its bitter taste anyway. A nervousness jittered through him. Where was Elena? She had disappeared in the throng. He searched the deck but did not find her.

"Blue Star," a deckhand said. His friends turned, grinned. "They said you were coming."

"I told Maya she was full of shit—"

"I held hope—"

"—the way you slid up was badass—"

"—did you see the Ravani queen and her fire?"

Their questions overwhelmed him, but it was the last one that snagged him.

"Have you seen her?" he asked the man, his heart tremoring in his throat.

The deckhand smiled inwardly, and his friends grinned, some chuckling with a mischievous look in their eyes.

"The last I saw, she was heading to the captain's cabin. Something about making tea."

His heart quickened. "Thank you."

He clinked his beer against the deckhand's and hurried to the cabin, each step increasing his nerves, his excitement. Why did his belly feel as if it was filled with hornets? It was only Elena. *Only* Elena. He had just seen her. They had just spoken. Of course she would run off without telling him. That hard-nosed, impossible woman—

He came to the entrance of the cabin and stopped.

Elena looked up from bandaging her arm, her eyes meeting his.

His heart stuttered, slowed. Then flared up again, quicker than a tempest.

"Y-you're hurt," he said.

Her gaze slunk down his shoulders, his chest, his legs, and Samson felt hot and cold all at once. The edge of her lip curved into a soft smile. "So are you."

He stepped in and did what he had wanted to do the moment he had seen her within the inferno: He swept her into his arms and crushed her against his aching chest. She laughed, and the rumble of her laughter against his skin thrummed through him like quicksilver, bright and joyous.

"Samson, you brute," she said, her voice muffled by his shoulder.

"Elena, you terror."

She smelled of ash and blood and sweat. She was dirty and covered in grime that clung to his clothes, his skin. But he did not care. He only held her closer, his face buried in her hair, his arms wrapped around her small back, and felt, for once in his life, a lucky, lucky man. Finally, after some time, he pulled away and she looked up, smiling.

"I should have known it would not be easy getting rid of you," she teased.

"You'll have to try harder next time."

Though she remained smiling, he noticed something change in her eyes. That quick shift. That look he could never catch but ached to know. There was so much he wished he knew about her, so much he wished to rectify. All those arguments, all those fights, seemed petty now. He saw the faded marks on her neck and swallowed his hot tide of guilt.

She touched the rim of her nose and drew away flakes of blood. "Strange," she muttered.

"What is it? Did the Jantari hurt you? Did they..." He trailed off. He could never forget the muffled screams of women as Jantari officers pulled them from their beds within the mines. The taste of his bitter rage, the acidity of his own helplessness.

Elena caught the look in his eyes. "No," she said gently. "It— I am just tired, that's all."

Out of habit, he reached for her Agni. And recoiled. It was like touching a beam of steel, baked in the sun. But then the feeling passed, the pain subdued with a corded disquiet, and he tasted something spoiled. *Wrong.* There was a taint in the immaterial shape of her spark, small and nearly translucent. He would have missed it had he not been familiar with her Agni. If Elena felt something amiss, she did not show it. She sighed and rubbed the blood off her fingers, and he thought, *It's because she's tired* and *She still cannot sense when I probe our connection.*

Elena turned back to the desk and reached for the kit.

"C-can I?" he said, pointing to her arm.

She sat on the edge of the desk as he unrolled a fresh strip of bandage. His fingers brushed the tender underside of her arm, and Elena stiffened. But his eyes fell to the sudden rise of her chest, the quick intake of her breath. He slowed. Kept his touch gentle, light.

"Doesn't look too deep of a cut," he whispered.

Elena turned, and he felt the intense heat of her gaze graze his jaw, his neck. He tried not to focus on how the soft hairs of her arm were brushed gold in the light, or how the lines of her throat quivered as she swallowed, or how his breath became smaller, shallower.

"Here, would you...?" He raised her arm and set her hand on his shoulder so he could wipe the dried blood on her elbow. Her fingers pressed into his skin, firm, warm.

"Who taught you medical aid?" she asked.

"Yassen, actually."

"Really?"

"I'm not sure where he learned, but once, when I was stupid and injured, he taught me how to clean my wounds."

"Stupid and injured. Sounds like the lot of us."

He chuckled, and he felt the tension slowly seep off her shoulders.

"I once bandaged Yassen's arm like this," she said with a wistfulness that sent an ache through him, not in jealousy, but because he could feel the memory of her pain beneath it.

"Yassen was jumpy about injuries. I bet he couldn't sit still."

"No," she laughed. "But to be fair, he required stitches."

"Oh, I'm sure Yassen had no problem being pierced by you," he said.

Her eyes lifted, crashing into his. "Would you?"

Somewhere between his chest and his throat, between his destiny and his desire, she caught him. Samson felt too bare, too seen. Heat licked down his neck and spine. But something else threaded beneath his discomfort. A breathless exhilaration, like the first time he had sailed. Or the first time he had commanded Agni and felt power rush through his veins. He felt hers now, still open, still unaware. How could she sit here so calmly and eviscerate him so easily?

As Samson looked into her eyes, he felt his despair surrender, his alarm heighten.

"You terrify me," he said softly.

She stilled. "Why?"

He imagined telling her the truth: That if she wanted, she could pry away his Agni. That he could do the same. They were each other's destruction, and he could not deny that there were days when he wished he could have it all. He had almost broken his restraint that night in the pit.

He almost told her.

"Because…" he began.

Almost.

"Because we may have a problem with the Yumi." He winced inwardly. He had agreed with Jaya to break the news together, after she had spoken with the Arohassin, but he'd rather tell Elena now than his own terrible truth.

He sealed off her bandage and stepped away. Elena tracked him with her eyes, and he felt a nervous, intoxicating sensation of being studied so intently.

"What happened?"

"Daz was going to retreat and race straight to Tsuana without the kill-doms. Jaya and I protested, but then he bound us, and we fought and, and…" He looked away. "Afira is dead. Rhumia jumped overboard. But Daz is still alive. We've told the other Yumi that he was injured and needs rest."

"Mother's Gold." Elena skated her hands through her hair. "Shit."

"You were right, though. About Jaya. She is useful."

"How is she?"

"Battered and bruised, but alive. I don't think I've seen Akaros this murderous before. If Yassen and I were harmed on missions, he could have cared less. But with Jaya…" He shrugged. "You should see her."

"I will." She rose and began to pack the bandages and salves back into the kit.

Samson watched, quiet. There was more he wanted to say, questions he wanted to ask. What would come once they reached Tsuana? How would they approach the council? But those were exigent questions. There was another one, a simple and possibly insignificant question, one he found himself returning to more often.

She caught him watching. "If you're worrying about the Yumi, I'll handle it. I can talk sense into Daz. Or we can keep him on the bounder, away from the others, until we're done in Tsuana."

"All right." He tapped the desk, hoping to drum up courage. Elena set down the kit carefully, stopped his drumming.

"What is it?"

He looked down at her hand on top of his. "I, uh, I." He shook his head, laughing bitterly. "Skies above, it was easier asking in your throne room."

He thought she would withdraw her hand, almost sensed her arm tensing, but Elena did not move away. Gently, firmly, she pressed her finger beneath his chin and forced him to meet her eyes.

"What do you want to ask me, Samson Kytuu?"

His heart stilled. He did not have courage, but she had given him it, and he almost asked her then and there.

"Will you"—*become my queen in marriage*—"have tea with me in honor of my name day?"

A slow smile bloomed across her face, and he forgave himself for not asking, if only to hang on to that smile longer.

"Your name day? Is it today?"

"Well, officially, it's a month from now on the fifteenth, but since we're in the mood for celebration—"

"A month?!" She smacked his arm, then grinned. "Fine. But only because we've won."

"You know, Samson is not my true name."

"Really? What is it, then?"

"Ruru."

"Ruru?"

"It's my middle name. Well, actually, it's Ru. But growing up, I used to say things twice, so my mother started calling me Ruru. It stuck."

Elena blinked, then laughed. "You liked to say things twice twice?"

"Quick and fast fast." He smiled. "I grew out of it."

"Ruru." Elena said the word slowly, curling the *r*'s as if to relish how the name rolled off her tongue. It sent a thrill through him. "What does it mean?"

"Son of the sea," he said. "But it also means lover. Tender-fleshed. He who would give half his life for his beloved."

"Ruru," she whispered, almost as if to herself.

Why did his born name on her lips sound like a prayer?

He wanted her to say it again. In his ear. On his lips. Again and again, until it was chant that reverberated through him with the sweet succor of the divine. Later, he would chide himself for not seeing it then. How her smile did not quite meet her eyes. How it faltered, just for a moment, before she righted it again.

"Well, Ruru." She waggled her brows. "Let me get the tea. One dollop of honey, yes?"

"Someone once told me it's better with two."

She blushed then. It sent an electric charge skating down his spine, vicious and potent. She showed him the captain's selection of tea and laughed when he told her she had given him too much honey, and as the night waned, as their laughter unspooled, easy and warm, Samson buried his earlier question. *Later.* When this was all over, when they were finally at peace, he would ask her.

CHAPTER 56

ELENA

I will not bend. I will not turn. I will endure and chant until the world knows my purpose. Agneepath, Agneepath, Agneepath!
—from the diaries of Priestess Nomu of the Fire Order

Elena waited as a Black Scale soldier unlocked the door of the former XO's quarters. Daz looked up from the bed as she entered. He seemed to have aged many suns, with rings of darkness shifting beneath his eyes like fading moon phases. He had not changed out of his jacket. Dried flakes of blood spotted his sleeves. Her eyes followed as he rubbed the soft skin beneath his wrist.

"Hello, little queen."

"General." He had not asked her to sit, and so she remained standing. Weak light filtered through the window, limning the hard angles of his face, the veins of his hand. Finally, she spoke, in a tired, hushed voice. "I am sorry for Afira."

Daz stilled for a moment, then continued rubbing his wrist, eyes fixed on the blood on his sleeve. "She was a warrior, and she died like one. That is all a Yumi can ask for."

"I know. There is no greater honor. Still, I—I am sorry for all of it. The blade that cut through Afira was of my man, and so her death is my responsibility. I will see that she is given a proper pyre, with all the rites—"

Daz looked up then, and the withering look in his eyes stopped her short.

"Do not grovel at my feet to seek forgiveness, little queen. We both know that is beneath you. You came here with a purpose. But first, I must know. How are my warriors? How . . . how many are left?"

"Twenty strong," she said.

"Am I a prisoner?"

"That is for you to decide, General."

He sat back, eyes hardened but dull, like old metal shined to hide its lackluster state. "What are my options, then, O queen?"

Elena winced at the jab, at the derision laced within her title. "I come here as a friend, Daz. Remember, it was *you* who erred when you decided to abandon our mission."

"You do not need to remind me of my folly, Elena," he spat, though the heat in his voice quickly died. "I did not know you were alive. Had I known, I would not have turned. I would— Afira would still be alive. Rhumia, Mother knows where she is, would be here. My grandnieces— they were queens in waiting. Do you think I would have endangered their lives willingly?"

"No. That is why I am giving you a choice." Elena straightened, meeting his gaze. "You can either come with me before the council as we agreed. We can fight against Jantar together. Or you and your warriors can stay here on this ship until the matter is done. Either way, you will be given the dignity of overseeing Afira's funeral. I do not seek a fight with you, Daz. Our sides have both erred, yours with abandonment, mine with violence. Let us make amends, then. I know Moksh and Ravence will be the better for it."

Daz laughed, low in his throat. "You call them choices. But in both, I am still a prisoner."

"I told you, that is for you to decide—"

"And what if I ask for your Butcher's throat? Will you give me that, *friend*?"

Elena eyed him carefully. "Whatever vengeance you seek, seek it with me. And seek it after the meeting of the council. We have fought long and far to get here, Daz. Do not let your anger tarnish your wisdom now."

"Wisdom?" Daz scratched at his wrist. "There is no wisdom in this bloody war. It died the moment I killed my sister for the throne. It died the moment you stepped onto Moksh. It died long, long before, when we started playing these vicious games. Can't you see, Elena? We are not moved by wisdom. We are moved by vengeance. Bloody, cruel, glorious vengeance. You want to revenge your father, I want to revenge my grand-nieces and every Yumi who suffered under my sister's rule. So come off it. *Open your damn eyes.*"

He stood suddenly, startling her. "You want vengeance against Jantar? Fine. I will come with you to the council. But I seek retribution too. I will fight the Butcher in the Yumi way, in the name of my grandnieces. Grant me that, and you will have my help."

Elena studied him, her jaw tight. She thought of Samson, of his soft touch and even softer words, of the pure, unadulterated relief in his eyes when he found her. She remembered *her* own startled joy when he had crushed her in that suffocating hug. It had been so *freeing*, to simply drink tea and not think of subterfuge or manipulation or what came next. Their laughter had rolled out, so warm, so easy, and she thought, for a moment, maybe Daz was wrong. Maybe vengeance was not her Agneepath, but a fork that disappeared like a path in the shifting sands. She looked at Daz, beginning to speak, and then stopped.

Because in his eyes, she saw herself too.

What could one tea do to assuage the months of agony she had suffered? What could one frivolous, achingly gentle night do to soothe the grief of her Ravani? What could one man do to quench her own thirst?

She still remembered the cruel crush of Samson's hands around her throat. The terrifying cold of his flames as they bit into her. If he had been given the same choice, Samson would have given her up too. He was a monster after all. And if all went to plan, then Daz wouldn't have to kill Samson himself.

The Jantari would do it for him.

"F-fine," she said, mustering more conviction than she felt. "You can fight Samson, but *after* the council."

Daz held out his bloody hand. "On your honor, then."

It died long ago too, she thought as she gripped his hand. "There is another matter I want to discuss with you. When we appear before the council, I…I want to propose Farin retreating from both Ravence and Seshar. I want us to fight for Ravani *and* Sesharian freedom."

Daz studied her. "You once told me that you wanted nothing to do with Seshar. What changed?"

The killdoms, the bloodbath, the anger and courage of Maya, the quickness of Tanmay, the cleverness of Ajira. The boy who had dared to show her kindness. Chandi, Akino, Akiri, even Visha. In her bitterness, she had lumped them with Samson and his thirst for power. In her selfishness, she had wanted to crush him, and by association, his home.

She had welcomed Sesharians. As long as they lived in Ravence, they were under her protection. But did she owe them more than that? Was she obligated to free their home, a home she had not seen? Her own was bleeding. Ravaged by war, splintered between faiths. How could she save another when she could barely save her own?

What did she owe Seshar?

"I think," she said, "I have been the biggest fool of a queen this continent has known."

Daz barked a laugh. "There have been worse."

"Perhaps. Or maybe they would have realized sooner that to punish a people for their leader, their god, is not justice. Not truly. My qualms, whatever they may be, are with Samson and Samson only. And my fight for Ravence…It is so much like Maya's fight for Seshar. Like Visha's. Like Chandi's. I would not be here today without the Sesharians. I owe them my life. The least I can do is fight for them, to show the other despots that Seshar is not alone. That she has an ally—a mad, biting, burning one."

Daz—his expression guarded, closed—dropped her hand. "You are slow, Elena. But at least you have come to realize I've been right all along. *Ravence and Seshar are the same.*"

"I know," she said, without malice, without anger. "I just hope I'm not too late."

To this, Daz said nothing. Moments passed, heavy, strained. Elena glanced out the narrow window.

"We will arrive at port soon. I will need you and Samson, eventually, as representatives of Moksh and Seshar. Can you remain…?" She trailed off.

"Civil?" Daz gave a cold, wry smile. "I have spent many suns swallowing my anger before my sister. I believe I can handle a week."

"Hopefully, we can make the council move in our favor within days."

He eyed her. "You have a plan."

"A mad one."

After she had told him of it, Daz studied her for a long moment, then said quietly: "The council is fickle, Elena. You come to them as an avenger, but some kings will see you as a rebel. Sympathizer to terrorists. Orchestrator of a genocide. Do you think Farin has forgotten the mines you burned? The ships you've taken? You are walking into the lion's den, little queen, and they are ready to eat even your bones."

"They will find thorns for bones within me."

"So what will you become, then, Elena? Villain, hero, or conqueror?"

Her voice was low, lush, vicious. "None. I will be greater than all three."

THE CONQUEROR

CHAPTER 57

ELENA

The council hereby finds King Kilis of Karven guilty of crimes against humanity of the first order. Punishment rendered: execution. Note: This is the first execution by council of a regent. May it be the last.
                    —from chapter 45 of *The Great History of Sayon*

The Tsuana harbor curved into the neck of a hammerhead shark, the long cut of the land stretching out toward the sea, Janoon, proud and resilient, rising like a sword within it. The pearl city, they called it. Pure and honorable, made from the richest Tsuani marble and strongest Jantari steel, a bastion of law and honor. The last time the council met, Seshar had bled red into the sea, and yet not one drop had marred the perfect face of the city.

Elena wanted to rake her blood through it.

They were led into the palace under guard. Janoon Palace was shaped into the contours of a conch shell, its exterior bright and white, its interior iridescent with hues of pink and lavender. Round doors made of stone and decked with nacreous chipped shells opened to tall, curved hallways. Fish swam beneath her feet through glass streams. Everywhere she looked,

Elena saw attendants dressed in soft, luxurious wraps and tinkling head-pieces. No dirt lined their fingernails. No soot speckled their wrists. What an image they made then, she and Samson, as they sauntered in with their bloodied and torn battlesuits.

"But, ma-madam, I mean, Your Majesty, the council is already in session," an attendant said as he stumbled beside her. "They haven't been informed of your arrival."

"Good, it'll be a surprise, then."

"But, Your Majesty, there is only one seat. Your guest—*esteemed* guest—must wait out here."

Elena came to a stop. She turned to the attendant, and he leaned away. "I believe my fellow council members will be interested in what he has to say, Ka Tirta."

Tirta flushed. "O-of course, Your Majesty. But you all are armed. I can't let you—"

Elena unclipped her slingsword, her pulse gun. Samson slowly unlooped his urumi and set it carefully in the attendant's hand.

Without waiting, Elena entered a long hallway lined with guards and staff members from the different kingdoms. Cyleoni, Karvenese, Ver-ani, Jantari. They turned as she marched, and Elena savored their startled gasps. Tsuani guarded the doors, but they paled at her approach.

"You're in my way, soldiers," she said.

One of the guards hesitated, the other looking to Tirta for direction. Suddenly, every guard quieted. The air tightened, sharpened, and Elena felt the weight of their stares, the nervous energy in which they touched their guns.

"Your Majesty," Tirta said. "Please. Why don't you rest for a moment? We will inform the council, let you properly introduce yourself—"

"I have sailed through the Black Pit, lost half my crew, and survived a mutiny and a drowning to come here, Ka Tirta. You can step aside, or I will add a felled Tsuani attendant to my list."

Tirta swallowed, hard. Then he waved his hand, and the guards stepped aside.

Elena pushed open the great heavy doors with a resounding boom.

Voices died mid-conversation as all the mighty kings and queens turned to scowl at the intruder. Their scowls gave way to confusion, then shock.

"Esteemed members of the council," she began.

The Verani king turned white, jowls open, as the Karvenese queen shared a look with Syla and the Tsuani monarch. The attendants who fluttered behind their regents stared at her as if she were a ghost, or a demon resurrected, their gazes snagging on her bandaged arm, her swollen face, her bloodied hands. Only Farin did not look shaken. Only he met her eyes, and a slow, amused smile crept across his lips. She returned it.

"I, Elena Aadya Ravence, have come to take my seat."

Without waiting, she settled into the empty chair designated for Ravence. Samson stood behind her. His Agni burned coolly, and she was grateful for its steady strength, its limitless wrath. The others simply stared.

Queen Risha of Tsuana was the first to recover. Her headpiece, an intricately crafted crown of shells and silver, tinkled softly as she said, "Q-Queen Elena. We thought—I thought—you were dead. How did you get here?"

"Now, that is an interesting question," Elena said, watching an attendant whisper quickly into Farin's ear.

The metal king sat very still, the cogs of his body hissing. Then, in a voice slick like oil, said, "So this was your surprise, Syla. *My enemy of the sea.* She comes sailing on my killdoms. My *captured* killdoms. Did you plan to tell me, or was this all part of your grand reveal?"

Syla started, protesting, and then Bormani chimed in, and then Risha tried to calm them *both* as they shouted over the other. *He is mistaken,* Elena thought, as Risha slammed her hand against the table and called for order. *I am not his intended enemy of the sea.*

"Really, Syla?" Queen Kysha of Karven said once the clamor quieted. She was a tall, thin woman, with long pale limbs and even paler hair braided to resemble crowns upon her head. She smiled, her black-stained lips peeling back to reveal gem-encrusted molars. "I didn't know you still plotted, old man."

The Karvenese queen sat across the round table, beside Queen Risha, but Elena felt as if the woman was right beside her, her voice and eyes pricking her skin with the delicacy of a snake bite.

"And with such a young thing," she mused. "Have you two formed an alliance, then? Conspired to make us look like fools?"

"Peace, Kysha," Risha said.

"How long have you been hiding her, Syla?" Kysha continued. "And who is the pet she brings?"

"You'd do well to remember, Kysha, who the pets are in this room," Syla said, looking between her and Farin. Kysha's face tightened, but her cool smile did not drop. She simply sat back in her seat, silent, watchful, but Elena caught how Farin's roaming metal eye skittered to the pale queen.

Jantar and Karven had a long-running alliance, longer than Ravence and Cyleon. Elena did not expect any support from the queen and her frigid country, but she wondered who held the power in the relationship. Was Karven a pet, like Syla insinuated of Veran?

"I had a pet once," King Bormani said mournfully. "A marjarah, with silver fur. Her name was Adria."

Kysha rolled her eyes as Risha turned to Elena. "Is it true you come sailing in on Jantari killdoms?"

"I come to you all with every intention of preventing a war," she said. "It will be up to this council, on the heads of all its kings and queens, if it comes to pass."

Kysha bristled, and even Bormani was bright enough to scowl. Though it was not a threat, it was clear: The blame would be on them, not her. An indelicate way to begin negotiations, but Elena had neither the subtlety nor the time to care.

"My family was murdered. My kingdom was taken. It's true that the Arohassin were behind it, but they were mere puppets. Controlled by another hand. A hand that controls all of you now."

Bormani guffawed. "No hand controls Veran, young queen."

"Nor Karven."

The Tsuani queen looked disturbed. "Elena, surely you are not suggesting we are puppets—"

Elena jerked toward her, and the sudden movement made Risha lean back as she responded, her tone acidic, "I do."

Silence thrummed, alive, intense. At once, the room shifted. Gone was their confusion, their half-curious amusement. The regents of the council looked nervous, or pissed. Slowly, Elena dragged her eyes across each and every one of them until, finally, she found the gaze of their master. She leaned forward, her voice full of all the loss and anger and grief of the past sun, sharpened into a blade, cutting deep.

"King Farin of Jantar, I accuse you of regicide. I accuse you of orchestrating the murder of my father and the attempt on my life through the Arohassin. You unlawfully invaded my country and thus stand in contempt of the Treaty of Borders. You are the master behind the carnage, the hand that pulls the strings. And I demand my reparations."

Risha inhaled sharply while Kysha scowled, as if now tasting the sour bite behind the skin of a fruit. Bormani looked sick. Only Farin remained composed, his hands folded placidly before him. His metal eye still roaming, seeking. His unfailing calm irritated her at best, infuriated her at worst, and Elena fought to keep her vision aligned. The hungry call of her Agni at bay.

He thought he could bury her. Silence her. Take her country like a thief in the night. Even now, with his unflinching composure, Farin believed he had the upper hand. But despite all his best efforts, he had not been able to kill her, and this undeniable fact gave Elena courage. Her Agni flared, and Samson shifted behind her in discomfort. She could almost taste it—her acidic desire for vengeance.

Elena sucked in a breath, savoring the ashen taste, and said, "I demand the freedom of Ravence *and* Seshar."

Chaos erupted. Bormani and Kysha spoke at once, shouting. Syla turned to Risha for help, who called for order, as the attendants around them fluttered in agitation, unsure of what to do.

"Seshar is not a kingdom that has been recognized—" Bormani cried.

"—it would jeopardize the metal trade—" Kysha interjected.

"Perhaps Ravence is founded, but Seshar—" Risha reasoned.

"You don't understand what you're asking," Farin said, his voice rising and silencing the rest.

At their obedience, Elena smiled inwardly, joylessly. Even if they did not know it, they were his puppets. Dancing along to his strings, his pauses and his whims, cajoling if only for more metal, more trade, more power and influence. Farin held an invisible influence over them all. Their sudden quiet was yet more proof.

"On the contrary. I know exactly what I'm *demanding*." She jabbed the table with a finger. "One, the removal of all Jantari troops from Ravence and Seshar. I do not want to see another zeemir within their borders. Two"—she jabbed another finger—"the nullification of all outstanding

Sesharian labor contracts in your regime, and three"—she held up her fingers, high and stiff, like a blade—"a head from your family. Your son perhaps. My father is dead, and I want blood for blood."

Farin hissed, and all the regents regarded her with something akin to terror and disgust. Samson remained nonplussed, but the tremor in his Agni gave him away. She knew she had taken him by surprise with her last demand. And she knew it was a ludicrous one. Farin would never agree to it. But it was not agreement she was after.

It was their fear.

Once, Queen Akira of Ravence had burned rebels and fed their bones to her dogs until the very idea of resistance had withered. They called her mad. Monstrous. Barbaric. Of course, she had only burned a few. But she had done it so grandly, so mercilessly, that fact became legend, legend became myth, and then the myth took a life of its own. Sometimes, the truth only took you so far. It was the threat of madness that took you to the end.

She wanted to seem merciless. Unhinged. If she could not have their friendship, she would have their fear.

Farin leaned forward, one hand braced on the table, the other against his chair, as if to stop himself from leaping on her. "You will *never* touch my sons."

"And yet you killed my father, and I am supposed to swallow my rage in silence." She laughed, adding an edge that made them all shrivel. "No, Farin, I think not. I want my bloody revenge."

She wanted him to walk away then. *Let the record show that, when offered peace, Jantar left first.* The other kingdoms would demand she be less preposterous, more reasonable. They had a metal trade to salvage, after all. But then she could move into her second phase, call in—

"You lost Ravence *yourself*, young queen," Farin said, his voice brimming with menace. "You could not protect it from the terrorists within its borders, and neither could your father. Rani fell because of the Arohassin. Terrorists who encroached into your palace, *under your watch*."

"Oh, come off it," she snapped.

But Farin continued. "What proof do you have that I was behind the attack in Rani? What, other than your own incompetence?"

Elena bristled as Risha interjected. "Now, this is a council. We will speak with each other civilly."

Farin held up his hands. "Of course, of course, Queen Risha. It's just, I have heard of some very *interesting* things about our young queen here. Her, and the people she associates with."

His gaze slid then to Samson, and she saw his metal eye finally still.

"Like the terrorist Samson Kytuu," he said, with such vehemence that Elena recoiled.

Samson's Agni trembled in instinctive rage. She could sense it: the metallic charge before a thunderstorm. He did not have his urumi, but he could still summon a spark... Elena half turned to stay him, but Farin's voice wrenched her back.

"He fashions himself a hero, and yet he killed hundreds of Sesharian laborers." Farin pressed the pod inset within his metal arm, and holos of the burned northern Jantari mines filled the close, stiff air. "Total tally of five hundred and sixty-six Sesharian laborers, spread across three mines. He killed them all in one night."

Behind her, Samson let out a choked sound, half snarl, half protest. It was still a fresh wound. And she knew how deep it ran, how thick the guilt congealed. *This is part of the game*, she reminded herself. The jabs, the accusations, the ripostes, and the diversions—it made up the grand theater of politics. But she found herself wanting to respond to Farin's cruel bait.

Samson beat her to it.

"I am no terrorist," he said. "*Your* killdoms have wrecked more families than I ever have. *Your* mines are death traps, *your* precious metal made of Sesharian blood. You said I killed hundreds of Sesharians. You have killed *tens of thousands.*"

"Queen Elena," Risha said quickly, "I must ask you to calm your attendant—"

"Pet," Kysha cut in.

"I am no pet," he spat.

"Careful, boy," Farin said coldly. "You are not a ruler and speak out of turn."

Samson started, but Elena rested a hand on his forearm. "Enough," she said quietly, fiercely.

"Tell them," he said, his voice low and intense. "Tell them I am not a terrorist."

But Elena hesitated. What did she care, how others saw him? She owed

Samson Kytuu nothing. Even if he had given her his secret name, even if he had offered a glimmer of vulnerability—she had never asked for it. Or for the way he looked at her now, wide, beseeching.

"Sam—"

"Tell them—"

"Leave." She would not let him jeopardize their negotiations because of an insult, however cruel, however harmful. She squeezed his wrist as guards spilled into the room at Risha's behest.

Samson stilled. But he was not looking at the approaching guards—he was looking at her. And the disappointment in his eyes, the betrayal, severe in its intensity, throttled her voice. She squeezed harder, her nails digging into his skin. Finally, Samson withdrew his hand and, with one last baleful look at Farin, stalked out the room.

"Like I said. He is no hero," the metal king said.

With her back still turned, Elena closed her eyes and took in a long, stabilizing breath before facing Farin. "Neither are you, Jantari."

Their eyes met, and in that brief impasse, Elena felt their shared enmity, the dark, dense quality of their malice. Everything else became meaningless. The council, the attendants, even Samson and the killdoms. They had no need to hide their hatred, but every reason to pretend civility, because this was the theater of grandstanding and subterfuge, and Elena would be damned if she lost to Farin, again.

She rose. "I come with three simple demands to prevent a great war. King Farin stands accused of regicide and breach of treaty." She turned slowly, meeting the gaze of each regent. "I have heard this council called spineless. Cowardly. But you as rulers have survived countless battles. You can *feel* when someone plots against you, or you would not be here. So, make no mistake, council members. This is an attack. One cutting to the very structure of our rule. I merely ask you to take on a little courage and cut the hand that controls your strings."

She walked out the door without waiting for their response. Let them stew. Let them believe she applied to their pride and ability as competent rulers. Let them believe they were safe. The doors clicked shut loudly behind her, and in their echoing ring, Elena felt the ache of her want grow, until her every cell trembled with it.

CHAPTER 58

JAYA

The most valuable soldier is not the warrior, medic, or leader. It is the strategist. She who sees the field and can turn it with the slightest touch.
—from *The Gamemaster Manual*

Jaya slipped onto the stone bridge and checked over her shoulder. The streets were empty, the canal below full of only darting fish, not boats. Janoon was a network of canals and alleyways that resembled the flowing locks of the goddess Tsuan, mother of the sea and the namesake of Tsuana. A goddess of peace, she was said to have ordained her followers to make a white city. A pure city, full of equality, justice. But the Tsuani guards had prodded Jaya like a market fish, and when they had finally let her deboard, she heard them whispering behind her.

"I've never seen a clipped Yumi," they had said.

Cheeks burning, she had left the port.

"Any alms for the poor?" an old woman had asked her. She sat on the corner, brown limbs wrapped in a faded white shawl. An old headpiece of shells and rusted chains covered her rheumy eyes as she looked up at Jaya.

Jaya snorted. "Equality my ass," she muttered and slid out her smaller pulse gun.

The woman's eyes widened as Jaya pressed it into her hands.

"Now go off whichever bastard forced you to beg on the streets, ma," Jaya had said.

The woman stared at Jaya, and then smiled. Jaya grinned back.

She had headed north then, past the twisting canals, beyond the merchants and tourist quarters. The streets began to widen. Quieten. Jaya had checked to see if someone had followed her, just in case, but there was no one else when she stepped onto the appointed bridge.

There was a strange silence in this part of the pearl city, the white buildings like stoic, luminescent knights in the falling sunlight, too still, too perfect. She wondered if they were waiting for the sword to fall.

Across the bridge, a small temple chimed softly. Jaya held her breath. Celestial ikara adorned the marble walls of the temple, their scales flashing iridescent then gold as the sun shifted behind the buildings and cast the street into a pale, silver shadow. Jaya waited. Slowly, the stone fish began to move.

They rose and fell like the crest of a wave, spinning gold in their wake. The bridge began to rumble. Jaya took in a long, deep breath before the stone pulled back and she dropped into the canal.

She plummeted, down, down, down.

So long, she thought it would never end.

But then she crashed into a tiny but deep pool, coughing and sputtering, and Akaros looked down, unimpressed.

"Did you close your eyes again?"

Jaya clawed herself up onto the tiled floor. A strand of seaweed stuck to her hair, and she attempted to grab the slimy tendril, but her fingers slipped over its oily surface.

"I thought you said you cleaned the chute," she said, attempting to sound angry, but her voice came frail, cracked. She rubbed her chest, trying to remember the sensation of warm wholeness before the drop had sucked the air out of her.

"If you haven't noticed, I've been a little busy." He held out his hand, and with a sour grimace, Jaya took it. Gently, Akaros untangled the seaweed from her hair and threw it aside.

She followed him down a dark hallway, boots squelching with each step. Moss furred the walls. Jaya tried not to think of what else skittered in the shadows before they came to a steel door.

Akaros rapped thrice.

The door hinged back with a screech, and Maya stood in the entryway. Behind her, Jaya spotted the bank of panels, the glass wall, and her heart trembled at the thought of what lay beyond.

"I trust you weren't followed," Maya said.

Jaya shook her head as she took the offered towel. "No. I spent four fucking hours wandering around this stinking city, bored out of my mind. The Yumi are depressed on the ship, the Black Scales too drunk in the city to care."

"Good. Elena and Samson are still in the palace, so we have a few hours before they notice you missing." Maya turned as the door to the adjoining glass chamber slid open, and a thin, dark-haired man entered. "Taran has command."

Jaya and Akaros snapped to salute, their fists slamming against their chests. "Master Taran."

The leader of the Arohassin fixed them with red eyes and smiled. "I have waited a long time to see you three."

"Everything is in place, sir," Maya said.

"Our agents have secured the Jantari ships, sir," Akaros added with an earnestness Jaya had never heard from him before. Gone was his carefully relaxed composure. He stood ramrod straight, arm stiff and angled like a tanker wing.

"And you, Jaya?" Taran asked. His accent was Ravani, western Rani to be specific, where sandscrapers gave way to the wide, rolling dunes. It sounded like a soft desert wind, the one that lulled you into the basins before the sands shifted and a sandstorm erupted. Even after all these suns, his voice still prickled her skin. She had never heard him raise his voice, never seen him without his hair tied back in a neat ponytail or his black velvet jacket without a gulmohar flower, crimson like his eyes, in its third button.

"I—I am ready for whatever task you have for me, sir," she said.

Taran studied her. "Show me what you've collected so far."

Jaya nodded vigorously, jamming her hand into her pocket. She withdrew her holopod, only she gripped it so tightly that her dry skin stretched over her knuckles, cracking. "It's in here. All—most—whatever I could manage." She stopped suddenly, frustrated at her sudden anxiety. Her lack of control. Taran always made her feel just outside of her depth, though through no fault of his own. It was just that she had seen his game designs, his battle flows, drawn so exquisitely—so *ingeniously*—that she felt a choking cry of jealousy, not of him, but to be *like him*. Poised, perfect—flawless. Taran Arya was the most gifted and creative gamemaster she had ever come across, and no matter how hard she tried, no matter how many times she wrung herself to find creative gasps of genius, her talent paled in comparison to his. It had annoyed her—until Taran used those same designs to help her brother.

He smiled kindly and took the pod. "Well, let's see what you've got."

He placed it on the panel, and the holos decoded, then sprang up around them. Footage of Elena's and Samson's Agni, their temperature readings, the flashpoints of their fire, the pattern of their flames, the speed at which they traveled—it was all there. Taran studied the holos, and she studied him, her heart thumping so loud it was a miracle they all did not hear it.

"Jaya," Taran began, and she thought suddenly, despairingly, *I fucked it up. He hates it, he hates—*

"This is marvelous work. Did you get this all from your lotuses?"

She blinked. Her throat had run awfully dry. "Y-yes?"

A slow smile spread across his face, his eyes wide with wonder. "Ingenious."

Pride—warm, fierce—bloomed in the pit of her stomach. She did not need Taran Arya's validation to know the worth of her work, but still.

But still.

Div would joke that she had a professional crush, but it wasn't like that. She did not crave Taran. She did not crave anyone, except maybe the alarmingly beautiful, devious vishkanya with eyes so sharp, so intelligent, she put the masters to shame— Jaya shook her head. Her cheeks had suddenly gone hot, and Taran had noticed.

"No, truly," he said. "This is splendid, Jaya. You should be proud of your work."

Akaros rolled his eyes, and Maya smirked, but Jaya knew they hung on to every word, as if, just by osmosis, they could be touched by his benediction.

She smiled, despite herself. Taran continued studying the holos, the blue light washing over his face, making the shadows under his eyes deeper, starker. She began to point out how she had used the Janani Game Theory to capture Elena's signature heat flare when Taran said, softly, "Then we are ready."

At this, Jaya froze. Akaros had heard, and she saw him stiffen, saw Maya realize the truth behind Taran's quiet exclamation. He never raised his voice. But they heard his excitement, so rare these days, and the fact sobered them.

He turned to her. "I want it to be you."

Her hand trembled. "M–me?"

"Out of the four of us, it must be you to play the game."

"B–but why not you?" Jaya said, her voice hitching. She could stage the field, draft game designs, stun her fighters. But play the game herself? No. There was a reason it was Samson's blade that cut through Afira and Rhumia, not hers. She looked to Akaros for help, then Maya. "You were on the ship with Elena, Maya. You fought those Jantari bastards alongside her. Surely, you could—"

"There's still Samson, Jaya," Akaros said. "He would never play with Maya in the field. She fucked that up a long time ago."

"Oh please." Maya scowled. "If it weren't for me, we wouldn't have learned he was Fireblood as early as we did. Maybe if *you* had done your job better, we could have used the two of them long before—"

"Enough." Taran's voice, spider soft, echoed like the ring of a sword against a metal beam.

They stilled. But Jaya could feel her heart thumping wildly, in her chest, her wrists, her head. She was no warrior. Why did they expect her of all people to carry out the worst?

"S–sir, if I may," she said. "I believe I can speed up the process in awakening the asset. All I need is a reading of Elena and Samson's intertwined Agni. Then Div—I mean the third . . ."

She trailed off as Taran gave a sympathetic smile.

"Ah, I've forgotten how long it's been. A sun now, hasn't it?"

Jaya swallowed, her throat suddenly tight. "One sun, four months, nineteen days, and two hours."

Her voice floated through the air, up into the haze of the shimmering holos. Taran held out his hand.

"Come, child. See your brother."

Jaya took his arm, her heart ratcheting up to a roar as they approached the glass wall. In the chamber below, two metal tubes were attached together by three pipes: oxygen, microfluids, and blood.

It ran like a slow, steady river between the two coffins, and in one of them, through the small glass pane, Jaya saw the face of her brother.

Her parents had thought they were going to have another girl, and so they chose Divya to match Jaya. Radiance and victory. *With both in our household, why would we ever want for more?* her mother had said. But when her sibling came out kicking with a scream so loud it frightened the sol-priest, Jaya had said, almost without thought:

"Div."

Later, when they had cleaned and wrapped him, she held him for the first time. He looked like an alien, forehead wrinkled, nose smooshed, lips puckered and twisted for another cry. Jaya had never seen such an ugly thing. He was perfect.

And he still was, albeit he looked gaunter than she had last seen him, skin sucked tightly along the curve of his cheekbones and the line of his jaw. His long dark hair blossomed like a flower around him, the strands soft and luxurious. He had never had the heart to wield it like a weapon. Were it not for the tubes and the holos before her, Jaya would have thought Div was asleep. Lost within peaceful dreams.

"He is doing well," Taran said gently. "They both are. Had Div not been his blood type, we would have lost the asset. But soon, we'll be able to wake him. We can reconstruct Div's body with your sands and his fire. We can give him a better life."

Jaya nodded. Her throat suddenly felt too hot, her chest too small to speak. Her gaze traveled to the second tube, and she felt a tightness lace up her shoulders, her spine—a buzz building in her ears with the sound of a thousand ringing swords—as she met the glazed golden eyes of the third.

She did not believe in destiny. Fate was a religious man's dream, and chaos his bitter reality. She had lost her faith the day it had crushed her mother and father into a tangle of severed limbs, and she had come to learn the world held no reason. But power? Power controlled chaos, and she knew better than most how even the slightest advantage could turn the field. And the third Agni was control itself.

She pressed her hand against the glass. Div slept soundly, peacefully. When he woke, she would tell him how their past had been a bad dream, that his new body was a testament to all they had suffered, all they had survived. She removed her hand, leaving smudges on the glass.

"The reading," she began, and Taran shook his head, almost good-naturedly, or as much as a crow could manage a grin. He pressed the pod into her hand.

"If you insist, then get it. But it should not come in the way of your mission, Jaya. Remember: *Be clever, be wicked, be ruthless.*" The old adage of the first gamemasters, the first Ravani. "Come home safe, and we'll wake the asset together."

She met his red gaze. "And then Div."

It was not a question.

Taran nodded, his smile edged. "And then Div."

She fisted the pod. "Tell me what to do."

CHAPTER 59

ELENA

*The gods gave us Agni. In turn, we promised them death. Who, then,
the real victim? Who, then, the real tyrant?*
　　　　—from the diaries of Priestess Nomu of the Fire Order

Elena stood underneath the warm spray of the shower as rivulets of
blood trickled down her arms, her legs. *You lost Ravence yourself.* She turned
the heat up, increased the jet sprays, but neither the heat nor the water
could drown out Farin's voice. He was wrong. *He was wrong, damn it—*

Abruptly, she yanked open the shower door and stepped out onto the
cold tile. Her reflection, morphed and ghostly in the fogged mirror, stared
back at her like a vetala from the stories of old. A maiden turned into a
monster.

She hastily whirled away from the mirror and grabbed a robe, flung it
on as there was a knock, then her door opened.

"Oh, hello." Jaya eyed the water dripping on the tile. "Don't you want
to…dry off?"

"No time. I need to see Syla." She turned to her bed, where a Tsuani attendant had left a blood-orange organza sari. "I need us both to round up the rulers. He'll deal with Bormani, I'll take Risha. We're going to vote this evening. Where are the others? Akaros, Maya? Are you— Oh." She remembered they had agreed for Akaros and Maya to stay out of sight. As top Arohassin operatives, they were no doubt in intelligence databases. Jaya, on the other hand, was too low in the chain to trip alarms. Still, Jaya watched her silently. "What is it? Is something wrong?"

"I know how to sway the council." Jaya softly closed the door. "Remember how you and Samson blended your Agnis within the Black Pit?"

Elena eyed her, unease tightening her muscles. "What of it?"

"What if you were to do it again, before the council? Show them how Ravence and Seshar are linked inextricably. *Become the threat.* If Farin does not retreat from Rani or Seshar, you'll burn his ships, like you did with his killdoms. You'll destroy his remaining mines. You'll ruin his country. Games aren't always won through battle. Sometimes, the presence of a threat is enough."

Elena stared at her with cold, dawning horror. "You want me to hold the council hostage."

"No," Jaya said. "Just show them who you are, Elena. *What* you really are. They're going to find out soon enough, so why not show them on your own terms?"

"I am not a monster," Elena said, her voice suddenly thin, strained. *I am not like him.*

"You want the rulers to listen? This will make them," Jaya said.

"I'm not going to threaten to burn them alive if they don't listen to me," Elena snapped. "I have other means to make them kneel. Besides, I'd have to contend with what comes *after*. *After* Jantar retreats. *After* Ravence is free. If I hold the others hostage, I will jeopardize Ravence's future by making more enemies. They will never trust me again."

"And you trust them? Now?" Jaya said.

Someone rapped on the door, but Elena stood rooted, glaring at Jaya. "I cannot afford a long war, Jaya. Our soldiers barely survived the crossing. If I make an enemy of Syla, or Risha, then who will send us food? Aid? Ravani will never be welcomed in other kingdoms ever again."

Jaya scoffed as the knocking increased. "Are you forgetting Seshar?

You'll find ready soldiers among the rebels. Among the miners, willing to revolt against Jantar. This war won't be short, Elena."

"It *must*—" Elena began when someone slammed open the door, and Samson stalked in.

"Mother's Gold, Elena, answer your fucking—" he said and stopped. For a moment, he stared at her, dripping wet in her robe, her hair undone. There was a hungry, almost ardent look in his eyes. And then he shook his head. Swallowed his hunger until only a cold, vicious violence remained. "I need to talk to you."

Jaya looked between them. "I should leave—"

"Jaya, stay," Elena said, not removing her eyes from Samson. He glared at her, but there was something beneath his anger, something unbridled and raw. She was almost afraid to know it. "Share your proposal with Samson."

Jaya thumbed the pod in her hand nervously. "I can come back later. Once you two have fuc—"

"Please, enlighten me," Samson said, his eyes still holding Elena's. A muscle ticked in his jaw, as if he was keeping control by the tips of his fingers.

Elena finally looked to Jaya. "Tell him."

Jaya hesitated, her large amber eyes dark and unreadable, before she stiffly turned to Samson. "Summon your Agnis before the council and threaten them if Jantar doesn't retreat from Ravence and Seshar."

He barked a laugh. "But that would mean our queen consorts with terrorists."

"Sam—"

"You did not correct them when they called me one," he snapped. "Why?"

"*Because it wasn't important!* You said yourself in your grand speech that they would call us despicable names. So who cares what those idiots think about you? Who cares if they hurt your fucking feelings? Get over it."

For a moment, Samson held still. It was as if all his muscles had locked into place, all his emotions—his wrath—sharpening, tuning. She knew that look. He wore it that day they had fought in the rain. It frightened her, but that fear had become familiar by now, twisting into a dark and delicious validation. Because she was right. Because he was *the* monster.

Because despite the pleasantries and the semblance of comfort he had given her, Samson Kytuu was a butcher and a brute. He would always bite first, and then she would. She felt a cold satisfaction in that certainty, along with a sour sorrow that tickled the back of her throat like the ash of a dead flame.

"I know why," he said, his voice dark and venomous. "You want to paint me the bloodthirsty brute. The *Butcher.*" He stepped forward, and Jaya shifted away, but Elena forced herself to remain rooted. "You think you're some saint. A Burning Queen, fighting valiantly for her people. But you are just as vicious and ugly as *me.*"

"We are not the same, Samson," she whispered.

"You're right." He took another step forward until he stood only a hand's width away. "You're even more ruthless."

Elena felt winded, her lungs so tight she wondered how they did not collapse and pierce her heart. *He is wrong,* she thought weakly, hopelessly. If he were in her position, if he had been given the choices she was given, he would have chosen the same.

"I know how to handle the kings and queens of Sayon," she said.

"And I don't because I was born on some backwater island?" His eyes ripped into her, hard and unkind. "I am not a terrorist, Elena. I am a free-dom fighter. Everything I do, everything I must do, is for Sesharian azadi. But how would you know? You were born a queen, raised in a palace, attended by simpering fools who called you brilliant. What do you know of my suffering?"

"Ravence is occupied by metalmen, and you say I don't understand your suffering?" she said. "That's rich, Sam. Really."

He smiled then, and his smile was so full of grief and bitterness, an anger so potent that she felt it hook into her rib cage and slowly pull until she was peeling apart at the seams.

"You still don't understand, do you? If they cannot respect me, then they will not respect Seshar. We will not gain Sesharian freedom. Your people might get azadi, but mine will be left behind to till the earth until we die. But I refuse. Seshar's reckoning has finally come because *I* demand it," he said, each word sharp and vicious like the snaps of a whip. "And *I* am a god."

Samson gripped her chin. "Your kingdom has been occupied for how many days? A few months? Mine has been ruined for *decades.* You have only tasted the misery my people have suffered. You can't even begin to fathom my loss. So, spare me your moral arguments. They have no purpose here."

She spoke against the crush of his fingers, keeping her voice steady. "We must play our cards carefully—"

He stepped back, as if struck. His throat trembled, and that look from before, a raw vulnerability she did not deserve, darkened into a dull heaviness that hit her in the chest like a fist.

"You disgust me," he said, his voice thick. And then he left without another word, without giving her a chance to, what, argue? Ask for forgiveness? A means to salvage her self-belief of her moral superiority?

He is wrong, she thought, but the words rang hollow.

Jaya watched her quietly. "What are you planning, Elena?"

Elena drew a long, tired breath. "I am going to make a play for both Ravence and Seshar, but he is an idiot who—"

"He is right."

She stilled. "What?"

"Samson is the symbol of Sesharian independence. If you allow Farin to smear his name, then you allow him to smear all Sesharians. The councilors already believe Sesharians are pitiful. Now, you'll give them an excuse to turn their pity into hatred. They'll call Seshar a country of terrorists and killers, not of bravehearted freedom fighters. They'll never want it to be free."

"They will." Elena turned, reaching for her sari. "But first, I need to speak with Risha. If we want to protect Ravence and Seshar—"

"You're only serving yourself," Jaya said softly. "*Your* throne. *Your* legacy. You don't give a damn about anyone else."

Elena huffed. "I am the queen. Of course I care."

"You aren't a queen," Jaya said. "Not really. A true queen fights for everyone before she fights for herself. Including for Samson Kytuu."

"You are Arohassin," Elena said, meeting her eyes. "You know nothing about fighting for anyone but yourself."

But Jaya was already moving away. "You are not my queen."

Elena watched her go, her words ringing in the empty room.

The glass walls curved around the tall chamber, stretching from floor to ceiling, so high that Elena had to crane her neck to see the top. The ikara flashed in the dark waters as if the radiance of the moons were captured in their silver scales. Queen Risha watched them. She had changed into a kinetic headpiece with delicate white petals that fluttered like the gentle fins of a sea creature. With every turn of her head, the ikara followed. Back and forth, up and down, like an orchestra before a conductor.

"How did you train them to do that?" she asked.

Queen Risha did not turn as she answered, but the fish stilled as if in wait for her response. "You'd be surprised how quickly you can train the devoted."

Elena watched as Risha picked up a bell from a side table and rang it, twice. At once, the ikara ribboned into a double helix formation. They spun, faster and faster, a long silver chain of quivering scales, and Elena was spellbound, unable to look away, unable to see the dark shadows of the room move until her Agni quivered in warning. She spun, tensing— but it was only Risha. She stood so close that Elena could see the blue glow of the waters reflected in her eyes.

"Strange," she murmured.

"What?" Elena asked. Her heart clanged against the cage of her chest, and she fought to keep her voice flat, unperturbed.

"The ikara have no hold on you." Risha frowned. "When Bormani watched, he was drooling by the end. He'd forgotten the time and where he was."

"Is that your play, then? Hypnotizing the others?"

Risha laughed, a soft tinkling sound, like bells under water, cold and forlorn. "No, dear Elena. The ikara tell me who can and cannot be easily swayed. And you prove to be stubborn."

Elena blew out a steadying breath to calm her racing heart. She had thought—for a moment even feared—that Risha had another objective. But the shadows were free of Jantari warriors, and she did not smell the infamous grime of Farin's oil.

"How did Farin fare?"

There was no noticeable change in Risha's face, but Elena caught how the ikara reared away as if in disdain. Or was it fear?

"He said you would come to me, seeking help."

A distant despair rang through her chest. Had Farin already beaten her to it? Had he met with the councilors and offered deals or threats they could not ignore? She forced herself to meet Risha's observant gaze with cool detachment.

"And what kind of help did he say I would seek?"

"He wasn't sure." Risha cocked her head, her headpiece swaying. The ikara fluttered above them. "He told me I would be a fool to help you. But I've never seen Farin so flustered."

At this, Elena smiled. "He is not as invincible as you think."

"And yet, you've asked for a private meeting, away from the prying eyes and ears of the council. Are you afraid of the council's judgment, then?"

"I just worry about the sway he has over you. Over you all." Elena gestured to the ikara. "He points, and the rest of you follow."

"You think Tsuana is spineless, then."

"Oh, not spineless, dear Risha." She waved her hand carelessly. "Just shrewd. You always side with the strongest opponent, the one you know you have no chance beating. For a while, that was Jantar. But what if I were to tell you that Ravence will decimate Farin before the war is even at its end?"

Risha examined her slowly, and above, the ikara crowded forward, their pale, pupilless eyes watching her. "You mean with the warlord Samson Kytuu and his army?"

You disgust me.

His voice rang in her memory, and Elena felt her throat constrict. So be it. It would be better for him to hate her. It would be easier to drive the blade between his eyes like she had intended, like she had promised, but Elena found herself miserable at the thought. Why did he affect her so? He was nothing. *Nothing.* And yet his voice slithered in the gaps between her thoughts, pursuing her.

She felt Risha watching, and Elena forced herself to reel back her thoughts from the treacherous slip of Samson Kytuu.

"Not him," she said.

"Then that is quite a presumption."

"Say, for the sake of argument, it's true. Say someone else has entered the game. Someone even the Jantari fear. Who would you pin your bet on then, the metalmen or the ones who can cut through steel?"

She saw the wheels turning in the queen's head as the ikara dispersed in agitation, shooting from one end of the tank to the other, a whirlwind of anxious silver. There was only one army with the strength to cut through steel. If the Yumi entered the war in aid of the Ravani, the Jantari would lose. Maybe not at once. It would be a slow death, a cruel death, one that drained the coffers and public morale until the people grew desperate and angry. And the Jantari would not be the only ones to suffer. Tsuana would too, with her dependency on the metal trade. Their fates were tied inextricably.

Elena watched Risha consider this, noting how her observation now took on a tinge of resentment, of fear.

"We've defeated the Yumi on this continent once before," Risha whispered sullenly. "The Jantari have new weapons. New metal. We can beat—"

"Last time, you had the Prophet. But there are no prophets on your side, Risha. And neither you nor Farin can afford a long and costly war. None of us can." She met her gaze. "But *you* can change the fate of your nation. You do not need to make an enemy of the Yumi. Tonight, when I push for the vote, remember that."

She turned to go when Risha cried out, "But Seshar! Surely you cannot demand freedom for it too. It is not your fight. Forget it. It will only drown you and Ravence. You finally have the opportunity for peace, and you should not squander it."

Elena froze. How could she tell the queen the cost of that peace meant the subjugation and humiliation of a million other lives? Ravence would be free if Seshar remained chained. That would be her legacy. Her cruel, vicious legacy.

You're even more ruthless.

Slowly, she turned to face the older queen. "You are right. Seshar is not my fight. It is not yours, or Bormani's, or Syla's. But neither is Ravence your fight, or your obligation. Yet, here you are, willing to listen. And that is all I ask from you, Risha. To listen to the Sesharians and hear their cry for freedom. We have ignored it for so long, me, you, my father, our ancestors. We can't continue, or else there will be a day when someone less merciful than I will come to take what he is due."

The ikara followed her across the chamber, and when she slipped out the door, she still felt the ghostly pinpricks of their white, pupilless eyes, measuring her.

CHAPTER 60

ELENA

The last rays of the sunset seeped in from the windows, catching the
river of pearls and seashells. Her attendant glanced nervously over his
shoulder, but Elena did not slow, her sandals slapping against the tiles with
a resounding clack, her pallu billowing behind her like a blazing flag.
No rulers without a seat were allowed in during a vote, but Elena did not
mind if it meant avoiding Samson. Or her own guilt.

Instead, she focused on how the guards snapped to attention, how the
attendant waved for the doors to open, how a low, heavy groan echoed
through the hall as the doors swung in and she entered the cold council
room once more.

Syla, Risha, Bormani, and Kysha were already seated, talking quietly.
She did not see Farin, but they still had a few precious minutes before the
vote began.

Elena slid into a seat beside Syla, who broke from his conversation with his attendant and turned to her.

"Did you meet with Bormani?" she asked softly.

He nodded. "He's convinced. Risha?"

Elena looked across the table, catching the gaze of the Tsuani queen. Risha did not smile, but she gave a singular nod.

"We have it, Syla," she said.

Before she could say anything else, the doors opened to reveal Farin and his retinue. She tried to decipher his expression, to look for clues on how he had spent the last few hours, but the metal king's face was cold and remote as he took his seat. He met the eyes of no one, spoke to no one. He dismissed his attendants with a wave of his hand, and they shrank back like kicked shobus.

He's pissed, she thought delightedly.

"Now that we are all settled, let's start," Risha called. "Let the records state we begin at five past the sun's zenith, in Tsuana with Queen Risha presiding. We will take attendance..."

As each ruler answered for attendance, Elena observed, noting how Kysha's gaze kept sliding toward Farin, how Bormani tapped the table in an uneasy rhythm, how Syla sat with his shoulders tensed, as if in anticipation. They all knew what was coming. Like sharks in water, they could smell the iron-rich promise of blood.

"Ravence?"

"In attendance," she said.

"Then we have all members of the council here today," Risha said. She paused, as if now realizing the sudden gravity in the air, the compressed charge building around them. The attendants shifted nervously too. For a moment, Risha closed her eyes, steeling herself. Then she turned to Elena. "Queen Elena, we left off with a...proposal from you."

Proposal was a delicate way of dressing up a threat, but Queen Risha was nothing if not diplomatic.

Elena slowly pressed her hands on the table. "Thank you, Queen Risha. Like I said in today's earlier session, I come with three demands: one, the removal of all Jantari troops from Ravence and Seshar; two, the nullification of all Sesharian labor contracts in Jantar; and three, the head of Farin's youngest son." She paused then. Her father had always taught her the value of silences. Elena used one now to give them time to consider the implications of her demands, and she saw them all stir in unease. "I understand it is a lot to contemplate, so I have a new proposal. I motion that we add a new seat to the council. Another king, to help us evaluate and understand the stakes."

Farin snarled. "I am not going to allow some Sesharian scum—"

"On the contrary," Elena said sharply. "I propose adding a new seat not for Seshar, but for another kingdom. A prudent and powerful one. A kingdom that will play a critical part in the future of the second continent."

"And who would that be, young queen?" Kysha snorted. "A kingdom of the Sky People?"

"No," Elena said, as the great doors groaned open. "The kingdom of the Yumi of Moksh."

Daz entered, flanked by two Yumi warriors with unbound hair that prickled and shivered like a weapon unsheathed. Gasps sounded around the room. Kysha grew alarmingly pale, and Farin stared, his mouth hanging agape. Bormani looked as if he were about to faint.

Daz stopped just a few feet from the table. He had cleaned up well. Gone was the blood on his wrists, the tears in his clothes. He wore full regalia, the trident of the Goddess flashing gold above his chest as he carefully inclined his head.

"Esteemed members of the council," he said, "I humbly offer my request to join your ranks. For too long, the kingdom of the Yumi has ignored the affairs of her brothers and sisters of the second continent. But with such conflict abroad, we believe it is our duty to help steer the future of the continent."

Farin made a strange choking sound. The attendants closer to the Yumi soldiers shrank back as their hair twisted in the air, tasting their fear.

Elena spread her hands. "Shall we vote, then?"

"I motion we grant a seventh seat to the esteemed General Daz of the Kingdom of Moksh," Syla said, as they had rehearsed.

"I second it," she said.

Risha, who had seen this unfold so quickly within her palace, swallowed hard. Then, in a small voice, said, "We move to a vote."

"Yes," Syla said.

"Nay," Kysha hissed.

"Nay," Farin said, his voice strained.

"Yes," Bormani said.

"Yes," Elena said, her heart leaping up her throat as she turned to Risha, the last and final vote. Tsuana, as host of the council, did not usually partake in its affairs. But if a vote to add a seat was called, then all members, even Tsuana, were compelled to cast their ballot. They would need an overwhelming majority to create a new seat. If Risha called nay and ended the vote in a tie, Daz could not join.

And Elena's final plan, her hope for a vote on Ravani and Sesharian freedom, would fail.

Risha looked at Elena one last time.

Elena breathed out slowly. *Remember*, she mouthed.

"Tsuana votes," Risha began, and Elena edged forward. The awful noise of her clamoring heart drowned her ears. She felt stretched thin, as if all her life, all her past actions, all her sacrifices and losses had led to this small, terrible moment. This simple space of seconds.

"Yes."

For a beat, Elena had not heard her. But then Syla slammed his fist against the table, and Bormani rapped the table with his knuckles, and Daz leaned forward, resting his hand next to hers.

"Thank you," he said.

Elena blinked, and then it came all at once, the vicious, heady thrill of victory. She looked to Farin, saw the wheels turning in his head. With Moksh on her side, she had the voting majority: Cyleon, Veran, Ravence, and Moksh. Farin had only Karven on his side. Tsuana could not vote except in matters of council structure or in the event of a tie. If Elena were to call a vote for Ravani and Sesharian freedom, he would lose, unless he turned not one, but *two* councilors against her. She saw him assess this with deep resentment, and when he met her eyes, she could not help but feel vindication, savage and high.

"Queen Risha," she said over the noise of the flurried attendants, never breaking her gaze, "I call for another vote in favor of Ravani and Sesharian independence. None of us want a long, costly war that disturbs the metal trade. If we agree to the removal of all Jantari troops from Ravani and Sesharian territories, then perhaps the trade can be restored and the costs salvaged."

"Moksh stands in favor with Queen Elena," Daz said, and she felt them all quail underneath his discerning gaze. "We stand against Jantar, who seeks only to expand its power until other kingdoms are brought to their knees. But Moksh refuses. We will fight for freedom, however bloody the cause."

At this, Elena finally allowed herself the pleasure of a self-satisfied smile. She turned to the members of the council, this time making no move to mask the threat. "Ravence and Moksh stand united in favor of Ravani and Sesharian independence. How do my fellow council members vote?"

"Cyleon stands with you," Syla said.

"As does Veran—"

"Veran?" Farin said suddenly, loudly. "Are you sure, Bormani? Even after the Arohassin tried to kill you?"

Bormani frowned. "How is that related, Farin?"

"The Arohassin sent a man by the name of Yassen Knight. Surely you remember him."

"I know him well," he growled.

Elena stilled. Her heart began to beat in a slow, inexorable march, like the beginning of a desert storm. Syla touched her arm. "Queen Risha, let us proceed. We must hold Jantar accountable for attempting to assassinate a council member and breaking the Treaty of Borders."

But Farin ignored him, turning to Bormani.

"Did you ever find the assassin? Did you find *where* Yassen Knight ran off to?" he said, his eyes meeting hers. And Elena felt her heart seize, because she understood, in that instant, she had lost.

Bormani carefully tracked Farin's gaze to Elena. "Where did he go?"

"To Ravence, of course," Farin said. "Right into the arms of our dear queen here. They were lovers."

Silence—sudden, claustrophobic—squeezed the room. Bormani stared at her with confusion while Risha pursed her lips, as if tasting something foul. Kysha smiled cruelly.

"I found them in my mountain, right before the attack on my southern mines. You said you don't work with terrorists, young queen. Fine. Perhaps Samson Kytuu is not one. But Yassen Knight?" Farin tutted. "He tried to kill our friend."

"That is not true," Syla snapped. "Right, Elena?"

She could deny it. Throw Yassen in the mud and pretend she had never loved him, never ached for him, never cared. That she had planned to execute him as soon as he had served his purpose.

But he died trying to save her. On that mountain when she had felt lost in the storm of her grief, he had helped her find safe passage. He had stayed.

She could not ruin his memory. She would not.

I am not as ruthless as you think, Sam.

"Yassen Knight chose to repent for his crimes and seek a second chance," she said. "He was a man of honor, even until his death."

"Honor?!" Bormani shot up in his seat. "He snuck into my home like a thief in the night and tried to kill me. There is no honor in that. There is no honor in opening your fucking legs to a criminal, *you whore!*"

"Bormani!" Risha hissed.

He raised a shaking finger. "*How dare you.* How dare you come to us seeking help when you offer refuge to that assassin. You are not fit to sit on this council. I refuse to even be in your presence."

"Bormani, wait—" Elena began, but he slammed his fist on the table, and she jumped.

"You are in no position to plea," he growled.

He wrenched open the doors, scaring the guards outside, and stomped out.

Kysha rose smoothly from her seat, her silver dress skimming across the floor as she left with a smirk. Elena called to Risha, but the Tsuani queen ignored her. For a wild moment, Elena thought of calling her Agni and forcing them back in, trapping them in the room until they listened, until they saw, until—what? They agreed? They would more likely turn their armies against her and hunt her down to the far reaches of the continent.

How quickly the world could turn, in a matter of a seconds.

She rose quickly, meaning to go after Bormani, to explain, but Daz stopped her.

"Let me take Bormani," he said. "Syla, you handle Risha."

Syla nodded, but his face was drawn, his shoulders stiff. "I know we've recruited the Arohassin, but Yassen Knight? You did not tell me you were so . . . close."

"He's *dead*, Syla," she said, with more anger and hurt than she intended. "In the end, Bormani had his justice."

"Come," Daz said to the Cyleoni king. "Let us wrangle the fools."

As she watched them go, Elena felt a numbness spread down her arms and legs, a heavy sinking sensation. After all she had done, after all she had suffered, they still saw her as *less*. How easily Farin had maneuvered the conversation around her. How easily he had taken her accusing finger and turned it to blame her as the perpetrator of her own torments. And she hated herself because what if he was right? Elena remembered the people crushed at the wall, the mountain, burned alive on the ships. What had she to prove other than her own wretched wrath?

"Why don't you sit down, Elena?" Farin said.

Slowly, she turned to find Farin still seated. Without his attendants, without his guards. The two of them, alone at last. "Perhaps it is time you and I settle this."

Elena eyed him warily. She did not sit.

"I have a proposition for you," he said. "A fair one where we can all win."

"I doubt it."

"I will remove all my armies from Ravence. I will even sign a new treaty with you, tonight, to prove my conviction. I will give you back your kingdom, as long as you stop this farce about Sesharian independence."

"I think you've already proved how much you value treaties," she sneered.

He waved his hand. "The Treaty of Borders is old and needs to be rewritten. Besides, my order will go out today. Tonight. By tomorrow morning, you can go back to a free Rani, Elena. You can go home."

Home. The word struck at the very depths of her, in the secret, dark place of her guilt, her shame, her anger and regret. She longed for Rani. She longed for her palace and her dunes and the mountains beyond. She missed the courtyard where her father and mother laughed beneath the banyan trees; the gamefield where Ferma had taught her about hand-to-hand combat; the studio where she had danced to her heart's delight under the guidance of her guru. Was she so monstrous, then, for considering? For dreaming, however briefly, of her home restored to her?

"Think about it, Elena," Farin pressed. "The war will be over, just like that. You will have fulfilled your duty in ensuring the peace and protection of your people. They will love you. Celebrate you. Forget Seshar. You owe it nothing. But you owe Ravence and your people everything."

You owe Seshar nothing.

Wasn't that what Syla had advised her? What Risha had hinted? The expression Farin wore now was the same subtle aversion that somehow snuck through the armor of polite society at the mention of Sesharians. Elena could not help but feel that quiet disappointment—in herself, in her friends—grow. When had they all turned so cruel?

"I will not abandon the men and women who fought alongside me," she said somberly. "I've let you all try to tell me that Ravence and Seshar are different, that one deserves freedom over the other. *But we are the same.*" She gripped the edge of the table to stop her hands from trembling as she thought of the Sesharian father and son in Magar, the Black Scales trapped in Ayona, Maya and the rebels who had saved her and fought valiantly to take the ships. She had been a fool. Selfish, ignorant, unwilling to accept the truth of their shared fate, but as she stood before the maker of their misery, Elena realized that her unwillingness did not come from ignorance, but fear. She was afraid of losing it all. And so was Farin. She saw his distress alter his face, his body, the way his gears slowed and his face tightened into a bleak, harsh expression.

This time, when she spoke, it was not with anger, or cajolement, or duplicity. It was past the hour for that. She met the gaze of the metal king, and her voice was soft with the grief of all that had come to pass, and the grief of what was to come.

"You have spent this past sun trying to grow your empire, but it has been crumbling from within for quite some time," she began. "Your coffers are nearly dry. Your steel production is down, your trade ruined. And your workers rebellious. I may have taken only two of your ships, Farin, but I have given the Sesharians something you cannot kill: hope. They will rise. In your mines, on your ships, in your cities and small towns. You cannot hold them down much longer. You cannot hold Ravence. Do not let your pride get in the way of your pragmatism, Farin, or you may find yourself losing your own kingdom while trying to conquer another."

"Is that a threat?"

"No," she said without pretense. "It is only the truth. Ravence and Seshar are one. I do not need a treaty from you tonight to win the war in the end. I need only to allow you to tear yourself apart. This war will be long, Farin. You may have your metal, but I have the Yumi. I have rebellion. I have the hearts and bravery of thousands of Sesharians already posted within your kingdom. And when your Jantari become frustrated by the growing costs, the burning mines, the captured ships, perhaps one of your sons will move against you. He will depose you, in a desperate attempt to calm your public. Or maybe the people will do it themselves. So you see, Farin, I do not need to defeat you. I need only to outlast you."

The metal king considered her for a long time, his eyes unblinking, his body so still that she thought he had turned *off*—but then slowly, slowly, he extended his hand.

"I will withdraw from Ravence and Seshar—on two conditions. Declare yourself regent of Seshar. If you rule both Ravence and Seshar, then I will be forced to retreat from your territories."

She nodded. "Done. And the second?

"Denounce Samson Kytuu as a liar, a murderer, and a terrorist. Then help me capture and execute him."

And there it was.

Farin had played right into her hand, but this time, Elena did not feel the heady swell of vindication. Only deep dissatisfaction. She had always meant to rid herself of Samson, and who better to enact her revenge than the king he abhorred? It was a cruel, delicious twist. When she had plotted it in Cyleon, she believed it would bring her relief. But guilt shored up in the waters of her heart, and as she eyed Farin's metal hand, anguish burned her throat.

So she remembered the biting rain. She remembered feeling small, and alone, and *weak*. She recalled the livid loathing in Samson's eyes as he gripped her chin and said *You disgust me.*

So what if he had spoken a few soft words? So what if his execution by the Jantari sent a cold ache through her? So what if she had to kill her own hope?

Elena sank her teeth into the dark fruit of her hate—that black twisted thing that had grown roots and fed on her desires—and remembered her promise to herself, her father, her kingdom. She would do anything for their azadi. Even if it came at the cost of the death of one man. One devious, ardent man.

Finally, she sat down.

"He means that much to you?" she asked.

A strange thing happened then. Farin's voice broke into something ragged, raw. "Far too much."

A disquiet wormed through her. She knew that Farin had treated Samson like a son, that his betrayal had hurt, but she had not known how deeply, how viciously. How important was he that Farin was willing to stop a war for his capture? But Elena swallowed her unease.

Samson Kytuu was not her worry.

Carefully, warily, Elena raised her hand and clasped his metal fingers. "Peace, then."

"Peace and freedom," Farin echoed.

CHAPTER 61

SAMSON

To awaken the Great Serpent, first you must sing a song. Then you must give a gift: one of blood, or one of fire. Choose wisely. For a gift given can never be saved.

—from *The Legends and Myths of Sayon*

Samson sat on the seashell-studded beach as the moons climbed the winter night. He buried his hands in the sand and closed his eyes, attempting to focus more on the rough grains brushing against his skin than his own traitorous heart. But even behind his eyes, he saw her. Why could he not rid himself of her as easily as she had cast down his hopes? Samson flung open his eyes and stared intently at the horizon. The killdoms were docked within the harbor, their metal hulls glimmering in the moonlight. He could just faintly make out the black burns streaking down the bow, the portside, and he thought of the men he had lost to capture those ships.

Deep down, he had known that the council would fail. That freedom through peace was but a hollow promise. He had forgotten his own instincts in favor of hope, that vile, capricious thing, and actually *believed*. Even when he had left those miners, even when he had abandoned his men, he had believed—desperately—that there was a *reason* behind all of this. Samson clenched his hands into fists, squeezing so tightly he could feel the grains of sand digging into his fingernail beds. They had destroyed the mines to pressure Farin, taken his ships to prove their strength—and for what? For him and his like to be considered terrorists? He had hoped for Sesharian azadi, but then Elena had yanked it away with her simpering platitudes, and he did not know if he felt sorrow or anger or disgust or heartbreak. Perhaps all of it.

Perhaps this was grief—not a grief of loss, but a grief for what could have been. He wished he had never dreamed of a softer future, a happier one, when she had rested her hand on top of his and asked him to be brave. He wished he had never learned of two dollops of honey.

It was nearly dawn by the time Samson rose to his feet. Sand sprinkled down his arms. Merchants and dockhands were slowly returning to the docks, their voices rising into a swell, louder than before, but he ignored it. Out of the corner of his eye, he saw the golden emblem of Tsuani palace guards. They were watching him. Normally, Samson would reach for his urumi, but it was within the palace, and frankly, he could care less about piss-pant Tsuani.

Samson looked out across the horizon and ached for home. Seshar was but two days' journey from Tsuana. He had always imagined returning to his birthplace with the promise of azadi unfurling from his tongue like a ribbon for all to see. Music would fill the streets. They'd pour wine into the sea for the ones they'd lost and then drink their sorrow and happiness into the warm depths of the night. They would eat until their stomachs swelled from gluttony and not famine. They'd drink and sing and laugh and cry, and then do it all over again the next day. No man or woman would look over their shoulder for the glint of a zeemir. He would not be called a rustblood. He would be deemed a hero, worthy of his promise.

But his promise was worth nothing now.

Samson turned away from the sea and began to walk up the beach when he heard a shout. Visha and another figure were running toward him.

"What is it?" he asked, panicking.

And then he recognized her companion. His throat closed. *"Akino?"*

The master of arms drew to a stop as Visha bent over, sucking in air loudly.

"We were looking for you," she panted.

"H-how?" he asked Akino. "How did you escape? The miners—were they—"

"They declared me dead when they pulled me from the rubble, but by some twisted grace of the skies, I lived," Akino said softly. "I was not fit to mine, so they sent me to work the killdoms."

Heat leached from Samson's face. He did not know what to say. How to make up for the lost time, or his own failings.

"I…" he tried.

Akino stared, quiet. An awkward silence stretched between them, large and unwieldly. Even Visha shifted uncomfortably, her quick smile forgotten.

"I…" he tried again.

"It's like you hoped," Akino said, his voice edged, but there was warmth beneath it, a soft yielding. "I lived, Sam."

Without warning, Samson pulled him into a fierce embrace. Akino squawked in surprise. Samson gripped him tight, his voice trembling.

"I'm sorry, brother. I shouldn't have left you behind. You were right—"

"Sam, Sam, I need to breathe," Akino laughed, and when he pulled back, a small smile lighted his lips. "I'm here now. We are free."

Samson let him go, dropping his hands. "We are not. It seems I keep failing, brother. Seshar is lost—"

"Lost?" An enormous grin split up Visha's face, radiant as lightning. "Where have you been? Haven't you heard?"

"Heard what?" he said, looking between them both.

"Elena called an emergency session last night. Apparently, Farin signed a treaty with her to retreat from both Ravence and Seshar, starting next week."

She grinned up at him, expectant, but he only stood there, bewildered. Visha sucked her teeth.

"Gods damn it, Sam! We're finally free! Seshar and Ravence are free!"

"It's true, Sam," Akino said softly. "It is done."

He stared at them in stunned disbelief. He could not think of a reason for Farin to suddenly change his tune.

Visha laughed at his silence. She grabbed him by the shoulders, shaking him gently as she said, "Farin cannot afford a long war. He bled his treasury dry trying to feed his armies and quell rebellions at home. And then we destroyed his mines. And then we took his two killdoms! He caved."

"Farin does not cave," he said.

"Apparently Elena imposed a threat he could not ignore," Akino said.

"Do you think they struck an under-the-table deal?"

"Sam, wake up!" Visha shook him hard. "We are free! The treaty is signed, Tsuana has approved, and Farin has already sent out the orders. It's official! We will have azadi on the fifteenth of next month."

"Fifteenth?" His heart trembled. The fifteenth of next month was his name day.

"Elena specifically requested it," she said, waggling her brows. She then touched his cheek, her voice softening. "You should find her."

Samson stood there, caught between the fraying edges of his pride and his hope. He had spent the entire last day furious and grief-stricken, and honestly, he felt unwilling to give up on the bitter addiction of his self-pity. But Visha's grin only grew wider, and he heard the first pops of fireworks breaking through the city. Colors lit up between the white towers. It was only then that he noticed the change in the voices of the merchants, the new energy and urgency that seemed to charge the air.

"Special deal on this special day!"

"Historic low prices, just for today! Two for one!"

"Newly minted fireworks with vivid new colors! Celebrate in style!"

He turned in a slow, stunned circle, gawking as the merchants hawked their old wares with a new gusto, as a Sesharian immigrant dockhand sat on his parcel, drinking rather than working, with two other dockhands. Samson stumbled up the beach, gasping as he saw holos in the beach storefronts showing Elena and Farin over a table, signing on rare paper with the honorary red fountain ink meant solely for treaties.

"Do you believe us now?" Akino said.

"No," he said, his voice floating through the air, "I don't."

Visha elbowed him, and he found himself unable to grimace any longer. A smile snuck across his face. This was real?

This is real.

"I have to find her," he said.

"There's going to be a big celebration tonight with all the rulers and their attendants. And we're invited, not as Ravani dignitaries, but as *Sesharian representatives*." Visha shook her head in disbelief. "Can you believe it? They wouldn't even recognize us at the council, and now we're seen as our own."

"'Change can be swift like a tempest, and just as ruinous,'" Akino intoned.

"Let us hope this is not ruinous," Samson admonished.

"Ruin for Jantar, not us!" She grabbed his elbow, pulling him forward. "Come on!"

He followed her and Akino into the city and marveled at its gleaming marble towers. Had it always been this bright, this beautiful? Or was this a reflection of how he felt? Everywhere he turned, Samson saw exuberance: in the golden rays of the sun bouncing off the spires; in the musical notes of small boats puttering through the canals; in the people who seemed no longer to be uptight and righteous, but friendly, warm. He was appalled. Overjoyed. And even a tiny bit afraid.

Hope burbled in his chest with a contagious effect. He had gone for so long without it that he did not know whether to trust its phantomlike wings beating within his chest. He allowed Visha to steer him through the city until they arrived at the palace. As Akino hailed a guard, Samson saw movement on the right, and then Elena walking through the western gates, alone.

"I'll be just there. I need to—" he said, catching a flash of Visha's smirk and Akino's knowing gaze as he turned away. He hurried into the courtyard, his boots striking against the warm stones.

Elena turned, stiffening. "Samson."

There was something odd in her voice, something that made him slow and come to a stop just before her. Purple veins ringed her eyes, as if she had not slept, and her face seemed slightly puffy. She wore no regalia, no color. Even her white kurta seemed ill-fitting, hanging off her curves rather than hugging them, her dupatta draped haphazardly over her shoulder rather than with the stylish deftness he had seen her wear before.

The wings within his chest stuttered, and alarm snuck into his voice. "Elena, what's wrong?"

She looked up at him for a long moment, her face shuttered, her eyes dark and unreadable. She looked exhausted. She looked despondent. She looked as if she had lost someone, and he could not imagine why, on the eve of their victory.

He softened his voice, hoping to put her at ease. "Are you all right?"

She blinked, slow, long. Then Elena took a quick shuddering breath as if to expel unwanted thoughts.

"I'm fine. Just tired."

"I heard about the emergency meeting," he said, watching her face. "About the treaty. Did—did you really free both Ravence and Seshar?"

"Yes," she said, "I did."

"How? What did you say to make Farin agree? What happened in the meeting?"

"I gave him an offer he couldn't back away from." Her words were forced, short, as if it took enormous effort to say them. "With the pressure we put on him, the mines, the ships, the council, he folded. Seshar is free now, Samson."

Different emotions rang through him, each enormous and powerful, but within the clamor of his elation, guilt laced up his throat again. He remembered their last argument. His brusque, harsh words; her bright, wet eyes. They were always arguing, and he found himself powerless and wounded to be caught in the same vicious cycle again where, at an impasse, he felt the brunt of his shame, the knife of her judgmental silence. Samson flexed his hand, unsure.

Elena watched him, quiet, unmoving.

Finally, after a few beats, she spoke, her voice thick and coarse. "You should go and find the Black Scales. Start arranging for your journey to Seshar."

"What about you?" he asked. The thought of returning to Seshar without her after all they had done, after what *she* had done, depressed him into a thick gloom. "Where will you go?"

"Home," she said, her voice hollow. "We both have to return to our homes, don't we?"

He hesitated. She was right, and she was wrong. Seshar could be her home, just as Ravence could be his. They had fought and bled for each other for so long, and so much, that he did not where his began and hers ended. They were interlinked. Viciously, horribly—ravishingly. He knew Elena at her worst, just as she knew him in his deepest, darkest throes. No. He could not leave it like this. It was a disservice to their nations, their men, themselves.

"Come with me," he said suddenly, urgently. "Ravence and Seshar— they are both yours. Seshar would love to meet the queen who freed them."

"Don't say that," she whispered. Why would she not meet his eyes? "Seshar is not mine. It will never be. Please, Sam. Go home."

"Seshar is your home too." He paused. Cold sweat broke out on his arms, and his tongue stuck to the roof of his mouth. There it was again, that question, lodged in his throat, refusing to move. Elena turned, and his heart ratcheted a few degrees as her eyes dragged up his face. Maybe it was fool's courage, or maybe it was his frustration overpowering his hesitation, but Samson found himself reaching out and raising her face to his. "Let me show you."

"Sam—"

"Marry me," he said.

Her eyes crashed into his. *"What?"*

"We were already engaged. Why not take it a step further? Marry me, Elena, and Ravence and Seshar will become one kingdom. We can rule it together, you and I. We will make sure Farin never again comes for our homes, our people—"

She pulled back. "I can't."

His heart wrenched. Silence beat in his ears, and then, in a soft voice, "Can you honestly tell me that you have not considered it? Power, absolute. People, worshipping at your feet. Our feet. You and I will make the most wondrous, powerful team, Elena."

"I— Ravence is my home. I must go back to it first."

"And Seshar." He smiled. "You must see it. The wide beaches, sand so white it feels like pearls spilling between your fingers. We'll have fresh nut-roast coffee in Ajgar. There's a mangrove forest, not too far from my home, filled with little pools of fish so beautiful—"

"No," she said, voice cold in its finality.

He stopped, his bite-sized hope fizzling out like a snuffed flame. "Elena, what is it? Why are you suddenly so— What have I done wrong?"

"This isn't about *you*, Samson," she snapped. Her anger slid into him with its familiar pain, its lasting sting. He felt himself beginning to rise to it, like a puppet jerked by a string, bound to his old habits, but he caught himself just at the end.

"Think about it, Elena."

"Go to Seshar. Leave me be," she said.

He watched her go, entrapped by a sudden feeling of helplessness to know he could say nothing to call her back.

CHAPTER 62

JAYA

We cannot save the dead, but we can free them.
　　　　　—from the introduction of *The Great History of Sayon*

Jaya crept through the darkened wings of the palace as the sun, sinking from its zenith, transformed into a cold silver light that bisected the hall with the vehemence of a sword. When she passed through it, Jaya felt it cut into her flesh. Her hand sweated around the metal lotus. She forced herself to steady her breathing, to recall Akaros's training, but her heart, that devious little creature, bounded ahead.

Jaya turned the corner and almost jumped at the sight of the two Tsuani guards down the hall. She dashed back, then faltered forward. *Don't look suspicious*, she thought as she straightened herself.

She forced herself to look ahead, to measure her steps. She wore the emblem of the Ravani Phoenix on her breast to indicate herself as a servant of the queen, and when she neared the guards, she gave them a slight smile. Instead of returning it, a guard frowned.

"What are you doing down here?" he asked.

"I'm on my way to the courtyard," Jaya said, trying to push confidence into her voice. Behind her back, she gripped the lotus.

"What for?"

"I need—I must—check the grounds before tonight's celebration for—" She thought quickly. Why would a servant of the queen be sent to investigate a courtyard? To see if the lilies were to her liking? That the musicians played her favorite song? It all sounded so vain. But wasn't that in keeping with the royals?

"Hello?" The guard peered down at her. "Did you understand what I said?"

"Of course I did," Jaya snapped, then paused, recognizing her mistake. She plastered on her most appeasing smile. "Your Hind is accented, that's all."

"First we're forced to host you lot, then speak your tongue," the other guard grumbled. "Better if we all spoke Tsun. Better if Tsun was the language of the continent."

"Yes, well, can't change history in a day," Jaya said lightly, but the guard's frown only deepened.

"Your queen just showed us that you can," he said as his eyes fell to the emblem on her chest. "Why did she send you here?"

"Uh, her—her entrance!" Jaya exclaimed as the idea popped into her head. The guard arched a brow, and the other did not look convinced. "She wants to make a grand entrance. Very official. Songs and flowers and all. She did just change history in a day, like you said. Needs all the pomp. So, I—I'll just be on my way…"

She tried to sidle past the guards, but they did not move from her path.

"I hear all the liberated Sesharians on the killdoms were invited to join the celebration tonight. They're under your queen's charge. But if I see one of them trying to steal even a plant…" The guard trailed off, patting the charged wincer at his waist. If Jaya listened closely, she could hear its low, dangerous hum. She had only seen one in action once, when Maya had flung the projectile cuffs at an unlucky initiate during training. It had clamped down on his bicep, the other on his neck, and he had screamed like a shobu with its tail shorn off.

Jaya met the guard's gaze, her smile cooling into something bitter and edged. "I wouldn't pick the Sesharians for thieves. King Bormani would stage a heist for the jelly-filled mooncakes in your kitchen, and King Farin would take your ships, if he had the chance. The real thieves are at the top, boys. We're just here struggling for the scraps."

"Hmph." The guard considered this, while the other scowled.

"If I see anyone stealing so much as a napkin, I'm taking my wincer and shoving it down their—"

"Yes, okay, ka, we get it." The guard rolled his eyes. He nodded at Jaya. "On your way, then."

She moved past them before he could reconsider, the other guard arguing that he wasn't trigger-happy, he was *attentive*, that they needed to be, with all these foreigners in their home...

Their voices faded as Jaya entered the courtyard. Palace workers dashed around her, setting tables, as the musicians plucked their strings and tuned their instruments and groaned that no, they didn't know the folk dance of the Karvenese, no one did, their set list was long enough with all the other nations requesting their national songs. Foreign attendants flitted about, worrying over the dinner menu. She heard one complaining to a flustered Tsuani kitchen staffer that they needed to warm the Verani garlic soup *exactly* twenty-three minutes before serving, or else Tsuana would disrespect Verani cuisine and their king. Complaints, demands, even sobs choked the air. Her head throbbed. Were they all like this? The rulers vain and selfish, their attendants hysterical and stressed? She had never seen Elena act in such a way, but then again, she had never seen the queen within the soft, luxurious abode of her palace. Power made everyone into a glutton. Ravenous, beseeching, always craving more.

In the center of the courtyard, the bronze seal of the council floated serenely. The emblems of the seven nations corded together, but Jaya was struck by how, even on the eve of victory, there was no sign of Seshar.

"You see it missing too, don't you?"

Jaya stiffened as she heard Maya's cool voice. The Arohassin strategist sidled up to her, dressed in Tsuani creams, the blue streak in her hair dyed black.

"I thought you and Akaros were going to wait outside the city," she hissed.

"I was, but then Taran asked me to keep an eye on you," Maya said, and Jaya's skin prickled.

Did Taran not believe she could do the job? Would he cut off Div's life support? Why did he send Maya over Akaros?

Maya, as if reading her mind, laughed. "Don't stress, gamemaster. I come as your exit strategy."

"What about Akaros?"

"He's moving our assets," she said, and Jaya knew she meant Div as one, but she winced at hearing her brother be considered so coldly. "Have you finished?"

"I just have one left," Jaya said, flashing the metal lotus tucked in her waistband.

"I'll give it to you, Jaya. They are a masterful creation. Better than anything I've created. You should have come under my wing, not Akaros's. I could have taught you more than just Ambari."

Jaya tried not to roll her eyes. She was tired of Maya's and Akaros's long-running rivalry. She had kept to the edges, avoiding being subsumed unlike other poor initiates.

"You're hovering. We'll attract attention," she said quickly, hoping to rid herself of Maya. "Go. I'll recon with you—"

"What do you plan to do after all of this?"

Jaya stopped, stunned by the question. "What do you mean?"

Maya's eyes slid to hers with a slyness that Jaya disliked. "After you have Div, what will you do?"

A cold, singular bell clanged through her as she met Maya's calculative gaze. Did she suspect? Did she know? Jaya studied her, but the strategist revealed nothing other than a cutting curiosity.

"I—we—will continue fighting with the Arohassin," Jaya said, her voice dry.

"Yes, Akaros said the same," Maya mused.

"And you?"

Maya looked up at the floating seal. "I think you'll go wherever Div does, should he survive."

Jaya swallowed. Her fingers fluttered at her sides, as if grasping an invisible weapon. She had no killer instinct—Akaros had complained about this before—but in the moment, Jaya wished she had a pulse gun. Or a sword. She wanted to drive it into Maya's back because it was that last part, the thinly veiled threat, that sent a surge of vicious fear and dark anger through her. Div was no chess piece. He was not someone to be manipulated like the kings in their obtuse political games. He was her *brother*. Of flesh and blood, or whatever remained of it.

Jaya calmed herself, and when she spoke, her voice was steeled. "We go with the Arohassin. We are indebted to Taran, after all."

Maya turned to her, eyes cutting down like a blade. "You'd do well to remember your debt, then."

She owed the Arohassin more than her dreams of revenge. She owed them her brother's life.

He had told her that his body did not feel right. That for suns, it had never felt right. And on that fateful day, when he had told their parents, she had stood, gripped with a delayed shock, as Div screamed his name, and her mother had responded with Divya.

"I don't understand," her mother had wailed. "You are my beautiful Divya, my darling girl. My radiance. I—I don't see why you would want to be something else."

"Have we done something wrong?" her father beseeched. "Did we treat you cruelly?"

"No," Div said, his voice thick with frustration. "This is me! ME! Mama, do you remember the stories you told about the warriors who created the Unsung? How they were Yumi? How they passed their teachings on to warriors that were neither men nor women, but a divine third that—"

"Those are legends," her mother growled. Her hair lashed and swung, agitated. "This is my fault. I should have returned to Moksh. Made you a temple attendant so you could see the beautiful lineage of what you are, Divya. You are a Yumi. Why would you clip your own hair?"

Jaya understood then that it was not Div himself that bothered her parents, or the idea of what he was, but the implication that in becoming his true self, he would relinquish the one gift their Great Mother had bestowed upon him. Hair of power. Hair of legend, of ancestry. The gift she had never been given.

"I am not less," Div said, his voice shaking. He jabbed a finger toward Jaya. "Look at Jaya. She is clipped, but you've told us all our lives that she's no less than you."

"You know that's not what I meant," her mother snapped, and it was this admission, this small, errant remark, that had stung Jaya the deepest. She *was* less. She was born Yumi but was not truly one, could not serve and protect like her ancestors, could not swear allegiance to their Great Mother because she had been born bereft of Her blessing. Jaya's eyes stung. Div turned to her, and maybe it was jealousy toward her sibling, who had been born whole and did not want it, or maybe it was her anger toward her mother, but Jaya looked at him and said, quietly, "You will become less."

Silence rang through their small home.

Tears welled in his eyes, and Jaya immediately regretted it, but he was already moving, leaving. Her parents called too, but Div had rushed up to his room, and then she was alone with them and their confusion, their ire. She had not heard the gold caps over their shouting. Did not hear the strike of a match, the flare of a flame.

By the time they noticed, it was too late.

Smoke clogged their home, trapping them inside. Her mother had roared with fury, but her voice was drowned out by the gold caps, and then they were all choking from the lack of air as the flames grew higher. The gold caps were going to burn them alive. Small mercy, then, that her family had been buried when the house caved in.

A gold cap had dragged her out by her hair, and Jaya had thrown herself on him. She had screamed until her lungs were hoarse. But nothing compared to the screech that ripped from her throat when she saw Div.

He had been burned terribly, his face marred, his body an incomprehensible mash of flesh and bone. It was a miracle he was still alive. A miracle Akaros made sure she did not forget.

"We can keep him alive, Jaya," he had told her after Div had slipped into his coma. "He is special, and in time, you will see how."

Every mission, every game, she thought of Div. Asleep in a bed, then trapped in a tube, then floating in a tank as his blood fed the third, and the third fed him.

She thought of him now as she placed the last lotus in the shadow of a pillar in the courtyard. In her pocket, the holopod sat heavy, cold. Maya nodded, then disappeared into the bustling mass of attendants. Jaya stepped back as an attendant rushed past, shouting at another to place the flower display *over there, not in the corner.*

She had no qualms about what was to befall the kings and queens. She did, however, feel a strange twisting in her chest as she watched the attendants, the musicians, and the guards. This was not their fight. The strange feeling increased as she thought of Elena and Samson. They, like the gold caps, held vicious prejudices. So what if they did not draw the sword now? They would eventually.

Right?

Jaya stepped farther into the shadows, gripping the pod tightly. *They will,* she affirmed to herself. *They're all the same.*

She pushed back her guilt and thought of Div. When he awoke, she would give him a new body. And they would go into the mountains beyond Magar, deep within the glens. She had already arranged the barrels of sand needed to sustain him. They would live undetected, in peace. War or no war, once she had Div, she had no intention of staying.

She gripped the pod tighter, her chappals slapping purposefully as she strode out of the courtyard. *Here is my courage, Div,* she said silently. *I give it all for you.*

CHAPTER 63

ELENA

I have always suspected a deep, rotten thing at the heart of me.
—from the diaries of Priestess Nomu of the Fire Order

Farin held out a golden kamarbandh. "This is for you."

Gingerly, Elena avoided his metal fingers. "What is this for?"

"For tracking. I want you to lead Samson to the beach between the docks. Tell him you have something to show him on the killdoms. My men will handle the rest."

Elena examined the waist belt. Precious emeralds and pink diamonds were set delicately into patterns of lotuses and jasmine. Intricate thread-work twined around the band, shaping vines, trees. She turned it around and stopped, her breath catching. A golden Phoenix, eyes ablaze with rubies and wings flared to the heavens, rose in the middle of the kamar-bandh as if ready to take flight. It reminded her of her coronation neck-lace. How heavily the Phoenix had sat on her chest. Perhaps it had been a warning of all the burdens she would come to bear.

Carefully, she turned the belt around, swallowing the sudden bitterness in her throat.

"Where is the tracker?"

He tapped a metal finger against the Phoenix with a sharp *ping*. "Right here."

Of course he would put it in the Phoenix. Elena met his eyes, and Farin gave a cold, simple smile that stoked the ire in her belly. "Do you want to see if it fits?"

"It will," she said, stepping quickly away from him.

Farin watched her for a moment, his robotic eye still. "Don't tell me you're having second thoughts."

"None." She kept her face remote, impassive. "The quicker we get this done, the better. I have a lot of work to do in Ravence after the ruin you caused."

"And I in Jantar, after the destruction you created in my mines." This time, his smile was edged. "So I say we're even."

She thought of her father, falling into the flames. Her city, scorched. Her people, lost. War had cost her everything, and still, it was not enough.

"No, Farin," she said softly. "We are not even. But it will have to do."

Back in her rooms, Elena cinched the kamarbandh around her waist. Despite all the jewels and gold, it remained light, weighed down only by the Phoenix. The tracker lay tucked within its hollow underside. Elena tugged the kamarbandh tighter, wincing as it began to cut into her skin. She draped her golden pallu down her arm when a sudden thud broke the quiet. Elena stiffened, the pallu drifting to the floor. Cautiously, she turned. A shape appeared outside her balcony, becoming more solid, drawing close, and she carved her hands into the Lotus, a flame sparking between her fingers when the door opened and the high sister stepped through.

"You?" Elena gasped.

"I told you we would meet again." Sura pulled down her hood with an amused smile as she saw the flame in her hand. "Is that meant for me?"

Elena snapped her wrist, and the flame vanished. "What are you doing here? Did Daz send you?"

"No, I am not here at the general's request but my own." Sura sat on the edge of the bed. "Sit."

But Elena could only stare. The high sister looked completely at ease despite dropping in with no warning, and Elena did not know what startled her the most. The Yumi priestess here, in her room, or the fact that she wore a plain Tsuani longcoat instead of her robes. Perhaps both.

"H-how did you get here?" Elena said, still standing.

"After you left, my sisters and I arranged for my journey to Tsuana," Sura answered. "First across the bay to Nbru, then on a merchant trade ship to Tsuana. They really do have tasty fried okra here."

"B-but," Elena said, her mind skittering between the priestess's odd appearance and her travels, "why?"

"The flames told me to," Sura said simply. She looked around the room. "Do you have it? The feather?"

"The feather?" Elena began, and then she remembered the crystallized feather and Samson's fading eyes. How he had fallen to his knees upon touching it. How it was the high sister who had told her to give it to him.

"You—you knew." The priestess watched calmly as Elena trembled. She remembered the biting cold in his body, the pallid skin of his chest. But most of all, she remembered how that numbness had tried to drown her. "It almost killed him. You said it would help me take his Agni. You did not warn me—"

"I wanted you to establish a connection with his Agni," Sura said gently. "Can you sense his now?"

Elena paused. She turned inward, searching. She perceived the ghost of Samson's Agni, though the sensation felt hazy, as if trying to grasp a flickering shadow. The more she concentrated on it, the flimsier it became. "I—I can, sort of. It is easier when he's closer."

Concern ringed the priestess's voice. "Can he lock onto yours? Have you tempered your end of the connection?"

"He did once." She remembered the sudden rush of heat as Samson had reached for her Agni on the boat, and then how everything had faded, muted after. "We melded our Agni together to sail through the Black Pit."

Sura inhaled sharply. "And he did not take all your Agni? Oh, Great Mother. Then perhaps there is a chance."

"Chance for what?" Elena said, frustration pushing into her voice. "Why are you here? Who are you seeking? What is this connection you speak of?"

"I have come seeking the third, Elena," Sura said. "It is here. I know it."

"What makes you so sure?"

"Because your Eternal Fire has rejected your Prophet, and mine now burns black with the grief of the Goddess. The time approaches. You and Samson Kytuu *must* find and break the Serpent's cage. The third will wake then. Hurry, Elena. Let us go at once—"

But Elena was no longer listening. Her heart crashed against her ribs with the wild abandon of waves beating the shore. She staggered to a seat. It felt as if she were drowning, clawing for the surface, struggling for air, only for the waves to beat her down again.

Suddenly, she felt the sharp contours of the kamarbandh around her waist, the heaviness of the Phoenix and its intended purpose. *Lead Samson to the beach.* She had no room for priestesses and their raving dreams of gods and fire. This was her purpose. She did not care about dead gods. She did not care about unity or great divinity. Ravence was at the end of this long, arduous journey, and she was too exhausted to entertain anything else.

"Stop," she whispered.

"—the fires will dance in unison! A new holy age shall begin! You are the Goddess's vehicle of change and—"

"STOP."

Sura froze. Slowly, Elena rose to her feet, and as she did so, she remembered her father and how he had told her of priestesses' mad rants. Their incessant need to *shove* upon others. Was this how he had felt, scraped to the bone, drained beyond belief, as he had listened?

"Samson Kytuu is not my responsibility," she said. "After tonight, we will go our separate ways. Ravence does not need its god. It needs its queen, and I intend to return to build it."

Sura sucked her teeth. "Are you afraid of divinity?"

"I am not," Elena said truthfully. "But I am tired of these talks of distant gods. Neither the Phoenix nor your Goddess helped me when Ravence fell. The Serpent did not help us when Seshar fell. The gods are just that, Priestess. Distant, uncaring, unyielding. It is better you go back to your temple now. Your general will return soon, and I'm sure he will be curious why you will not be there to greet him."

Sura studied her for a long moment, then said, quietly, "Do you honestly not crave such divine powers?"

Elena thought of the killdoms, of how she had reached for and wrenched out all the bright, essential parts of the captain until he had become a shriveled mess of blood and bone. She remembered the heat of power rushing through her veins then. The glory of it. The beauty of it. She closed her eyes, inhaling, then spoke. "I do. I have. On the ships, I saw the chakra points within another and could bend his heat to destroy himself."

When she opened her eyes, she found the high sister still, her face marred with both horror and intrigue.

"Was this after you connected with Samson?" she asked softly. Elena nodded, and Sura ran a hand over her bald scalp. "I have read of the ability only in legend, only wielded by those of Agni. But it is within the Serpent's nature to ruin all that She touches."

Suddenly, Sura grasped her hands, squeezing so tightly that Elena winced.

"When you wield such power, it bites into your own. For every life taken, you shave off a sun of your own. How many have you taken with such powers, Elena?" When she did not answer, the priestess shook her. "How many?"

"I—I don't know," Elena gasped.

The priestess dropped her hands, moving back. "Then pray you find your faith again. The third will rise, Elena. And it is up to you to seek unity or wither into chaos."

Elena entered the courtyard, her mind still ringing with the baleful prophecy of the high sister. After she had failed to convince her, Sura had slipped out, and Elena felt no urge to call her back. She was weary of Agni and the mad dreams it produced. Or the people it endangered. She thought listlessly of her purpose, her fingers fluttering over her belt.

One man for two kingdoms. One monster for freedom. Surely, she could pay that exchange. Surely, she could bear that price.

Elena slipped between attendants and foreign aides, the end of her gold-and-orange sari fluttering in the breeze. Yumi, Sesharians, Tsuani, Jantari, all people of the kingdoms celebrating the brokering of peace. She tried to find Daz but found the general nowhere. Lights sparkled above with the warmth of distant suns. People chattered, laughing loudly, drinking freely, but somehow, even on the eve of victory, their happiness could not budge the dark weight that had settled in her stomach. She avoided the food, too sick to eat. She instead wandered to the musician's stage just as they began to play another tune.

A flute began the first notes, followed by a deep, steady drumbeat. Elena turned as she saw Sesharians forming a circle. The others pushed out to watch, and Elena had to crane her neck to see as someone started a song. It was Tanmay, the deckhand, singing in a low, throaty voice. Laughs sparked up and around the circle as people linked arms and began to kick. Suddenly, Visha appeared at her side, tugging her forward.

"No, no, I don't want to—" Elena began but she was pulled in. She found herself skipping along in rhythm with the drumbeats. The beat quickened and they went in, then out, again and again, turning in a large circle, twirling in place. The circle widened. More confused people were pulled in. More laughter filled the courtyard. Despite herself, Elena giggled as a Karvenese aide kicked so high he almost knocked his knee into his nose. A warm, hearty flush crept up her cheeks, and for a moment, she forgot the kamarbandh biting into her flesh. More people began to sing. She knew only a few Ambari words, but she found herself shouting them all the same. Beside her, Visha laughed.

"You're off-key!"

"You're off-beat," she shouted back.

Visha grinned, and when the circle drew back, she spun to face her. Elena clapped her hands against Visha's, then laughed as Visha kicked back into the circle. In the middle of the floor, Tanmay balanced a drink on his head. He shimmied his hips, turning in place and eliciting hoots from the crowd. Elena wet her fingers and blew a whistle. He chortled, then panicked as the glass began to slip. Elena bit back a roar of laughter as he tried to regain his balance, and then she was swept up in the circle again. They began to kick higher, skip faster. Her cheeks burned from grinning, sweat beading down the back of her blouse as she spun to the quickening rhythm.

She twirled, clapping her hands with Visha again, and then turned to clap the person on her left. In her flush, Elena did not recognize him until she felt his familiar calloused fingers against hers. She startled. Samson held her hands for a beat longer. Elena felt time slow, the music and the laughter seeping out until she heard only her racing heartbeat, his sharp, sudden intake of breath. His throat quivered. The others danced around them, but Elena stood rooted to the spot, her hand in his. His eyes on hers. When his long fingers grazed her palm, she felt the air tighten, as if a string connecting them both had been struck with the bold resonance of a sarangi. There was a heat in his eyes, one that made her feel flustered and annoyed and ravenous. His voice was a low hum in his throat.

"Dance with me," he said.

She should not. She should put as much distance between her and him until the appointed hour. She should tear her eyes away from his and forget the look she had seen in them, forget the feelings it had elicited within her.

But Elena felt her hand closing around his, and she allowed him to lead her into the center of the circle. Samson's hand slipped down to the small of her back, his touch light, barely there. The other hovered right above the nape of her neck. Elena swallowed. If he touched her neck, would he feel the sudden rush of heat that overtook her body? Or did he already sense it, flaring within her ribs?

The music slowed. He spun her out, and when she came back, she turned inward. His arm looped around her, and she could feel the warm contours of his muscled chest against her upper back. Elena twirled out to face him. In the warm glow of the lights, his eyes were softer, like a sea soaked by the sun. Resplendent, beautiful. *But they are cursed*, she reminded herself as they drew apart. *A warning from the desert.*

Elena danced around him, her hand trailing across his chest, and she tried not to notice how it suddenly gave under her touch, how his hand trembled as he drew her closer. Was it just the drums, picking up the pace, or was that her pulse, jackhammering?

"You've been avoiding me," he said, his voice oddly hoarse.

"I have not," she said, though she felt something within her tighten with the lie. "I just have other matters to attend to."

"I can tell when you're lying," he said, and her blood thinned.

No, she thought sadly, desperately, *you cannot.*

"I shouldn't have pushed," he said. "Seshar will be there for you whenever you choose to visit. I will be there."

"Is that a promise?"

He met her eyes. She had the sensation that perhaps she had asked too much, given away too much in that question, but it was too late to take it back now.

"For you? Of course, my rani." He leaned closer, and her breath hitched as she felt his tickling her ear. "Meri rani."

Meri rani. She shivered at the sound of ancient Herra rolling off his tongue. He drew back, and Elena saw a soft, almost hopeful smile flickering across his lips.

Stop it, she chided herself. *Do not give him hope. He deserves nothing from you.*

Elena turned, half looking for an escape, half wanting to hide her face so he could not see her crestfallen expression. Her fingers slipped from his.

"I have to go," she said.

"Elena, wait."

But she hurried away, hot guilt bubbling up her throat like bile. She could hear him calling after her. She did not turn.

Elena broke into the cool expanse of the hallway, and she took a deep, shuddering breath. Tears cropped her vision. Angrily, she wiped her eyes. What a fool she was. Weak, sniveling. *Focus*, she berated herself. The beach, she needed to take him to the beach.

Elena glanced up at the moons, full and brilliant in their ivory throne. It was not time yet, but perhaps Farin would not mind if she was early. She could bear it no longer.

When she heard footsteps behind her, Elena steadied her breath. She did not turn as the footsteps faltered. She did not turn as she felt his hand on her shoulder, gentle, kind. Samson walked around, facing her.

With his ring finger, he gently wiped the tears from the inner corners of her eyes. She watched as he sucked on his finger.

"There," he said. "The salt of thine is the salt of mine. Your grief is my grief."

"*Sam.*" Her voice trembled under the weight of his name. "Please."

He watched her face closely, his voice quiet. "Are you running from me because you have chosen not to become my queen?"

She opened her mouth to speak, when footsteps at the other end of the hall made them both turn. Jaya froze when she saw them.

Elena spotted something metallic in her hand as Jaya gave a nervous laugh and flipped off her hood, striding forward.

"Good, I've been looking for you two," she said. "I have a favor to ask."

CHAPTER 64

JAYA

The most accomplished gamemasters understand this: The greatest games are played not in our arenas, but in the world outside.
—from *The Gamemaster Manual*

Elena and Samson stared at her, and for a moment, Jaya wondered if she had intruded on something soft and intimate, something she did not earn. She fixed an uneasy smile on her face.

"Oooor I can come back later," she began when Elena stepped forward.

"No, it's all right," she said, her voice rough. She quickly dabbed her eyes. "What is it, Jaya?"

Jaya saw something dark and wounded cross Samson's face. She was definitely intruding. One thousand percent.

"Um, I just needed, well." She feigned ineptitude as she watched Elena carefully avoid Samson's gaze. Slowly, she took out her device, a metal orb no bigger than her palm. "I was wondering if I could get an infusion of your Agnis. I'd like to study it."

Samson shook his head. "It's too dangerous. Agni can be unstable without a wielder, and two at once could be catastrophic. No, Jaya, perhaps another time."

But she turned to Elena, keeping her voice steady, reasonable. "I don't mean to experiment now. I just need the melding, before you two go your separate ways." When Samson frowned, she added, "And I will report to you all my findings. Everything. You will know all the developments firsthand, and if it proves too dangerous, we can shut it down."

Elena seemed to consider this, her eyes flitting from the orb to her. Samson turned to her, his voice low.

"Elena, this is a bad idea," he began.

"Do you not trust me, Sam?" Jaya said loudly. "After I saved our hides on the killdoms? Do you really not believe me?"

He whipped toward her. "That was different. This is dangerous. You could harm yourself, or others, or—"

"When can you run an experiment?" Elena said.

Jaya pretended to make a show of it, counting on her fingers, drawing out the silence. "Three, maybe four days. If I have your Agni tonight, then two."

"Then you can tell us your initial findings before I depart for Ravence." Elena stepped forward, but it was Samson that Jaya watched. It was his look of pure, utter pain that suddenly made her twist in sympathetic agony.

Elena held up her hand, and a flame flared out with a soft hiss. "Sam."

When he did not move, she softened her voice a fraction. "Please."

With a deep sigh, Samson came forward. He held his palm under hers, and Jaya watched, her breath held, as a second flame burst to life. They were so bright compared with the darkness of the hall that Jaya had to look away for a moment, blinking rapidly. When she turned back, she saw the flames twine together.

Quickly, she raised her orb. Held it over the dancing, growing fire.

"Easy," she whispered.

The heat of the inferno beat against the back of her hand. It felt like a needle, piercing her flesh. Jaya bit back a hiss of pain as she brought the orb closer. "Easy."

Elena guided her hand up, Samson following, and together, they tucked the flame into the orb. Jaya snapped it shut quickly, and then hugged it to her chest, afraid they would change their minds.

But Elena only stood there for a moment, stock-still, as she watched the intertwined fire in the orb.

"Take good care of it," she said, her voice oddly distant. She left then, her sari fluttering behind her like a dying, fading flame.

Samson hesitated. Jaya noticed how his eyes tracked her down the hall, how he always searched for her in any room they entered. She did not know if Samson Kytuu loved their queen. But perhaps that was love— obsession. The desperate urge to make sure the one thing you desired most was always within your reach.

They stood in silence, and when Samson finally spoke, his voice cracked with the weight of unsaid emotions.

"Be careful, Jaya," he said, looking down the hall at Elena's fading form. "Fire is more than just power. It is resonance. It drives us to do mad things."

And with that, he followed in pursuit of the queen.

Jaya watched him go, her neck crawling with that strange sensation of being watched, but when she turned, there was no one there. *You're being paranoid.* She hugged the orb closer. Dully, she felt a pang of guilt, then moved quickly to bury it. She thought of Div, of the freedom they would have, the one almost within their reach. The flame beat against the orb. Its heat pricked her skin, but Jaya only held on tighter.

CHAPTER 65

ELENA

Our stories are full of fools who, in agony, drive the blade deeper and call it love.

—from The Legends and Myths of Sayon

She slipped out of the palace, following the moonlit canals toward the shore. The moons, yellow and soft like the heart of a lotus, swelled over the horizon. Music trilled in the distance as the city celebrated, but unlike before, Elena no longer felt the urge to dance.

A large park floated along the port, and beyond it, Elena could see the silver stretch of the beach gleaming like an oiled blade. Her steps slowed. For a moment, Elena stood transfixed as the tide crashed into the shore with steady, even sighs. But then her gaze drifted to the killdoms out in the bay, and the moment passed. She shuttered her wonder.

Just one more night, and then we can all go home.

Elena walked down the hillside to the park. She had time before the hour, and she knew, as she wandered through the still gardens, that he would come. She knew before she even felt the faint edges of his Agni flickering in her mind's eye. Birds of paradise fluttered in between the trees, and Elena kept her eyes trained on one as she felt him approach.

"Elena."

She closed her eyes. Drew in a bracing breath, and then turned.

There was no warm light in his gaze now, no flirty smile. He stalked forward with the slow gait of a predator, and she thought, dully, that this was the Samson Kytuu she knew. Not the tender, beautiful man who asked her to dance and dressed her wounds. Her Samson was a monster.

"Why are you following me?"

"Why are you running?" he asked.

"I am not running," she said, and he stopped a pace before her. She could see the silver glint of his urumi. Ironic, that they both wore weapons around their waist.

"I think you are," he said. "I think you're afraid, but I don't understand why."

She barked a laugh. "I am not afraid. I told you, I am tired. There is so much to do, with so little time, and I can't spend it dancing."

"But you want to," he said, and his voice struck her cold. "You want to and you're denying yourself. Why, Elena? Why are you leading us both on this chase?"

She swallowed, gooseflesh prickling up her arms. Through the trees, she saw the silver gleam of the beach. Farin's men would be coming with their boats soon. Perhaps she should bring Samson down, toward the shore—

"I know why," he said, and her eyes lifted to his. "You are afraid that if you admit how you feel, you will also admit some fault of your own. You are afraid of yourself, Elena Aadya Ravence. That is why you're running."

"That is not true," she said, heat rising to her face.

"It is. And you will deny it because it is in your nature. Because for whatever reason, your pride outweighs your honesty."

She scoffed. "Is this why you followed me? To tell me off?"

"*No*," he said, and his voice quivered under the weight of unsaid things. She froze, suddenly unsure. She did not want him to go further. If he did, she would regret it, and her regret would claw her until she was bleeding from within. How then could she heal from self-inflicted wounds?

"Samson, listen. Whatever you may feel about me, about us, forget it."

She drew in a shaky breath as she felt the cool press of the kamarbandh around her waist. "It will be better that way. Trust me."

He watched her for a long moment, the shadows of the fluttering leaves dancing across his still face. When he spoke, they rippled over his lips. "I don't believe you."

Her pulse quickened as he stepped forward, his voice low, intense.

"And I don't love you, Elena Aadya Ravence, I despise you. You're idealistic to the point of self-destruction. You throw yourself into danger for the sake of your country, but you don't stop to realize the consequences. You're self-righteous, thickheaded, and vain to the point that I cannot fully trust you.

"So why," he said, his eyes dragging to hers with a fresh wave of pain, "can I not stop thinking about you? Why, when I try to make myself hate you with every fiber of my being, do my thoughts betray me? Why, Elena, can I not *forget* you?"

A roar filled her ears as if she was standing on a cliff, the wind buffeting her forward. Everything felt distant and pointless all at once, the beach, the kamarbandh, her promise. She had the strange, peculiar sensation of teetering on the edge, afraid of falling, but also curious to know how it felt. To fall.

For him.

His eyes, always a mask, always hiding some terror in their dark depths like an ocean drowning its secrets, were clear with desperation—to the point of vulnerability. His openness terrified her. His words pulled her in.

She trembled as he came closer and touched her chin with a gentleness that shocked her, if only because of its incongruity with the violent passion in his voice.

"*You,*" he said, his voice trembling. "You vex me, Elena. Every second, every moment you're near, I cannot think clearly. And yet I cannot stand it when you stay away."

The roar in her ears reached a keen as he tilted her chin up, bringing her face to his so that when he spoke in a hushed whisper, his breath brushed her lips.

"Why must you haunt me so? Why can't you leave me be?" He grazed his thumb against her lower lip, shaking. "Tell me. Please."

Because you and I are the same, she almost said. *Cut from the same fabric by the same cruel gods. Vain, self-righteous, horrid. Because you are the monster I see in me.*

But the roar in her ears crushed out all sound and lodged the words in her throat. To say them was to speak a truth she'd rather ignore. Better to leave them unsaid than acknowledge her own corruption. If she did not speak, she could pretend the events that had led them to this point, this precipice where they stood now, was only of his making. She was blameless, honest, true—like the queen she had always yearned to be.

But even as she thought so, Elena knew it was not true. She was just as monstrous. Just as desirous and desperate for power, so much so that it would have made her laugh, if not for the sudden tightness in her throat. The Burning Queen and the Butcher. The odd pair. Monsters of the same coin.

She had as much blood on her hands as he had on his. And she could suffer for it on her own, because even in suffering she was vain, or—and this was a deadly, incriminating *or*—she could share that suffering. Find someone to bear her burden of sins if only to have companionship. If only to be a little less lonely.

Elena looked into Samson's eyes as he cupped her face, her chest twisting with a terror that made her feel like she was already plummeting, the wind raging in her ears as she fell—to what, she did not know.

And she realized she no longer cared. What was the point in denying herself, if destruction was her ultimate path?

"Sam," she gasped, and she felt a great weight break upon her shoulders, her voice cracking upon his name. The plea in her voice registered across his face as he breathed in quick. His fingers trembled on her cheeks. "I can't stay away either."

She touched his chest and felt his heart thrum beneath her palm, matching the racing rhythm of her own heartbeat. Her skin prickled, hot. He seemed to shudder at her touch, his eyes fluttering closed for a moment and then snapping back open.

"Elena," he whispered.

His lips, warm, soft, and near. Glistening as his tongue darted forth to wet them.

"You," he said.

She swayed in his arms. "You."

"You are my ruin. And I want to be completely, utterly ravaged by you."

He cupped the back of her neck, his caress sending a thrill down her spine. His other hand dropped to her waist, and it felt like the dance all over again, but this time, she pressed willingly into his touch. Her hips brushed his, and she felt the cool slick of his urumi against her belly. Warmth flared down her legs, making her weak. Elena shuddered against him, her lips just a breath before his.

"Then ruin us," she said.

He kissed her. Hot, slow, taking care to taste her lips and dance his tongue along the edges of her teeth. Elena gave a slight moan. She was falling, falling.

She forgot about the beach, her promises, her failures, as she raked her fingers through his hair and tugged him closer. He moaned into her mouth. Ran his hands over the bare curves of her stomach, as if to memorize every inch. His mouth became hungrier, harder. She bit down on his lip, and he gasped, his chest quaking against her fingertips. She wanted to tear him apart, to peel back the layers and see what lay beneath. To see the monster and bare her own.

The desire to see him fully filled her with a heady yearning. She grasped at the buttons of his shirt. With a simple, effortless pull, Samson tore it in two. She saw the faded scar running down his chest to the ridges of his upper abdomen. When she traced it, Samson hissed against her neck. She wanted to take it away from him, the memory and the pain it carried. She kissed his neck, his chest, his scar until he growled low in his throat.

"Elena."

Samson pulled her back up, kissing her with a renewed passion that made her knees buckle as his hands cupped beneath her. She gasped as he hoisted her up with a sudden strength.

She wrapped her legs around his waist as he shielded the backs of her thighs from his urumi. He kissed her neck, her breasts, his chest pressing into the curve of her stomach. When he nipped at the soft skin beneath her collarbone, Elena groaned.

"Sam, wait," she said.

He paused, his eyes glazed and unfocused. "Do you not want—"

"No, *no.*" She pressed closer, shivering as she felt his hardness press against the inside of her thigh. "Just…not here. We should leave and go—"

Where? The palace? Farin would find them there. His men were already on their way to the beach. No, they needed to leave Tsuana. Now.

"The bounders," she began, when a sudden sound to their right made her stiffen. Samson stilled beneath her, his voice coming out in short, hot gasps.

"What is it?" he said.

His lips were slick and wet underneath the moon. Instinctively, she wiped the corner of his mouth, when the sound came again. A sharp crack, like branches snapping underfoot.

This time, Samson heard it too. He dropped her immediately and pushed her behind him, reaching for his urumi, but it was too late.

A pulse ripped through the night, shattering the quiet. Samson dove, pulling her down with him. He draped his body over hers as the night erupted with shrieking birds and pulse fire.

"Sam," she cried in warning.

She saw a shape out of the corner of her eye, and suddenly rough hands were pulling him up, pulling her away.

She yelled, kicking, hands sparking. Elena drove forward, kneeing her opponent as her flame roared to life. She twisted, calling for Samson, when someone rammed the butt of a gun against her temple.

Her head whiplashed back. A high ringing filled her ears. She tried to turn, but then a soldier punched her in the liver, and she crumpled in two like a fallen petal.

"Sam," she rasped.

Shapes spun in her vision, quick and efficient with violence. Something flared, and her vision cleared for a moment to see Samson, half-dressed, summoning a flame. It rippled down his urumi with a crack that thundered through the garden. He whirled, the twin blades cutting through a soldier with a vicious, practiced beauty. Another brought up his zeemir, but Samson cleaved it in half. He was a flurry of motion and fire and god-given rage. A monster, and hers alone.

"Sam!" she cried.

He whipped around at the sound of her voice, and in that moment she would remember forever, in that moment she would come to regret, his eyes crashed into hers. She saw his blazing fury, his wrath—and his tenderness. Even in ruin, he had love for her.

And it would haunt her forever.

The soldier came from the undergrowth, from the other side. She saw the glint of silver, a flapping sleeve. Samson spun, trying to dodge his attacker, but he was off step, off rhythm.

The dagger cut clean through his chest—through his scar.

Samson gasped.

"No!" she screamed.

His eyes widened in shock as he looked down at the curved blade. At his blood, already dripping.

Samson sank to his knees.

Elena screamed again, trying to pull herself up, but her hands slipped in the slick dirt. With a violent shove, the soldier pushed Samson onto his side. The pulse fire stopped then, plummeting them into a horrible silence where the only sound was that of Samson's rasping breath.

"No, no, *Sam*." She reached with bloody fingers. *"Ruru, please."*

But the Jantari dragged her away as his eyes—those terrible, wonderful, cursed eyes—shuttered, their light fading fast.

CHAPTER 66

JAYA

In the long history of Ravence, very few rulers have lived to old age, or seen the coronation of their grandchildren. Historians point out family ailments, while locals call it Alabore's Curse.

The burden of death.

—from chapter 38 of *The Great History of Sayon*

Jaya hugged the orb close as she hurried through the palace, moonlight razoring the hall into strips of black and white. Even the fish in the glass stream below her nipped at her heels. She checked her pod. Twenty minutes. She had only twenty until—

Jaya halted abruptly as a lotus, the one she had placed in the courtyard, suddenly blinked off. It couldn't be. She refired the commands, but the lotus remained eerily unlit.

Shit.

She could go back. It was possible the lotus had become unlinked from her pod, and she could reconnect them. But then she would have only ten minutes to escape. Barely enough time to jump into the awaiting canal boat. *Better to leave it.* Jaya began to walk when her pod chimed again. She watched in horror and disbelief as another lotus blinked off, then another. Three of the five were now offline. A startled cry escaped her lips, like a sparrow caught in the shadow of an eagle.

The realization cut into her quickly, drying her throat.

Someone was taking out her lotuses.

Someone knew of her plot.

Jaya swiveled sharply, but no one lurked in the passage. She could faintly hear laughter and song in the distance, the bright swell of a cheer, but there was a strange, stilted silence in the air, like a forest fallen quiet at the approach of a predator.

She started forward, her pace brisk and controlled, then long and hurried, then broken, until she was half running, half jogging. She looked over her shoulder. The shadows seemed to surge closer, pricking her with vicious delight. She ran faster. Down the hall, ducking around a corner. She just needed to get to her rooms. There was a garden outside her window, the canal flowing beyond its walls. She could almost hear the quiet lapping of the water against the boat's hull, the low rumble of its engine vibrating beneath her fingers. Just a little farther—

A wet hand grasped her wrist, at once cold and piercing, and her imagination ran amok as she imagined long nails biting into her skin, a demon's face appearing out of the darkness, but then she saw the familiar tilt of that sardonic smile, the amber of her eyes, and Jaya bit down a cry as Rhumia yanked her back.

"Always running in the shadows, aren't you, little bird?" she said.

"H-how?" Jaya said as she took in Rhumia's dark ripped clothing, her unrestrained hair curling like a thousand snakes. And then in Rhumia's other hand, she saw her bent, crumpled lotuses. "It was you."

Rhumia twisted her arm, and Jaya yelped as pain seared up her wrist. She kicked Rhumia's shin, but the Yumi only yanked her around, slamming her into the wall. Jaya gasped. The orb slipped from her broken fingers, bouncing once, twice.

"What have we here?" Rhumia said as she picked up the orb with her hair.

Jaya twisted viciously, suddenly. Her teeth closed around the Yumi's ear. Rhumia jerked away on instinct, Jaya pulling. There was a sickening crunch, then a tearing, then hot, metallic blood flooded her mouth, her tongue. Rhumia howled. She staggered back, clutching her torn ear as Jaya spit out her flesh, gagging. The orb came loose. She tried to grab it when shouts sounded down the hall.

Two guards sprinted toward them. With a sinking sensation, Jaya recognized them as the guards she had encountered before.

"Call for reinforcements! We have two assailants—"

Rhumia dragged her back, and Jaya screamed as she felt a strand cut into her shoulder.

"I am of the Kingdom of Moksh," Rhumia called out, "and I have caught this assailant under the command of my general. Stay your guns—"

A pulse ripped through the air, missing them. Rhumia snarled. Her hair lengthened, sharpened, and as it did so, she relinquished her pressure on Jaya. Jaya twisted immediately, ducking under her reaching hair and vaulting forward.

Pulses fired behind her. Jaya covered her head with her arms, her heart a flightless thing, pumping wildly in her chest. She saw the orb. Ten paces, five, three—but then a pulse slammed and shattered the glass.

"No!"

The flame roared forward, sensing the pulse shot's heat, swallowing it, growing. Jaya shrieked.

This couldn't be happening. She was so close. *She was so fucking close!* Panic, desperation, fear swallowed her alarm, her pain, as she tried to scoop up the flame, tried to save it. *This can't be happening. This isn't—*

A pulse flared past her ear, singeing her skin. Jaya fell back with a cry. More pulses shredded the air, and she crawled forward, glass biting into her hands and knees as the flame cackled, leeching heat from the pulse fire. Dimly, a part of her noted how strange this was. An Agni flame usually could not live without a host, or a sustained environment like the orb, but then Jaya heard Rhumia's curses and the wet, startled cry of a guard.

She did not turn back.

She ran.

Down the hall, into her room, slamming open the window, and tumbling into the garden. Her hand swelled with pain. But she did not stop. She rushed to the wall and shimmied up with her good hand. She was halfway up when she felt a hand on her ankle.

"You little bitch," Rhumia snarled.

Jaya kicked wildly, and her ankle connected with the stub of Rhumia's ear. The Yumi screamed, falling back, and Jaya used the last of her strength to pull herself up and over the wall. She fell into the canal, water surging up her nostrils, into her ears. She broke the surface, retching.

"JAYA!"

Rhumia's voice thundered above her, and Jaya saw a black shape reflecting off the water. For all her worth, all her training, Jaya failed to find a clever strategy now. She swam desperately, messily, her limbs screaming with effort, with pain, fueled only by her wretched instinct to survive above all else.

Her broken hand smashed against the hull of the boat, and Jaya inhaled sharply to scream. A mistake. Water flooded her mouth, and she coughed, her nose stinging with pain, when another splash sounded down the canal. She turned to find Rhumia, swimming toward her with the awful elegance of a shark.

Fear swept up her pain, and she hauled herself onto the boat. A bridge curved above them, empty for now, but Jaya knew the guards would come racing down in minutes. Blearily, she fired up the panel.

"Come on, come on, *please.*"

With a groan, the boat rumbled to life. Her heart soared, beating with a wild, senseless hope, when a wet thud came from the back.

She whipped around to see Rhumia slowly clambering onto the boat.

"Jaya," she said.

Her voice echoed underneath the bridge, seeming to come from everywhere all at once.

"Jaya, stand down. Now."

Maybe it was her fear, or her grief, or the sudden, vicious desperation to salvage what had been lost, that moved Jaya as she opened her holopod. Holos sprouted to life. In the blue light, she saw Rhumia's eyes widen.

"Jaya, don't—"

"You should have left me in peace."

A sudden, terrible roar reverberated through the air. Rhumia dove into the canal, turning back to the palace, toward her general, and Jaya zipped forward into the canal without waiting to see her lotuses bloom.

CHAPTER 67

SAMSON

The Sesharian is, at his heart, a coward. That is why their rebellions never see a full moon's cycle. They lack the spine and cleverness to rise against us.

—from *A Manual on Employing a Sesharian for Jantari Gentlefolk*

Samson woke with the rancid taste of metal on his tongue. Leather straps cut across his cheeks, shoving the bar into his mouth with an increasing pressure. He groaned. A sour, putrid stench wafted up, and he realized he had pissed himself. Wincing, he attempted to twist out of his bonds, but his knees brushed against the stone wall, his back scraping against the wall opposite.

He was in a box, trapped.

Samson grunted, flexing his bound hands, willing his Agni to spark. He felt heat course through his veins, but then the metal bands around his hands and feet cut deeper. He cried out, choking. He wanted to throw up, found that he already had. Dried gobbets caked the floor. When Samson looked down at his chest, he saw the faint outline of stitches, smelled the cutting bitterness of antibiotics.

It was dark in the box, and still. He strained to hear any noise, but only a thundering silence answered him. Vaguely, he remembered the taste of blood. Elena's scream. The glint of a silver blade.

Then pain.

Then darkness.

Samson whimpered, curling into a ball as the metal bands tightened around his limbs. He felt as if they would saw through his bones.

Sudden, blinding light. He gasped, pressing into the wall, trying to make himself as small as possible as a figure approached.

He smelled oil, heard the whir of gears.

A memory flitted through the fog in his brain. He recalled a ballroom lit with chandeliers. A curtain of roses. And the half-metal man who had greeted him with a bent smile.

"Hello, Butcher," Farin said. His green eye glinted in the dark. "Look at what a mess you've made."

Samson stared, blood draining from his body. The metal bands notched up a degree, and he gasped.

"Cunning things, aren't they?" Farin said. His nose wrinkled as he took in the vomit. "But I confess they can get rather messy."

He raised his hand, and someone placed a chair at the doorway. It was then that Samson realized he was not in a box, but in a cell, the ceiling sloping down so it felt like he was pinned to the ground. He tried to crawl forward, but the bands ratcheted tighter, and he hissed in pain.

For a while, Farin said nothing. He sat perfectly still, the quiet hiss of valves and motors filling the cell.

"You were like a son," the king said finally.

The words struck Samson with a weight he had not expected. They were cruel and false. *I was never a son. Not truly.* He was Jantar's outcast, the black sheep.

"I suppose every son must rise against his father someday, but I had higher hopes for you, Sam. So many hopes." Disappointment skittered sideways across Farin's face like a spider. He leaned forward, and Samson shrank back, but then Farin gripped his chin. Turned his head up as he loosened the leather straps. The metal rod fell to the stone floor with a sharp ring that echoed in the small cell.

Samson closed his mouth, wincing. Pain cricked down his face and neck. Behind his back, he tried to rub his fingertips together to create friction, heat, but the bands only clenched tighter around his wrists. He winced.

"They're sensitive," Farin said. "Every time they detect a slight increase in temperature, they constrict. Quite useful against fire fanatics."

"Wh-where is Elena?" Samson croaked. His voice sounded thin, several shades less than his usual booming timbre.

Farin's metallic eye pierced through him. His stomach twisted.

"You have cost me quite a lot, Samson," he said quietly. "Six mines, hundreds of men, never mind my stolen metal. I would have let that go. But then you and your rebels forced me to give up my most prized possession." Farin reached inside his coat, withdrew a dagger. With a start, Samson recognized the jagged blade. It was the same dagger his attacker had used. The hilt was shaped like a metal dragon, the blade lancing out of its jaws. Farin turned the blade over, traced its point. He pressed his metal finger against its edge, swiped, and showed Samson his hand. There was no scratch.

"Seshar was created by my forefathers. It took years to build, decades to perfect. But you snatched it away in one night. You, with your red queen and black devils." Farin lowered the dagger. The blade hovered inches above Samson's toes. "I gave you sanctuary from the Arohassin. I let you raise an army. I even gifted you an entire mountain to build your mines."

"That gift was a blood gift, and you know that," Samson said, even as his toes curled. His hands shook behind his back. "You gave me protection in exchange for a bond. An army, in exchange for all the metal I mined. Everything you gave, Farin, came with a cost."

"Such is compromise." Farin tapped the metal band around Samson's legs with the tip of the dagger. "There are always costs."

"Where's Elena? Where are my men?"

"Dead, or imprisoned," Farin said flatly.

He had feared the worst, but to hear it out loud, after floundering in the dark, filled him with a sense of hopelessness he had never felt before in his life—not even when he watched Seshar burn. His hands slackened. There was no heat, no sparks, no fire.

He had lost.

"Why?" he said softly, for if he spoke louder, Farin would hear the tremble in his voice. "Why pretend to play peacemaker if you intended this?"

Farin paused. His green eye ticked back and forth from Samson to the dagger. His thumb curled around the dragon's roaring mouth.

"Because your queen chose instead to give you up," he said finally, and for once, his voice was not monotonous. It was laced with pity. "I gave Elena Seshar and Ravence in exchange for you, and she took the deal all too willingly."

"You're lying," he whispered.

Farin's eyes cut to him. "I lied about Seshar. But not about your queen, Samson. She lied to you herself."

He remembered the heat of her lips, the quiver of her chest as she gasped into his mouth. She would not betray him. Not when she had looked at him with such desire and hunger—

But the truth in Farin's eyes made him grow cold and wretched. He had not the energy to feel anger. Only a dead hopelessness. A despair so heavy it threatened to rip through his chest and stomach, disemboweling him.

Samson could not even feel the spark of his Agni.

He simply stared, with the slow realization that he had believed, however fiercely, in a lie. Elena had never loved him. She had never seen him as her equal. He was disposable, a pawn on her board, a sorry soldier for her games, and now that she had gotten her use, she had cast him off.

Broken, and alone.

Farin sighed, tucking the blade into his jacket. Gears popped and wheezed as he rose.

"You fought well, son of mine. Now it's time for you to join your brethren."

The door slid closed behind him. Samson listened to his fading foot-steps until silence swallowed him once more.

"Too late," he whispered into the darkness. "They have already for-saken me."

CHAPTER 68

ELENA

I will burn and burn until I have become a shred of myself.
—from the diaries of Priestess Nomu of the Fire Order

She dreamed of Yassen dying again. He was caught in the flames as they built in power, and no matter how quickly he twisted, they lashed him. His yelps of pain threatened to sunder her. Elena lunged for him. The inferno beat her back, and despite her efforts, she could not control it. The flames were silver and stark and sharp like swords, like a row of teeth. Suddenly, they swiveled to her.

You disgust me, they sang, except it was not their voice, not Samson's, but Yassen's. His lips curled into a sneer. *You destroy everything between heaven and earth.*

No, she sobbed, trying to tear away the flames. He was dying, couldn't he see? *Please, I am not like that.*

You are a monster, he said, and his voice bent, morphed, until she heard both their voices, Yassen's and Samson's, condemning her. *You disgust me.*

Elena woke to iron bonds around her hands and feet. Her heart thundered with the force of ten thousand rivers rushing at once. Vestiges of the dream evaporated, but she could not shake the grim, accusatory sensation throttling her neck like a vise.

You disgust me.

A heavy metal collar hugged her neck, bearing down on her shoulders with a subtle but substantial weight. She was in a cell, the white walls rounded and bare. A silver screen separated her from the hall. Shaking, Elena rose to her feet when she heard footsteps.

"Hello?" she croaked. "Risha? Syla? *Sam?*"

Her voice broke under his name. She remembered his rasping breath, the flutter of his fingers as he had reached for her. Wretchedly, she searched for his Agni and found not even a shadow, not even a spark. A deep despair filled her then. A bleakness that suffused her limbs so that she could barely register the stir of air as the silver screen flickered off.

I'm sorry, Samson.

A guard appeared before her, holding a chain. "Come with me, Your Majesty."

"Where?" she asked dully. "What is this?"

But the guard clipped the chain to her shackles and tugged hard. Elena stumbled forward, almost losing her balance. She moved in a daze, tripping over her feet as they went down a long white hallway as bare and empty as her cell. She heard no song. No sounds of celebration. Nothing but the rataplan of their footsteps.

Two armed guards stood at a black door at the end of the hall, and it was when she saw their bright oiled spears, their gruff, scornful looks, that Elena finally felt a delayed sort of panic. She stopped.

"Where are you taking me?" she asked. The guard yanked on the chain, but she dug in her heels—like she had done countless times when she danced—and remained rooted to her spot. "Tell me."

But then the other guards grabbed her arms. Elena cried out as the door swung open. She twisted, kicking, cursing, as they hauled her into the dark, cavernous room. She could see nothing. Not the ceiling or the walls. Just a brooding, living darkness.

They shoved her forward, and Elena fell to her hands and knees with a yelp. The pallu of her black sari fell from her shoulders, and she could not remember when she had donned such a thing, when the lights flared.

Their brightness seared her vision, and she blinked blearily as a figure stood.

"The Kingdom of Tsuana calls this tribunal," Queen Risha said.

Another light flared, this time to her left. Queen Kysha rose. "The Kingdom of Karven attends the tribunal."

Another light, this time Syla. He looked wary, and afraid, his expression pinched, his eyes heavy. Daz appeared next, his face stoic, unreadable. Farin came forward, his metal voice grating through the large room, and when the last spotlight flashed, Elena turned, expecting Bormani, but his chair remained empty.

She stared at the vacant seat, dread threading up her spine.

"We call this tribunal to assess the crimes of Elena Aadya Ravence, queen of the Kingdom of Ravence, and give judgment according to the degree of her transgressions," Risha said, her voice oddly remote.

Elena slowly raised herself to her feet. She stood in the middle of a long circular table, and she could now see the outlines of tall, grand windows, shuttered shut. Surely, she was still dreaming. She gritted her teeth, pinching the inner skin of her thumbs, but the figures did not melt or bend around her. This nightmare did not lift.

Risha continued. "Elena Aadya Ravence, you are charged with conspiring with terrorists and the murder and assassination of King Bormani of Veran. How do you plead?"

Elena blanched. "Th-this is a mistake. Syla. Daz," she called, but they either turned away or flinched. "What has happened? Where is Bormani?"

"Obliterated to pieces because of your bombs," Risha said, and her voice, so controlled, buckled under the strain of her anger. Or her disgust.

"Bombs? I have planted no bombs," she said. "Risha, please. Unbind me—"

The door opened again, and Elena turned to see a Yumi hobbling through, followed by guards. Her mouth fell open in recognition.

"Rhumia?"

Though the Yumi stood tall, Elena saw pain in the dent of her brow, and then she saw the bloody stub of her ear. Rhumia refused to meet her gaze.

"Rhumia of Moksh," Risha called out. "Tell us what you saw."

Rhumia said nothing, her eyes flitting to Daz. The general stayed silent, his face impassive. Perhaps it was her imagination, but Elena thought she saw regret lacing his jaw. But then something seemed to pass between them, because Rhumia squared her shoulders.

"I found an Arohassin operative planting bombs throughout the palace," Rhumia said, her voice dead. "I attempted to apprehend the assassin, but she escaped through the canals."

She.

A slow terror beat through Elena, like the awful march of an army creeping to the battlefield.

"And were you able to identity the operative?" Risha asked.

"Her name is Jaya, a gamemaster of the Arohassin," Rhumia said, and then, after a beat, "of Ravence."

A guard stepped forward, holding a twisted metal scrap that Elena belatedly recognized as one of Jaya's lotuses.

"We encountered the operative earlier, Your Majesties," he said. His voice was strong, filled with a conviction only the righteous could conjure. "I found her coming from the direction of the Ravani queen's chambers. When the explosions began, strange fires burned through the queen's rooms. All from this device.

"The fire was unnatural. Quicker than anything I've seen. It burned half of the western wing before we could stop it. A similar fire was found in the lower second wing. It also sprouted from a similar device, though this time, the flames were blue and came from Samson Kytuu's room.

"We found five of these...metal lotuses in total. Had three of the five not been deactivated by the Yumi, we would be dealing with far more deaths."

"What are you trying to say?" Farin purred, his voice knifing through Elena.

The guard, emboldened, stepped forward. "All evidence proves that Queen Elena and Samson Kytuu sought to assassinate the members of the council with the help of the Arohassin operative."

Something shattered within Elena. Her heart plummeted, like an arrow loosed. She remembered Jaya in her rooms, telling her how to sway the council. Handing her the lotus. Asking to study their Agni with an earnestness Elena now recognized as subterfuge. Had she really been blind, all this time? She had come to tolerate the gamemaster, even trust her. But now Elena saw the past in a different light, and everything became colder, starker. She remembered Jaya flicking off her hood. Clutching the orb with a strange possessiveness. All those details, rendered anew with the brutality of truth.

It hurt to swallow. Elena blinked away hot, frustrated tears and forced herself to hold her head high, her chains rattling.

"Jaya is no friend of mine," she said hoarsely.

But the guard ignored her. He turned to Syla and Daz, the awful lotus glinting in his hands. "We also believe she was aided by other accomplices."

Daz caught the accusation. Slowly, he leaned forward, resting his hands on the table. "We Yumi of Moksh were not aware of Queen Elena's conspiracy with the Arohassin. We aided Queen Elena solely for the purpose of brokering peace."

Kysha snorted. "She was half-Yumi, wasn't she? She was *one of you*. And she killed one of our own. Bormani sat with us not a day before. I say we give her head to Veran, let her blood seep into their soil and give Bormani's soul justice."

"She was no Yumi," Rhumia snarled. "She was clipped. A blasphemy upon our Great Mother."

Daz threw her a warning glance. "If I must stand tribunal, then I will do so to prove my innocence. Queen Elena alone conspired with the Arohassin."

He looked at her then. There was no change in his expression, no quiver within his stoic facade. But Elena understood that he was giving her a choice. His imprisonment, perhaps even his death, rested now in her hands. If she implicated Daz, or Syla, if she even admitted they had known of the Arohassin, then they would be standing here like this. Perhaps, by giving her a choice, Daz was showing her mercy. Or hedging his bets.

Silence stretched between them. Elena squared her shoulders, forcing her voice to sound steady, convincing.

"Moksh and Cyleon had no relationship with the Arohassin. And I have deceived no one," she said. "I came here only seeking peace. It is I who Jaya has deceived. I did not know of her true—"

Farin laughed, a high grating sound, like gears grinding together. "Did she deceive you like Yassen Knight deceived you? Or was she a woman of honor like Bormani's failed assassin?"

Elena froze. Syla and Daz said nothing, their faces shuttered. Rhumia shifted away from her. Like animals sensing disease, they were already distancing themselves.

"You say you came seeking peace. I say you wanted to help the Arohassin end what they started," Farin growled. "You let the terrorist into the palace. You pretended she was your aide. And when these . . . *lotus bombs* were set off, you and Samson Kytuu were found not in the palace, but at the shore, conspiring."

"That is not true—"

"Why did you leave the palace, then, Elena, when everyone was celebrating?"

"Because I—"

I was there to give Samson to you.

And then it struck her.

This had been Farin's plan all along.

Perhaps from the very beginning, when Samson had destroyed the mines. Had Farin signed the peace treaty knowing it would all lead to this? *He* had instructed her to bring Samson to the beach at the appointed hour. *He* had swiftly agreed to her demands of freeing both Ravence and Seshar. She had been so caught up in her guilt and regret that she had not seen his acquiescence for what it truly was—subterfuge. She had fallen into his trap, like an insect in the web of a patient spider waiting for its dinner. And now he was ready to gorge.

"I revoke the treaty between our countries," Farin said, his voice booming through the chamber. "And I vote that we sentence Queen Elena to death."

She stilled. All her racing thoughts, her hammering heart, her rushing fear, were muted as she watched the cold faces of the regents before her.

"I second," Kysha said.

Daz and Syla made no move, and Elena's gaze settled on Risha.

The tiebreaker.

The queen of Tsuana stared ahead, eyes glazed and distant. Mouth set. She said nothing for a long time. In the deafening silence, Elena felt herself weaken, buckle.

The seashells of her headdress tinkled softly as Risha finally met her gaze. There was no kindness in her eyes. Only grief.

"Bormani could be overbearing, but he was also a friend." She seemed to brace herself, her jaw tightening. "We do this in his memory, to serve justice for Veran."

She raised her hand.

Elena had imagined that at her death, the temple bells would clang in mourning. The desert would stir with storms of sorrow. People would fill the streets, weeping, laying malas upon her pyre.

But she was a long way from home.

Only the sounds of the lights shuttering filled the air. Only the soft footfalls of the guard as he came forward, his face an expression of pity and resentment.

No, a small voice within her whispered. It grew stronger as the guard clipped his chain to her cuffs, as the regents rose from their seats. A deep-rooted, floundering desperation clawed up her throat with the asperity of the damned. She would not die like this. She *refused*.

"If you have already sentenced me, dear kings and queens, then please, afford me this one reprieve.

"Syla, Daz," she called, and they froze at the unnerving calm in her voice. "Would you be so kind as to see to my belongings on the killdoms?"

Syla hesitated, but Daz knew the look in her eye. Unlike the Cyleoni, he had seen her fight, seen her fires, and before Syla could argue, he quickly gripped the man's elbow and tugged him forward. "May the Mother's Light guide you."

He hurried out the door, Syla in tow. Risha frowned at their sudden departure, and Elena saw unease flitter across her face. Kysha merely crossed her arms. "Is that all?"

Beside her, the guard fastened a second chain from his hip to the shackles on her feet. He tugged, satisfied.

"One last request," Elena said, and her gaze found Farin, her vision splitting into the eyes of her Agni. "The next time you plan to execute me, make it quicker."

With a sudden jerk, she whipped around, startling her guard. She threw herself forward and tackled him to the ground. Shouts sounded. She heard the sudden thunder of more boots, but she had found his dagger, and with a wrench, Elena flung it toward Farin.

The metal king sidestepped, and the blade clattered harmlessly against the wall.

"Take her to the cells," Farin sneered.

They dragged her to her feet, but Elena smiled grimly, her blood already roaring, her Agni surging forth as she saw the golden points of his chakras and the flows of his nadis, and pulled.

"*Pick it up*," she snarled.

Farin stiffened suddenly. His eyes bulged, and his body clacked, the gears whining in protest. He resisted her instinctively, like an unbroken horse bucks its rider, but Elena surged her awareness through the heat of his veins, the bright essence within. "I said, *pick it up*."

With a cry, Farin snatched up the blade. The guards shouted, some rushing toward Farin, the others searching her, looking for a device, a tool. *The fools.* The greatest weapon she had was herself. Jaya had been right. They would never see her as their equal. To them, she was Elena Aadya Ravence, terrorist, warmonger, the awful and monstrous Burning Queen. Her story and the stories of all abused Ravani and Sesharians were but mere noises in the grand symphony of their power. Who cared about the dead Ravani? Who cared about the oppressed Sesharians? As long as someone else suffered, as long as the metal trade survived, the regents were satiated. They would never listen to her—even if she brought them peace. Even if she played to their benefit. No matter the threats she crafted, no matter the alliances she forged, they would always see her and her like as nothing more than a country of fanatics, lost and broken and poor. They would always find her wanting.

Who even are you, alone?

She was the sum of her people's hope, and the object of their disdain. She had been a liar and a fraud, hero, villain, and conqueror, but Elena knew one thing for certain—she was no coward of an empire.

Wrath—absolute, complete—ripped through her. With all her power, all her worth, Elena summoned her Agni until she was nothing more than a singular desire to *burn*.

She jerked Farin toward Kysha with a twisting of limbs. The Karvenese queen tried to run, but her dress caught in the legs of her chair. She stumbled, and then Farin's metal hand flashed, and she screamed as his blade cut through her upper back.

Risha shrieked and rushed for the exit, but Elena flared her Agni forth and snagged into her prana. Risha floundered, caught. Her limbs twitched as Elena forced her to turn around, to face Farin.

The metal king ripped out the blade from Kysha's shoulders. Blood dripped down the point. The guards moved from her to Farin, one grabbing his arm, the other his leg, but the king was half machine and moved with a brutal strength.

"Farin, please," Risha said, her body frozen.

"Stop this, Elena," Farin cried as he moved forward.

But she could not hear him over the terrible ringing in her ears. A pressure built behind her eyes, her mouth. Blood trickled from her nose, and Elena could taste something wet and hot in her chest, but she did not care. They had brought this upon themselves. *They had done this.*

A guard, bright enough to recognize her control, darted toward her.

Elena felt for his heat, the distinctive prana of his heart, and tore.

Flames ripped up from beneath his skin. He crashed, aflame. Screams cleaved through the air, from Risha, from Farin, from the guards who finally began to understand the horror before their eyes.

"Witch!"

"Sorceress!"

"Bitch!" they called her, and Elena could only laugh, her voice high and brittle.

"Better to be a bitch than a bechari."

She raised Farin's arm and threw the blade. It sank neatly into Risha's chest. The Tsuani queen let out a loud, wet gurgle, her eyes catching Elena's with a look of such confusion, she almost felt pity.

The queen toppled to the floor. Her guards cried for a medic, for help. Their voices rose in a chorus, panicked and hysterical like birds trapped in a smoking tree. It slammed into her. And for a moment, Elena swayed.

She remembered the burning mountain. She remembered her burning city. She had felt this fear—this immutable, irrevocable premonition of death.

This had been her, once.

But over the chorus of their screams, Elena heard the song of her power. The delicious, devastating thrum of her Agni, deep and resonant, like dawn breaking over a burning sea. Like beauty over horror. A goddess over men.

So she drowned that feeling.

She drowned her fear.

Elena wrenched her Agni forward and burned.

The guard closest to her shrieked as flames licked down his leg. He hopped back, kicking. Another tried to pin her to the ground, but Elena yanked the flames, and he howled at their vicious bite. She began to rise—but pain razed down her wounded leg. She gasped, crashing back to the floor.

The pain swelled—white-hot, unwieldly. It traveled up her leg, her chest, to the upper reaches of her throat. Elena bit back a scream as her control wavered. Farin jerked free, shouting for the guards to pin her down, goddamn it! They rushed forward, meaty, cruel hands clenching around her arms, digging into her skin. She fought them. Hard. With all her strength—but that too was fading fast.

Elena cried out as she was shoved onto her stomach, her chin clacking against the floor. Blood filled her mouth. Faintly, she smelled the ash of her dying fires. Someone tugged her up, and she caught Farin's spiteful, frayed face.

"Bury her," he spat, spittle flying from his lips. "I want her fucking entombed in the mountain."

But she could smell his fear, taste it even now, and Elena laughed and laughed as they dragged her back to her cell.

CHAPTER 69

SAMSON

"Come home," his mother says. "Come home, for my eyesight grows weak." But the son of sea marches on to his deadly purpose.
—from A Lament of Seshar: A People's History

Samson drooped, his bones heavy, his mind fogged from the drugs they had pumped into him. Cold, biting air slid across his hands, his wrists. There was something familiar about it, something familiar about the smell of pine and earth and...

He woke to the icy shock of water. Samson sputtered, coughing, but then the guard threw another bucket. The water slapped his face, hard like cement. Samson crashed back against the wall.

"All right, he's clean now," the guard shouted.

An officer marched in, but as he drew closer, his nose wrinkled.

"Mountains, he still smells like shit."

"Don't get too close, he'll bite," the guard laughed.

"Oh, I don't think so." The officer studied Samson. A smile cut across his face. "Look at him."

Samson slid farther down the wall to edge away from their gazes. Shame and anger roiled through him. He felt small, powerless. Water dripped down his naked chest, his thighs. Blood still ringed his wrists and ankles, and his teeth chattered.

Look away, he wanted to shriek.

The guard chortled. "No fight left."

The officer unhooked the chain and tugged forcefully. Samson stumbled. He landed on his right knee, biting his tongue and letting out a muffled cry.

The guard sniffed. "Can't even walk straight."

"Up," the officer snarled. He kicked Samson in the shin, hard.

Samson crawled onto his hands and knees, but he did not get up.

"Useless." The officer yanked the chain, sliding Samson's arms out from under him.

He hit the stone floor. It was slimy and cold, dirt caked into the grout. The texture was revolting, and Samson had the urge to scrub himself until his skin was raw, but he did not move.

He knew it was useless protesting, useless to fight. But still. He would rather die than follow a Jantari's orders ever again.

The officer hauled Samson up and roughly pushed him against the wall. He was shorter than Samson, but wider, with hands that dwarfed the large coconuts found on Seshar.

"Now listen, islander," he hissed. "You *will* walk. Or I will drag you face-first through your own dirt and piss. Either way, you're coming."

Samson closed his eyes, wavering. He wanted to annoy the officer, petty as it may be. Even now, irritation settled on the officer's face, deepening his scowl. *He's going to hit me*, Samson thought dully. And yet, Samson was not afraid of the blow. The officer's irritation gave him satisfaction. However small. It was the only victory he could manage.

The punch nearly took him out.

The officer hit the bruise on his chest, and Samson gasped. His head knocked against the wall, white spots searing across his vision. Skies above, it *hurt*.

"Now move," the officer growled.

This time, when he pulled, Samson followed.

A plain black uniform was laid out on a bench outside the cell. The officer ordered him to put it on. Samson donned it wordlessly, holding out his hands as the officer undid the cuffs to slip on the sleeves. When the cuffs unlocked, Samson did not try to charge or even to run.

What was the use, when all he had left, all the people he had loved, were gone?

"This way."

They went down a stone corridor that smelled of old, dried blood and musty sweat. A few cells held remainders of their past occupants. Samson spotted a torn patch of fabric, possibly from a jacket. An orange splotch, hastily scrubbed, adorned the floor of another. In one corner, he found a decaying toe.

The tunnel began to veer upward. Guards stood before a metal door, and faintly, Samson heard the clink of metal and the rumbling of earth beyond it.

"Officer Ren," a guard said with a salute. His lips twitched into a scowl as he looked at Samson. "Islander."

"We're to take the islander to Rhea's Chamber and wait for the king," Ren said.

"But, sir, the chamber isn't fully stabilized—"

"It's the king's wish," Ren said, his voice edged, and the guard shut up quickly. He opened the door. A cold, sudden draft whipped past them, and Samson felt a low moan reverberate through his bones.

It was only then that he registered where he was going. *The mines.* Great Serpent, they were taking him *back.* Fear, true fear, leapt through Samson. It zipped up his spine, metallic and harsh.

"No," he croaked.

It was the first time he had spoken.

The officer turned. "What?"

Samson shook his head, the effort itself making him dizzy. "I won't go."

At this, Ren laughed. "Oh, you will."

He pulled, but Samson locked his legs, surprising himself. He did not know where this strength came from. Maybe it was panic, desperation. He tugged back, eyes wide.

"I won't go," he repeated, voice high.

But Ren yanked him forward. He kicked, floundering, and Ren slapped him across the face.

His neck whipped to the side as pain exploded down his cheek. Samson stumbled, and then Ren wrenched his face toward him, his breath hot and rancid across his burning cheek.

"Remember. I will fucking drag you."

The bastards had brought him to *his mine*.

He saw the silver serpent snaking down the gates. Recognized the milky-white stalactites hanging above the tall cavern. From the tunnel on his right, he could hear the echo of machines, the shouts of men, the ringing of tools.

And beneath it all, he heard the whisper.

It was like a stream that ran beneath the stones, everywhere all at once. How many suns had his men spent mining for Farin while trying to find the source of that voice? Power lay beneath this mountain. He had sought it for so long as a free man. It was with a sick sense of irony, then, or fate perhaps, that they would lead him back here now, chained and broken.

Ren and a soldier led him through a tunnel he did not recognize, the muffled shrill of drills and the thump of hammers growing louder. He did not remember his men ever mining this area. They had kept it untouched, instead mining up north while secretly exploring passageways that dove deeper into the mountain. But the thrumming beneath his feet was unmistakable. The Jantari had found his secret.

The walls hunkered closer. The shadows slunk down, latching around his ankles and pulling him forward with cruel delight. They grew bolder the deeper they went. Licking his face, his hands, his feet. Encroaching on his vision. Samson trembled, his breaths short and panicked. His eyelids felt hot, feverish, and he tried to touch his face, to somehow open his mouth and shove air into his chest because, skies above, *he could not breathe—*

He crashed to his knees, gasping. Ahead, the Jantari soldiers turned. He tried to call out for help, to tell them he could not breathe, but Ren simply grabbed him and threw him over his shoulder. Samson struggled, but Ren marched on without pause into the access shaft.

They dropped, fast. Samson whimpered as the sound of machinery grew closer. When the platform abruptly stopped and the doors opened, it hit him full blast.

The screech of drills, the sharp barks of overseers, the tired grunts of laborers. Samson tried to twist out of Ren's grasp, but the officer held him tight. The indignity and hot shame of being lifted and carried like a sandbag knifed through his gut. He still had his pride, damn it.

Ren dropped him suddenly, and he landed on his hip. Samson hissed in pain. By the time he regained his bearings, he realized the mine had fallen silent, save for the whispery drip of water.

Butcher, it crooned.

Through bleary eyes, Samson saw his brethren. The miners had stopped working and were staring at him, some surprised, others troubled, a few already retreating in horror. He could not tell who was more crushed.

Him, realizing that he had returned to this place of terror.

Or the Sesharians, realizing with shock that their hero, their tormentor, was trapped just like them.

Samson saw their hope perish in their eyes.

And he hated himself even more for it.

"Samson Kytuu has returned to die," Ren called out. "So. Let's give him a warm welcome home."

Samson could not bear to meet their eyes, but he could feel their weight. Their disappointment.

Ren paraded him past. Samson tried to hold his head high, to look brave, but their gazes hooked into him, peeled him apart. One Sesharian caught his attention, then quickly looked away. They could do nothing to help him, and neither could he do anything for them. An acidic lump rose in his throat. He tried to call his Agni, to save whatever shred of dignity he had left, but the iron bonds tightened around his wrists, cutting off his blood flow.

He tried not to shiver, found he could not stop shuddering. His legs cramped. A wave of exhaustion suddenly struck him, and Samson swayed. He closed his eyes. For a moment, he wondered if it would have been better to die in Tsuana. Better to bleed out on a beach than the cold, hard stones. Better to die a martyr than a failed hero.

Samson opened his eyes, his chains rattling behind him as he continued his march.

And then a young girl stepped forward.

She was a child, too young, too small for the dark confines of the mine.

Dusty black curls crowded her forehead, but her eyes shone with a light that would give the Jantari pause, if only to remind them of what they could not kill.

Hope.

"Blue Star," the girl said in Ambari, and knelt.

The Sesharian beside her, a tall, worn-looking man, followed. As did the next. And the next. All along the line, his people spoke his name. Officers rushed forward. Shouting, raising zeemirs, the blades glinting in the low light. But the Sesharians did not get up. They did not flinch. And Samson muscled down his horrified cry because to waver now was to squander their bravery. He marched on, his chains rattling, shrieks filling the air, to his death.

The tunnel delved lower than he had ever gone, deep into the heart of the mountain. The walls shook as another rumble reverberated through the tunnel. *They are drilling too deep*, he thought. But he knew why. Ore pulsed around them in shades of azure and sapphire and cerulean. Shadows pooled around his feet. He felt as if he was treading through a shallow river. Water seemed to rush above, below, all around.

And beneath it all, the whisper.

Butcher, it called.

It zipped through him like a physical force, rattling his bones. He felt water stain his clothes, his lips, but when he touched them, they were dry.

Butcher, Butcher, Butcher. The singsong whisper itched his ears. *You have come at last.*

A chill prickled up his spine. His teeth were chattering violently now, the fingertips of his right hand an alarming shade of blue. Ahead, Samson saw the flash of doors sliding back, and a silvery light filled the tunnel. He knew, with the deep certainty of the dying, that whatever lay ahead would be his undoing.

He concentrated on fire, on warmth. On memories, bright and true.

Chandi, walking beside him amid the canyons. Visha, slinging her arm around his, the smell of wine strong on her lips. Elena, threading her fingers through his hair as she kissed him.

But it was the memory of Yassen that he latched on to. It was the day they had stolen from the bakery. He had been chewing on his broken lip when he found Yassen, the food already half-eaten. He had every right to be angry, but it was Yassen's face—the immediate regret, the shy hesitancy—that had made him fold.

For Yassen, he would take any blow.

Samson focused on that memory, and as he walked forward, the whisper rising, he thought he saw a pair of golden eyes watching him. He blinked, and then they were gone.

They entered a tall chamber. Milky-white stalactites stretched down from the ceiling. A long, silver pool reflected them, doubling them, and Samson had the uneasy sensation of entering the mouth of a diseased, dying beast. When Samson looked beyond, he fell to his knees.

The skin of a great snake lay coiled in the center of the chamber. Silver amrithi—raw, unspoiled—glimmered within its scales with such radiance, it was as if the moons had been brought down from the heavens and sliced into tiny discs of luminescence.

"Great Serpent," he gasped.

The bastards had found Her. After all these suns, after all he had sacrificed, it was Farin who had unearthed the chamber in the end. *A metal so fine it can cut through steel.* He had hoped to find it first, to use the amrithi for himself, but as Samson saw the Jantari guards lined up along the stone harbor and the sensors spaced out around the pool, he realized with a slow, thickening despair that Farin had beaten him once again.

Suddenly, the mountain rumbled. Dust and loose stones splashed into the pool as the guards shouted. Samson dove to the side. He crashed onto his back, and his chains strained, snapping. Feeling rushed back into his fingers just as terror locked his chest as he imagined the stalactites raining down, the mountain cracking, his god screaming in agony—

At once, the rumbling stilled. Samson stared up at the ceiling in the stilted silence that came after, his pulse thundering in his ears.

Butcher, Butcher, Butcher, the whisper sang, *have you come to free me?*

"Stay where you are," Ren commanded.

It was then that he realized his hands were no longer bound. Samson blinked, then shot forward as Ren reached for his zeemir. The blade screeched. He reached for his Agni, pressing his entire will into his desperate plea, and he felt heat skate up his arms, his Agni rising to answer with a ferocity that made him almost cry in relief as he twisted his hands and—

"Move another muscle, Samson, and I will execute your queen."

He stopped cold at the sound of Farin's oily voice, and Ren struck him.

Samson gasped, falling to his knees. His vision wavered. When he looked up, he saw the guards shove Elena, and the sight of chains fastened around her neck, of her face streaked with blood, made all the fury within him still.

"Elena."

His tormentor. His queen. She had betrayed him. So why was she here, then? Why was she bound? Why was she suddenly crying? There was so much he wanted to say, so much he wished to know, emotions swelling within him like a wave breaching, anger and bitterness giving away to confusion and fear, but then he saw Farin's sardonic metal sneer, and he realized, with a cold, final clap, that she was here for him.

To die.

"Samson," she cried.

"I thought I'd bring your queen to watch you bleed," Farin said as a guard offered him a zeemir. He took the weapon and ran a metal finger down its spine. "You have led me on quite the chase, Samson. I have been looking for this place for decades, led astray by twisted myths and your false reports. Funny, then, that the man who helped me find it was one of your own."

Samson stilled. "Mine?"

"Akino, I think," Farin said. "He makes such fine weapons, like the horned dagger."

And then Samson remembered. In the dark of the trees, in the slivers of moonlight, a dagger with a dragon's mouth had sunk deep into his chest. He remembered that his attacker had looked familiar. That the hand, gripping the hilt, had often crafted and molded weapons of his own.

"No," Samson said, trying to stand, his body already realizing what his mind was slow to comprehend.

"He also told me the curious tale of this monster here," Farin said, pointing toward the translucent snakeskin with the zeemir. " 'Blood of the son of sea will give rise to thee.' Isn't that how your prayers go? Have your tales always foretold that your blood will activate the amrithi?"

"Farin, please," he choked out. It was not his blood, but his fire. "If you kill me, you'll only anger the goddess—"

A soldier shoved Elena forward, and she bit down on a cry. Despite himself, Samson's heart lurched. He moved to catch her. She grasped his arms, her grip tight, her eyes wide with, what—relief, regret, grief?

"I'm sorry, Ruru," she gasped.

Farin motioned to the guards. "Bring him to the pool."

"No—" An officer pulled her back, and Elena yelped as the cuffs tightened around her wrists. "Samson, run!"

At the sound of her pain, at the sight of the king's nonchalance, something snapped within Samson. In that moment, he did not care about her lies, or Farin's, or his own. In that moment, in the stony hell of his oppressors, he saw only a familiar face, calling to him.

Samson roared, surprising Ren. The Jantari officer tried to block him, but Samson rushed forward, slamming him down as the others shouted. Elena twisted, reaching.

"Sam!"

"Elena," he cried.

He grasped her hands, then her face, trying to commit to memory the touch of her skin on his. Elena clutched his arms, her grip like a vise. For a fleeting moment, their foreheads pressed together, and he whispered harshly, quickly, so only she could hear as the Jantari darted forward.

"Do you remember the boat? Do you trust me?"

She nodded, her nose brushing his. "For you? Anything."

In that moment, he loved her. It was not a pure, hopeful love, full of promises and beauty and softness. They had hurt each other far too much for that. Their love was carved from cruelty. Wrenched from betrayal, forged by anger. It was monstrous. Unholy.

But it was wholly, utterly theirs.

Her lips touched his—too quick for a kiss, too desperate to be meaningless, enough for him to crave more—and Samson reached for her Agni.

CHAPTER 70

ELENA

What if the three goddesses were to become one? Who then remains the most monstrous? The one who folds quickly, or the one who withstands the longest?

—from *A Critique of the Ancient Gods*
(note: debunked by historians)

Cold in the shape of a beast sank its teeth into her flesh, spearing her bones, snapping her veins, flooding her with agony.

Elena screamed.

It was as if she had been submerged underwater and set afire. She was only dimly aware of the mountain shaking horribly as Samson gripped her face, his nails cutting into her skin.

A deep crack echoed through the chamber. It sounded like a laugh, like a memory. Her Agni screeched, twisting, and Elena felt as if every cell within her body had been set ablaze twice over.

She could only clutch Samson.

She could only remember the earnest passion in his voice as he had grasped her face and asked her to trust him.

She could only give, because she had never learned to stop.

Her Agni surged forward at his call, and she felt the furious heat of his Agni swallow her own, growing in size, in strength.

Her vision split.

Elena saw two things at once.

She saw herself falling, her chakras blazing with the ferocity of a dying star, her Agni molten and vicious like the magma beneath the earth.

She saw Samson kneeling before a dead snake that was full of silver and shadows, his chakras a beautiful, horrid blue, like the deepest of oceans, the worst of terrors.

He said something. A word she knew, from a lifetime ago. A word that was both a promise and a curse, the beginning of her misery, and the end of it all.

Agneepath.

To her horror, the dead snake rose.

And it spoke with the voice of Yassen Knight.

"You stupid, beautiful idiots," it began.

CHAPTER 71

SAMSON

The Great Serpent is an ancient and capricious god. With scales like the moons and eyes like the terrible deep, She controls the seas and whips fire into obedience. Her power is mighty, and always, it comes with a price.
                              —from *The Legends and Myths of Sayon*

She gave it to him willingly. Her Agni flooded his senses with an intoxicating heat that made his veins strum as if plucked anew. Skies above, it felt *good* to feel power again. His Agni flared, licking up Elena's spark with eager hunger.

The mountain rumbled as the old god sensed the blending of the two Agnis.

Butcher, it sang.

He could not summon fire without his urumi, but with Elena's Agni, he did not need it. A blue flame, so strong and fresh it made him laugh in bewilderment, leapt from his palms. The Jantari rushed forward. Distantly, he remembered their faces. The condescending officer. The cruel king. The stupid soldiers. With an almost mindless ease, he flicked his hand, and his flames leapt.

Screams filled the air.

All the pain, all the abuse and loneliness and trauma, melted away as he felt the power of both his Agni and Elena's twine together.

Lock together.

Bind together.

Butcher, Butcher, Butcher.

Shadows rustled within the snakeskin, coalescing, wriggling. Suddenly, the dead snake began to *move.* It rose, silver scales flashing, and the hollow voice of an old god echoed through the chamber.

"You stupid, beautiful idiots," it said.

Samson reeled, stunned at the familiar voice. "Yassen?" he gasped.

Somewhere deep within the mountain, there was a laugh. Low, rumbling, like tectonic plates rubbing together. Its tremor carried up his knees to his head, his skull vibrating.

"Not quite," the old god said.

Shadows bled outward, forming a triangular head that seemed to sniff the air and shudder in pleasure.

"I speak through a voice loved and lost to the Agni," it hissed. "But a voice is only a voice. A voice is not enough."

The blue flame in his palm rippled, impatient. Samson curled his hand, and the flame grew, wrapping down his arm and torso. Elena whimpered in his arms. Her Agni flared, afraid. She must have realized he was drawing too hard, too quick, but Samson held on. Made her stay.

I'm sorry, he thought. *But I need you.*

He turned to the dead snake. The shadows had lengthened, forming a crown of antlers that towered above its head like jagged blades.

"Great Serpent, I have come to free you," he called.

It laughed. The voice, Yassen's voice, grew more distant, static, as if it came from the darkened bowels of the earth where the carcasses of old gods lay entombed.

"You do not have the power or the will to free me," the old god rumbled.

"I have Agni and a song," he said. "A song of the sea."

The snake sighed. It sounded like a low hiss, rippling down its body and the mountain. In it, Samson felt the old god's loneliness, its longing. So keen and familiar to his own. They both were strangers trapped in a foreign land. They both craved the open sea and the unending sky above.

"Sing it to me," it rasped.

He swept his arms, and his flames shot forth, engulfing the snake. The ore's light swooned in time with his inferno as his voice carried through the chamber.

"There lies a flame, blue as the sea,
True and strong, it remains in the deep,
Beyond the sun where only the shadows can reach,
Master of the realm is the one I seek."

The mountain trembled violently as Samson sang. Rocks cracked. Stalactites crashed with heavy booms, but he kept on as the Serpent hissed in pleasure, grew in power.

"Agneepath, Agneepath, Agneepath,
The path of the three.
The sand, the sun, and the sea.
Rise, Great Serpent,
Rise, O Preserver,
To Seshar, to the son of the sea."

A great roar rolled through the chamber, the mountains, and the land beyond. The old god laughed. It was working. The mountain shook, and the Serpent's voice shed its veneer for the deep truth beneath. Its scales darkened, took form. His flames twisted, crawling up its spine as something more solid replaced its ghostly face.

The old god opened an eye. It was deep and blue and terrible, beautiful and dark and unlike anything Samson had ever seen. It pinned him in place.

"It is you, Agni of three," the Great Serpent sang.

Its diamond-shaped pupil bore into Samson, but he did not waver.

Samson inhaled, drawing even more of Elena's Agni. He could feel her resisting, but she had already given him so much. He was like quicksand. The harder she struggled, the more he took.

"Sam," she whispered.

He should have felt guilt then. Remorse, even. To take and take, to do nothing but devour. But he had always been a hungry man.

He let her go and stepped forward.

Elena gasped, but he did not hear her. He did not see her limp body crash to the floor or the light fading from her eyes as he stood before his god and reached.

"My son," the Serpent crooned.

He touched Her scales. Suddenly, heat—white-hot, electric—zipped up his spine. The Serpent screeched, shadows exploding in shards of black and silver. But there wasn't triumph or euphoria in its voice.

There was *pain*.

A deep, heart-wrenching agony gripped Samson and twisted viciously. He howled, doubling over.

Meanwhile, the god thrashed, slamming against the wall, the ceiling. Meanwhile, the mountain shook as if it was not stone but water, and a rock had cracked its still surface.

Meanwhile, Elena lay curled at his feet, his name strangled upon her lips.

Samson felt something integral break then. A splintering.

He saw two things at once: Elena before a great fire that spoiled, a darkness growing within its core.

And a metal coffin with a lone figure, someone at once horrible and familiar. Samson felt *wrong* upon seeing it, as if he was trespassing on some ancient god's sleep.

But then the god stirred.

Two beautiful, awful golden eyes snapped open.

The Phoenix laughed, and Samson screamed.

CHAPTER 72

It began, as always, with the desert.

Dunes as high as mountains rolled out across the horizon, scraping the sky as if to catch all the stars. Oases sparkled within valleys. The sand was warm beneath his feet. Soft, as if he were bouncing off pillows.

The desert sighed, and he turned to see that the sky had darkened in the west. Night approached, suddenly and then all at once.

Strange beasts stalked through the terrain, their dark muzzles flecked with blood. Shadows grew where oases once lounged. They cut down the dunes with a strange, vicious hunger, but he felt no fear. Shadows, and even the beasts of the night, were a part of the desert.

The wind kissed his cheek, as if nudging him to look. In the north, he saw three figures. A man and two girls. A father and his daughters.

Shadows pooled around them, the sand around them oddly slick and wet. It was only when he peered closer that he noticed it was soaked with blood too.

A great blaze flared before them all, red and blue and gold and every color imaginable. In the inferno, he saw the faces of people he did not recognize but had the unshakable feeling that he had known long ago. He saw the world as it began. With a spark, a roar. He saw how it died. And he saw it repeat, again and again. The inferno grew taller, but the shadows did not draw back. They leapt into the blaze, and it bucked, hissing. Suddenly, a daughter fell. The other cried. The old man fell to his knees, but the deal was done, the sacrifice complete.

The blaze morphed, and he saw the colors seep away until something dark and terrible and horribly *other* appeared before them.

It reached, and he knew then of fear.

The abyss was deep and endless. It stretched before him, around him, past him, into the unknown future. He traveled mindlessly. There was no one beside him in this long, terrible deep. And the weight of that realization eventually overwhelmed him. He sank, the fabric of the abyss indenting around his knees. The long dark stared back at him, and he could bear it no more. He bowed his head, closed his eyes.

It was then that he knew of loneliness.

They came slowly, like flits of sunlight through a net, brushing his consciousness.

The memories of her.

Her leaning into his hand, his thumb against her cheek. Her standing on a dune, her shoulders outlined by the sun. Her brown eyes bright with fervor, with fire.

Stay with me. Fight with me.

Deep within, the darkness hissed. Deep within, he felt *its fear.*

Her frowning at him, eyebrows furrowed in annoyance. Her crying into his shoulder, her tears soaking the fabric, her sobs ripping through his chest.

In the distance, the fabric of the long dark rippled. Shadows ebbed. Spots began to appear in light patches of grey.

Her kissing him, her lips sweet as honey. Her laughing at him, her voice like a song from another life, lived in the shoes of another man.

The darkness growled, resisting. It sucked him in, dragged him back. Her laughter sounded, but it was too faint, she too far. What was the point?

I'll find you.

His voice rang through the abyss, and the memory of fire, of a promise rendered, rammed back against the dark.

You'd better.

You'd better.

You'd better.

A promise. He had promised her.

He moved forward. The darkness sucked at his limbs, alarmed, but he remembered *her.* Her laughter, her voice, her anger and desperation and fear.

Her love.

All the best memories were of her.

And he knew her face, even in the darkness of death.

The shadows dripped down from the sky, as if a hand was peeling back the facade. Her voice pulled him, tugged him. He latched on, like a starving traveler stumbling through the dark, and followed until he saw a light in the great abyss and reached for it.

It was then that he knew of hope.

CHAPTER 73

YASSEN

I have woken to a great and terrible transformation. I am the Sixth Prophet.
        —from the diaries of Priestess Nomu of the Fire Order

Yassen Knight awoke to the sound of her memories. The first thing he realized was that he had made a promise to find her. The second was that tubes were attached to his arms, his chest, his legs, pumping a rich red liquid into him. Faintly, he could hear the wheezing of someone dying. It took him a moment to discover that the wheezing came not from someone, but *something*. The large metal contraption around him shuddered. He touched its side, and it brushed against his palm as if alive. He shrank back. Panic—thick, drip-like—beaded down his throat, and he knew he should be screaming, trapped within a metal beast, but then the glass before him slid back with a hiss.

Slowly, he heard it.

The inferno.

He turned to where a tiny fire crackled along the back wall. It blazed

450

brighter beneath his gaze. The flames pulsed and lengthened, their tips curling upward toward him.

"You're finally back."

An all-too-familiar voice cut through the space. He forced himself to look away from the inferno to Akaros. Behind him stood a tall Yumi girl with eyes of amber and cheeks streaked with dried tears. Why had she been crying? Her eyes met his, heated, accusatory.

"Wh—" he began, but his tongue flopped in his mouth. His voice was a pale sliver of its former self.

"Think you can sit up for me?" Akaros said.

Before Yassen could respond, Akaros hooked his hands beneath his armpits and hauled him up. Pain gripped his body. Yassen moaned, leaning forward. Gently, Akaros brushed back Yassen's hair, his fingers lingering along his ear.

"Phoenix Above, boy, it really is you."

Akaros dropped his hand and stepped back, his eyes full of an emotion Yassen had never seen him wear before.

Hope.

Unbridled, untainted hope.

Why would he look at him this way?

Yassen began to speak again when the fire hissed. A stray flame rolled out and inched toward his metal coffin. Yassen pulled back in alarm, but a part of him, a deep guttural instinct, bade him to stay.

The flame's tip flickered, as if testing the air, and then latched around his ankle.

He yelped—but the pain did not come.

Yassen Knight found then that he did not burn.

He felt *alive*.

The flame's heat vibrated through him, from his bones to his very cells. It was like a comet, distant and sure in its beauty, but when he focused on the flame's touch, it became a bright blaze fueled by momentum and speed, careening to an end point he did not know, was afraid to know.

Slowly, carefully, he opened his hand. At once, the flame shot up and tightened into a small ball in his palm. He stared in bewilderment. It hummed, waiting.

"What..." he said, his voice foreign to his own ears. "What is this?"

Akaros's eyes glistened in wonder, but his lips curved into a cold, knowing smile, and Yassen felt more afraid of that than the fire that no longer burned him.

"We have been waiting for your return for a long time, Cass."

Yassen could only gaze at the fire, a slow dread building within him. This was a hallucination. A dream. He would wake up in the cabin again to find Elena puttering about in the kitchen, attempting to wrangle together a pot of tea. He dug his nails into his palms to wake himself. But the room did not change. Akaros's watchful gaze did not blur into Elena's honey-brown eyes.

"Please," he said, his voice scratchy, his tongue like sandpaper. "I—I don't know what you mean. Where am I? What happened?"

"What do you mean, what happened?" Akaros said. He gestured to the fire lapping at his feet. "Haven't you already figured it out?"

"But the last thing I remember was the cabin. No...there was something else." Yassen's voice trailed off as he looked down at his chest. Memories, bitter and frayed, swept through him as he remembered the explosions, the fire, Elena's desperate voice as she grasped his hand. *You'd better.* And then there was the sound of a bullet. The hot pain in his chest. The soft press of the earth beneath his back as he looked up at the flames... Slowly, Yassen pulled up his kurta and hissed at the scar, red and angry, slanting diagonally above his heart.

"*You* shot me," he said.

"And I saved you," Akaros replied. He paused then, glancing up to a silvered screen above them. "We saved you."

"*Div* saved you," the girl snapped, finally speaking. Yassen saw a quiet rage in her eyes, made only fiercer by the desperate angle of her lips, the tension in her jaw. She stood beside another metal chamber, as if protecting it. There was a shadow of a face in there. Young, boyish. He leaned forward to get a closer look, and she blocked his vision.

"Jaya," Akaros said, a warning in his voice.

"You said we would wake Div after the third," she said. Fresh tears formed in her eyes. "You lied."

"We will. Give him a chance—"

"Wake him up, then," she said.

"Jaya—"

"Wake him," she said, this time leveling her gaze at Yassen.

Despite the flame, Yassen felt a chill skitter down his spine under her glare. There was so much *anger* in her eyes, and he half expected her hair to rise and shred him into ribbons of flesh.

"I—I don't understand," Yassen said. "Why did you save me and not Elena?"

"Oh, for sand's sake, forget about Elena. I am tired of the world revolving around that fucking queen," Jaya snarled. "We rescued *you*. Div gave *you* his blood. Now it's your turn to return the favor."

"Elena survived on Sona," Akaros said quietly. "Can't you feel her Agni?"

"Agni?"

"Your inner fire," Akaros said, and at this, the flame coiled tighter around Yassen. Again, he felt that ancient instinct, like an opening inside him. Yassen raised his hand, and the flame zipped up his arm. He shuddered.

"You're one of three, Yassen," Akaros said. "You, Elena, and Samson. Maybe there are more, I don't know. I hope not. Fuck, you were trouble enough to get."

"Me?" Yassen sat forward, so quick that Akaros flinched back. "Did you find me on the mountain? Did you find Elena, then, too?" The sudden memory of her running through the ravine, flames at her heels, sliced through his chest and carved downward to his Agni, for he was already understanding that it was an essential part *inside* him.

He could feel her. He didn't know why, but he did.

When he focused on her, on her memory, Yassen saw a golden spark. It sat within him, below his belly button. Small and awfully bright for its size, sizzling with power. It pulsed as if it could feel his awareness turning to it.

"Keep your eyes closed," Akaros said in a hushed voice.

Yassen hadn't even realized he had closed his eyes. He obeyed, concentrating on his inner spark, his so-called Agni. It burnished from gold to bronze. Yassen reached for it, and as he did so, he felt something sharp and metallic in his throat, as if tasting lightning.

His Agni grew, and in its glaring light, he saw two infernos emerge. One was blue and small, so small that it barely even existed. The other was the color of deep reddish earth, as if soaked in blood and left out to wither and die. They felt familiar, and horribly, awfully *wrong*. He could taste something rotten in their core. Like spoiled meat, ridden with maggots. When he tried to feel for their warmth, all he felt was a blistering cold. So vicious it sank its claws into him.

Yassen recoiled. When he opened his eyes, he found Akaros and Jaya watching him intently.

"Did you find Elena and Samson?" Akaros asked.

"Can you siphon their Agnis?" Jaya said.

"I—I—" And then Yassen stopped, the realization stark and hard in its awful absurdity. "That was them? That *was* them. Their fires felt *wrong*."

Akaros frowned as Jaya turned to him.

"Their Agnis are linked, Akaros. If something is corrupting theirs, then it's only a matter of time before it reaches him. We need his Fireblood to wake up Div. Now," she urged.

"I don't know how," Yassen said. "This—this fire, this Agni, I don't understand—please, Akaros. Take me to Elena. She needs my help. She is in pain, I know it—"

"He is not ready," Akaros said.

"Like hell he isn't," Jaya snarled, reaching for him.

It happened so quickly. At the sudden jerk of her hand, her flashing eyes, the thought of her hair sharpening, burrowing into him, Yassen heard the cold, crisp warning of his Agni, and he reacted. He could not stop himself. It was instinctual, ineluctable. He snapped his wrist, and the flame shot forward and latched around her arm.

Jaya screamed.

It sounded from far away. Upon his fire touching her skin, he was suddenly overcome by a flood of sensory information. The heat of her skin, the map of her veins, the intricate loops of her nadis, the bright, sparking cores of her chakras. It was brilliant and beautiful and terrifying. Like gazing into the glare of a thousand blazing suns, only to know they could not blind him. It filled him with a dizzying sense of power. Control. He knew at once her hair was not a weapon. He also knew that she wrote with her left hand, that she had a recent injury on her right leg, that she hated him, feared him, even desired him.

"Stop!" Akaros cried from a long, long distance.

With an almost detached curiosity, Yassen delved deeper. He saw the layers of her mind. Memories with their own heat signatures, sparks snapping in her brain with every thought, every emotion. He saw Div. Her parents. Akaros. Samson. Elena—*Elena*. He snagged. The sight of her, in Jaya's memories, hit him cold.

Yassen yanked away. The flame curled back to his wrist as Jaya crumpled and Akaros rushed to her side. She was still screaming.

But it was the smell of her burning flesh that arrested him. He suddenly remembered the inferno searing his arm in the king's chamber. The white-hot pain. The coppery tang of his scorched skin. His horror made anew.

"No." Yassen fell forward, crashing to his knees. "No—no, no. I'm sorry, I'm sorry."

He saw the vivid molten red of her burns. The stutter of her chest. This was his doing. His error. His power. He reached for her, jerked his hand back.

"I'm sorry," he repeated.

"Enough," Akaros said quietly, forcefully.

He took off his shirt and gently wrapped it around her burnt forearm. Jaya moaned, her voice soft, but it sounded like a thunderclap. It struck Yassen down to the marrow, to the deep, ugly guilt rotting within him. He fell back, staring at his hands, his fire, in terror.

"What is this?" he said, his voice shaking. "What have you done to me?"

Akaros did not reply right away as he gently cradled Jaya in his arms. His face was drawn, tired. Yassen had forgotten how old he was, how old he had become. When Akaros turned, he looked at him with a cavernous sorrow.

"I have done nothing. This is what you are, Yassen Knight."

"N-no—"

"Guardian of the Phoenix. Creator of the desert. Third of the Agni. You are the Seventh Prophet."

EPILOGUE

THE THIRD AGNI

It was strange waking up as a forsaken god.

On one hand, Yassen felt like the sun had burned the clots of sin marking his skin and birthed him anew. Tender-fleshed, glorious. A godling still unaware of his deep and terrible power.

And on the other, in the dreams that would not wither, in the visions that pricked his eyesight like desert kair, he saw the ghosts. They had come after he had burned the girl. He did not know who they were. They did not speak or seem to notice him, but when he caught them edging the shadows, a cold, vicious dread beat through his chest. He felt as if he knew them. Not from now, but from several lifetimes ago, a slow pouring of souls who all bore the prints of burning on their skin.

This is a mistake, he thought. *I should be dead.*

"Are you ready, Prophet?"

Prophet. That awful word again.

"Don't call me that." Amid his visions and confusion, they had dragged him to a gamefield. Yassen had no idea of how much time had passed, only that Akaros sauntered toward him now.

"It is what you are," Akaros said. A ghost flickered in his shadow.

456

Yassen could not see her face, but he saw her burns, a glowing red map of pain sprawling down her chest and abdomen. Reflexively, he touched his own stomach. But his skin lay intact, whole and strong.

"I am no god," he said.

"We will teach you how to become one," Akaros said as the sand hummed. "First, we'll start off with summoning a simple flame."

Yassen jerked back as shards shot up like a flock of crows cawing with anger. They stopped suddenly, sharp edges glinting over their heads.

"Elena and Samson used a channel," Akaros said. "Something to help them center and focus their energy. Elena's was dance. Samson's, an urumi. We need to find yours."

The shards plunged down. Yassen yelped and stumbled back, raising his hands above his head. The sand smacked into him, beating him into the ground. *Thump. Thump. Thump.* He buckled, smashing onto his knees.

The sand collapsed. Grains rained down into his hair, beneath his collar, as he peered blearily through his fingers. Akaros studied him, unimpressed.

"Again."

The field hummed as another flock of shards streaked through the air. Yassen barely had time to get onto his feet before they slammed into him. He was brought to his knees much quicker this time.

"Again."

This time, Yassen ran. He sprinted across the field, the shards hissing behind him as Akaros shouted in a clipped, bored voice.

"Focus on your Agni, Cass. Its shape. Its heat. Call to it."

"I don't know—*heugh.*" A shard slammed into his chest, and he crumpled instantly.

Black leather boots edged his vision as he lay there in the sand.

"The more time you spend squealing like a bitch," Akaros said, "the less time Elena has left."

Her name zipped through him like lightning, and Yassen felt himself rising to it, aching for her. What right did Akaros have to take her name? What right did any of them have to her memory? Anger replaced his confusion, fueled by a vicious, desperate longing. Yassen shot up with a snarl. Akaros jerked away in surprise, but Yassen pitched forward, slamming him into the ground. They struggled in the sand, wrestling for the upper hand. Yassen scrambled up—trying to get to his feet—and a boot rammed into his face.

Heat burst in his nose. Yassen cried out, gagging as blood dripped down his lips. Akaros shoved him off and then pulled back his foot for another kick. Yassen saw it. He tried to cup his bleeding nose, to move away, but the heat was spreading. Down his head, his neck, into his shoulders and chest. Vicious and metallic like a slingsword, searing like lightning. And all he could think, as he saw the grim menace in Akaros's face, the promised violence in his coiled momentum, was how familiar this was. This *pain*. He had lived with it all his life. From the hunger that had gnawed his bones while stealing bread, to the grief that gripped his throat as he clutched a bleeding Samson, to the quiet sorrow lacing his ribs when he told Elena to leave him behind. He was no stranger to pain. It thrummed through his veins, made up the very structure of his bones. It was old and acute and intimate, like a secret. Like a dream, promised.

So he reached into it. He reached for his pain and its heat and he felt his Agni rush up, singing. Like the desert come to life under the summer sun. Like the beat of a million sweeping wings, it roared through him. Yassen opened his palm. A flame, brilliant and brutal and beautiful, whipped forward. Its long tongue lashed against Akaros. He jerked back, howling, but Yassen did not feel remorse.

Blood dripped steadily from his nose, darkening the ground. Yassen rose. He felt lightheaded and dizzy and triumphant. He felt exhausted.

A spider-soft voice rang through the speakers.

"His channel is pain."

He whirled around in surprise, recognition peeling away to shock as he saw a thin, tall figure, wreathed in black.

A ghost, he thought. But unlike the others, this ghost had seen him.

"Taran?"

The leader of the Arohassin regarded him slowly, languidly. His red eyes had always unnerved Yassen, but today, they seemed to pierce into the very bleating, ruinous mess of him.

"It's been a long time, Yassen," Taran said.

"Taran, how——" he began when he felt a sudden strange breathlessness. He turned as Akaros stamped out his flame. It squealed in pain, and his body ached as if Akaros had stomped on him.

"Stop it," he gasped.

Akaros kicked the pile of ash. "See, Prophet? Fire is your spawn."

This is a lie. This is a dream.

Yassen stumbled, but Taran steadied him. His voice, always spider soft, eased through his clamoring thoughts.

"You must feel overwhelmed, coming back from the dead. But you are among friends, Yassen. We will help you understand your powers. We will teach you how to hone it."

"Am I a hostage?" Yassen said. "Is this hell?"

Taran laughed. Bright, genuine, a laugh that should not belong to a man like him.

"Hell has always reigned on Sayon." He shook his head. "But you are here to set it right."

He gestured to the glass wall where, beyond, Yassen could see the dying boy's metal coffin. "Div's blood is a unique match to yours, and he's kept you alive. He's been comatose for over a sun because of a gold-caps riot."

He pointed up, to the silver screen. "Jaya dedicated a whole sun to studying the nature of Agni, and she's helped keep you alive. She almost lost her life because of some jealous, power-hungry kings."

He raised another finger. "There's Akaros. You've known him all your life, blamed him for your miseries. He's kept you alive. He almost lost his student earlier because of you."

"Taran—"

"And then there's Maya. She's been working with the Sesharian rebel groups for months to overthrow the Jantari. She's kept you alive. And she almost lost her life too because of the same jealous, power-hungry kings."

"Taran, please," Yassen said.

"You are here because we decided to save you, Yassen Knight. You are not a hostage. You were a choice. And we have sacrificed so much, and will continue to sacrifice much more, to keep you alive."

Yassen stared at him. He felt lost, stuck. Like he was standing in the pit of a dune, the sand slowly sucking him in. Pressure built up in his spine, his limbs. He knew better than to trust the Arohassin. How many times had they manipulated him? How many times had they plucked him from the brink of death only to find that their touch had left scars? Their promises only ruin. But he saw the boy whose blood pumped through him even now, and he felt a sudden guilt then.

"Why?" His voice came out strained, broken from exhaustion and the sinking feeling that whatever the answer may be, it would leave him wanting. "Why would you do all of this?"

"Because you are the Prophet. Because, with you, we can finally end the reign of all kings. Because you are now a symbol of hope. And they will hate you for it. They will fear you, Yassen Knight, and one day, they will even come to love you."

His heart hammered as his Agni stirred and sighed as if in agreement.

"You asked where Elena is. And I will answer honestly. Jaya tried to kill both her and Samson, along with the kings and queens of the second continent, under my orders. She succeeded in only killing one. Bormani. Remember?" Taran smiled as Yassen shuddered. "But can I tell you the truth? I made a mistake. I underestimated Farin."

Yassen froze as Taran met his eyes. "He took Elena and Samson as his prisoners. They are to be executed. Seshar and Ravence will be subsumed by Jantar, your desert ruined, your people oppressed. And the other kings will do nothing to stop him. The last we heard, the council voted to execute Elena. Do you see now why the reign of kings must end? They will continue to demean and kill the ones we love until they grow fat with power, and even then, it will not be enough. It will never be enough.

"But you, my friend, have been given a gift. By the gods, by nature, by fate, whatever you want to believe in. *You* can change history, Yassen. Avenge your friends. Help me bring Farin to his knees."

Elena. Samson. Yassen took an involuntary step forward.

"I must go to them," he said.

"After you have done something for me," Taran said.

Yassen stilled. A cold, familiar dread wormed down his throat. How many times had he heard this from the Arohassin?

Just one last task.

One more job.

"What do you want?" he asked warily.

"I would like to collect more of your blood. Fireblood, actually. You see, Jaya has made these lovely lotuses that we will arm with your... essence."

"Weapons," Yassen said. "You want to make weapons with my blood."

Taran smiled. "Not weapons, Yassen. Advantages in our war against kings."

"No." He had already seen the destruction his inferno had wrought. He did not wish to burn someone else when he knew so intimately of its pain. "I need to find my friends."

Taran's face did not change. His smile did not quiver. In fact, he delivered his response with the same gentle tone as before, but Yassen felt the fire's warning, a raw, instinctual danger rising from his stomach to his throat, as Taran slipped his hand into his pocket.

"I am not asking, Yassen."

He felt a strange, sudden sundering then, like an axe cutting his thoughts in half. His mind emptied. An absence echoed through him, and he could not tell why he was here, standing in a gamefield that smelled faintly of ash.

"Wh-what?" He looked to Taran, who simply watched him, a pod balanced delicately in his slender hand. Yassen lunged for him, tripped, and crashed to his knees.

"You—you." He scratched the ground so hard that his nails dug into his skin, drawing blood. He tried to rise again, fell. "You can't force me."

"Oh, Yassen," Taran said, and for once, his voice changed to reveal sorrow. "I can make you do anything."

He turned the pod. Yassen shrieked as pain blistered down his right arm. White-hot, electric. Reflexively, almost immediately, he drew upon it, and a fire bloomed in his hand. Twisting, Yassen attempted to fling it at Taran, but he tapped the pod, and Yassen gasped as he was cut off from all sensation. He could not feel anything—his hands, his feet, his pain, or his Agni. Only a deep, aching absence. Like a rose snipped from the stem, he wilted.

"No," he whispered. He stumbled forward, his hand catching on Taran's sleeve, and it was then that he noticed the sensor blinking beneath his skin. In his forearm. The drug moved quickly. Yassen sagged. His head rolled, and then he was falling.

Elena, he called.

But only Taran knelt above him. It was he who gently brushed back his hair as Yassen's vision sank.

"Sleep now, Prophet," Taran whispered. "We have much to achieve together."

The story continues in . . .

Book THREE of the Ravence Trilogy

GLOSSARY

Agneepath: The path of fire.

Agnee Palace: The royal governmental home of the ruler of Ravence.

Agnee Range: Mountains that create the western border of Ravence. The Agnee Range is lush and covered with diverse plant species. It stands in sharp contrast to the Ravani Desert.

Agni: The very spark and essence of fire. It is the primordial power.

Ahi Sea: A large body of water that splits Sayon in half.

Alabore's Passage: A long lane that runs east to west in Rani.

Alabore Street: A long lane that runs north to south in Rani.

Alabore's Tear: A long, dark valley north of Palace Hill. Legends say that it was created by Alabore Ravence himself when he met the Phoenix.

Ambari: The native language of Seshar. Scholars have traced its lineage back to a mix of indigenous first-continent languages and Herra.

Amrithi: The ancient ore that creates an undefeatable metal. Amrithi is found only in the dead skin of the Great Serpent, but it exists in a precarious state. To mine amrithi, it must first be activated by the son of the sea.

Arohassin: An underground network of criminals and terrorists who are known to assassinate leaders and take down governments. The leader of the Arohassin goes by the name of Taran, but no one truly knows his name.

Ashanta ceremony: A fire blessing ceremony used to bestow the ruler(s) of Ravence with the power of the Phoenix.

Astra: The closest advisor and right-hand man of the ruler of Ravence.

Ayona: A large island nation in the northern Ahi Sea. The Ayoni do not welcome outsiders.

Azadi: A Herra term that means freedom. It is also the name of the capital of Moksh.

Azuri: A delicate tree whose white branches are often used to build pyres.

Banyan: A tree that can grow to be several feet wide, while its roots can be several miles long. It was introduced to the desert after intense years of environmental development under the rule of Queen Tamana.

Bechari: A Hind term that means "a helpless woman." Note: The masculine form, *bechara*, means "a helpless man."

Beuron: A southern city of Cyleon.

Birdsong: A small festival celebrated before the official opening day of the Fire Festival. It is meant for the Ravani to open their hearts and fill their spirits with song.

Black Scale: A soldier of Samson Kytuu's army. Known for their strength and skill, Black Scales have never lost a war.

Brenni: Furry, llama-like animals. They are often used to transport heavy loads in the Sona Range.

Chakra: Energy centers of the body. It is said that Firebloods, or wielders of Agni, are able to open their lower chakra to access the power of the gods.

Chakram: A circular Ravani weapon. It can be used for close combat or thrown like a disc.

Chand Mahal: The moon palace, otherwise known as the abode of Samson Kytuu.

Chhatri: An elevated, dome-shaped pavilion often found within the architectural style of Ravence.

Claws, the: Curved metal fixtures that are stationed around the track of a hovertrain station. When a hovertrain docks, the Claws latch on to the sides of the train and recharge its engines.

Clipped: A derogatory term that refers to a Yumi who does not have the power of her hair. Such a Yumi is considered a godforsaken abomination.

Coin Square: A popular square in the Thar district of Rani.

Cruiser: A floating vehicle used to traverse the desert.

Cyleon: A kingdom that lies north of Ravence. Cyleon has been an ally of Ravence for nearly two hundred suns.

Desert Spiders: The band of female warriors chosen by Alabore Ravence to protect the Ravani kingdom.

Desertstone: A fine, purple crystal found within Ravence.

Dhol: A large drum used in Ravani music.

Diya: An oil lantern fixed at the end of every petal in the Temple of Fire.

Dupatta: A long scarf.

Enuu: An entity considered to be the evil eye by the Jantari.

Eternal Fire: A large inferno that burns within the Temple of Fire. It is said to have been created by the Sixth Prophet to remind men of the wrath of the Phoenix. It needs no fuel but demands sacrifice from all those who wish to claim its power.

Featherstone: A large gem that contains the only Phoenix feather given to man. It rests in the center of the Ravani crown.

Fire Festival: A weeklong festival that celebrates the founding of Ravence by Alabore and his followers.

Fire Order: A religious order of priests who serve the Phoenix and protect Her temple.

Five Desert Wars: Five bitter years of war between Ravence and Jantar during the reign of King Fani of Ravence and Queen Runtha of Jantar. Both kingdoms lost thousands of men, but Ravence emerged victorious in the end.

Floating bladers: Metal and/or wooden boards that hover slightly above the ground. They are powered by batteries and can go up to thirty miles per hour with a full charge.

Fyerian: A bush that grows within the Agnee Range and produces vivid red flowers.

Fyrra: A large white wolf known to live in the Sona Range.

Gamemaster: A trained official who can code gamesuits and create obstacles within the training field.

Gamesuit: Thin yet sturdy armor that is specifically programmed to fit its wearer. Gamesuits can reknit broken bones during training sessions. They can only be used within the constraints of a training field, due to the magnetic fixtures that help power the suit.

Ganja: Marijuana.

Goddess, the: The goddess of fire who is worshipped by the Yumi of Moksh. Also known as the Goddess Mother, the Mother, the Great Goddess, and the Great Mother.

Gold cap: An ardent supporter of King Leo. Gold caps fiercely believe that King Leo is blessed by the Phoenix and has the divine right to rule Her desert kingdom. They are often vocal (and sometimes violent) in showing their support.

Gujiyas: Sweet pastries that are stuffed with sugar and crushed nuts, like pistachios, almonds, and cashews, and then fried for the perfect treat.

Gulmohar: A tree with fiery red leaves found within Ravence.

Herra: An ancient language that used to be spoken in Ravence. It is the language that the first priests of the Fire Order used when creating scrollwork within the temple.

Hind: The common day language spoken in Ravence.

Hiran: Deer found within Ravence.

Holopod: A small, circular handheld device that is activated by scanning one's fingerprint. One can store personal data, money, images, videos, and more in this device.

Holosign: A floating, holographic poster and/or advertisement.

Homeland dock: The main dock within the port of Rysanti. It is full of shops, restaurants, and entertainment. It is often a newcomer's first glimpse of Jantar.

Hoverboat: A boat that hovers slightly over the sea.

Hovercam: A camera that can float in the air and is controlled via remote.

Hoverpod: A powered flying vehicle shaped like a large black ovoid. These vehicles vary in size, depending on their escort type: civilian, governmental, and/or military.

Hovertrain: A train that flies through the air. They can travel a great distance if properly charged (see **Claws**).

Iktara: A southeastern city of Ravence known for its fine artisans and scholars.

Immortal: Ancient beings of Sayon who never die, such as the Phoenix.

Jantar: A kingdom that shares the southern and eastern borders of Ravence. Jantar is known for its metal and brass cities. Jantar was founded before Ravence and believes the desert should be a part of its kingdom. Throughout the centuries, Jantar has waged countless wars against Ravence, but it has never won.

Jantari: The people of Jantar. They are known for their pale skin and white, colorless eyes.

Kamarbandh: A long chain or belt designed to be worn around the waist. It is often worn with Ravani attire.

Karven: A kingdom that borders Cyleon and Jantar. It has been a steadfast ally of Jantar.

Karvenese: The people of Karven.

Kavach: A gamesuit designed by the Arohassin.

Khajas: Flaky, layered pastry that's dipped in chocolate and garnished with crushed pistachios.

Kurta: A long, loose collarless shirt commonly worn in Ravence.

Kymathra: An ancient fighting style of the Ravani.

Laal Joon: National Ravani holiday to celebrate the founding of Ravence.

Lehenga: A large, embellished skirt commonly worn in Ravence, often paired with a choli (blouse) and dupatta (scarf).

Lilliberries: Berries that grow off the deep roots of a skorrir bush.

Loyarian sparks: Floating specks of light that appear in shadowed areas during the summer in Ravence.

Magar: A southwestern city of Ravence known for its red canyons and bountiful gems.

Makhana: Foxnuts.

Mala: A flower garland often used during Ravani ceremonies, celebrations, and funerals.

Mandur: A kingdom across the Ahi Sea that borders Nbru and Pagua. It is well known for its outstanding army. It has been in constant conflict with Pagua.

Mero/a/i: A term of endearment spoken in Jantar. Its masculine form means boy; its feminine form means girl; and its third form means a genderless person.

Metalmen: A colloquial name given to the Jantari.

Mohanti: A horned, winged ox, the national symbol of Jantar.

Moksh: A kingdom across the Ahi Sea that borders the volcanic region of Pagua.

Molorian: A tree with purple leaves and dark bark found in the Sona Range.

Monora: A northwestern city of Jantar.

Monte Gumi: A mountain within the northern parts of Veran.

Moonspun flowers: Lavender buds that bloom when touched.

Moonspun ganja: A mild psychoactive drug often smoked with a pipe. It is harvested from the ganja plant, found within the Sona Range.

Mutherwood: A pine that grows within the mountains of Seshar.

Nadi: The channel or pathway through which prana flows throughout the body.

Nagini: A Sesharian priestess.

Nbru: A kingdom across the Ahi Sea that borders Mandur and Pagua. It is often the peacemaker between Mandur and Pagua, and never participates in wars.

Neverwood: A thorny plant that grows beneath the underbrush in the Sona Range.

Pagua: A kingdom across the Ahi Sea that borders Nbru, Mandur, and Moksh. It is well known for its stealthy air force. It has been in constant conflict with Mandur.

Pakhawaj: A two-headed, barrel-shaped drum often used in Ravani dance.

Palace Hill: The large rise north of Rani upon which the Agnee Palace sits.

Palehearts: White flowers shaped like tiny hearts that grow within the Sona Range.

Phoenix, the: The fiery god known for Her vengeful fire and penchant for justice. The Phoenix is said to choose a Prophet when the world is full of strife. She is worshipped by the Ravani.

Prana: The life force or heat energy that exists in all things.

Prasad: A Ravani temple offering, often food, blessed by the Phoenix and then given to devotees.

Prophet: A man or woman chosen to enact justice as ordered by the Phoenix. The Prophet can wield fire and cannot burn.

Pulse gun: A weapon that shoots out "pulses," or bursts of lasers. Depending on the size and weight of the gun, some pulse guns can cleanly cut off limbs.

Radhia's Bazaar: A large, teeming network of shops, restaurants, and alleyways located south of Rani's city center.

Rakins: Thorny bushes that grow around the Temple of Fire.

Rani: The capital of Ravence.

Rasbakan: A port city that lies on the eastern border of Ravence.

Ravanahatha: A wooden stringed instrument popular in Ravence and used in traditional dances.

Ravani Desert: A large swath of dunes and canyons. The southern desert is lusher and better suited for crops; the northern desert is harsher. Desert storms are known to appear and disappear suddenly within the northern regions.

Ravence: A desert kingdom founded by Alabore Ravence three hundred suns ago. The kingdom is considered to be part of the holy land created by the Sixth Prophet. Alabore Ravence named the kingdom after himself, bestowing upon his bloodline the burden of maintaining his dream of peace.

Receiving dock: An immigration and customs dock within the port of Rysanti used to check non-Sesharian visitors.

Red Rebellion: An uprising within Ravence led by rebels who wished for a democratic government. It was crushed by Queen Akira.

Registaan: A six-month-long desert test in which the Ravani heir is given no food, water, shelter, or protection. It is a rite of passage in which the heir must learn the sands of her home and why it runs through her veins.

Retherin: A pine with a velvety blue trunk and tawny orange leaves located within the Sona Range.

Royal Library: A tall chamber built underneath the Agnee Palace that houses ancient scrolls and texts.

Rustblood: A derogatory term that refers to a Sesharian traitor.

Rysanti: The Brass City of Jantar; it is a port city and popular immigration access point. All of its buildings are made out of brass, glass, and shining steel.

Sand raider: A Ravani soldier who is skilled in operating a cruiser and fighting underneath the surface of the Ravani Desert. Sand raiders were formally a unit within the army; however, Queen Jumi created a separate branch for the sand raiders after expanding the kingdom's underground tunnels.

Sandscrapers: Tall buildings made of sandstone and steel within the Ravani kingdom.

Sandtrapper: A large, scaly tree found within the Ravani Desert.

Sarangi: Instrument that resembles the violin. Its sound is said to most closely resemble the human voice.

Sari: A garment of unstitched fabric that is wrapped around the waist and draped over the shoulder, exposing the midriff; it is commonly worn in Ravence.

Sayon: The name of the world.

Seat, the: The center dome within the Temple of Fire.

Serpent, the: The dragon deity and goddess of fire who created Seshar and the monsters of the Ahi Sea. She is worshipped by the Sesharians and believed to be part of the Triagni. Also referred to as the Great Serpent.

Seshar: A nation of three islands that lie within the middle of the Ahi Sea. Jantar invaded the country, turning the three islands against each other. Jantar emerged victorious and has maintained a seventy-sun colonial rule over Seshar, forcing its citizens to work within the mines of the Sona Range.

Sesharians: The people of Seshar. They are known for their raven-black hair and insurmountable strength.

Shagun: Presents given by the bride's father to the groom and his family.

Sherwani: A long coat-like garment often worn by royals in Ravence.

Shobu: A small dog with two tails and the mane of a lion, often found within Ravence.

Silver feathers: A colloquial name for the capital police of Rani.

Sixth Prophet: A priestess of the Fire Order believed to have existed five hundred suns ago. She burned down the forest beyond the Agnee Range, creating what is now known as the Ravani Desert. The Sixth Prophet killed many kings, queens, generals, and Yumi as punishment for constantly waging war. After many suns of burning, the Sixth Prophet disappeared.

Skorrir: A thorny bush found within the Ravani Desert. Its buds recede when a predator walks by.

Slab grenades: Explosive devices that shoot out spikes; they are detonated by pulling out a pin.

Slingsword: A weapon with a long, sharp blade and a trigger in the hilt. When pulled, the trigger releases the blade. The blade is connected to the trigger via a steel rope. A user can recall the blade back to the hilt by pulling the trigger again.

Sona Range: A mountain range located within the southeastern regions of Jantar. The mountains have a rich deposit of metal ore. Before the Invasion of Seshar, Jantari miners worked the rigs. Now, Sesharians work the mines while Jantari soldiers keep watch.

Spear: The head guard of a Ravani royal.

Sun's breath: Dawn.

Tabla: Twin drums often used in Ravani music.

Tanker: Military aircraft.

Temple of Fire: The place of worship of the Phoenix. Shaped like a large white lotus with a dome in the center, the temple was built by the first priests of the Fire Order.

Teranghar: A southern city of Ravence known for its rolling hills and training bases for Ravani and Sesharian soldiers.

Thar: A southern district of Rani.

Triagni: The three manifestations of the fire goddesses: the Phoenix, the Great Serpent, and the Goddess. It is said that the great goddesses once lived in harmony, but then an ancient quarrel ripped them apart.

Tsuana: A kingdom that borders Veran. Like Nbru, the country has sworn off war. Peace treaties between other countries are often signed with Tsuana.

Unsung: An ancient fighting style of the Ravani.

Urumi: A long, whiplike sword that has become the symbol of Sesharian resistance. It is said that the greatest warriors added multiple "tongues," or blades, to their urumis. The most ever recorded was seven blades.

Veran: A kingdom that lies east of Jantar.

Vermi: A type of tea grown within the Agnee Range.

Vesathri: An ancient, mythical creature with the body of a scorpion and the head of a stag.

Vetala: A vampire or monster of Ravani lore.

Vishkanya: A female assassin trained in the art of poison. These Sesharian women were taken by Jantari soldiers at birth and forced to ingest poison. Those who survived developed antibodies and the eventual ability to poison others. Their methods of poisoning vary, but the most popular is by touch.

Visor: Made of plastic and/or fiber sheath, visors are used to shield the eyes from blinding Jantari metal.

White Lotus: A large, lotus-shaped sculpture that sits directly in a garden in the heart of Rani. A gas-powered flame burns in the center of the sculpture.

Windsnatch: A game in which two opposing teams ride floating bladers. The goal is to get the ball into the opposing team's net.

Yeseri: A desert lion.

Yoddha Base: A Ravani military compound that sits along the Ravani southern border.

Yron: A type of cigarette only found on the black market. Its nicotine is harvested from the Beldur plant, which can be found within the volcanic regions of Pagua.

Yuani: A sand-colored desert bird.

Yumi: A race of skilled fighters. The Yumi women are known for their long, silky hair that can suddenly harden into sharp shards; their hair can cut through diamonds. The Yumi men are known for their healing abilities. Once plentiful, the Yumi were nearly wiped out by the fires of the Sixth Prophet. Now, many serve as soldiers, guards, or mercenaries.

Zeemir: A long weapon with a sharp blade and the butt of a gun. They are often used by the Jantari army.

ACKNOWLEDGMENTS

This book was a feat. Not because it's a legendary, life-altering piece of literature, but because it taught me the meaning of endurance. I had to fight and claw for these words. There were days when I became undone, buried underneath the staggering weight of the task ahead, of a future I could not see, could not even imagine. But it came. Slowly, stubbornly. And now here we are, at the end of yet another story, another book that feels like a blessing to even exist.

I have many people to thank for this book, and the unfortunate task of trying to give them all their flowers in the limited space of these pages. I would like to thank my editor, Angelica Chong, who patiently read through all my messy drafts and saw the gleaming silver underneath. Your astute observation and whip-smart suggestions helped me navigate through the quagmire of sequel writing, and I am lucky to have found a new champion of my works.

To my stalwart agent, Lucienne Diver, thank you for supporting me and being a voice of reason and encouragement. You really are the best in the game.

To the entire Orbit team, thank you for pushing diverse tales and spoiling us with artwork *in our books*. Who says adult fantasy can't have pictures? I especially want to thank Tim Holman, Jenni Hill, Ellen Wright, Alex Lencicki, Nazia Khatun, Rachel Goldstein, Natassja Haught, Alexia Mazis Pereira, Lauren Panepinto, and Lisa Marie Pompilio. To Priyanka Krishan, thank you for believing in my story and bringing it to Orbit in the first place.

Speaking of pictures, I need to give this artist her due. To Ngoc

Nguyen, thank you for the gorgeous interior artwork within this book. We have both come such a long way since the days of *The Boy with Fire*, haven't we? I love working with you, and I hope we can join forces again in book 3.

To my author friends, specifically Kritika H. Rao, Gabriela Romero Lacruz, Essa Hansen, Elyse John, M. J. Kuhn, Chelsea Conradt, and Hannah M. Long, thank you for sprinting with me in the long hours of the night and being a constant source of encouragement and kindness in this industry. To Ronnie Virdi, thank you for being a trailblazing cheerleader for all kinds of South Asian fantasy.

To my family, I love you. Please read my books *before* they become movies. I will quiz you. To my David, I would wander the long dark in search of you. You are my beacon in the dark, my strength and my courage. If I were to count my best memories, many of them are with you.

To my readers who have been with me since the *Boy with Fire* days, thank you for sticking around. Thank you for your kind messages, your gifts, your fan art and cosplays. I am a lucky and spoiled writer. And to my newer readers who have just discovered these characters, I hope you'll find them as lovely and twisted and beautiful as I do.

MEET THE AUTHOR

APARNA VERMA was born in Rajasthan, India, and grew up in the United States. She graduated from Stanford University with honors in the arts and a BA in English. When she is not writing, Aparna likes to lift heavy (arm days are her favorite), dance to Bollywood music, and find cozy cafés in which to read myths about forgotten worlds.

Find out more about Aparna Verma and other Orbit authors by registering for the free monthly newsletter at orbitbooks.net.

RAISING READERS
Books Build Bright Futures

Thank you for reading this book and for being a reader of books in general. As an author, I am so grateful to share being part of a community of readers with you, and I hope you will join me in passing our love of books on to the next generation of readers.

Did you know that reading for enjoyment is the single biggest predictor of a child's future happiness and success?

More than family circumstances, parents' educational background, or income, reading impacts a child's future academic performance, emotional well-being, communication skills, economic security, ambition, and happiness.

Studies show that kids reading for enjoyment in the US is in rapid decline:

- In 2012, 53% of 9-year-olds read almost every day. Just 10 years later, in 2022, the number had fallen to 39%.
- In 2012, 27% of 13-year-olds read for fun daily. By 2023, that number was just 14%.

Together, we can commit to **Raising Readers** and change this trend. How?

- Read to children in your life daily.
- Model reading as a fun activity.
- Reduce screen time.
- Start a family, school, or community book club.
- Visit bookstores and libraries regularly.
- Listen to audiobooks.
- Read the book before you see the movie.
- Encourage your child to read aloud to a pet or stuffed animal.
- Give books as gifts.
- Donate books to families and communities in need.

BOB1217

Books build bright futures, and **Raising Readers** is our shared responsibility.

Follow us:

 /orbitbooksUS

 /orbitbooks

 /orbitbooks

Join our mailing list
to receive alerts on our
latest releases and deals.

orbitbooks.net

Enter our monthly
giveaway for the chance
to win some epic prizes.

orbitloot.com